THE
PARIS
PROMISE

BOOKS BY SUZANNE KELMAN

SUZANNE KELMAN

THE
PARIS
PROMISE

Bookouture

Published by Bookouture in 2025

An imprint of Storyfire Ltd.
Carmelite House
50 Victoria Embankment
London EC4Y 0DZ

www.bookouture.com

The authorised representative in the EEA is Hachette Ireland
8 Castlecourt Centre
Dublin 15 D15 XTP3
Ireland
(email: info@hbgi.ie)

ISBN: 978-1-83790-531-7
eBook ISBN: 978-1-83790-527-0

Dedicated to the countless women who sacrificed their minds and bodies for the cause of freedom. Some of your names we know; others we may never learn. Yet, we remain forever indebted to all of you, who ventured into realms darker than our deepest nightmares, lighting the way toward liberty.

PROLOGUE

Antoinette

In the dim, candlelit suite in the beautiful Majestic Hotel, a haunting melody echoed through the stillness. Antoinette's fingers danced over the strings of her violin, each note a desperate plea for deliverance.

The stench of alcohol and dread permeated the room, mingling with the chill that seeped through the walls, making Antoinette shiver beneath her flimsy nightdress. The world outside was as silent as her captor, who watched from the shadows with an unnerving intensity. As the final note reverberated through the darkness, she lowered her instrument, her mind consumed by one burning question: how long would he take to die?

'Exquisite,' the Nazi slurred as his eyes roamed hungrily over her. 'You are everything I ever wanted.'

The cloying scent of sweat filled the air, making her nauseous as she leaned back and clung tightly to the sheets, trying to shake off the disgust that consumed her.

For her plan to succeed, she had to lure him in, pull him

closer with each calculated move. It was vital he remained unaware of the trap tightening around him.

Forcing a smile onto her face, she hoped it resembled the slow, seductive one her husband always adored. The thought of René, the love of her life, stung her. He had been taken away by the Nazis to a labour camp, on the orders of the very man who stood before her.

Antoinette suppressed the rising terror, as slowly he peeled away his grey tunic embroidered with a white cross of valour.

His gaze traced every curve of her body, his satisfaction so palpable and sickening that she struggled to suppress the bile rising in her throat.

Antoinette focused on the dim light above his shoulder, envisioning her kind and loving husband's face in its glow. With every breath, she reminded herself that this was for him and their son. Even though if René ever found out, it would break his heart.

As Commander Otto von Falkenberg slithered towards her, her body tightened with loathing. Nervously, she stroked the indent on her finger where her wedding ring had once sat. The soft skin provided some small comfort in the face of this unspeakable betrayal.

The Nazi's menacing voice cut through the tense silence.

'From the day I first met you I knew you were always meant to be mine,' he hissed, possessively.

Sitting on the edge of the bed he reached out, his touch cold and clammy against her warm skin. Antoinette closed her eyes, trying to block out the reality of the situation, pretending she was somewhere far away, back on the rooftop of her apartment, once again safe in her husband's embrace. But as the Nazi's rough hands trailed down her arm, leaving an icy dread in their wake, she couldn't help but slip her hand beneath her pillow to seek the assurance of the cold knife she had hidden there.

His lips crushed hers, oppressive and uninviting, the Nazi's hot breath washing over her, his fingers tracing a path down her back like a spider crawling on her skin. His touch became more possessive, each movement rougher than the last, his need urgent; she clenched her fist and braced herself: she had to endure, he needed to be tired if this was to work.

As he continued, she clutched the knife with white-knuckled determination, its sharp edge cutting into her palm as she prepared to strike.

The thought of killing a man in cold blood sent shivers through her whole body, but she had planned this for too long to back down now.

Once he was finished the room descended into a suffocating silence, broken only by the ragged, disjointed rhythm of their breath. The faint flicker of the lamp cast long, distorted shadows across the walls, as Antoinette stood on the brink of her moral precipice, teetering perilously between light and dark, life and death.

This was her chance. She had to do it now.

With shaking hands, she raised the knife above her head, its handle smooth, its weight heavy in her palm. The blade caught a sliver of moonlight, glinting momentarily like silver lightning as she prepared to strike.

Could she do it? Take a life and lose herself forever? A tear slipped down her cheek, knowing the next moment would plunge her into unfathomable darkness – from which she might never return.

1

WALES, 2012

Deanna

Deanna climbed the creaking ladder to the attic, her fingers tracing lines through the thick layers of dust that had settled over time. She pushed open the heavy trapdoor, releasing a familiar musty smell that carried memories of the past – memories she wasn't sure her heart was ready to confront.

The attic was a cluttered snapshot of her father's past. Every corner pulsed with the essence of a life lived. 'Hold on to the past, but don't let it weigh you down,' her mother's words echoed in her mind. She would never have let it get to this state. But in the twenty years since her mother had passed, her father had neglected to stay on top of his clutter.

Deanna moved to the window, opening it to let in fresh air. Her reflection caught in the glass – those wide, blue eyes, so like her grandmother's. A wave of longing washed over her.

'I wish you were here, Grandma Netty,' she whispered to the still air. 'I hope I'm doing the right thing for Dad.'

With a deep sigh, she began sorting through the piles. Broken items went into a cardboard box – no hesitation. Keepsakes and family photos set aside. She found her grandmother's violin in its battered case; she would see if her dad wanted to keep it or give it away. With his move to assisted living looming, nothing could remain.

Hours later, sweat-drenched and dusty, she carried the box of keepsakes downstairs. Placing it on the kitchen table, she stepped outside, enjoying the coolness of the fresh air.

Her father, Ben, was in the garden, shuffling uncomfortably among the overgrown plants. His fingers, once nimble, now struggled with the shears. Watching him, her heart went out to him as she saw the toll time had taken on his body. He had slowed down so much, especially in the last year. Resolving to make this transition as gentle as possible for him, she assured herself she was doing the right thing. His new house and garden would be much more manageable.

'Ready for some lunch, Dad?' she called. His broad smile and usual wave warmed her heart, melting some of her concerns. In the kitchen, she made him a sandwich with extra pickle, just how he liked them. As he joined her, his gaze landed on the dusty box. 'Is there anything here you want to keep, Dad?' she asked, her voice hopeful yet gentle.

He rummaged through the box, pausing on a faded photograph. A young couple, old friends, now dead, who beamed up at him, radiant with joy. Clearing his throat, he managed, 'I don't think so, love. You can get rid of it all.' His voice carried a weight of sadness.

Deanna moved beside her father as she placed his sandwich in front of him, her hand squeezing his shoulder reassuringly. 'It's going to be nice having a fresh start, Dad. You'll make new friends, new memories,' she comforted, her tone soft and supportive.

Deanna's fingers brushed against the smooth wood of her grandmother's violin in its battered case. 'This can find a new home.' She smiled as her father agreed.

She pictured a young musician discovering the instrument, fingers dancing across the strings, filling their life with the same music that had once echoed through her grandmother's world. A legacy passed on, she thought, as the violin prepared to begin its next chapter.

The next day, Deanna drove into town, the violin beside her. She entered a cosy music shop, filled with the scent of mahogany and rosin.

The shop owner, a stout man with a kind smile and round, red-framed glasses, greeted her warmly.

She placed the dented violin case on the counter, feeling self-conscious about its appearance. In the harsh light of day, and without her feelings of sentimentality from the day before, it seemed even more forlorn and battered than it had when she had found it. She probably should have cleaned it up a little before bringing it in.

'I, uh, have this violin that used to belong to my grandmother,' she began, a hint of uncertainty in her voice. 'I wanted to know if you knew of someone who may want to play it that I could give it to. I know they can be expensive.'

'Ah, let me take a look.' He examined the case with a casual smile, clearly not expecting much. But as he carefully opened it and lifted out the instrument, he drew in breath. Awe and disbelief flickered across his face.

She instantly regretted bringing it to him. She braced herself for him to throw it back at her, to tell her to take it to the charity shop where it belonged.

But his voice was barely above a whisper as he spoke. 'Where did you say you got this?'

'I found it in my father's attic,' Deanna replied, taken aback by the man's sudden change in demeanour.

'Do you mind if I...' He signalled to her his desire to play it.

'Of course, go ahead,' she said, curiosity mingling with her nervousness.

The shop owner took the violin with reverence, adjusting the bow and tightening the strings. He positioned it under his chin and began to play. The first few notes filled the room with a rich, haunting melody and the sound was unexpectedly beautiful. He was obviously an exceptional musician; his eyes were closed as he played, lost in the music that seemed to flow effortlessly from the old instrument.

Finally, as the last note faded into silence, the shop owner opened his eyes and turned to Deanna with a look of wonder on his face. He placed the instrument back reverently in its case and excused himself for a moment.

While he was gone, Deanna rubbed furiously at the top of the case with the corner of her T-shirt, attempting to clean off some of the dust.

The shop owner arrived back at the counter with a book about musical history. His voice was filled with excitement as he flipped through the pages. 'This is no ordinary violin,' he said softly. 'This, I believe, is a Stradivarius, an incredibly rare and exquisite instrument.'

He highlighted a page for her to read. Deanna's eyes widened in astonishment as she stared at the photograph and read the information about the priceless violin. The shop owner explained to her that these violins were crafted by the renowned Italian luthier Antonio Stradivari, and were considered some of the most exceptional and valuable instruments in the world.

Deanna was speechless.

'I can't be sure,' he continued. 'I've never seen one before. That's why I went to get my book, but the craftsmanship and the sound it produces... I would be willing to bet my entire shop that this is the real deal.'

Deanna's head was spinning as he continued to speak. 'It

would be best if you got it professionally valued. Do you know of anyone?'

'Maybe,' Deanna finally stuttered. 'My friend works at Sotheby's in London; she may know someone.'

'Perfect,' the man said, running a tender finger across the bridge. 'This has been such an honour for me to have held such a treasure in my hands. Thank you for coming in; you made my day!'

Deanna left the music shop in a daze, the weight of the Stradivarius violin case feeling heavier than before. How could something so extraordinary – so impossibly *rare* – have been forgotten in her father's attic?

It didn't make sense. Her grandmother wasn't wealthy, and her family had no connections to speak of. The violin didn't belong in their story – or at least, not the story Deanna thought she knew. Had it been a gift? A chance acquisition? Or... was there something darker she didn't know about her grandmother's past?

She felt a knot form within her as questions twisted through her mind. For the first time, it occurred to her that the woman she'd idolised might have carried secrets more remarkable than she dared imagine and a chill ran through her despite the warmth of the morning sun.

She placed the violin gently on the passenger seat and slid into the car, her fingers gripping the steering wheel as she drove. Her reflection flashed in the rearview mirror – wide, blue eyes that once reflected her grandmother's calm resolve now shone with unease. Had she just stumbled upon an heirloom, or had she unknowingly opened a door to something far bigger than herself – something her grandmother had fought to keep hidden away?

2

PARIS, JUNE 1940

Antoinette

In the heart of Paris, beneath the exquisite canvas of a Parisian summer sky, Antoinette stood paralysed at her apartment bedroom window, watching in terror as endless waves of Nazi soldiers marched through the cobbled streets below. They moved as one, in a chilling display of determination and power, like a swarm of grey locusts that suffocated the life out of the city, consuming every ounce of warmth and colour in their path.

Her breath was shallow as she gripped the edge of the window frame, her knuckles white. Antoinette's gaze flicked down to the street, then back to the room behind her, where the faint melody of René's piano-playing drifted through the open doorway. The music was achingly familiar, yet today it felt laced with a sorrow she couldn't bear. The thought of losing him – to danger, to darkness, to the relentless machine of hatred closing in on them – was a weight she couldn't dislodge from her chest.

Pulling herself away from the window, she paused in the doorway to watch him, her heart-shaped face framed by a halo of blonde curls. Her blue eyes, usually filled with warmth, now brimmed with the same gut-wrenching mix of emotion that haunted her husband.

He sat at his piano, fingers dancing across the keys in a melancholic melody that filled the room like a soft lament. Tall and thin, his dark hair fell in unruly waves around his pale face, his hazel eyes intense and focused as he played. She loved him fiercely, but in this world where being Jewish was a death sentence, his brilliance meant nothing. And as she looked at him, vulnerable and exposed, she couldn't suppress the terror that consumed her. The man she cherished, loved with all her being, was now in grave danger, and she didn't know how to protect him from the growing hostility around them.

She looked around her apartment, trying to anchor herself to all that was beautiful and good. It was modest, but filled with the charm and elegance befitting two musicians who had studied and fallen in love at the Paris Conservatoire. Sheet music and manuscripts were scattered across the polished wooden table, and framed certificates of their accomplishments decorated the walls, alongside black-and-white photographs of their performances. A violin rested on a stand near the piano, its polished wood gleaming in the soft light that filtered through the lace curtains.

As René finished playing, he turned to Antoinette with a sad smile, his eyes reflecting the same worry that clouded her thoughts. 'I take it our Nazi guests have arrived,' he surmised, lighting a cigarette with practised ease as he leaned back from the piano, looking both weary and defiant, his long legs stretched out in front of him.

Antoinette moved closer, joining him on the piano bench and resting her head on his shoulder. She reached for his hand, seeking solace in his touch.

'Yes, they've arrived,' she whispered, her voice barely above a murmur. 'It's all happening so fast, René. I'm scared for us, for our son. What will it all mean?'

René squeezed her hand reassuringly. 'We will get through this together, Antoinette. You, me and Benjamin, we always have.'

She drew strength from his words, but this time felt different, more ominous. As the clipped marching feet pounded the street and the deep rumble of tanks rolled through the city outside, the sound vibrated through the floor beneath them, signalling that something about this challenge felt insurmountable.

After Benjamin had gone to bed, Antoinette had been asleep for a couple of hours, exhausted, before René gently woke her.

'Antoinette, my love,' René whispered, his voice barely audible in the darkness of their room.

She stirred, blinking away the remnants of sleep as she gazed up at him, his silhouette outlined by the faint moonlight filtering through the window.

'Is Benjamin sick?' she asked, her heart quickening with unease.

He took her hand, his touch warm and reassuring as he shook his head. 'Nothing like that, come on,' he urged, as he pulled her dressing gown from the door. 'I have something to show you.'

Antoinette followed René through the silent apartment, the floorboards creaking softly beneath their bare feet. He led her to the window overlooking the cobblestone street below, where the moon cast a silvery glow on the deserted road lined with shuttered windows and shadowed doorways. Silently, he lifted it and stepped outside onto the tiny balcony.

'What are you doing?' she hissed.

'Come on,' he said. Antoinette looked at him warily as she

followed René out onto the balcony, the night air cool against her skin. A small ladder was propped against the wall, leading up to the roof. He encouraged her to climb as he followed her. At the top of the ladder, the most beautiful sight greeted her. Dozens of candles were aglow, scattered around the rooftop. A rug on the ground with pillows and blankets created a cosy, intimate space under the starlit sky.

Antoinette's breath caught in her throat as she took in the scene before her, a mixture of astonishment and delight washing over her. The blanket of stars bathed the city in a soft, ethereal light. From their vantage point on the rooftop, Antoinette could see the Eiffel Tower looming in the distance, its silhouette a stark reminder of the city's resilience in the face of adversity. The sounds of the night were a symphony around them, a mixture of distant voices, the soft rustle of the wind through the trees, and the occasional bark of a dog echoing in the stillness.

'Oh, René,' she breathed, her voice barely above a whisper. 'It's *beautiful*.'

He pulled her close as they stood together beneath the starlit sky. She turned, and her lips met his in a tender kiss.

'What is this? It isn't my birthday or anything.'

'I wanted to show you that there is still beauty to be found in our world.'

They sat down on the makeshift bed of pillows and blankets, and René's hand found hers, fingers intertwining as they looked out over Paris. The world felt far away in that moment, she felt suspended in time as they clung to each other, seeking solace in their love and the fragile peace of the night.

'I remember the first day I met you in class. I knew in that moment I was going to marry you, even though I could tell you were very angry with me,' he whispered with a grin.

Antoinette chuckled softly, the memory of their first

encounter at the Conservatoire bringing a warm smile to her lips as she settled against his chest.

'I *was* angry. You were late for the class, had forgotten your music, and came rushing in trying to find your seat. I thought, "He isn't going to last long here." And then I heard you play the piano, and everything changed. René, it was as if the whole world faded away, and there was only the melody you created.'

René reached out to gently brush a lock of blonde hair from her face.

'I was trying to impress you.' He chuckled. 'You were the brightest star in that room, Antoinette, though once I got to know you, it was obvious you were also by far the most wilful woman I had ever met. But it was in that first connection I knew I was meant to love you. As I became accustomed with your wilfulness I grew to understand it was your strength, your passion for life and love; it captivated me from that very first moment.'

Leaning into his embrace, Antoinette sighed, comforted by the steady beat of his heart. 'When you proposed so soon after, it felt like madness.'

René wrapped his arms around her, holding her close as she shivered with the memory.

'When I asked you to run away with me and get married just six weeks later, I was sure you would refuse. Any regrets?'

'Only about my family.' She sighed. 'They were so hurt that we eloped. But I knew we were so young that they would never have agreed.'

René chuckled, 'I am glad they have forgiven us. I thought your father was going to have me shot when we showed up on their doorstep, married and barely out of our teenage years. But here we are, years later, with a family of our own.'

A dark thought tightened her chest, her voice laced with fear and uncertainty as she asked, 'Are you afraid because we are Jewish?'

René's steady gaze held hers, his dark eyes meeting her with unwavering resolve.

He took her hand in his, squeezing it gently as he gently kissed her forehead. 'I won't lie to you, my love. I am afraid. But I refuse to let that fear control us. We have each other, and we'll do whatever it takes. We'll find a way through this, together.'

Antoinette's brow furrowed in worry. 'But what can we do to protect ourselves? Our son?'

'There is talk at the Conservatoire of forming a resistance, a group of like-minded individuals who are willing to fight against the oppression that is creeping into our city. I've been approached by some of my colleagues, and I believe it's our best chance to make a difference, to stand up for what we believe in.'

Antoinette's eyes widened with a mix of fear and awe. 'But, René, that sounds dangerous. What if you're caught?'

'I won't let anything jeopardise our family,' René vowed, his grip on her hand tightening. 'I'll be careful.'

As they lay on the rooftop, wrapped in each other's arms, a sense of resolve washed over Antoinette. She leaned into René, her voice steady as she spoke. 'Then we must join them. We cannot stand idly by while our city is torn apart by hatred and fear.'

As they lay together in that moment contemplating all that was ahead, the flickering candles around them seemed to dance with newfound energy, casting long shadows across the rooftop as a gust of wind ruffled their hair.

René leaned down and kissed his wife deeply. In response, she pulled him closer, their bodies wrapping around one another in a familiar tangle of limbs.

All at once, a distant rumble of thunder echoed in the night sky, a prelude to the storm gathering on the horizon. It was like an ominous warning of the challenges that lay ahead. But in that moment, on the rooftop beneath the starlit sky, nothing mattered except that moment in time. As she held her husband,

Antoinette felt a deep sense of peace settle over her. She knew that whatever trials awaited them, they would face them together, united.

Gentle raindrops began to fall, snuffing out the candles with a hiss one by one as the storm finally broke over the city. The rain fell in a steady rhythm, and they laughed as they quickly gathered pillows and blankets, their bodies soaked with rain as they hastily retreated back down the ladder and into the safety of their apartment below.

Inside, the sound of thunder echoed through the night as they stood laughing and shivering from the chill of the rain that drenched them to the bone.

Antoinette looked up at René, his soft hazel eyes shining with mirth and love, and she reached up to run her hand through his rain-soaked dark hair.

'I love you, you crazy pianist.'

'I love you too, my fearless rebel,' René replied, his eyes sparkling with mischief as he kissed her wet cheeks.

As they towelled off and collapsed into bed, the laughter from their rooftop retreat lingered faintly, like the fading notes of a melody. Yet, despite René's warmth beside her, sleep proved elusive for Antoinette. The weather outside was a cruel reminder of the chaos closing in around them. Each roll of thunder felt like an ominous drumbeat, heralding the uncertainty of the days ahead.

René's steady breathing soon signalled that he had drifted into sleep, his arm draped protectively around her waist. She turned her gaze toward the dim light spilling in from the moon outside, her thoughts pulling her away from the fleeting joy of the evening. Her mind raced to their son, Benjamin, slumbering peacefully in his small room just down the hall. He was so young, so innocent, and utterly unaware of the dangers that threatened to uproot their lives.

The weight of responsibility pressed down on her chest like

a stone. How could they possibly shield him from the relentless hatred that now prowled their streets? Would his childhood be stolen by fear, by violence, by loss? The ache in her heart was almost unbearable. She had promised herself she would protect him at all costs – but *how*? Could love and courage be enough in the face of such overwhelming darkness?

Her thoughts flickered back to René, her brilliant, defiant husband, who had vowed to fight for them, for their family, for their city. The thought of him risking his life, joining the Resistance, filled her with dread. How could she ask him to stay safe when she knew he would never turn away from a fight for justice? How could she accept the possibility of a future without him, if her worst fears came true and his defiance cost him his life?

Tears pricked at her eyes, but she refused to let them fall. Instead, she turned her head to watch René, his face softened in sleep, his dark hair still damp and curling against the pillow. She reached out and gently brushed a lock from his forehead, her fingertips lingering on his skin as if trying to memorise every detail of his handsome face.

'I love you,' she whispered into the stillness, her voice breaking under the weight of her fear. 'Please stay with me. Please stay safe.'

As the storm raged on, she curled into him, drawing comfort from the steady rhythm of his heartbeat against her cheek. For a fleeting moment, she allowed herself to imagine a future where the war was over, where their family was whole and happy, and where Benjamin could grow up, unburdened by fear. But as lightning lit up the room and thunder shook the walls, that dream felt like it was slipping further from her grasp.

Eventually, exhaustion claimed her, pulling her into a restless sleep. Her dreams, like the weather outside, were turbulent and relentless, filled with fractured images of René and

Benjamin slipping through her fingers as the sound of boots echoed in the distance.

The last thought she clung to before the darkness fully enveloped her was the promise she made to herself: no matter what it took, she would fight for them both. For René, for Benjamin, for the family they had built, and the love that bound them together.

Whatever sacrifices lay ahead, she would make them, for the sake of her family.

3

WALES, 2012

Deanna

The next morning, Deanna paced her kitchen, her nerves getting the best of her as she waited for Sotheby's to open. She had already called Felicity at home, but it had gone straight to voicemail. Typical Fee, Deanna thought with a smile. Her friend never answered the phone before her third cup of coffee after she got to work. As soon as nine o'clock hit, she dialled Felicity's office number, her eyes flicking nervously to the violin case sitting on the kitchen table.

She lifted the lid carefully, revealing the beautiful instrument nestled inside. In the daylight streaming through the kitchen window, she could appreciate its elegance. She wondered how many hands had once played this instrument. She thought of her grandmother's fingers dancing across the strings, but now, there was a deeper question haunting her – how did it end up here, in this house?

Her thoughts were interrupted by a familiar voice on the other end of the line.

'My goodness, Deanna Kaplan! I was starting to think you'd forgotten me. How's it going?'

Deanna's face broke into a grin at the sound of her friend's warm, familiar tone.

'Fee, I need a favour. And... this is huge. Remember the library? Yeah, bigger than that.'

Felicity's laugh echoed through the phone. 'Bigger than breaking into the library to rescue my thesis? You've got my attention. What's so big that it compares to our legendary heist? Please tell me it involves less climbing through windows.'

'No windows this time, but definitely something of that scale. I found a violin in my dad's attic, and the guy at the music shop thinks it might be... a Stradivarius.'

There was a pause on the other end of the line.

'Is this a joke? A Stradivarius? Deanna, that is *highly* unlikely.'

'No, I'm serious, the man at the music shop showed me a picture, he said he would bet his shop on it.'

'But if this is real, you just stumbled onto something... priceless.'

Deanna could hear the excitement building in Felicity's voice. 'Yeah, I know. I was hoping you could help me figure out what to do next. I need to get it appraised, right?'

Felicity didn't miss a beat. 'Bring it to me at Sotheby's. I'll set up the appraisal.'

The laughter between the two friends eased the tension Deanna had been feeling all morning. By the time they hung up, she felt a sense of relief wash over her. Felicity always knew how to make things feel lighter, no matter how serious things were.

Her father had been initially sceptical when she told him they were heading to London to get the violin valued. The idea that it could be a priceless artefact crafted by the legendary Antonio Stradivari seemed beyond belief to him.

'But where on earth would my mother have got such a thing?'

She had to admit that the thought had crossed her mind as well. 'I'm not sure, Dad, but I have a feeling we're about to find out.'

On the train the next day, Deanna watched her father, who sat beside her with a distant look in his eyes. She had a feeling he might be lost in memories of his mother and the precious times he had with her.

'Are you okay, Dad?' she asked, placing a comforting hand on his arm.

Ben turned to look at her, his eyes clouded with memories. 'I'm fine, love,' he replied softly. 'You know... the last time I had this violin on a train, it was... well, it was during the war. Things were... different. Nazis everywhere, and I left my mother behind, not knowing if...' His voice trailed off as he remembered a darker time.

'Did you have any idea this might be valuable?'

He shook his head. 'My mother handed it to me as I boarded the train, telling me to keep it safe, and that one day I might need it. At the time, I thought it was her own. The one she played so beautifully for me.' His voice trailed off before saying under his breath, 'I miss her.'

Tears misted his eyes as he spoke, and Deanna reached out to grasp his hand in reassurance. She couldn't imagine the weight of his memories, the fear and uncertainty he must have faced as a tiny boy during those tumultuous times. Deanna felt a newfound closeness with her father, a deeper understanding of the silent battles he had fought in his past. She had battled a few herself.

As she looked out of the window watching the countryside rush by, memories of her painful breakup from the year before resurfaced, causing a weight to settle on her chest. She and her partner Glen had been together for years, their relationship seemingly strong and steady. But then, out of nowhere, he had announced his need to find himself and had walked out of her life without a backward glance. Deanna had been left reeling, trying to make sense of what had gone wrong. Especially when she had found out that 'finding himself' had actually meant 'finding himself in the arms of long-time friend Laura'.

She pushed the pain away, focusing on her dad; it was all about him now.

On arriving in London, Sotheby's stood tall and imposing, a world of history and luxury encapsulated within its walls. She was so proud of her friend and all that Fee had accomplished in her career at the prestigious auction house.

Felicity stood in the foyer, eagerly waiting for Deanna and her dad to arrive. As soon as she spotted them, her eyes lit up with excitement. She gave Deanna a big hug, followed by one for her father. 'Hello, Ben! Or should I call you Aladdin, with that magical attic of yours? How have you been?'

Felicity's teasing made Ben chuckle, his eyes sparkling with amusement. 'Not pushing up daisies yet, and as I get older everything I own seems to become an antique,' he joked.

In Felicity's office a distinguished man, with a keen eye for detail, carefully examined the instrument. He ran his fingers over the wood, inspected the craftsmanship, and peered inside with a tiny flashlight. Deanna held her breath, waiting for his verdict.

After what felt like an eternity, he finally spoke. 'We will need to do more testing and trace its history, but this appears to be an authentic Antonio Stradivari violin.' His tone was reverent. 'It's in remarkable condition. Can you tell me more about how it came into your family's possession?'

Deanna's father, who had been silent until now, took a deep breath. 'It belonged to my mother. She was a musician in Paris during the war.' His voice faltered slightly. 'She wasn't wealthy, so I don't know how she came to own something like this.'

The appraiser sat back, considering Ben's words. 'During the war, the Nazis confiscated instruments of value. It's possible this violin was taken from a wealthy family and passed into other hands. Was there any known connection between your mother and the Nazis?'

Ben's face tightened, his voice strained. 'My mother despised them. She fought with the Resistance. My father was taken by them to a camp, and my mother did everything she could to protect me.'

The expert nodded thoughtfully. 'Would you be willing to leave it with us for further research?'

Deanna and her father exchanged a meaningful glance, silently communicating their decision. 'Yes, we need to know the truth.'

'We will take good care of it,' Felicity assured them, as she squeezed Ben's arm.

The appraiser continued. 'If you are sure you have claim to this, it would be advisable for you to maybe do your own research. There is a new Ancestry website; it might provide you with more information that could connect your family to the previous owner.'

Antoinette said goodbye to her friend, who encouraged her to go and buy a bottle of champagne.

As they stepped out of Sotheby's, the cool London air brushing against their faces, Deanna stole a glance at her father. His expression was a mix of shock and anguish as though the weight of his mother's past was suddenly pressing down on him. For the first time, she truly understood that this violin wasn't just an artefact – it was a bridge to her father's history and memories of his mother. And to a mystery she now felt compelled to unravel for him.

. . .

A week later, Deanna was scrubbing the cupboard under the kitchen sink when her phone rang. She wiped her hands and answered, her heart immediately sinking at the tone of Felicity's voice.

'Dee, we've found something about the violin... and I think you should come to London. Alone.'

A wave of apprehension swept over her. 'You can't just tell me now?'

The silence that followed only deepened her worry.

'It's complicated. There are things I have to show you and it will be too hard to explain it all over the phone. Please, just trust me.'

'Did we pop the champagne cork too early?' she enquired with a hint of humour.

'Not *exactly*. But just come down as soon as you can, and we'll talk in person.'

'Okay,' Deanna stuttered, trying to digest everything her friend was implying. 'Dad has a doctor's appointment tomorrow, but I think I can come the day after.'

'That sounds great.'

'You sure you won't need him?' Deanna was starting to feel a gnawing sense of unease creeping up in her chest.

'No,' Felicity replied hastily. 'I believe it would be best for you to share this with him later at home.'

The call ended with those ominous words, leaving Deanna in a whirl of anxiety and speculation. What could be so significant about the violin that necessitated such secrecy and caution?

4

SEPTEMBER 1940

Antoinette

The streets of Paris, once alive with laughter and music, had fallen silent under the oppressive shadow of occupation. The vibrant City of Lights was now cloaked in an eerie quiet, the rhythmic march of Nazi boots echoing through the deserted boulevards and empty cafés. The once-beautiful city now seemed like a ghost of its former self.

Since the Nazis had taken over Paris, Antoinette and René carried on the best they could. René continued to teach piano at the Conservatoire, and Antoinette took care of their son, Benjamin, and gave private violin lessons to young students from their little apartment.

One evening, she went with Benjamin to meet René, who was working late. Benjamin was talking in his young, animated way, telling her all about his day at school.

Antoinette smiled as she listened to her son's lively chatter, his innocent enthusiasm distracting her from the way Paris was changing. The war was seeping into every corner of their beloved city, and she hated it.

As they turned towards the Conservatoire, Benjamin's words faltered. 'My teacher said that my picture was very good and...'

His eyes became fixated on a huge swastika looming above the doorway. Antoinette followed his gaze to the ominous symbol of hate.

'Why is there a red flag with a black spider at Papa's work, Maman?' Benjamin asked, confusion evident in his innocent voice.

She knelt down to Benjamin's eye level, a forced smile on her face as she tried to mask her growing apprehension. Not wanting to confront this dark reality head-on, she decided to tell her son a white lie.

'Because the Germans want to learn to play instruments too, my love. They have heard about your papa's amazing talent.'

Obviously not totally appeased by her explanation, she could see the fear and confusion in her son's eyes, but she knew she couldn't burden him with the truth. 'But it's nothing for you to worry about. Now, how about we go inside and surprise Papa?' she suggested with a hopeful smile.

Though his mind appeared to be reeling with confusion, he nodded numbly and grasped his mother's hand tightly as they entered the building.

'I don't understand, Maman. Why do they want the red flag with the ugly spider? Do they not like our flag with the blue, white, and red stripes?' he whispered, unable to let it go.

She hurried him inside the doorway, wanting to reach her husband to distract him. 'Our flag is special to us, and their flag is special to them,' she replied vaguely, trying to navigate the delicate balance of shielding her son from the harsh realities outside their door, while also preparing him for the world that awaited.

Inside, the grand hallway enveloped them in an aura of

timeless elegance and history. The air was tinged with the faint
scent of polished wood and resin. Tall, arched windows allowed
streams of soft, golden sunlight to flood the space. Along their
way, the walls were filled with portraits of distinguished musicians and composers, and as they passed by practice rooms, the
sound of music floated through the air, soothing and familiar.

But when she found her husband's room, instead of the
usual piano music that usually filled the space, she was met
with an eerie silence. As she pushed open the door, she found
René huddled in a corner with two other teachers. They startled when she entered, their expressions grave.

René quickly stood up and came to greet her. Benjamin let
go of her hand and rushed towards his father.

'Papa!' he exclaimed as he embraced him.

René knelt down to hug his son tightly, his expression
weighted as he caught his wife's gaze over the little boy's
shoulder.

'What is wrong?' she mouthed.

In response, René shook his head slightly, implying he
didn't want to talk in front of their son.

'Why don't you go and find something in the percussion
basket, Benjamin?' René said, giving his son a gentle nudge
towards the corner of the room where musical instruments of all
shapes and sizes were neatly stored. As Benjamin eagerly
dashed off to explore, Antoinette turned her attention back to
her husband and the two teachers, a sense of dread rushing
through her body.

She folded her arms across her chest. 'What's happened?'

René hesitated, searching for the right words. 'We have just
heard from the secretary that our director, Professor Rabaud,
wrote to the Nazis, offering to help "cleanse" the institution of
Jewish musicians. He feared that if he didn't, the Conservatoire
might be shut down altogether.'

Antoinette's face paled. 'What do you mean by "cleanse"?'

'Apparently, unbeknown to us, he conducted an inquiry to determine how many Jewish students and staff were here at the Conservatoire. Out of five hundred and eighty students, he identified twenty-four Jews and fifteen half-Jews.'

She drew in a breath. 'You included?'

René nodded solemnly. 'Yes, I am on the list, as well as several other professors and our students.'

Antoinette's eyes filled with tears. 'What does it mean?' she asked, her mind racing with all the implications.

'We don't know yet.'

Antoinette squeezed his hand, trying to offer comfort. 'How could he do such a thing? How could he betray his own teachers and students?'

René shook his head, a mixture of anger and helplessness in his eyes. 'He claimed it was to ensure the Conservatoire's survival, but at what cost? The very soul of this place will be torn apart.'

'What can we do?'

René's expression softened as he looked at her. 'We continue to teach, and we resist in any way we can.'

Antoinette's breath hitched as a wave of panic surged through her. 'But, René, is it safe? Staying here... teaching under their watchful eyes... isn't that exactly what they want? What if it's too risky?'

He took her other hand in his, his gaze steady and unyielding. 'If we leave, we lose everything. The students, the music, the hope – we can't abandon it all. They need us, Antoinette. This place is worth fighting for.'

Antoinette bit her lip, torn between the logic of his words and the growing knot of fear in her chest. She wanted to believe him, to draw strength from his unwavering determination, but the shadow of danger loomed too large.

All at once, Benjamin arrived back with a tambourine in hand, his face beaming with excitement. 'Look, Papa, look what

I found!' he exclaimed, shaking the tambourine to make it jingle.

René managed a weak smile at his son's innocent enthusiasm. One of the other teachers, Dr Samuel Cohen, who taught strings and was also Jewish, approached them both.

'We need to get all the affected faculty together,' he said in a hushed tone, out of Benjamin's earshot. 'We must make a plan to protect ourselves and our students.'

'You can come to our apartment tomorrow night,' René offered.

Dr Cohen nodded. 'I will get the word out.'

Antoinette held Benjamin's hand tightly as she and René made their way home that evening. They hadn't said anything to each other, but she knew she and her husband were both thinking the same thing: if the director of something so benign as a musical conservatoire could so easily succumb to the pressures of the occupying forces, what chance did they have to protect themselves and Benjamin?

In the dim light of their cramped apartment that night, Antoinette tucked Benjamin under a cosy quilt, pressing a kiss to his forehead and turning off the light. His innocent face, serene in sleep, was a heartbreaking contrast to the fear of their fate that gnawed at her inside and consumed her thoughts.

She straightened, glancing around the tiny room – the peeling wallpaper she had planned to change, the worn rug she had been saving up to replace – but none of it seemed to matter now. It was all a constant reminder of the life they may never have together.

At the kitchen table, René poured two cups of dark, bitter coffee. He reached across the scrubbed surface, taking her hand, his fingers cold yet gentle. 'I'm so sorry,' he murmured, his voice barely more than a whisper in the silence.

Antoinette's brow furrowed. 'For what?'

'For putting you and Benjamin in danger just because I was born Jewish.' His voice cracked, as if the words were tearing something vital from his soul. He looked away, a shadow of shame clouding his eyes.

Her grip tightened around his hand, her gaze fierce. 'Don't you *dare* apologise for who you are, René Kaplan. You're the man I fell in love with, every part of you. I'd do it all over again, a thousand times.' Her voice held a defiant tenderness, her words defying the world that demanded they live in fear.

René's eyes softened, but worry etched deeper lines into his face. He paused before he continued, the pain lingering in his eyes. 'I need you to start using your maiden name again. Valette is safer. It's... for you and Benjamin.' His voice was pleading, each word weighted with the love and dread only a husband could feel.

Antoinette set her jaw, fire blazing in her eyes. 'I will not hide who I am, nor who I'm married to!'

'But you must,' he urged, his voice dropping to a hoarse whisper. 'If they find out about me, they'll come for you too. You and Benjamin are all I have in this world. Please, Antoinette.'

Her resolve wavered, tears pooling in her eyes. She looked down, fighting the knot of fear and anger building in her chest. 'I am proud to be your wife, René. Changing my name feels like surrender, like letting them win.'

René reached out, cupping her face, his thumb gently brushing away a tear. 'You are the bravest woman I know. If it were just us, I'd fight by your side until the end. But we have Benjamin. His life depends on the choices we make now.'

Antoinette leaned into his touch, closing her eyes as a single tear traced down her cheek. 'Every day feels like a nightmare,' she whispered, her voice trembling. 'When will it end?'

He pressed his forehead to hers, a quiet strength emanating

from his touch. 'I don't know, my love. But we will endure it. For our son.'

She took a shaky breath, her defiance softening into a resigned resolve. 'For Benjamin,' she whispered, her voice steady even as her heart raged. 'But it doesn't mean we have to forget who we are. I will always be a Kaplan inside, no matter what name I use.'

René kissed her forehead, his lips lingering, as if to anchor them both to the love that kept them going. 'As long as you're safe, I can bear anything.'

That night, they held each other close, cocooned in a love that defied the darkness around them. And as Antoinette drifted into a restless sleep, René's words echoed in her dreams.

'I love you, my darling, with all my heart.'

5

LONDON, 2012

Deanna

The train screeched to a halt, jolting Deanna from her anxious thoughts. As she glanced out, she could see rain pelting down in sheets, hammering against the windows, blurring the city into streaks of grey and black. She sighed, buttoning up her coat and stepping off the train onto the slick platform as her umbrella fought back, refusing to open as the rain soaked her through.

'Brilliant,' she muttered to herself under her breath as she wrestled with the stubborn thing.

It finally popped open, but the damage was done. By the time she reached Sotheby's, she was thoroughly drenched, leaving puddles in her wake.

Inside the auction house, Felicity was waiting, arms crossed, a familiar smirk tugging at her lips.

'You still haven't figured out umbrellas?' she chuckled. 'It's been, what, fifteen years since we were at uni? And you're still not good at dealing with the rain,' Felicity teased.

Deanna shot her a mock glare as she justified herself. 'I can't help it if this umbrella has a personal vendetta against me.'

'Sure, Dee. That must be it,' Felicity quipped as they exchanged a soggy hug.

Felicity led Deanna through the bustling halls of the auction house, past locked glass shelves displaying exquisite artefacts from all corners of the world, until they reached her private room at the back.

Stripping off her coat, Deanna collapsed into the comfortable office chair with a dramatic sigh as her friend offered her a hot cup of strong tea and a plate of biscuits. She also handed her a towel from her own gym bag, and Deanna began drying off.

'Okay, I'm moving here. I'll live in this chair, and you can bring me tea and biscuits daily. It would be better than cleaning out my dad's house.'

Felicity gave her a sympathetic smile as they slipped into their usual banter, reminiscing about late-night study sessions, last-minute essays, and that one disastrous pub quiz where Deanna had confidently answered every question wrong. But eventually, Felicity's laughter faded, and she started fidgeting with the papers on her desk, avoiding any eye contact.

Deanna set down her cup, her senses on alert. 'Okay, Fee, what's going on? I know that look.'

Felicity's shoulders tensed, and she took a deep breath. 'Right, I've been doing some digging on the violin.' She hesitated, then met Deanna's gaze. 'Dee, what I found... it's complicated.'

Deanna raised an eyebrow. 'I'm getting nervous here. Just tell me.'

Felicity handed her a folder, her fingers trembling slightly. 'The violin has distinguishing markings on the scroll, confirming its identity. This proved to be a crucial clue in unravelling its past. The more we dug, the more we found... As our expert had insinuated in our last meeting, it was in the possession of a high-ranking Nazi officer during the war.'

'God, I wonder how my grandmother even had it?'

Felicity pressed her lips together, clearly struggling with the next part.

'I think I might know. The man who stole the violin was called Otto von Falkenberg.'

Deanna shifted uncomfortably. Felicity was using her serious voice, the one she kept for delivering bad news. Deanna opened the folder, and as she flipped through the pages filled with old photographs, documents, and faded letters, a sense of unease washed over her. Felicity's investigation had been thorough.

She paused on the first image, which was of a man, unmistakably dressed in a Nazi uniform, holding the violin. His features were sharp, arrogant, and – unsettling.

Felicity nodded toward it. 'That's Falkenberg.' Her friend then went into a potted history of his military career, but Deanna tuned most of it out as she stared at the picture of the same violin that had been in her family's possession for years.

Deanna blinked, her mind racing. 'But that doesn't explain anything about my grandmother.'

Felicity handed her a letter, her voice soft and tentative. 'There's a letter – one that suggests your grandmother was involved with him... *romantically*. Maybe even his lover...'

Deanna froze, her breath catching in her throat. The words hung in the air like a bomb waiting to detonate. Her mind raced, refusing to process what Felicity had just said. The pounding of her heart thundered in her ears, drowning out the sounds around her.

Her hand trembled as she reached for the letter, but she stopped herself, her chest tightening with disbelief. 'No,' she said sharply, her voice rising. 'No way. My grandmother was part of the Resistance. She would never—'

Felicity's face was full of quiet sympathy, her eyes flicking between Deanna and the letter as though bracing for the inevitable fallout. Deanna hesitated for a moment, her fingers brushing against the paper as she nervously unfolded the copy of a letter translated from German, her pulse roaring in her chest.

Dear Commander,

I hope this letter finds you well in these tumultuous times. I write to you in an unofficial capacity today with a matter of utmost urgency and grave importance. I'm sure by now you are aware of Commander Otto von Falkenberg's fate. As you know, our esteemed officer has been a dedicated collector of fine art and rare artefacts. Among his most prized possessions was a Stradivarius violin of exceptional beauty and value.

It is with great distress that I must inform you of its theft. The violin was stolen from Commander von Falkenberg by none other than his French lover, Melodie Buchet. This woman, whom he trusted implicitly, has betrayed him in the most despicable manner. She absconded with the violin, and her whereabouts are currently unknown.

This loss is not merely a personal affront but a significant blow to our efforts to preserve and secure valuable cultural artefacts for the Reich. We are determined to retrieve the violin at any cost, and I have been tasked with coordinating the search.

I implore you, Stephan, to use all available resources to assist in locating her and the stolen violin. The importance of this task cannot be overstated. Any information or assistance you can provide will be greatly appreciated and duly rewarded.

Please respond with any leads or suggestions you may have. Time is of the essence, and we must act swiftly to rectify this situation.

Yours sincerely,

Captain Johann Vogelmann

'Who is this woman? This *Melodie*? Did she know my grandmother?' Deanna asked, already afraid of the answer.

Felicity pulled another photograph from the file and slid it across the table.

It showed a faded image of a young woman with striking features, dressed in elegant attire as if at a party, a woman with the very same features, blonde hair, and body shape as Deanna. A man had his arm around her shoulders as he kissed her cheek. Even though his face was in profile, it was obvious the man, wearing the uniform of a high-ranking Nazi officer, was Falkenberg, his bearing haughty and self-assured. Deanna's heart clenched as she turned the photograph over. In a messy script were written the words: *Otto und Melodie*.

Deanna tried to push away the terrible reality in front of her as memories of her grandmother flooded back – images of a woman with a warm smile and a gentle touch, her hands always busy teaching her how to cook. Deanna remembered the stories of the woman who had faced the harshest of times with unyielding strength and grace. How could that same woman have been entangled with a *Nazi*?

Felicity reached across the table, her voice gentle. 'Dee, I know how hard this is. I know you idolised her. I even met her a couple of times when she came to visit you at uni. She was amazing. But you have to consider the possibility that she had secrets – ones even your dad doesn't know about.'

Deanna let out a hollow laugh. 'Secrets? That's the understatement of the century. She was always this hero to me, this unstoppable woman. My grandfather was taken away to a prison camp; she was left alone, and she managed to survive. Her story gave me strength in my most challenging times,' Deanna continued, her voice filled with a newfound realisation. 'What am I supposed to do with this?'

'People made hard choices to survive,' Felicity acknowledged softly.

'Hard choices are like living without chocolate, not sleeping with Nazis.'

'You don't know that she did that for sure,' Felicity interjected abruptly. 'One thing I have learned while doing research is that history is rarely black and white. People who are seen as heroes may have made questionable decisions, and those deemed villains might have had moments of compassion. We can't judge the past by our current standards; it was a different time, with different pressures and challenges. Besides, there may be much more to this story that we haven't uncovered yet. I just felt you needed to know what we have found out so far.'

'God, I hope there's more,' Deanna sighed, running her fingers over the edges of the photograph. 'I just don't know how I'll tell my dad. He adored his mother.'

'I'll help you. Whatever you need. And don't worry about the violin – if you want us to hold on to it to keep it safe, we will. Take your time.'

As Deanna left Sotheby's, the rain continued to pour, but she barely noticed. She clutched her bag under her arm, the infamous folder inside, her thoughts swirling with every unanswered question. The train ride back was quiet, save for the sound of raindrops pelting the windows. Deanna couldn't stop thinking about the letter, about her grandmother, and about what it all meant for her family.

And through it all, one thing was certain – she was determined to uncover the whole story, no matter what.

6

SEPTEMBER 1940

Antoinette

The city was blanketed in a hazy, orange glow as dawn broke over the horizon. Antoinette stirred from a restless sleep and carefully slid out of bed, tiptoeing out of the room to avoid waking her slumbering husband.

She made her way to the window, pulling back the heavy curtain to reveal the world outside. The first rays of sunlight filtered through the delicate lace curtains, casting a warm glow on everything they touched. In the streets below, she saw a young woman being stopped by a Nazi soldier as he demanded her identification papers. The woman fumbled nervously, her hands shaking as she searched through her bag.

Antoinette's pulse quickened in fear as she watched the scene unfold, a stark reminder of the dangers that lurked just outside their doorstep. Her mind drifted back to their wedding day. She remembered the promise she made to René, to stand by him through anything. That promise felt heavier now, laden with the weight of their current struggles but she felt a surge of anger, a deep-rooted instinct to protect her family at all costs.

Quietly retreating from the window, Antoinette made her way to the kitchen, the floorboards creaking softly beneath her feet. As she started to prepare breakfast, the events of the previous day weighed heavily on her mind, casting a shadow over the warmth of her familiar home.

She thought about René's suggestion to change her name to keep herself and Benjamin safe from the Nazis. The idea of erasing that identity felt like a knife twisting in her heart, a betrayal of her marriage vows and everything they had built together. But she knew it was a necessary sacrifice. The image of Benjamin growing up without his parents, or worse, being torn away from them by the cruel hands of their enemy, haunted her.

Soon, the rich aroma of brewing coffee filled the small kitchen, mingling with the faint scent of toasted bread. As she went about her morning routine, the warmth of the stove that flickered a glow on the walls, making the shadows dance, provided a brief solace. She cherished these small moments of normalcy, knowing now how fragile and fleeting they were.

Entering his room, Antoinette gazed down at her sleepy-eyed boy, his hair adorably ruffled on one side. She gently brushed a hand through his soft curls, feeling a wave of protectiveness and love wash over her. Benjamin stirred slightly, blinking up at her with innocent curiosity, his wide eyes searching hers for reassurance. She leaned down to kiss his warm forehead, whispering a silent promise to herself to keep him safe.

'Good morning, sweetheart,' she said softly, her voice laced with tenderness as she tucked a stray lock of hair behind his ear.

'Morning, Maman,' Benjamin replied, his voice still heavy with sleep as he rubbed his eyes and let out a small yawn. His innocent smile brought a fleeting sense of peace to Antoinette's troubled heart. She hugged him tightly for a moment longer than usual, savouring the brief respite from her fears.

As he sat at the breakfast table later, swinging his legs back and forth, Benjamin chattered away with the innocence of youth about the tambourine he had found the day before. His eyes sparkled with excitement as he described the sounds it made, but Antoinette listened absently, her mind still preoccupied with the upcoming meeting that evening.

René soon joined them, his eyes heavy with concern and lack of sleep, as he poured himself a cup of coffee.

'Did you sleep at all?' René asked softly, his voice filled with concern as he reached out to squeeze her hand. The gentle pressure of his touch was a comfort.

Antoinette managed a small smile, though it didn't quite reach her eyes. 'Not much. I couldn't stop thinking about everything,' she admitted, her voice trembling slightly.

'What about you?' She saw the same weight of worry mirrored in his eyes, as he shook his head, knowing they were both fighting the same silent battle.

René left early, the door closing softly behind him as he headed out to teach his classes at the Conservatoire.

Antoinette's heart ached as she watched him disappear up the road, passing the area where the girl had been stopped. She held her breath, but the soldier had moved on, and she sighed with relief.

Turning back to the quiet apartment, she pressed her hands to her chest and prayed silently, not just for René's safety, but for the strength to carry them through another day. She worried about the meeting that night – who would show up, what they might discuss, and, more terrifyingly, who might betray them.

The risks loomed large, but the resolve to fight back against the growing darkness burned bright in her heart.

That evening, the Jewish music teachers of the Conservatoire arrived at Antoinette and René's tiny apartment, their faces etched with exhaustion and worry. The atmosphere in the small space was palpable, a mix of fear and defiance. Their clothes were rumpled, their eyes haunted, but amid the tension, there was a flicker of camaraderie and shared persistence that brought a fleeting warmth to the room.

As the apartment filled with people, Antoinette's anxiety grew. Each knock at the door sent a jolt of fear through her, the possibility of the wrong person showing up looming in her mind. Her heart raced as she glanced at René, who seemed calm on the surface, his movements deliberate as he arranged chairs to make space. But she knew him too well – his shoulders were tense, his jaw set tighter than usual.

Their home was soon packed with people, each seeking refuge from the uncertain world outside. Some were young musicians who had recently joined the Conservatoire, their faces still fresh with youthful hope, while others were seasoned members of the community, their eyes reflecting years of struggle and resilience. Despite their varied backgrounds, they all shared a common trait – they were Jewish. As they gathered in the front room, their whispered conversations quickly turned to their uncertain futures and the desperate need for a plan.

Antoinette moved quietly through the room, serving wine and cheese with a smile that she hoped masked her turmoil She caught snippets of conversations – words like 'arrests', 'raids' and 'forged papers' – and unease rippled through her, tightening like a vice.

These teachers and musicians were more than just colleagues; they were family. And the thought of losing even one of them was unbearable.

'These are hard times,' René said solemnly. 'We are facing challenges that will test us, but we must find strength in each other.'

'We must not lose hope,' Antoinette interjected, her voice steady but her hands trembling slightly as she set down a tray.

'At the Conservatoire we have built something beautiful together, something they cannot take away from us. We will stand strong, and protect what we hold dear.'

She saw the fear in their eyes, but also the flicker of determination that her words ignited.

'What should we do?' asked Monsieur Leclerc, an older teacher with a wizened countenance and eyes as sharp as a hawk. He had been teaching at the Conservatoire for over three decades. 'Hitler's hatred of Jewish people is legendary. I've heard stories of them arresting Jewish people for the slightest reasons. We need a plan, and we need it now.'

A murmur of agreement rippled through the room as worried glances were exchanged.

'You are right, we need to have a plan,' René added, his voice unwavering. 'We cannot wait for the worst to happen before we act. We need to be prepared, now more than ever,' he said firmly, his eyes locking onto each person's gaze, underscoring the dire urgency of their situation.

Antoinette felt her chest tighten as she listened. René's confidence bolstered her, but it also terrified her. The idea of him taking such risks made her palms sweat. She glanced at Benjamin's closed bedroom door, imagining their son waking to an empty house, their lives upended by a single misstep.

'But what else can we do?' asked Professor Chevalier, a bold teacher with a marvellous handlebar moustache. He was a violin instructor who had taught Antoinette and whose hands shook as he spoke. 'We are musicians, not soldiers. How can we possibly stand up and fight against the Nazi regime? How can we protect ourselves, and our families?'

Antoinette felt the weight of their vulnerability. They were outmatched in terms of their enemy, but she knew they possessed a strength within them that the Nazis could never understand.

'We may not have weapons,' she began slowly, 'but we have

our music. Our music has the power to move hearts and inspire courage like nothing else. It can reach places that guns and bombs cannot. Maybe we can find a way to become invaluable to the Nazis in a different way,' she continued, her voice gaining strength. 'We can use our talents to become indispensable, to make them see our worth, and to protect our lives through the beauty and power of our art.'

The room fell silent, the weight of her words settling over them all as every sombre face turned to look at her with fear.

René's voice rose in fervour as he shared his plan. 'Listen, my friends. I propose we organise a series of concerts at the Conservatoire, inviting high-ranking officials to attend each one. It will take a little time for planning, but while they are focused on this distraction, we can work behind the scenes to figure out our next step, secure forged documents for new identities if needed, and find safe houses for us to live.' René's eyes sparkled with new-felt enthusiasm as he spoke, a glimmer of hope shining through the desperation in his words. His passion was infectious, and for the first time that evening, a flicker of hope lit up their faces.

Antoinette watched him, pride and terror warring within her. She knew his passion would inspire them, but she also knew it could draw dangerous attention to him and their family.

As René outlined his idea, the group exchanged glances, some with hesitant smiles, others with nods of encouragement, feeling the first stirrings of optimism that had eluded many of them since the beginning of the occupation.

'I will approach the director tomorrow morning,' René continued, his voice filled with conviction. 'I will propose the idea to showcase the incredible talent of our students and faculty. We will make it an event to remember, one that will capture the attention of not only the Nazis but the entire city. I will play upon his pride and his need to impress them to ensure its success.' His confidence was unwavering, and the group could feel the potential of their plan taking shape.

'In the meantime,' he continued. 'we must be prepared for the possibility that we could do all this and still face unimaginable consequences. But I do not want to run like a coward from the fight.' His words resonated deeply, filling them with a renewed sense of purpose and determination.

The group continued to talk until before the curfew, their voices rising and falling as they debated musical pieces, shared ideas of resistance, and explored every possibility. The air buzzed with conversation and decisions, but also with a sense of camaraderie.

After everyone left, René turned to his wife and took her hands in his, his eyes filled with the vulnerability he truly felt, that he had kept hidden from the other teachers.

'Do you think we are doing the right thing?'

Antoinette met her husband's gaze, her own eyes reflecting the same mix of emotions. She squeezed his hands tightly, drawing strength from his presence.

'I believe we are,' she said softly, her voice unwavering despite the turmoil inside her. 'We have to try, René. We can't sit idly by and watch as our world crumbles around us. We have to fight back in whatever way we can, using whatever means are at our disposal.'

As they prepared for bed, the gravity of their decision hung heavy between them. The prospect of taking on the Nazis was daunting, but they were fuelled by a shared sense of purpose and a deep-rooted belief in the power of music to bring about change.

As she lay in her husband's arms that night, Antoinette felt the fear coursing through her veins, a cold and relentless current. Her mind raced with every possible scenario – arrests, betrayals, loss. She clutched René tighter, whispering a silent prayer that he would stay safe, even when he was beyond her sight. The thought of Benjamin growing up in a world where they had not fought for his freedom was unbearable.

7

WALES, 2012

Deanna

The evening after she arrived back from London, she found Ben lounging in his favourite armchair, his eyes fixed on the TV screen. Deanna stood in the doorway for a moment, gathering the courage to approach him and share what she had uncovered. With a deep breath, a prickle of unease coursed through her as she forced herself to step forward.

'Dad,' she began tentatively, her voice soft and tinged with nervousness. 'Could I talk to you for a moment?'

The room fell into an uneasy silence as Ben, sensing something serious, clicked off the TV and turned toward Deanna. His smile was warm, but his eyes, showing a flicker of concern, told her that he knew whatever she had to say wasn't going to be easy.

'Of course, love,' he said, his voice steady though his fingers gripped the armrest, belying his calm façade. Deanna sat next to him, her thoughts racing, unsure how to begin.

'I discovered something about Grandma Netty yesterday,' she started, her words slow and deliberate as his body stiffened.

'What?' he asked, his voice quiet, apprehension leaking into his tone.

Deanna hesitated, then gently placed her hand on his arm, feeling the tension ripple through him. She explained what Felicity had found out as she handed him the photo and the letter about Falkenberg, holding her breath as she watched him unfold it.

Ben's eyes darted across the page, his breath shallow as the elegant script detailed the theft of the violin and the shocking mention of Antoinette being romantically involved with Falkenberg. Deanna studied his expression, searching for any hint of recognition, denial, or understanding.

When Ben finished reading, he set the letter down, his hand trembling slightly. His gaze met Deanna's, darkened by a surge of emotions – confusion, anger, and hurt.

'Did you know any of this?' Deanna asked, her voice barely a whisper. The air in the room felt thick with the weight of the revelation, suffocating them both.

Ben's face twisted in anguish, his voice strained as he spoke. 'It's lies, it has to be. My mother would never – *could* never – have been involved with the Nazis. She loved my father. I… won't believe it…' He shook his head, his voice trailing off in disbelief.

Deanna's heart broke as she watched the man she had always known as strong and unshakeable struggle with the shattering of his mother's image. She could see the little boy in him, clinging to the idealised version of Antoinette, the mother he loved so deeply, now painted in a new, horrifying light.

'I know this is hard to hear,' Deanna said, her own voice shaky as he held the photograph of Antoinette. His fingers traced the faded outline of his mother's face, now frozen in a moment of intimacy with a man wearing the uniform of the enemy.

Tears brimmed in Deanna's eyes as she continued, 'But

there are things in these letters that we can't ignore. Felicity warned me we that we won't be able to keep the secret of the violin forever. And when it comes out, so will Grandma's story. I didn't want you to hear this from someone else.'

Ben's voice trembled as he responded, 'My mother was a *hero* – a member of the Resistance. She fought for France. This letter... this man... he's twisting the truth! He must be. Or there is a mistake.'

Deanna reached for his hand, but he pulled away, his body rigid with anger and hurt.

Ben stood abruptly, his voice hoarse, his emotions raw and exposed. 'I need to prepare for my garden club meeting tonight.' His jaw was clenched, a sign that the conversation was over. He hurried out of the room, leaving Deanna alone.

She watched him go, her heart aching with the unresolved tension between them. The pain in his eyes reminded her of the time when her mother had died, and she realised with sudden clarity that until they uncovered the truth about Antoinette, this shadow would haunt her father forever.

After he left, Deanna sat down at her computer, determined to uncover as much of the truth as she could. With a deep breath, she began to search for any information about her grandmother.

First, she ran a search for her grandmother's name. As she waited, she pictured the beauty her grandmother had been – blonde hair, a heart-shaped face, mischievous and full of fire. She couldn't reconcile the woman in the faded black-and-white photographs with the person described in Vogelmann's letter.

As she sifted through search results, a particular article caught her eye. It was a historical piece about a daring heist orchestrated during World War Two involving valuable artefacts stolen by high-ranking Nazi officials. Deanna's pulse quickened as she read about the missing violin that Vogelmann had mentioned – a priceless piece of art that had mysteriously disappeared during the chaos of war.

The article detailed how the Nazis systematically looted cultural artefacts from occupied countries, often using them as bargaining chips or personal treasures. It also mentioned the Resistance's efforts to recover these stolen items and return them to their rightful owners.

Could her grandmother have been one of these unsung heroes, risking everything to defy the tyranny of the Nazis? Or was she, Deanna thought with a shudder, just a Nazi's mistress trying to survive, who had been caught in a dangerous game of love and betrayal?

Deanna's mind spun with possibilities as she delved deeper into the article. The lengths the Nazis went to in order to steal and hoard precious artefacts were staggering. According to historical research, several Stradivarius instruments had gone missing during World War Two and were still lost.

Had one of those missing violins been in her parents' attic all this time?

Deanna was so absorbed in the research that she lost track of time. When she finally looked up from her computer screen and glanced at the clock, she realised with a pang of worry that Ben had been gone for longer than she had expected. Heading into the kitchen to make a cup of tea, she noticed a light on in his potting shed.

Setting the tea aside, she wound her way down the garden, the evening air cool against her skin. Reaching the shed, she hesitated for a moment before gently pushing the door open. The soft glow of a single bulb illuminated the space, casting shadows on the walls.

'Dad?' Deanna called out softly, her voice trembling with a mix of concern and urgency.

He was there, just sitting at his potting bench, staring into space. Ben looked up at her, his eyes red-rimmed and weary.

'Dad, are you all right?'

Ben let out a heavy sigh, running a hand through his hair. 'I just needed some time to clear my head,' he replied, his voice rough with emotion. His shoulders sagged, as if burdened by unseen weights.

Deanna stepped into the shed, the scent of earth and plants enveloping her. She approached her father from behind, wrapping her arms around his broad shoulders and kissing the top of his soft downy head. She inhaled the soothing scent of sandalwood and musk aftershave that he had worn since she was a child.

'You don't have to face this alone, Dad. We can figure this out together.'

He nodded and squeezed her arm. 'As I get older, memories from my past seem to come into sharper focus,' he confided. 'The little details are what stand out the most.' He closed his eyes for a moment as if trying to summon those memories. 'I can still remember the vivid red of the Nazi flags fluttering in the wind. And the bustling sounds of the train station when I first left Paris. The distinct scent of my mother's perfume that always lingered on her clothes. And the way she looked at me when she handed me what I thought was *her* violin.' A small sigh escaped him, filled with bittersweet nostalgia.

'I can still hear the intensity in her voice as she handed it to me. "Take care of it, Benjamin, you may really need this one day if anything happens..." And I still remember wondering why she was giving me a violin, of all things. Her violin – surely, she would need it. I had never shown any interest in playing the instrument; I always wanted to play the piano like my father. By then, he was already in a camp. It was such a terrible time when he was taken. I was just a boy, barely old enough to understand what was happening. But I remember the fear, the uncertainty.

My mother's screams as they hauled him away.' Ben's voice was thick with unshed tears, his memories threatening to overwhelm him.

Deanna listened intently, her heart aching for the pain and confusion darkening her father's face. As he recovered his composure, he continued.

'At the time, I didn't question it. I was just glad to have a little piece of her with me, something to remember her by when she was so far away.'

His eyes clouded with pain. 'But now, with this Nazi's letter, I am afraid it will open the door to a terrible secret, the kind of secret a son should never know about his mother...' Ben's voice trailed off, lost in a wave of memories that threatened to drown him.

Deanna reached out and took his hand, trying to offer some comfort. 'We don't know for sure what happened,' she said softly. 'There could be an explanation for all of this.'

He turned to look at her. 'Then why did she hide it? Why never ask for it again? Why, if she was working for the Resistance, did she not hand it back?'

Deanna squeezed his hand reassuringly; her mind had been racing with the same questions that plagued him. 'Maybe she was trying to protect you, Dad. Who knows what people had to do during a war to stay alive? Maybe there was a reason she couldn't tell you the truth,' she offered, her voice gentle and soothing.

Ben stared at her for a long moment, his eyes searching hers as if seeking solace in her words. 'You may be right, Deanna. But the uncertainty is what's tearing me apart,' he admitted quietly.

'Then we will find out the truth, Dad,' Deanna vowed, her voice filled with determination. 'We owe it to Antoinette's memory and to ourselves to uncover the whole story, no matter how difficult it might be.'

Ben nodded, a sense of purpose flickering in his eyes. She ran her hands down his arms, noticing he was chilled to the bone.

'Come on, let's go inside and have a cup of tea.'

He agreed and, struggling to his feet with a weary sigh, Ben followed Deanna out of the potting shed and back into the warmth of his cosy home.

As she boiled the kettle, Deanna watched him shuffle into the front room to his favourite chair by the fire, and her heart broke for the sadness she saw in his eyes. Right then and there, she knew until she got to the bottom of this, he would never be free from the shadows that now threatened to consume him.

8

MARCH 1941

Antoinette

It was well past midnight when the knock came at the door – a sharp, urgent rap that shattered the silence of the night. Antoinette bolted upright in bed, her heart racing as the chill of the night enveloped the room.

René swiftly put on his dressing gown, his hands trembling slightly as he met Antoinette's eyes, then rushed to the door. Antoinette's mind raced with possibilities. Who could be calling at such a late hour?

She joined him in the hall as René opened the door to find Professor Chevalier standing on the threshold, his distinguished handlebar moustache drooping with sweat and fear. His usually well-groomed hair was dishevelled, and panic was evident in his stance; his wife, Juliette, clutched their daughter, Claire, tightly, the little girl's face pale with terror.

René invited them inside without hesitation.

'René, I didn't know where else to go,' Professor Chevalier whispered, his voice trembling. 'They came for us.'

The elderly man's words were a desperate whisper. 'We

were asleep when our neighbour warned us. Gestapo officers were demanding to search the apartments, claiming a tip about illegal activities and specifically seeking me. I knew it was a set-up. We barely escaped in time and have nowhere else to turn.'

Antoinette and René exchanged a glance, understanding the gravity of the situation, and the possibility of what could happen if Professor Chevalier and his family were caught by the Nazis. Without a word, René beckoned them into the warmth of the front room. Still in their night clothes, Juliette and Claire were visibly trembling, so Antoinette quickly fetched some thick blankets to wrap around them.

'We cannot let them take you,' René declared, his jaw set firmly, his voice carrying a conviction that left no room for argument. 'We will help you escape.'

Gratitude filled Professor Chevalier's eyes, tears spilling over as he clasped René's hand. Juliette nodded, her own eyes brimming as she pulled her shivering child even closer, her body a shield against the world's cruelty.

Antoinette stood rooted to the spot, blood pounding in her ears. It was clear to her – they had to help their friends. But even as determination bloomed within her, a sharp edge of fear cut through her resolve.

What if they were caught? What if someone betrayed them? The consequences were unthinkable. Images of René taken away in the dead of night or Benjamin growing up without his father flashed through her mind, and she felt a tremor in her hands. She wanted to reach for René, to draw strength from his calm certainty, but she stayed still, forcing herself to stand tall. She knew this was the right thing to do. She wanted to do it – *needed* to do it. But the weight of the decision, the risks it carried, pressed heavily on her chest.

Antoinette met Juliette's gaze, the other woman's silent plea for help cutting through her fear like a blade. Taking a shaky breath, she nodded. 'We'll do whatever it takes,' she said softly, her voice steady, despite the turmoil raging within her.

Antoinette put the kettle on, the hiss of steam cutting through the tense silence. As she steeped the tea, she noticed René buttoning his shirt in the bedroom. She followed him inside and quietly shut the door.

'What are we going to do, René?' she asked, her voice tight with anxiety as the walls of the small bedroom seemed to close in around them under the weight of their fear.

René paused, organising his thoughts as he fastened his shirt. 'We need to get them out of the city,' he stated calmly, though his eyes betrayed his concern. 'I'll take them to my brother's farm in the countryside. It's isolated enough to hide until we can figure out a long-term solution.'

The thought of Pierre's remote farmhouse offered a sliver of hope, despite the perilous journey that lay ahead.

'How will you manage without a car?' Antoinette's voice was barely a whisper, filled with doubt.

'I know someone,' René replied, turning to her and speaking decisively. 'A student of mine, whose parents run a bakery on the outskirts. They have a delivery van that might just work to transport the Chevaliers discreetly. It's risky, but it might be our best shot.'

Antoinette's mind raced with the logistics, her resolve hardening despite the fear. A wave of defiance rose within her. 'I'll pack some food,' she stated firmly. 'We must act quickly.'

Back in the front room, she handed out tea and draped a shawl over Juliette's shoulders, placing a small coat around Claire for the trip. 'Drink this, it'll help warm you up,' she urged, scanning the room for anything else they might need. 'We've come up with a plan.'

Professor Chevalier took the cup with shaking hands. Although the warmth of the tea was minimal against cold dread, the gratitude in his eyes bolstered Antoinette's courage. Juliette sipped her tea, trying to soothe Claire, who still clung to her, eyes wide with fear. 'Thank you,' Juliette murmured, her voice laden with emotion. 'I don't know what we would have done without you.'

As Antoinette packed supplies, René joined her in the kitchen, glancing at the clock. 'We need to leave before dawn,' he murmured. 'It's our only chance to avoid the morning patrols.'

'But the curfew?' Antoinette asked, urgency colouring her tone.

'We'll have to risk it,' René said, unrelenting. He stepped closer, his hands resting lightly on her arms, grounding her in the midst of their shared danger. His gaze softened, holding hers with an intensity that spoke what words could not – a silent vow, unbreakable.

René leaned in, pressing a kiss to her forehead, his lips lingering as though memorising her warmth. 'I will return,' he whispered, the words barely audible but ringing with quiet determination.

Antoinette swallowed against the tightness in her throat, nodding as she fought to keep her composure. 'Stay safe,' she whispered, her voice breaking.

Watching from the doorway as René and the Chevaliers disappeared into the night, Antoinette felt chilled with fear. She closed the door behind them, wrapping her arms around herself for comfort as the sound of their footsteps faded away.

Benjamin appeared in the hallway, rubbing his eyes, his small body shaking slightly. 'What's going on, Maman? Where's Papa?'

'We had visitors who needed our help,' Antoinette soothed, offering a gentle smile to mask her anxiety. 'Papa is making sure they're safe. Now, let's get you back to bed.'

. . .

Later, as dawn crept through the blackout curtains, Antoinette awoke in Benjamin's bed, disoriented and stiff. She tiptoed out of his room, careful not to wake him, and checked the house. René was not yet back and it was nearly nine when he finally returned, visibly exhausted and strained.

Her heart wrenched at the sight of him. 'What happened?'

René's expression was grim. 'We were spotted by a Nazi patrol en route to the bakery. I managed to hide Juliette and Claire, and they're on their way to my brother's place. But the professor... they caught him.'

Antoinette's breath caught, the gravity of the situation crashing down on her. 'What will happen to him?'

René shook his head, his eyes shadowed with regret. 'I don't know. But this shows we aren't safe either. Once this next concert is over, we have to disappear too, to avoid any suspicion.'

'Leave everything behind – our home, my sisters, and parents?' Antoinette's voice broke over the words.

'It may be our only option,' René replied solemnly. 'The Nazis are tightening their control, and staying here grows more dangerous by the day. We have to think of Benjamin – of his safety first.'

Tears blurred Antoinette's vision as she embraced René, seeking comfort in his presence. The decision to leave was harrowing, but protecting their family was paramount. As they held each other, the determination to face whatever lay ahead solidified, fortified by their love and the shared resolve to protect their son at all costs.

9

PARIS, 2012

Deanna

The following week, Deanna set out for Paris, driven by an unshakeable need to uncover the secrets of her grandmother Antoinette's past.

Antoinette's sister, her great-aunt Madeline, once a stalwart wartime bookseller, now lived above the same quaint shop, even at the age of ninety-six. Her grand-niece Chloe managed the shop now, and Deanna hoped Madeline held the key to the mysteries that had haunted her since she found the violin.

As Deanna stepped into the quaint Parisian bookshop, a wave of nostalgia washed over her. The scent of paper and ink transported her back to childhood summers, where she had curled up in corners reading picture books on holidays at her favourite great-aunt's home. The familiar atmosphere wrapped around her like a cherished memory, evoking a deep sense of belonging.

Chloe looked up from the counter and greeted her with a warm smile. Her auburn hair, tied loosely at the nape of her neck, glinted under the soft light, framing a face with delicate

features and bright, inquisitive green eyes. Her style was effortlessly Parisian, a simple navy blouse paired with high-waisted
trousers that accentuated her lithe figure. She carried herself
with the understated elegance that seemed to come naturally to
French women, her every movement purposeful, yet unhurried.

'*Bonjour*, Deanna! It's been far too long since we've seen
you. I was so surprised to get your call.' Chloe's soft, melodic
French accent charmed Deanna as they hugged each other
deeply. 'Aunt Madeline is so looking forward to this,' she said as
she led Deanna up the creaky wooden stairs to Madeline's cosy
apartment.

Gently knocking on the door, Chloe announced her arrival
in French. '*Tante Madeline, Deanna est ici!*' The door creaked
open slowly, revealing her great-aunt Madeline seated in a
comfortable armchair by the window. Her silver hair, pulled
back into a loose bun, framed her wise eyes that sparkled with
recognition and warmth as she gazed at Deanna. The room
seemed to hold its breath, the past and present colliding.

'*Ah, ma chérie, Deanna!* It's so wonderful to see you,' Aunt
Madeline greeted her warmly, her eyes lighting up with joy that
seemed to dispel the years. She motioned for Deanna to come
closer, her voice reflecting her joy. 'You have no idea how much
I've missed you,' the older woman said as she stood to hug her
great-niece.

Then she pulled back and studied her. 'It is remarkable how
much you look like your grandmother Antoinette,' Aunt Madeline whispered, her voice barely above a breath.

Chloe spoke. 'I need to return to the shop, but I'll fetch
some tea.'

As the two women sat facing each other, the afternoon sun
streamed through the window, casting a golden glow that
seemed to wrap them in a cocoon of warmth.

The soothing aroma of lavender and leather enveloped
Deanna as she sank into the plush sofa, surrounded by an

eclectic mix of literary treasures that adorned her great-aunt's living room. Her eyes traced over the shelves, filled to the brim with weathered volumes and old-fashioned knick-knacks scattered across every surface.

Black-and-white photographs lined the walls, capturing moments from a different time – her great-aunt's four sisters posing in their elegant 1940s dresses, and her late husband, immortalised in a honeymoon snapshot before the war. Comfort and nostalgia washed over Deanna; this room was a time capsule, preserving the memories of those who had come before her.

They made small talk, catching up on family matters as Chloe brought in a tea tray and poured fragrant jasmine tea into delicate china cups. Deanna grew quiet as she listened to her great-aunt catching her up on all the family news. Madeline was very proud of all her nieces and nephews and their children, and wanted to update her great-niece with all their comings and goings.

'Well, that's enough about me,' Madeline said after a while, placing her cup in its saucer with a delicate clink and fixing her gaze on Deanna. 'Tell me, my dear, what brings you to Paris after all this time? Your call was such a pleasant surprise.'

Deanna smiled nervously before placing down her own cup as she tried to decide how to begin.

'I have a mystery to unravel, Aunt Madeline. A mystery that I hope you might help me solve,' she said, her voice tinged with emotion. Madeline listened intently, her bright eyes never leaving Deanna's face. Deanna chose her words carefully as she relayed the story, not wanting to shock her elderly great-aunt with the less savoury details of her suspicions.

'Do you know anything about it? Or her involvement in the war, Aunt Madeline? All I know is she was separated from my father for most of it but, beyond that, I know very little.'

Madeline looked at her with surprise. 'My goodness, Deanna. That is an unbelievable story.'

'Would you have any idea how the violin came into Antoinette's possession?' Deanna asked.

'No,' Madeline said slowly, her expression thoughtful. 'Your grandmother was a child prodigy. She attended the Paris Music Conservatoire at a very young age and showed great promise as a violinist. But she abruptly stopped playing after the war, and no one knew why. It was a great loss to the musical world – many believed she could have been a virtuoso.' Aunt Madeline's voice held a touch of sadness as she remembered her sister's incredible talent. 'But as I recall, her violin was just a simple instrument she played; my father gave it to her for her twelfth birthday.'

Deanna's mind raced with possibilities, each one more perplexing than the last.

Aunt Madeline reached for a weathered photo album on the coffee table, flipping through its yellowed pages. She paused at a faded black-and-white photograph of a young Antoinette, her eyes alight with passion as she cradled a violin in her hands. 'You see, *this* was her with her violin,' she said, her voice tinged with nostalgia.

Deanna stared at the picture, her gaze narrowing as she studied the instrument in her grandmother's hands. It was a modest violin, its surface dulled by use, the varnish uneven, and its simple craftsmanship a far cry from anything remarkable. The fingerboard looked slightly worn, evidence of years of devoted practice, and the strings were taut but not pristine. It was the kind of violin one might expect from a young girl with big dreams and limited means – cherished, but ordinary.

Her thoughts returned to the violin they had unearthed in the attic. The intricate craftsmanship of Antonio Stradivari was unmistakable in every curve and detail. The scroll was a work of art in itself, its delicate spirals so finely carved they seemed almost alive. Even the grain of the wood told a story of meticulous care and unparalleled skill. It was a masterpiece – a relic from another world – light-years away from the simple, second-hand instrument captured in the photograph.

Deanna's mind raced, trying to piece together the puzzle. How had a young woman from a modest family traded that unassuming violin for a treasure so rare it was almost mythical? Who had placed it in her grandmother's hands, and at what cost?

Deanna looked back at the photograph, her heart heavy with questions she didn't know how to ask.

'Here's another one; this was taken just before she got married,' Aunt Madeline explained. 'She eloped at a very young age. Headstrong and determined, she caused quite an upset. But when the war came, everything changed. Antoinette's husband was taken to a camp, leaving her alone with a young child. She did what she had to do to survive, even if it meant making choices others might not understand.' Aunt Madeline's tone hinted at something darker, her eyes reflecting pain and admiration.

'What do you know about that?' Deanna asked meekly, her words laced with uncertainty as she braced herself for the answer.

Aunt Madeline took a moment to gather her thoughts, averting her gaze and appearing to choose her words carefully. 'Antoinette was a woman of extraordinary courage and sacrifice. She joined the Resistance, risking her life to fight against the occupation. After the war, my parents got word that she was dead. The farmhouse she had been living in had been attacked as the Germans retreated. But in the end, it turned out not to be true, thank God. She was always fiery and secretive. I'm not sure what else she did, but there were rumours...' Aunt Madeline's voice trailed off, the weight of her memories pressing down on her.

'What kind of rumours?' Deanna pressed, the intensity in her voice mirroring the urgency she felt inside.

Madeline's eyes flickered up to meet her gaze, a haunted look in them. 'Surely you don't want to know all the sordid details of the past, my dear,' she said, taking a sip of her tea. 'Sometimes it's better to remember people for who they *were*, rather than what they *did*,' Aunt Madeline cautioned softly, her tone filled with a mix of protection and reluctance, a barrier against the painful truths of the past.

'There is a reason I'm asking,' Deanna said, her voice steady but tinged with urgency. She went on to explain what they had found, hinting that her grandmother might have had an affair with the Nazi who owned the violin. Aunt Madeline's face paled, and the silence between them seemed to stretch endlessly, charged with the gravity of Deanna's words.

Deanna leaned forward, her hands clasped tightly in her lap. 'I need to know the truth,' she said, her voice softer now but no less determined. 'Not just for me, but for Dad. He's lived his whole life with this image of his mother, never knowing what she endured, what sacrifices she made – or what she might have been forced to do. If there's even a chance that the violin and her past could give us answers, I owe it to him to find them.'

'An affair with a... *Nazi*?' Aunt Madeline finally repeated, her voice barely above a whisper. Memories flickered behind her eyes, and she seemed to age before Deanna, the years catching up with her in an instant. The once vibrant woman now appeared frail and burdened by the weight of her words.

Deanna watched as emotions warred within her great-aunt's gaze – disbelief, sorrow, perhaps even a trace of guilt. She reached out to gently touch her great-aunt Madeline's arm, offering comfort, her touch a silent promise of support.

'I never knew,' Aunt Madeline finally whispered, her voice trembling. 'Your grandmother... she always carried so much with her. If she did what you're suggesting, it must have been out of desperation or to protect someone she loved. When she went missing, we were so afraid for her life, but an affair...' She shook her head. 'The war forced many of us to make unimaginable choices. I can't believe that of her, but something did happen that hardened her, and she became very secretive after her husband, René, was taken away. But a mistress to a Nazi? *Never!*' Aunt Madeline's voice was firm.

Deanna nodded, feeling the enormity of the revelations and the assurance of her great-aunt's words. 'I just want to understand her story. Maybe then I can find some peace with it all. And peace for Antoinette's son.'

'How can I help you?' her great-aunt asked, her voice filled with empathy.

'I need to track down people who knew her during that time, anyone who can help me unravel the mysteries of her past. Do you know of anyone?'

Aunt Madeline looked despondently at her great-niece. 'So many people are gone now,' she said, her eyes sad, then suddenly lighting up with a spark of memory. 'But there is one person who might be able to help. I met her a few years ago. She volunteers at the Holocaust Memorial here in Paris. Her mother was a member of the Resistance during the war. She told me her mother and Antoinette had been in the Resistance together. Her name was... Florence, I believe.'

Aunt Madeline reached for a pen and a piece of paper, jotting down the name and address of the Holocaust Memorial where Florence's daughter volunteered. Deanna took the slip of paper, feeling a rush of hope.

She placed the paper into her bag and they moved on and spoke of other things: her father's move to a new home, and life at the bookshop.

At the end of the afternoon, Deanna embraced Aunt Madeline tightly, feeling a deep sense of connection and gratitude for this living link to her grandmother's past. She left her great-aunt's home promising to share any new information she uncov-ered. A newfound sense of purpose propelled her forward, her single-mindedness bolstered by her great-aunt's adamant refusal to believe that Antoinette could have done what was being suggested.

As Deanna stepped out into the crisp Parisian air, she reached into her bag and clutched the slip of paper tightly in her hand. With the address as her first clue, she resolved to uncover the truth, not just for herself, but for her father and the legacy of the woman they both loved.

The answers were out there, and Deanna vowed she wouldn't stop until she found them.

10

APRIL 1941

Antoinette

It had been a month since Professor Chevalier was taken. René and Antoinette had made their arrangements to leave Paris, and planned to slip away after the final concert.

Despite the urgency of their situation, René had insisted on staying until then, believing his continued presence and leadership at the Conservatoire would help protect the remaining Jewish musicians and students still under suspicion. More than that, he had been working tirelessly with the Resistance to secure forged papers, safe houses, and escape routes for those left behind. It was a dangerous and delicate operation, one that consumed his nights and filled Antoinette with both pride, and an unrelenting fear for his safety.

Antoinette hadn't argued, though the decision weighed heavily on her. She knew how much the music and the Conservatoire meant to René – it was their lifeline to normality, to purpose – but it also tethered them dangerously close to the tightening grip of the Nazi regime.

Antoinette's mind buzzed with all she had to do the next

day as she and Benjamin sat in the audience at the final concert at the Conservatoire. The concert hall was bathed in soft, dim lighting as she sat waiting for the concert to begin, her thoughts racing. Their bags were packed; tomorrow, they would flee to René's brother Paul's farm. Yet, the uncertainty of what lay ahead for Professor Chevalier, his family, and themselves filled her with dread. Benjamin sat beside her in his best clothes, his small hand gripping hers tightly, offering silent, yet profound, reassurance.

The concert had barely begun when, suddenly, chaos erupted at the back of the grand hall. Heavy footsteps marched down the aisle, the sound ricocheting off the white marble floors and amplifying the growing tension. Antoinette spun around, her breath catching, to see uniformed Nazis flooding in, their ominous presence shattering the concert hall's refined elegance.

Along with members of the French police, a Nazi commander, his posture rigid and his gaze both piercing and unyielding, strode to the front of the grand hall, interrupting the performance. By his side stood the director of the Conservatoire, looking pale and guilty.

The room fell into hushed silence as people tried to make sense of the upset. Antoinette's heart clenched – surely, they wouldn't cause trouble with so many innocent children present? The atmosphere was thick with tension, everyone holding their breath, waiting for what would come next.

The music stuttered to a halt as the conductor, a middle-aged man with wild grey hair and a professional stance, stepped back, his eyes flickering with shock.

The Nazi commander's voice boomed through the hall, demanding attention. 'Ladies and gentlemen,' he began coldly, 'we have received word that there are traitors among you. We are here to root out these enemies of the state and ensure the safety of this nation.' His words hung in the air, a chilling promise of the horrors to come.

With a cold nod, the commander signalled his soldiers to begin their ruthless search. Panic erupted as women screamed and children wailed, clinging desperately to their loved ones. Armed men stormed through the room, yanking innocent individuals from their seats as the director pointed them out.

Antoinette's mind spun as she watched her friends and colleagues being dragged away, their pleas piercing the tense air. She locked eyes with René, who had risen from his piano, a steely defiance in his expression. In that brief, desperate moment, their silent communication was clear and powerful: they had to stay strong for Benjamin, no matter the cost.

As she stood, her grip on Benjamin's hand tightened, his small fingers trembling. She could see the terror in his wide eyes as he clung to her side, seeking a reassurance she could not give.

The sound of her husband's name being called sent a jolt of fear through her whole body, and her heart dropped like a stone into the pit of her stomach. She watched helplessly as René was pointed out and then violently yanked from his piano by merciless soldiers, as she stood frozen with terror.

Instinctively, she screamed out his name, but her voice was lost in the cacophony of noise all around her. Tears bubbled up as their eyes met, communicating a silent message of love and devotion as he was dragged away. She fought through the crowd, pushing and shoving against the tide of panicked bodies as she followed him outside, her hand still clasping her son.

Finally, breaking free from the grasp of the crowd, Antoinette burst into the frigid night air, the sounds of orders and cries still ringing in her ears. The cold air bit into her skin as she desperately scanned through the crowds looking for René, her breath coming in ragged gasps. And then, in the distance, she caught a glimpse of him being loaded onto a truck along with other members of the Conservatoire, looking so out of place in their three-piece suits. With renewed urgency, she rushed towards him, her young son's legs struggling to keep up with her frenzied pace.

She reached him as he was being hauled up onto an idling truck by two Nazi soldiers. Ignoring their shouts and warnings, she lunged forward, her hand outstretched towards René, tears streaming down her face.

'René!' she cried out, her voice raw with desperation. His eyes met hers for a fleeting moment before he was roughly pushed up into the crowded vehicle and was lost in the sea of faces. Benjamin clung to her leg, sobbing as she called out her husband's name over and over again, her voice cutting through the chaos around them.

Antoinette flung herself towards the truck, ignoring the slew of guns pointed in her direction. She slammed her fists against the cold metal exterior with all her might, each blow sending a jolt of pain up her arms. 'René! René!' she screamed, her voice raw, her eyes searching frantically for her husband amidst the chaos of soldiers and bodies.

At last, she caught a glimpse of his face through the mass of bodies, twisted with anguish and disbelief as he registered her presence. 'Antoinette, I love you!' he shouted towards her, his voice barely audible above the screams of the crowd and the roar of the engine.

Tears stung her eyes as she yelled back, 'I love you too!'

René's hoarse voice echoed through the chaos, his words laced with fierce determination. 'Protect Benjamin; don't worry about me. Be strong for him.'

Antoinette scooped up her trembling child and held him close to her chest, trying to muffle his sobs. She frantically reached out for her husband, desperate to touch his face one last time before they were torn apart. But a merciless Nazi officer materialised from the darkness, yanking her back with a grip of steel as he barked orders at her to stay away. Her anger built as she struggled against his unyielding hold, fighting with every ounce of strength in her body as he dragged her further and further away from René's reassuring presence.

Suddenly, without warning, he lifted his gun and slammed the barrel into the side of her head. The impact sent shockwaves of pain ripping through her skull, blurring her vision and threatening to send her crashing to the ground. She fought against the darkness creeping in at the edges of her consciousness, determined to stay awake despite the world spinning out of control. The soldier's grip was like steel, digging into her arm with inhuman strength.

He flung her to the ground and, through the haze of agony, she could see Benjamin's terrified face staring back at her, his eyes wide with fear and confusion. Summoning every ounce of strength within her, Antoinette pushed through the pain and reached out for her child, pulling him close to her chest in a protective embrace. The soldier loomed over them, his expression cold and unyielding as he towered above the pair. He raised his hand to strike again, but a commotion behind him diverted his attention and saved them from that blow.

In that brief moment of distraction, Antoinette leapt to her feet, clutching Benjamin's hand tightly. Her head throbbed from the soldier's merciless blow as she pulled her son back into the frenzied crowd that swallowed them whole. She stole one last look at the truck, where René stood frozen in terror, watching, their eyes locked in a desperate promise of love and resilience. With gritted teeth, she mouthed the words, 'I will find you, René. I promise. Stay strong.' The truck roared to life, spewing out thick clouds of black smoke before vanishing into the night, ripping her beloved husband away from her.

The searing pain in her heart matched the pain throbbing in her head and was unlike anything she had ever felt before. As she sat down on the floor, panting, Benjamin touched his hand to her temple, blood staining his tiny fingers.

'Maman, you're bleeding,' he whimpered, his voice cracking with fear as he looked up at her with wide, tear-filled eyes.

Antoinette took a deep breath, trying to hold back her own tears of agony and loss as she whispered through trembling lips, 'I'll be all right, my love.' She gasped, her hands frantically searching for something to stop the bleeding. A kind woman offered a handkerchief, which Antoinette gratefully pressed against her wound, determined to remain strong for her son, despite the fear coursing through her veins.

René's words of love echoed in her mind. With renewed strength, she got to her feet and pushed back through the suffocating crowd, every step feeling heavier than the last. Exhausted and drained, she made her way from the Conservatoire, her heart aching with the knowledge that her husband was gone. But even as she struggled to keep moving forward, Antoinette refused to let go of hope. She would do whatever it took to protect her son, and promised herself that one day they would be reunited with René.

She would not succumb to the darkness that threatened to consume her; she would fight with every fibre of her being for the sake of her family. The Nazis may try to strip away her freedom and humanity, but Antoinette would never let them take her soul.

11

PARIS, 2012

Deanna

An hour later, Deanna gazed up at the imposing façade of the Holocaust Memorial in Paris. She took a deep breath, feeling the weight of history as she pushed open the heavy wooden doors and stepped inside.

The museum was a sombre place, its walls lined with memories captured in black-and-white photographs and preserved artefacts of World War Two.

She arrived at the information desk, where a gentle-faced woman with kind, understanding eyes greeted her. Deanna hesitated for a moment, her fingers tracing the edge of the polished desk, trying to work out where to begin.

'I'm looking for a woman who is the daughter of a Resistance agent named Florence,' Deanna began, her voice tinged with nervousness. 'She volunteers here, I believe. I'm hoping she might be able to help me with some research. Do you know who that might be?'

The woman's face softened into a warm smile as recognition

dawned in her eyes. 'I know exactly who you're talking about,' she replied. 'Florence's daughter, Yvonne, is here today. Let me take you to her.'

Deanna followed the woman through the museum, her mind racing. Being here made everything feel so... real. She couldn't help but feel a sense of awe as she passed by exhibits detailing the bravery and sacrifices of those who fought against the atrocities of war. It was a stark reminder of the darkness that had once engulfed the world, and she found herself wondering how her own grandmother fitted into this intricate tapestry of history.

As they approached a section dedicated to the Resistance fighters, Deanna felt her emotions swell. The sight of the displays brought a lump to her throat, knowing that her own grandmother had been among them, despite the shadows now clouding her legacy.

They reached another volunteer's desk where a middle-aged woman sat surrounded by pamphlets and books. Yvonne looked up as they approached, her eyes alight with curiosity, the light catching the edges of her auburn hair.

The woman from the information desk introduced her. Yvonne's eyes widened, and she gestured for Deanna to take a seat opposite her. Deanna felt a mix of nervousness and excitement as she settled into the chair, her fingers gripping the edge of the seat for support.

'I was told that you might have information about my grandmother's involvement in the Resistance during the war,' Deanna began tentatively, her eyes searching Yvonne's face for any hint of insight. 'Her name was Antoinette Valette, but she might have gone by the codename Melodie Buchet.'

Yvonne's eyes brightened. 'Why, yes, I know of Melodie. She was very close to my mother. My mother, Florence, often spoke of your grandmother with great respect. They were comrades in arms, fighting side by side.'

Deanna listened intently as Yvonne recounted stories of courage and sacrifice, of secret missions undertaken under the cover of darkness, and of bonds forged in the crucible of war.

When Yvonne paused, Deanna spoke. 'There is something more serious I need to know about.' She cleared her throat and began, 'During the last months of the war, my grandmother went missing from Paris. Do you have any information about what might have happened to her?'

Yvonne listened and then, from below a glass case, pulled out a worn black leather journal, pages covered in faint, spidery script.

'This is my mother's diary, written during the war,' Yvonne said softly, sliding the pages across the desk to Deanna. 'She mentioned your grandmother in a few entries. Perhaps this will shed some light on what happened.'

Deanna's heart raced as she picked up the fragile pages, her hands trembling slightly.

'Here is the time you are talking about,' Yvonne said, pointing to a specific entry in the diary dated 1944. Yvonne translated from French to English as Deanna's eyes scanned the words, her palms sweating as Yvonne read through it. '*I finally confronted Melodie on the inevitable and she confessed to me what was going on. I was shocked, to say the least. I never would have expected this of her, but I understood why she had done it. I told her I would help her any way I could because her husband must never know.*'

As Deanna listened to the words scrawled in Florence's diary, her mind raced with possibilities. With her thoughts drifting to Falkenberg, she asked Yvonne, 'Does it say anywhere in the diary what she was keeping secret from my grandfather?'

Yvonne's brow furrowed as she flipped through the diary's weathered pages. After a moment, she paused, her finger landing on a particular entry dated several months later. 'The only other entry about your grandmother is this: *I tried to reason with Melodie about her decision, but she was adamant this was the only way to protect her family, especially her husband. I promised to keep her secret, knowing the consequences if it ever came to light. She was in tears, and my heart ached for the burden she carried.'*

Deanna's breath caught as she absorbed the weight of her grandmother's situation. Perhaps the Nazi had some sort of hold over her due to her husband, which was why she had started the affair with him.

'Do you have any idea what decision she might have been referring to?' Deanna asked, desperate to know more.

Yvonne shook her head. 'I myself have always wondered.'

A memory of the picture of Antoinette and the Nazi flashed through Deanna's mind. She hesitated, unsure if she should reveal the photograph to Yvonne. But the need for answers outweighed her reservations, and she reached into her bag to retrieve the image she had brought for her research.

'I have this picture,' Deanna said, handing the photograph to Yvonne. As Yvonne's eyes fell upon the image, she caught her breath, her expression shifting from curiosity to shock.

'This is my grandmother, and she is with a man called Otto von Falkenberg. He was a notorious Nazi officer, known for his cruelty during the war,' Deanna informed her.

Yvonne stared at the photograph in silence. Deanna watched her closely, waiting for any sign that Yvonne knew more than she was letting on.

After what felt like an eternity, Yvonne finally spoke in a hushed tone. 'Your grandmother must have been in a precarious position if she was involved with him.' She reached out to grasp Deanna's hand, offering silent support. 'I understand now why you need to uncover the truth about your grandmother's past,' Yvonne said softly, her eyes reflecting a mix of compassion and sorrow. 'I have numerous letters my mother wrote during that period and after the war at home. I will comb through them for any clues about why she was with this Nazi. If I find anything, I will let you know. I will give you a copy of the whole journal; there may be something in there that can help you.'

'Thank you, Yvonne,' Deanna said gratefully, as Florence's daughter went to copy the pages of the journal for her. Her heart was heavy with the impact of all she had learned. Instead of proving her grandmother's innocence, it seemed to confirm that her grandmother had indeed been entangled with a high-ranking Nazi officer. What else could have been so shocking and needed to be kept a secret?

As she said goodbye to Yvonne, Deanna's mind swirled as she clutched the copied pages of Florence's diary. Each word seemed to add another layer to the mystery, another possibility she hadn't considered. The image of her grandmother with Otto von Falkenberg burned in her mind, a stark contradiction to the brave Resistance fighter she had envisioned.

Could it be true, as Yvonne suggested, that her grandmother had willingly been involved with such a man for the sake of her family? Or had she been forced into a situation where no choice was truly her own? Deanna felt a ripple of unease at the thought, but as she pieced together the fragments of what she had learned, a glimmer of understanding began to emerge.

Antoinette had done what she had to do – what anyone might have done – to protect those she loved. Deanna's gaze dropped to the pages in her hand, and she felt the weight of her father's legacy settle on her shoulders. But she knew no matter how painful or complex, her grandmother's story deserved to be told in full.

As she left the museum, the Parisian air felt heavier, but somewhere deep inside her, a quiet determination took hold. Antoinette Valette's life had been far more than a collection of photographs and faded memories. Whatever the truth was,

Deanna was determined not to judge, but to understand. Still, a lingering concern gnawed at her.

The image of Antoinette, a fierce Resistance fighter, now forever tainted by this dark connection to the enemy, seemed to haunt every memory she had of her grandmother.

12

APRIL 1941

Antoinette

As Antoinette stumbled through the chaos of the crowd, she clutched Benjamin tightly in her arms, her breath coming in ragged gasps.

Blood trickled down her temple, warm and sticky, blurring her vision as it mingled with the cold sweat on her face. Her head throbbed with a relentless pounding, each beat a cruel reminder of the blow she had taken moments before. Her thoughts raced, a torrent of fear, pain, and loss threatening to consume her, but she refused to give in to despair.

The sharp cries of frightened voices and the deafening clamour of boots against stone surged around her, a cacophony that mirrored the chaos in her mind. She felt Benjamin's tiny hands gripping her coat, his face pressed tightly against her chest as though seeking refuge from the nightmare unfolding around them. She drew strength from the weight of him in her arms, the steady warmth of his body grounding her even as terror clawed at her resolve.

Antoinette blinked hard, willing her focus to sharpen

despite the haze of pain clouding her senses. She had promised René she would stay strong for their child, and that was exactly what she intended to do, no matter the cost. Even as her knees threatened to buckle and her heart pounded like a war drum in her chest, she pushed forward, her every step fuelled by a desperate determination to keep her son safe.

Without realising where she was going, Antoinette found herself at her parents' home in Montmartre, and she frantically knocked on the door. When her younger sister Charlotte opened it, her eyes widened in shock at the sight of Antoinette's dishevelled state, her dress torn, her body dirty and blood-streaked, her face a mask of anguish and tear-stained.

'Oh my God, Antoinette!' Charlotte gasped, pulling her inside with a force that belied her small frame. The younger sibling wrapped her sister in a fierce embrace, as tremors coursed through Antoinette's body.

'You're bleeding, what happened?' Charlotte's words cut through the fog in Antoinette's mind. She reached up and touched the wound on her head, feeling the sticky warmth of blood mixed with the throbbing pain that had been overshadowed by her overwhelming emotions.

Antoinette's sobs were so intense she could barely speak. She took a deep, shuddering breath before finally finding her voice. 'René... they took him,' she managed to choke out, her words heavy with grief and disbelief. Her tears fell freely, mingling with the dirt and blood on her cheeks.

All at once, the door opened again, and their parents, Bernard and Delphine, entered, their laughter from a concert they had attended abruptly silenced as Charlotte explained what had happened. Bernard's face turned ashen, and Delphine's hand flew to her mouth in horror.

Ushering their daughter and grandson into the front room, Bernard quickly built up the fire, that cast a warm glow contrasting sharply with the cold dread in the room.

Charlotte wrapped a blanket around Benjamin, handed him a toy, and set the kettle to boil. The room was filled with the comforting aroma of chamomile tea as her mother dealt with Antoinette's injury.

Tears flowed unchecked from Antoinette as she huddled with her family, recounting the harrowing events of that night through stuttering sobs. She described the brutality of the soldiers and the heart-wrenching separation from René as her family listened to her story in shock.

As she finished dressing the head wound, Delphine's hands tightened around her daughter's, a silent promise of unwavering support and love in the face of unspeakable tragedy, but the crackling fire and the scent of brewing tea did little to soothe the raw pain that filled the room.

Bernard was furious, his eyes blazing with an unshakable purpose as he studied his family, his voice angry as he spoke. 'I read about the Jewish round-up in the underground newspaper, but we will not let them win. We will fight back, together, as a family.' His brown eyes, once warm, now reflected the unshakeable tenaciousness of a man who had already fought through one war and had seen too much to be broken.

'How, Papa? How do we fight against such a strong and ruthless enemy?' Antoinette's voice quivered with despair. She knew the odds were stacked against them, but the fire in her heart refused to be extinguished. Bernard placed a comforting hand on his daughter's shoulder, his grip firm, his eyes reflecting his conviction. 'Every enemy has its weakness, we just need to find a way.'

Antoinette's mind began to turn over her father's words. She would find their weakness. She would bring her husband home.

. . .

That evening, for the first time in years, she slept in her old bed at her family home, Benjamin curled up at her side, his small hands clutching a teddy bear and the nightdress she had borrowed from Charlotte, afraid she would leave him.

She had a restless night, her dreams filled with fragmented images of René and the soldiers. But sometime early in the morning, a clear plan began to form in her mind, each step becoming more defined as dawn approached.

Her need to do something had only strengthened during the night, driven by a unwavering resolve to rescue René and make those responsible for their suffering pay. She could see each step clearly now.

As the first light of dawn filtered through the curtains, Antoinette's mind was clear, her heart decided.

She kissed Benjamin's forehead gently before slipping out of bed, leaving him sound asleep. She would start with the people from the Conservatoire that she knew were working for the Resistance. The memory of a whispered conversation with a cellist who spoke of hidden networks and safe houses came to her. One of the Jewish musicians, whose name was Emile, had talked about them at the gathering they'd had. She knew where to begin.

Leaving a note for her family, who were still sleeping, Antoinette ventured out into the awakening city.

The streets were quiet in the early hours of the morning, a stark contrast to the chaos of the previous night. She had borrowed some of Charlotte's clothes, the fabric still carrying the faint scent of her sister's favourite perfume. She made her way towards the street where she knew Emile lived.

As she approached the unassuming door, she hesitated for a moment before finally reaching out to knock. Her mind was a whirlwind of doubt and fear as the door creaked open to reveal a young man with tired eyes and a steely gaze.

'Antoinette,' he whispered hoarsely, a flicker of surprise crossing his face. He quickly scanned their surroundings before motioning for her to enter.

Silently, she followed him inside, the heavy door shutting behind her. The kitchen was sparsely furnished, with only a small wooden table and a few chairs scattered around it. The young man, Emile, motioned for her to sit down as he offered to make her coffee. Despite his calm demeanour, she could see the tension in the muscles of his arms.

Dressed in a black undershirt and crumpled trousers, his arm bore a tattoo of the French national motto: *Liberté, Égalité, Fraternité* – in this case a defiant symbol against the brutal Nazi regime. As he handed her a steaming cup of coffee, their eyes met in silent understanding.

'I wasn't there last night, but I heard about what happened at the concert,' Emile said gravely. 'And how they took René away. I'm so sorry. They rounded people up all over the city last night.' He shook a cigarette from its packet on the table and offered one to her, which she refused, before he lit it with practised ease. In that brief flame, she could see the weariness carved into his features – a reflection of the constant fear and struggle they all faced under occupation.

'What can I do, to get him back?' Antoinette asked with desperation.

Emile took a long drag from his cigarette, the smoke curling lazily in the dimly lit room. His gaze held Antoinette's, assessing her resolve. Finally, he spoke in a low, measured tone. 'We are planning an emergency meeting this morning, and discussing possible strategies.' Emile ran a hand through his thick, dark hair, a flicker of uncertainty crossing his face. 'It won't be easy, and it certainly won't be without risks, but I want us to discuss the possibility of a raid. Two of my other friends were taken last night as well.'

Antoinette felt a surge of anger coursing through her veins, pushing aside any lingering doubts or fears. This was her chance to do something, to fight back against the tyranny that had torn her family apart.

'Count me in. I'll do whatever it takes,' she said, her voice steady despite the rapid beating of her heart. Emile studied her for a moment, his eyes searching hers for any trace of hesitation or doubt. Finding none, he nodded solemnly.

'Good. We need all the help we can get,' he replied. 'But you must understand, the risks are immense.'

Antoinette met his gaze and nodded without flinching. She knew the dangers that lay ahead, but she was willing to face them head-on for the chance to save René.

Later that morning, other members of the Resistance arrived, including the leader of the cell in that area of Paris, Jacques. He came with an update as the group settled around the table together.

'There is talk of people being taken to a transit camp on the edge of Paris. If we are to attempt anything, we need information. As you may know, the Nazis have commandeered the Majestic Hotel, and apparently, all the transfers and information about the station are being handled from there.'

He paused and stared at Antoinette, apparently weighing her up. 'Emile tells me you want to help?'

Antoinette nodded firmly. 'Yes, I'll do whatever it takes to save René,' she said, her voice steady even as fear tightened like a vice deep within her.

Jacques continued to study her for a moment, his expression unreadable, before nodding his approval. 'Good. We need someone on the inside to gather information about when and where prisoners are to be taken from the transfer station. All the documentation is held there at the Majestic.'

'How would I get in without them suspecting me?' she asked.

He paused and narrowed his eyes before continuing. 'You studied at the Conservatoire?'

'Yes,' Antoinette replied, surprised at the change of topic. 'I am a violinist.'

'She is *brilliant*,' Emile chimed in, a glimmer of pride in his eyes, despite the gravity of the situation.

Jacques continued. 'Good. The Nazis frequently entertain dignitaries and visiting officers. A musician of your talent would be a valuable asset to them. If you can gain their trust, you might be invited to play at private parties on the second floor, where we believe their main suites and offices are located.'

Antoinette's chest tightened further as she listened to the leader's plan, her pulse pounding in her ears. Go undercover at the Majestic Hotel? Her mind immediately filled with images of narrow escapes and violent interrogations. Her hands trembled at her sides as she thought about the danger – what if she was caught? What if they found out why she was there? What if she failed to bring René back?

For a moment, the room seemed to blur, the weight of the proposal pressing down on her. But then she thought of René – his voice, his smile, his unwavering strength. She pictured Benjamin growing up without his father, and a fire ignited within her, burning through her fear.

'I'll do it,' Antoinette said, her voice steady despite the growing anxiety inside her. The words left her mouth before she could second-guess herself. She clenched her hands into fists to stop their trembling, forcing herself to meet Jacques's intense gaze. 'If this is what it takes to save him, I'll do whatever is needed.'

Jacques nodded, but his expression remained serious. 'This

will not be easy,' he warned. 'One misstep, and you won't make it out.'

'I understand,' she replied, though her voice faltered slightly. She straightened her posture, steeling herself against the fear clawing at her insides. But she had no choice. René needed her. Benjamin needed his father. And Antoinette would not let her family down.

The leader's eyes reflected both concern for Antoinette's safety and admiration for her bravery.

'We will provide you with the necessary documents and a cover story to get you inside,' Jacques said. 'But you must be cautious at all times. You will need to mingle with the Nazis, pretend you are one of them, and win their trust. The slightest slip-up could put not only yourself but also this entire Resistance cell in danger. If you are found out, you will be taken away, just like your husband.'

Antoinette thought of Benjamin, a wave of fear washing over her at the thought of him losing both his parents to the Nazis' cruelty.

But she pushed those thoughts aside. Even one day without René felt like an eternity. She was willing to face any danger, any hardship, if it meant bringing her family back together again.

'Come back tomorrow, and we will start training you,' Jacques instructed her.

With those final words echoing in her ears, Antoinette stepped out into the chilly day, the reality of her new mission bearing down heavily on her shoulders.

13

WALES, 2012

Deanna

That night, Deanna's phone buzzed with an unexpected call.

'Deanna, you won't *believe* this!' Felicity's voice crackled with excitement. 'I think we've found the original owner of the violin. He claims it was stolen from his family before the war!'

Deanna sat down. 'What? You're right, I really can't believe it.'

'He also brought up your grandmother,' Felicity continued, her voice dropping a notch. 'This could be a huge discovery, Dee. He might be able to fill in the gaps about your grandmother's life during the war.'

'Who is he?'

'His name is Carlos Rossi, and he's from Brazil. And he'll be in London on business next week.'

'How on earth did you find him?'

'It was a bit of detective work, really. During my research on the violin's history, I found the name of its last known owner, Giovanni Rossi. That led me down a rabbit hole of birth and death records. Eventually, I connected with a distant relative who mentioned their family had owned a valuable violin that was stolen during the war. Finally, I tracked down Carlos, Giovanni's son, who is also a dealer. And while he doesn't deal in instruments, he's very well connected in the antiques world.'

'That's why you did so well in your exams and I didn't,' Deanna admitted with a sigh. 'You always had that persistence, like a dog with a bone.'

'I can't help it, you know I love the thrill of solving a puzzle. It makes me feel like Indiana Jones, minus the hat and whip.'

Deanna's tone changed as she became more serious.

'Seriously, Fee, thank you for doing this. You know how much it means to both my dad and me. I'm truly grateful for all your help.'

As the call ended, Deanna set her phone down and leaned back in her chair, her mind swirling with questions. Could this man, Carlos Rossi, be the key to uncovering the truth about the violin – and maybe her grandmother's mysterious past? She held her arms tightly around herself, the weight of anticipation settling over her.

As promised, within a week, Deanna found herself back in London, sitting across from a strikingly handsome man in a cosy café by the Thames. The river sparkled in the afternoon light, while the aroma of fresh pastries and roasted coffee filled the air.

Carlos had risen smoothly as she'd entered, unfolding his tall frame with effortless grace. His tailored navy suit hugged his broad shoulders, and the crisp white shirt beneath it accentuated his sun-kissed complexion.

He extended his hand, his grip firm yet gentle, his thick, wavy black-and-silver hair perfectly combed. His piercing blue eyes held a hint of curiosity that radiated warmth.

Her first thoughts were: tall and brooding, a fiercely handsome yet kinder-looking Mr Darcy. Her gaze caught Felicity's, who was also communicating quite clearly to her friend that she thought Carlos wasn't terrible to look at.

Deanna cleared her throat. 'Mr Rossi, thank you for meeting with me.'

In response, his voice was smooth and melodic, with a hint of a South American accent that gave his words a lyrical quality. 'Miss Kaplan, the pleasure is all mine,' he said, his gaze golding hers with a warmth that was both disarming and intriguing.

Deanna smiled nervously, momentarily caught off guard by the intensity of his gaze. 'Please, call me Deanna.'

'Deanna,' he repeated, his accent lingering deliciously on the name. 'It's miraculous that this violin has resurfaced after so many years. My father informs me that my great-grandfather was gifted the violin by his grandmother, given to her from Antonio Stradivari himself. It held great sentimental value to him. When it was stolen, he said it felt like a piece of his heart had been ripped away.' His tone softened as he spoke, and Deanna couldn't help but notice the faint shadow of sadness in his otherwise composed demeanour.

He paused, then added, 'We are, of course, willing to pay a very good sum for its recovery.'

Felicity snapped out of the spell his presence was casting between them and went into business mode. 'Obviously, with an item this valuable and with such a rich history, we would need to ensure that the proper steps are taken in terms of authentication and verification before I would encourage Deanna to consider anything further.'

Carlos nodded in agreement. 'Of course, I understand completely,' he said, his expression thoughtful.

Deanna leaned forward. 'Is there anything else you can tell me about its past and its connection to my grandmother?'

Carlos's expression grew reflective. 'My father escaped Italy during the war,' he began, his gaze flickering with emotion as he seemed to weigh his words. 'The impact of that time has haunted him for decades. He lost his parents – my grandparents – and his younger brother. They were rounded up and sent to a camp, while my father managed to flee from his home in Italy and work for the Resistance in France. He had heard that the violin, which had been so precious to his family, had been stolen by Nazis and was somewhere in Paris.'

Deanna noticed the way Carlos's features softened when he spoke of his father, a tenderness contrasting with the commanding air he exuded, and the mix of strength and vulnerability was captivating.

'He refused to give up until he found it,' he continued. 'As a tribute to his father and grandfather, who had cherished it before him.'

Deanna's heart ached as Carlos continued. His passion and pain seemed etched into the very lines of his striking features, making it impossible to look away.

'He settled in Brazil after the war, met my mother, and tried to start again. But their marriage didn't survive. My mother was much younger, and the strain of my father's past created a rift between them. They divorced when I was still young, and I didn't see him for many years. I grew up with my mother, not really knowing much about my father's history. When we finally reconnected after my mother's death, it was through a shared love of antiques. That's when he started opening up to me about the war, about the violin, and about the people he knew back then – including your grandmother.'

Deanna's eyes widened. '*My* grandmother?'

Carlos nodded, his thoughtful expression illuminated by a flicker of admiration. 'He said they crossed paths many times in the Resistance. They worked together undercover in a hotel. She too was a violinist, and she vowed to help him find the violin. He told me an interesting story about her and her own violin. He mentioned she kept a page of sheet music inside with the word "always" scribbled on top. He never knew what it meant, but it seemed to have some personal significance to her.'

Deanna's breath caught. Liszt's *Liebestraum No. 3* – her grandfather's song, the one he had played to her when he proposed. The story her great-aunt had once told her about.

Deanna's mind raced. Could Carlos's father really have known her grandmother that well? The connection was undeniable.

'He's never forgotten her,' Carlos continued, his voice dropping into a softer, almost reverent tone.

Deanna's need to know more surged. 'I need to meet with your father. I have a lot of questions. Does he ever come to London?'

'He hates to travel; he's never left Brazil since he arrived there after the war. And unfortunately, as he ages, his hearing loss prevents him from talking well on the phone. But you would be most welcome to come to Brazil. I would be happy to pay for your flights – both of you. The violin is very important to us, and I think my father could tell you things about your grandmother that you've never heard before. His memory is sharp. It would mean the world to him.'

As Carlos leaned forward, the intensity in his blue eyes made Deanna momentarily forget her surroundings. She remained silent, still processing everything.

'You wouldn't be alone,' Carlos added, sensing her hesitation. 'My sister Maria lives with him at our family villa. She's wonderful – fiercely protective of our father, and she loves having guests. You'd be well taken care of. And if it makes you feel more comfortable, you could bring a friend or stay at a hotel. But be aware, Maria has a way of convincing people to stay at the villa once they meet her,' he added with a warm smile. 'She's... hard to resist.'

Deanna chuckled, feeling some of her apprehension melt away.

Carlos leaned in slightly, his voice soft but sincere. 'I know this might feel overwhelming, but I promise, this isn't just about the violin. It's about family, about history. I think you deserve to know the truth about your grandmother.'

Deanna smiled. 'Let me think about it.'

As Carlos departed, Deanna turned to Felicity, who was already eyeing her with that familiar look of playful scepticism.

'So?' Felicity raised her eyebrows mischievously. 'Charming, right? And that accent – very "tall, dark, and mysterious". You didn't even blush, I'm impressed.'

Deanna rolled her eyes, feigning exasperation. 'Oh, please. It was just a meeting. Besides, he's clearly only passionate about the violin.'

'Sure, Dee. *Just a meeting* where he offers to fly you to Brazil. Very average Tuesday for you, right?' Felicity grinned, tapping her chin.

'So,' Felicity said, folding her arms, 'you're considering hopping on a plane to South America, trusting Mr Handsome-and-Charming, and hoping you don't get abducted? Which, by the way, sounds like a solid plan.'

Deanna laughed. 'Okay, okay, point taken. But if I go, *you're* coming with me. He said I could bring a friend. There's no way I'd understand all this violin's history without you.'

Felicity grinned, leaning back. 'A tropical getaway? Count me in. I'll bring my sun hat and – oh, wait – I'm married. Such a shame.' She mock-pouted, raising her eyebrows dramatically.

Deanna smirked. 'Oh, come on. I'll talk to Dave. Besides, I'll make it worth your while if this whole violin exchange goes through.' She gave Felicity her best puppy-dog eyes.

Felicity sighed theatrically. 'All right, all right. Hey, if there's money involved,' she quipped, 'I know Dave would make an exception. He would sell me off if he thought he could make money. He'll happily just pack me off with a gallon of SPF 50 and strict instructions to behave.'

Deanna snorted. 'You? Behave? That'll be the day.'

Felicity placed a hand over her heart, feigning hurt. 'I am the very picture of marital responsibility! Just because I'm married doesn't mean I can't appreciate a handsome face.'

Deanna raised an eyebrow, grinning. 'Just remember who gets to flirt with Carlos – if she wants to. The *single* lady, thank you very much.'

'Deal!' Felicity shot back with a laugh. 'I'll be on my best non-flirting behaviour.'

Deanna drew a deep breath, steadying herself. The unknown stretched before her, vast and uncertain. But within that uncertainty was hope – a hope she couldn't ignore. She had to go. For her father, for her grandmother, and for herself.

As she stood to leave, Felicity fell into step beside her, their familiar banter momentarily quiet. Deanna couldn't help but wonder what the future held and how it might change everything she thought she knew.

Whatever awaited her in Brazil, she was ready to face it – no matter how difficult or extraordinary the journey might be.

14

APRIL 1941

Antoinette

The next day, after taking Benjamin to school, Antoinette returned to the Resistance safe house as instructed, her body tense about what lay ahead, but determined to save her husband.

Waiting for her at Emile's apartment was Jacques, his rugged features weathered by worry. Despite his short, stocky build, he exuded a quiet strength that Antoinette found both comforting and inspiring. His sandy-coloured hair was cropped short, his dark eyes sharp as they met hers. Today, he was dressed for combat in canvas trousers, sturdy boots, and a black turtleneck, making him appear formidable, ready for any challenge. They set off in his truck immediately.

'Today we start,' he informed her in a low growl as they travelled.

The rumble of the engine reverberated through her body as they left the city and drove past rolling hills and sprawling fields. With each passing mile, tension coiled tighter within her. She took deep breaths and focused on René and Benjamin, picturing their faces in her mind to steady her nerves. She was doing this for them, for their future.

They pulled up to a stone farmhouse, and Jacques cut the engine, casting a quick glance and tight smile at Antoinette before opening his door. His silent reassurance gave her a small measure of comfort.

Inside, she was greeted by a small group of members who obviously lived there year-round. Their faces were lined with experience, their eyes filled with quiet resolve. The other Resistance members bustled about, some cleaning weapons, others poring over maps spread out on the large wooden table. She had expected something intense, but the camaraderie among the group put her at ease. Laughter and banter mixed with their serious tasks, creating an environment of solidarity.

Someone made her a coffee, and they sat down at a large wooden farmhouse table as Jacques spelled out their plan.

'As I told you yesterday, we want to get you into the orchestra at the Majestic.' His voice was low and urgent. 'And as you earn their trust, you can gather information. Here we can train you in the skills you will need.' Jacques's eyes held a seriousness that made her understand the gravity of her mission and as she sipped her coffee she felt a sense of purpose wash over her. The group discussed the details of the plan, strategising the best way to train her for infiltration into the orchestra without raising suspicion. Antoinette listened intently.

All at once, Jacques met her eyes with his unflinching gaze, his expression serious. 'This won't be easy, Antoinette. You'll have to be vigilant at all times and trust no one but yourself. If you feel this is too much for you at any time, there is no shame in backing out now. Not everyone is cut out for this kind of work.' His words were a stark reminder of the risks involved.

Antoinette's jaw tightened as she responded. '*I* am,' she said defiantly. 'All my life, I have been strong-willed. In the past, I have often exasperated my family, but it's just because I've felt a fire burning within me for what is right.' She recalled moments of stubborn resistance that now seemed like preparation for this very task.

Jacques leaned back in his chair and gave a sly grin. 'I knew it. You have that fierce look in your eyes, like a wildcat. It will work well for you We will begin your training right away.'

Antoinette spent days immersed in intensive training with the members, learning the subtle art of deception and subterfuge.

She learned basic German, practised her codes, memorising intricate details about her cover story and even learning weapons and combat training. Every moment she wasn't with Benjamin was consumed by preparation for her mission at the hotel.

At the end of her eight-week training, the cell provided her with forged documents detailing her fictional background as a talented violinist who sympathised with the German cause. As she held the documents in her hands, the reality of her under-cover role sank in, and a shiver ran through her whole body.

She had perfected her understanding of Hitler and his ideologies, and mastered the mannerisms of a high-society musician. Every aspect of her role had to be flawless.

'How will I get into the orchestra?' she asked with curiosity.

Jacques exchanged a knowing look with his second-in-command. 'Well, the usual violinist is about to have a little accident, nothing life-threatening that could be traced back to us, but just something that will prevent him from performing for the foreseeable future. You will step in as his replacement,' her leader explained.

Antoinette's brow furrowed with concern at the mention of causing harm to a fellow violinist, even if it was minor. Her mind raced with thoughts of the consequences and the moral implications.

Jacques noted her change in expression and chuckled. 'Don't worry too much. Leo is a big supporter of the Nazi regime. He plays in the orchestra to gain favour with the officers. It is men like him who reported your husband.' The revelation sent a jolt of anger through Antoinette, overshadowing her unease.

'In order to keep you safe,' he continued, 'we have decided to give you a new name. We believe "Melodie Buchet" is fitting, given your musical abilities, and it will serve as a signal for other members of the cell. Are you prepared?'

She nodded. 'I am,' she said with an assurance she didn't totally feel in her body.

'Then your mission begins as soon as everything is in place.'

She returned home that day with a cover story already in place for her family. She had told them that since René had been taken away, she had been offered by the Conservatoire to perform at various events throughout the city. Her parents had agreed to help take care of her son, and Benjamin would stay with her parents and Charlotte overnight on the nights of her concerts.

Antoinette felt a pang of guilt for her lies, but she knew how necessary they were for her family's safety.

It had been more than three months since she had started her training and, when August arrived, she got a message from Jacques. She was to start the next evening at the hotel.

After she had dropped Benjamin off at his grandparents', she went home to get ready. Her mind was racing with fear as she prepared for the night ahead.

Antoinette slipped into a sleek black dress that hugged her figure, her hands trembling slightly as she fastened the clasp at the back. She could sense the weight of the forged documents in her purse, a constant reminder of the intricate web of deception she was about to weave.

Her long, curly blonde hair was artfully pinned up in an elegant twist, a few loose tendrils framing her face in a delicate manner, giving her a sophisticated appearance befitting the role she was about to undertake. As she applied a touch of pink lipstick, she took a deep breath to steady her nerves. She could see the fear in her blue eyes, as she spoke to the air.

'Oh, René, what have I gotten myself into now?'

She touched two fingers to her lips and brushed the smiling picture she had of him on her dressing table with a light kiss.

'I'm going to bring you home, my darling, just as I promised you.'

She picked up her violin, seeing the one piece of sheet music she always kept with it, which had the word '*always*' scribed in her husband's hand. The music he had played when he had proposed. She sighed as she tucked it away, knowing that, somehow, she would find him.

She arrived at twilight as instructed. The grandeur of the hotel was impressive, its imposing façade illuminated by soft lights. Its beauty, however, was overshadowed by the enemy's presence. The hotel was heavily guarded. She walked up to the foyer, carefully adjusting the gown she had chosen to wear. The fabric was cool and smooth against her skin, the deep black pearl trim shimmering softly in the light.

With practised nonchalance, she presented her forged documents to the guards at the entrance, her hands steady despite the racing of her heart. She felt a bead of sweat trickle down her back as she forced herself to remain calm.

The guard looked over the documents with a critical eye, his gaze lingering on her curves longer than necessary, making her a little uncomfortable. Finally, he nodded and stepped aside, allowing her to pass through. Relief washed over her as she moved forward.

The interior took her breath away. The elegant decor and extravagant furnishings were a stark contrast to the world at war outside its walls. She marvelled at the opulence that seemed almost otherworldly in its excess.

Chandeliers dripped with crystals, casting prisms of light across the marble floors. The sound of laughter floated through the air, mingling with the murmur of conversations in both French and German. Antoinette walked with purpose through the grand halls, her elegant gown whispering against the marble floors. The lavishness was a stark reminder of the disparity between those who enjoyed such luxury and the reality of the war-torn world outside.

As she entered the ballroom, a wave of anxiety washed over her. The room was filled with elegantly dressed Nazi officers and their companions, their laughter ringing hollow in Antoinette's ears. She could feel her pulse quicken as she scanned the room.

She spotted a stage at one end, where the small orchestra was beginning to gather, tuning their instruments in preparation for the evening's entertainment. She drew in a sharp breath as she realised this was the moment she had been preparing for, the moment where her courage and conviction would be tested.

Antoinette approached the orchestra leader, a stern-looking man with a military bearing and a swastika armband. With a polite smile, she introduced herself as the replacement violinist for the evening. The man eyed her sceptically as he spoke. 'What happened to Leo? He is our regular violinist.'

Antoinette remembered the response she had rehearsed. 'Unfortunately, he had an accident and wasn't able to make it tonight. The Conservatoire contacted me to replace him,' she replied smoothly, praying that her answer would satisfy him, grabbing her violin case a little tighter as she attempted to maintain her outward calm.

The man scrutinised her for a moment before nodding

curtly. 'Very well, take your place,' he ordered, gesturing towards the empty chair in the orchestra. Antoinette nodded gratefully, relief flooding through her as she seated herself among the other musicians – at least this part felt familiar to her.

Before they started, the orchestra leader approached her and thrust a Nazi armband at her with a cold stare. 'Wear this, in respect of our Führer,' he commanded, his voice low and authoritative. Antoinette's heart constricted as she stared at the armband, the significance of its symbolism heavy in her hands. She knew that putting it on would solidify her disguise but would also mean aligning herself with everything she despised.

Gritting her teeth and swallowing her revulsion, Antoinette forced herself to pin the armband to her sleeve, her fingers fumbling slightly. It felt like a betrayal of everything she stood for, every fibre of her being resisting the urge to rip the symbol of hatred from her arm and stamp on it. But she knew that in order to carry out her mission and find René, she had to play the part convincingly, even if it meant donning the emblem of the enemy.

People started to move into the ballroom for their meal, and the leader of the orchestra raised his baton, signalling the start of the evening's performance. Antoinette opened the music already on the stand, and her fingers tightened around the bow as she raised her violin to her chin. She felt the familiar weight of the instrument grounding her in the midst of deception. As she played and as the music flowed through her, she went over her mission in her mind.

In the break between pieces, a distinguished officer approached the orchestra, his uniform adorned with medals that gleamed in the soft light of the ballroom. Antoinette tensed as he stopped in front of her, his piercing gaze meeting hers with a hint of curiosity.

'You play beautifully, Mademoiselle,' he remarked in fluent

French, a faint smile playing on his lips. 'I don't believe I've had the pleasure of hearing you perform before.'

Antoinette returned his smile with practised charm. 'Thank you, it is an honour to play for such esteemed company,' she replied, feeling a twinge of disgust.

'What is your name?' the officer enquired, his eyes narrowing slightly.

Antoinette hesitated for a moment, her mind racing to remember the false identity she had adopted for this mission. 'I am Melodie Buchet,' she replied smoothly, meeting the officer's gaze with unwavering confidence. 'It is a pleasure to make your acquaintance, Commander...' She trailed off, waiting for him to provide his name.

The officer chuckled softly. 'Otto von Falkenberg.' His eyes twinkled with amusement as he extended a hand toward her.

Antoinette forced herself to take it, as she met his gaze. There was something unnerving about the way he looked at her, staring for longer than was natural as if trying to read her very soul. He also stood closer to her than she was comfortable with, his presence looming over her in a way that made her skin crawl. She plastered on a smile, trying to maintain her composure despite the unease that crept through her veins.

'Tell me, Mademoiselle Buchet,' Commander von Falkenberg continued, his voice smooth and calculated, 'how did you come to be part of tonight's performance? I don't recall seeing your face before.'

Antoinette steadied her gaze, recognising that this man was observant and not to be underestimated. She summoned her most charming smile and replied, 'A fellow musician who fell ill at the last moment. It is truly a privilege to fill in for him tonight.'

Commander von Falkenberg's eyes lingered on her for a moment longer before he nodded, seemingly satisfied with her response.

'A fortunate turn of events for us,' he mused, his tone contemplative. 'I must say, your playing is quite exquisite, Mademoiselle Buchet. It is rare to find such talent in Paris.'

He was so close to her now she could feel his warm breath on her cheek and hear the faint rustle of his uniform as he leaned in, his words sending a shiver down her spine. 'I wonder, would you do me the honour of joining me for a dance later this evening? It would be a shame for such beauty and talent to go unnoticed in the corner of the orchestra.'

Antoinette's heart raced. This was her chance to get closer to this Nazi, to gain his trust and potentially uncover valuable information for the Resistance. She forced a smile, batting her eyelashes in feigned bashfulness as she replied, 'I would be delighted, Herr Commander. But who would play the violin while I was gone?'

'I believe I have the power to ensure your fellow musicians can carry on without you for a brief moment,' he said, his voice filled with a confidence that sent a chill through her.

With a flick of a finger, he beckoned to the leader of the orchestra. The leader approached them, an expectant look in his eyes as he awaited Commander von Falkenberg's request.

'Fräulein Buchet here has graciously accepted my invitation for a dance later this evening,' Falkenberg announced smoothly, his gaze never leaving Antoinette's face. 'I trust you can spare her for a few moments to grace me with her presence on the dance floor?'

The orchestra leader showed obvious fear as he confronted the officer, a slight tremor in his voice. 'Of course, Commander von Falkenberg. We can manage without Mademoiselle Buchet for as long as you require her.'

With a nod of satisfaction, Falkenberg turned back to Antoinette, his eyes gleaming with a dangerous intensity. 'Shall we say, a waltz after dinner, Mademoiselle?' he suggested, already extending a hand towards her in anticipation of her agreement.

Antoinette forced herself to maintain a calm exterior, hoping a smile would hide the turbulent emotions swirling within her. This was her chance to gather information, to fulfil her mission for the Resistance. But everything inside her screamed with caution. There was something about his demeanour that set her teeth on edge, a darkness lurking beneath the polished surface that made her skin crawl. With a graceful nod, she accepted his offer. As the orchestra leader summoned the musicians back from their break, she took up her violin again and resumed playing.

She suddenly felt a chilling sense of apprehension wash over her. She just knew without looking that he was watching her. Glancing up from her music, across the crowded ballroom, there he was, his steely eyes locked onto hers with an intensity that made her blood run cold, his gaze unwavering.

She quickly averted her eyes, focusing on her playing, but tension coiled within her, sharp and unrelenting. She knew she was in danger of getting in over her head. And even though everything inside her body told her to run, to escape this perilous situation before it was too late, Antoinette knew that she couldn't abandon her mission, not when so much was at stake for René.

She took a deep breath, steeling herself against the fear and reminding herself why she was here.

15

RIO DE JANEIRO, BRAZIL, 2012

Deanna

Two weeks later, as their plane touched down in Brazil, Deanna and Felicity were greeted warmly by Carlos at the airport. Deanna couldn't help but notice how effortlessly handsome he looked, his captivating smile making her feel instantly welcome as they passed through the exit. She was struck again by his piercing blue eyes – they were just as mesmerising as she remembered from their first meeting.

But Carlos looked strikingly different here, dressed impeccably in a light taupe suit that accentuated his strong, relaxed physique. The cream linen shirt beneath and the stylish Panama hat completed the picture, exuding effortless charm. Deanna caught herself wondering how one man could combine such confidence and charisma, with an almost disarming warmth.

As if reading her thoughts, Felicity whispered, nudging Deanna playfully. 'He certainly knows how to make an entrance, doesn't he?'

Deanna grinned, her cheeks warming. 'Probably practises in front of the mirror.'

They both supressed a giggle as he strode towards them to greet them. His confidence shone as he navigated the bustling airport, engaging Deanna and Felicity with his quick wit and easy conversation, soothing any lingering nerves about coming.

In Brazil, Carlos was more vibrant and expressive than the reserved man they had met in London. His smile was freer, his eyes sparkled with passion for his homeland, drawing Deanna to this livelier side of him.

She suddenly felt very English and out of place, her fair skin and slightly awkward, reserved manner starkly contrasting with the vibrant backdrop of South America and Carlos's easy charisma. She felt a surge of gratitude for Felicity's presence by her side, her unwavering support a comforting anchor in this unfamiliar land.

Stepping out of the terminal, the heat of the Brazilian sun hit them like a wall, the air thick with humidity and the distant squawk of exotic birds adding an otherworldly feel. Deanna shielded her eyes from the sun, taking in the vibrant surroundings with a mixture of awe and apprehension.

'I guess we're not in Kansas any more,' Felicity quipped with a laugh, fanning herself with a magazine.

As they neared the car, Deanna noticed a tall, older man waiting beside it, his wide smile spreading across his face. He stepped forward with open arms, radiating the warmth and exuberance one might expect from a patriarch.

'*Ah!* Our beautiful guests have arrived!' Giovanni exclaimed, enveloping Deanna and Felicity in warm, welcoming embraces. His infectious joy and energy immediately filled the air with a sense of comfort and hospitality. 'Welcome to Brazil, and to our family home! You are most welcome here.'

Giovanni's attire – a crisp white linen shirt with sleeves

rolled up, beige trousers, and loafers – perfectly matched the warmth of his greeting. His neatly combed grey hair and lively brown eyes sparkled with humour, enhancing his tanned skin and tall stature, adding to his commanding presence, but it was his charm that instantly put Deanna at ease.

As Giovanni stepped back, his expression momentarily shifted; his smile faltered as his gaze lingered on Deanna, studying her more intently than seemed necessary. It was brief, but Deanna felt it – a subtle yet unmistakable shift in his body language. The brightness in his eyes dimmed as if he had seen a ghost, a shadow of the past reflected in Deanna's face.

Carlos, completely unaware of the moment, beamed with pride as he gestured towards the car. 'My father has been eagerly awaiting your arrival,' he announced cheerfully.

Giovanni quickly masked any trace of his earlier intensity, though a hint of something remained unsettled in his eyes. But before Deanna could dwell on it, his expansive exuberance reclaimed the atmosphere.

'Come! We have much to talk about, but first, you must escape this heat and enjoy some refreshments at the villa.'

Pushing away her momentary feeling of unease, Deanna was reassured by his genuinely welcoming nature, which fitted Carlos's descriptions of an Italian freedom fighter. She exchanged a knowing look with Felicity, who smiled back, equally taken with their hosts' warmth. They climbed into the back seat of the car, their initial nerves calming as the air-conditioned interior shielded them from the oppressive heat.

The drive to the villa was lively, filled with light-hearted stories from Giovanni and Carlos about the estate and their family's deep connection to the land. Giovanni's tales vividly recounted his memories of Brazil.

However, the brief, unsettling moment at the airport lingered in Deanna's mind. What had Giovanni seen in her face that made him pause? She glanced at Felicity, who seemed blissfully absorbed in the storytelling.

She pushed away her fear, forcing herself to absorb the vibrant scenes outside – street vendors selling exotic fruits and colourful trinkets, buildings adorned with intricate murals, and lively music weaving through the bustling streets – the journey felt like a transition into another world. They soon arrived at a magnificent villa nestled among lush greenery, the scent of blooming flowers enhancing the magical ambiance.

A young woman, presumably Maria, emerged from the villa. Her warm, curious eyes reminded Deanna of Carlos as she invited them inside.

'Welcome to our home!' Maria exclaimed, her voice as warm as her smile.

Deanna liked Maria instantly. Her long, raven-black curls framed her oval face, and her olive complexion glowed with youthful vitality. Maria's deep brown eyes shimmered with warmth, reflecting her adventurous and nurturing spirit. Dressed in a floral maxi dress that accentuated her slender waist, she carried a vibrant aura, complemented by simple gold jewellery and playful pink nails.

'Thank you, Maria. Your home is beautiful,' Deanna responded, genuinely impressed.

'We love to share it with guests,' Maria replied, leading them inside.

The villa was a testament to elegance and warmth. The grand entrance hall led into a lavish sitting room where art adorned the walls and antique furniture sparkled under the soft Brazilian sunlight streaming through large windows. The opulence of the decor, the intricate architectural details and rich tapestries told stories of a distant past, captivating Deanna's senses. The air was infused with the subtle scent of polished wood which blended seamlessly with the fresh, floral notes drifting in from the lush gardens outside and also, brought in through the open windows on the warm wind, the smell of citrus from blooming orange trees.

Felicity, who had been quietly observing the surroundings, whispered to Deanna, 'Imagine the history these walls have witnessed...'

Deanna nodded, her mind racing with images of grand events and intimate gatherings from decades past.

As they settled into comfortable armchairs, Giovanni, brimming with genuine joy, served them lemonade and raised his glass in a toast. 'It is a pleasure to have you here,' he said warmly. 'To new friendships, and to family.'

The afternoon unfolded with Giovanni regaling them with more stories of his life in Italy, his Resistance work, and his passion for music and culture. Maria occasionally added her insights, painting a complete picture of a man who had endured great losses yet found peace in this beautiful estate.

As the evening approached, Giovanni clapped his hands excitedly. 'Now, you must stay with us here in the villa. We've prepared beautiful rooms for you both, and Maria has planned a wonderful dinner – it will be a true Brazilian feast!'

Deanna hesitated briefly, considering their initial plan to stay at a hotel if they felt uncomfortable. However, with a nod towards her from Felicity, the overwhelming hospitality was hard to resist.

'We would love to stay,' Deanna responded, feeling a wave of relief wash over her as Giovanni's broad smile lit up the room.

'*Fantastico!* You'll see, once you experience Maria's cooking, you'll never want to leave!' Giovanni's laughter echoed warmly around them.

But a pause in the conversation allowed for a sudden, intense shift. Giovanni's gaze fixed on Deanna with a sharpness that startled her. He leaned in, his voice soft yet heavy with implication. 'Carlos told me that you brought my violin with you; is it true?'

'That is still to be decided,' Felicity interjected, her tone firm, signalling her role in determining the violin's rightful ownership.

Unfazed, Giovanni's piercing gaze remained locked on Deanna. Her heart fluttered under the weight of his scrutiny. 'Yes,' she admitted cautiously. 'I brought the violin.'

'Would you... show it to me?' His voice carried a deep, emotional undertone that piqued both her curiosity and her unease. 'I would love to see it once more.'

With a hesitant nod, Deanna retrieved the violin case from her luggage. As she handed it over, Giovanni's fingers reverently brushed the worn leather, opening it with an awe that spoke volumes. His breath caught as he beheld the instrument, his touch tentative as he traced its curves. 'It's... *beautiful*,' he whispered, awe colouring his tone.

A tense silence enveloped the room. Maria and Carlos watched, seeming to sense the profound connection their father had with the violin, a relic harbouring deep personal significance.

'Your grandmother fought hard for this violin. I've always wondered why she never returned it to me, given the price she paid,' Giovanni mused, his fingers caressing the violin lovingly. Lost in his thoughts, he seemed to traverse time, bridging the gap between past and present with his touch.

Finally, Giovanni's gaze met Deanna's, revealing an unguarded emotion that quickened her pulse. His voice, barely above a whisper, broke the silence. 'Would you... play it? For me?'

The request took Deanna by surprise, not merely due to its intensity but because of the palpable longing behind it. It was more than a mere request; it was a heartfelt plea.

'I – I don't play,' she admitted softly, the embarrassment evident in her tone. 'I never learned.'

Giovanni stared at her, his disappointment clearly etched across his face, making the silence between them heavy and uncomfortable.

'She doesn't,' Felicity quickly chimed in, attempting to lighten the mood. 'And don't ask her to sing either; she's practically tone-deaf.' The others chuckled gently, grateful for Felicity's attempt to diffuse the tension.

However, Giovanni seemed unaffected by the humour. With a solemn expression, he carefully closed the violin case, his body shaking slightly with the strength of his emotions.

Deanna felt a strange pang of guilt at his reaction, though she couldn't pinpoint why. 'I'm sorry,' she murmured, her words failing to bridge the gap his hope had created.

Giovanni dismissed her apology with a wave, though his smile didn't quite reach his eyes. 'No, it's not your fault,' he assured her, his voice heavy with resignation. 'It's just... seeing you with it, I almost felt as if she were here again. I saw her play at the Majestic, back when we were with the Resistance. She was... magnificent.'

Those words, laden with memories, struck Deanna profoundly. He was speaking of her grandmother Antoinette, a woman whose past was now intricately linked to her present through this violin.

For a moment, Giovanni seemed transported to another time, his features softening as if he were once again in the presence of a long-lost love. The jovial Italian patriarch had vanished, replaced by a man haunted by his memories and ghosts.

He gazed at the violin one last time before shutting the case with finality, his voice trailing off, leaving a palpable sense of longing and loss in the air. 'It was just a thought,' he concluded, the sorrow apparent in his voice as he handed the case back to Deanna.

Abruptly getting up, Giovanni excused himself, claiming fatigue. His departure left a silent question hanging in the air.

The siblings seemed uncomfortable, and Felicity exchanged a confused look with Deanna. The footsteps of the old man echoed on the stairs.

Deanna's grip on the violin case tightened as the air in the room grew heavier, as though the ghosts of the past were swirling around her, their whispers just out of reach. Despite her best efforts, she could not shake the feeling that something monumental had just occurred, leaving behind a deep disquiet that curled in her chest – an unshakable sense of foreboding, something dark and undeniable.

As she tried to make sense of it all, a chilling realisation dawned on her: the truth behind this violin was far more complex than she had ever dared to imagine. She couldn't escape the harrowing question: was she truly ready to uncover all the truths it carried?

16

AUGUST 1941

Antoinette

When the time came for the waltz after dinner, Falkenberg approached the orchestra and extended a hand to Antoinette. His grasp was possessive and unyielding, making her skin crawl as he led her onto the dance floor.

He stood at around six feet tall, his broad, muscular build hinting at years of rigorous military training. His face was sharp, defined by angular cheekbones and a strong jawline, softened only slightly by his closely cropped blonde hair. His eyes, ice blue, glinted predatorily, sizing up Antoinette with every glance. His uniform, meticulously maintained, epitomised the Nazi aesthetic – stiff, dark fabric adorned with multiple medals that clinked softly with each step he took. The Iron Cross hung prominently, a testament to his bravery – or brutality – on the battlefield. The uniform's high collar and tightly buttoned front added to his imposing presence, making him an unmissable figure in any room.

As he pulled her close, Antoinette's body brushed up

against his stiff Nazi uniform, a stark contrast to the soft fabric of her gown. They moved in time with the music, but Antoinette's mind was far from the elegant steps of the waltz. She could feel Falkenberg's calculating, predatory eyes on her, twisting her insides with apprehension. Her mind raced with her Resistance training, striving to remain calm under his penetrating gaze.

She forced a smile as he spoke, his lips close to her ear. His German accent was pronounced, sending a shiver of fear through her whole body. 'You are a fine violinist, Mademoiselle Buchet,' Falkenberg murmured, his breath hot against her skin. 'We were no doubt fortunate to get someone of your calibre at such short notice.'

With practised coyness, she replied smoothly, 'Thank you, Commander.'

'I must admit,' Falkenberg continued, his eyes piercing hers, his grip tightening ever so slightly on her waist, 'I am intrigued by your background. You play with such passion and skill, it's as if the music flows through your veins. Where did you learn to play?'

Antoinette felt a bead of sweat form on her brow as she maintained her façade, the weight of his scrutiny almost suffocating. She remembered the backstory she had practised with the Resistance. 'I have been fortunate to receive tutelage from a fine musician,' she said, her voice steady despite the turmoil inside her. 'My late mentor was a virtuoso violinist who instilled in me a deep love for music, and a dedication to perfecting my craft.'

'I would be interested to meet such a mentor someday,' Falkenberg replied, his interest piqued.

She carefully steered the conversation away from names and places. 'Surely you would enjoy meeting more interesting people, or talking about all that Paris has to offer,' she said with a quirk of her eyebrow. 'Besides, I would rather know more about you,' she continued, trying to sound in awe. 'You must have travelled far and wide to achieve such an esteemed position in the military. I imagine you have many fascinating stories to tell.'

Falkenberg's lips curled into a half-smile at her words, a glint of satisfaction in his eyes. 'Ah, the life of a soldier is not always as glamorous as one might think, Mademoiselle Buchet,' he replied cryptically, his voice low and smooth like velvet but carrying an undercurrent of coldness. 'But perhaps, I could regale you with tales of my exploits some other time.'

'I look forward to it, Commander.' Antoinette forced the words through a clenched smile.

His eyes roamed her face with intensity, as if weighing up whether he could trust her. The dance seemed to stretch on endlessly, and Antoinette's thoughts flew to René, her dear sweet husband. She had taken off her wedding ring and hidden it carefully under a floorboard in their small apartment before leaving. She missed the weight of it on her finger, the reminder of the love and commitment she and René shared. As the waltz came to an end, Falkenberg's grip on her tightened again for just a moment, his fingers digging into her waist almost painfully.

'Thank you for the dance, Mademoiselle Buchet,' he said with a smile that did not reach his eyes. 'I travel a lot for my work, but do come back here from time to time and I do hope we will have more opportunities to speak in the future.'

Antoinette took a step back, a sense of relief flooding through her. 'The pleasure was all mine, Herr Commander,' she replied with false sweetness.

Before returning to the orchestra, she needed a moment to catch her breath. As she headed to the bathroom, she could feel his eyes boring into her back, making her skin prickle. She closed the door behind her, leaning against the cool marble sink, her reflection staring back at her with wide, fearful eyes. She took a deep breath and splashed some cold water onto her neck, trying to steady her nerves.

She had to figure out how to use this connection to her advantage, how to glean information that would aid the Resistance in their mission. Walking the tightrope between loyalty to her cause and maintaining the trust of Nazis like Falkenberg would be a delicate dance indeed. She straightened her spine, steeling herself for whatever lay ahead.

As she dried her face, she thought how different it felt from the planning at the Resistance meetings to actually being in the arms of the enemy. The theoretical discussions and strategic planning seemed a world away from the reality of dancing with Falkenberg, feeling his possessive grip and sensing his intense gaze. The stakes were higher, and the danger more palpable than she had ever imagined.

As she opened the door and stepped back into the grand hall, Antoinette's eyes scanned the room until they landed on Falkenberg, who was engaged in conversation with a group of officers. His laughter echoed through the hall, a chilling reminder of the duality of his nature. She made her way back to the orchestra, her breath racing slightly as she picked up her violin. The familiar weight of the instrument was a comfort now, grounding her amid this uncertainty. As she took her place among the musicians, she felt a renewed sense of purpose. She was determined to play her part flawlessly, both on the stage and in the delicate game of espionage she was now entangled in.

The orchestra leader watched her with newfound respect, making her wonder if Falkenberg held more sway here than she realised.

At the end of the performance, she couldn't see Falkenberg anywhere. But as she slipped out of the hotel, a car was waiting at the kerb. As she approached, she recognised the dark silhouette of Falkenberg sitting in the back seat. He rolled down the window, his eyes glinting in the dim light.

'Mademoiselle Buchet, do you need a ride home?' he asked. 'My driver can take you anywhere in Paris. I would be happy to escort you safely. It is after curfew, and we don't want you to come to any harm, do we? It would be unfortunate to have you arrested when you have played so well.'

Her mind raced with her choice. He was right about the curfew, but getting into his car would expose where she lived. Antoinette weighed her options carefully as she stood on the kerb, the cool night air making the hairs on her arms stand on end. She could feel the intensity of his gaze on her, waiting for her response.

'Thank you, Commander,' she replied, her voice steady despite the anxiety twisting inside her.

She gave an address on a road some distance from her street, and the car pulled away from the kerb, gliding smoothly through the empty streets of Paris. Falkenberg's presence loomed beside her, his gaze intense as he studied her profile in the dim light of the car.

'You are most beautiful in this light,' he commented, his voice low and smooth as he gestured to the moonlight filtering through the window.

Antoinette forced a polite smile, her heart racing in her chest as she tried to keep up her façade of composure. 'Thank you, Commander,' she said again, shifting uncomfortably in her seat, the tension between them palpable in the confined space of the car.

'I spoke to the orchestra leader before I left,' Falkenberg continued. 'You will become the *permanent* first choice violinist for all our events. So, I can look forward to hearing you play again on my return, Mademoiselle Buchet,' he said, his tone almost possessive as the car slid through the streets of Paris.

'That is very kind of you, Commander,' Antoinette replied,

masking her unease with a polite tone. Inside, her mind was racing with thoughts of how she could use this newfound position to her advantage without raising suspicion.

'I trust you will be joining us for the next special event?' Falkenberg enquired, though it sounded more like a command.

Antoinette's chest tightened at the thought of having to spend more time in Falkenberg's presence, but she knew she needed to play her part convincingly if she was to gather any valuable information for the Resistance. With a tight smile, she nodded in agreement. 'Of course, Commander. I would be honoured to attend and play at any reception,' she replied, her voice steady despite the turmoil churning inside her. As the car came to a stop in front of the address she had given, Antoinette felt a rush of relief wash over her.

As she stepped out of the vehicle, Falkenberg ran his eyes over her form in a way that made her want to be sick. But she swallowed down her revulsion and forced another smile, thanking him for the ride. Falkenberg inclined his head slightly, a look of satisfaction in his eyes.

'Until we meet again then, Mademoiselle Buchet,' he said, and Antoinette watched as the car pulled away, the sound of its engine fading into the distance. She stood alone on the darkened street, anger and fear swirling inside her.

As she began the long walk to her home, a Parisian smoking a cigarette with his beret pulled down over his eyes spat out a string of expletives and slurs. She realised she was still wearing the swastika armband she had been forced to put on.

She ripped it off and shoved it into her bag, her heart pounding with adrenaline. She quickened her pace through the dimly lit streets, feeling empowered by her small act of defiance. Tomorrow, she would meet with her fellow members of the Resistance to discuss this new connection with Falkenberg and how they could use it to their advantage. There was only one lingering fear that gnawed at her inside.

How far would she have to go to keep up this dangerous charade, to gather valuable information for the Resistance and save René? The path ahead felt fraught with uncertain peril, and the cost of failure was unimaginable – not just for her, but for everyone she loved.

17

RIO DE JANEIRO, BRAZIL, 2012

Deanna

On her first morning in Brazil, Deanna stepped onto the balcony of her bedroom and let the scene below wash over her senses.

The lush gardens stretched out beneath her, vibrant with life even in the early morning. Yet, it was the heat that caught her off guard – a thick, humid wave that made the air almost tangible. She inhaled deeply, the rich scent of blooming flowers mingling with the distinct, earthy smell of the Brazilian vegetation.

Over the water, the sun was just beginning its slow ascent, igniting the sky with brilliant shades of pink and orange. It was a moment of pure, tranquil beauty, and for just a few precious seconds, the persistence of her worries seemed to dissolve into the warm air.

But then, a murmur of voices rose from below, interrupting the stillness. Curious, Deanna leaned over the railing and spotted Giovanni, surrounded by a small group of elderly men on the porch. There was something about their presence that felt unsettling. Instinctively, Deanna stepped back, retreating into the shadows of her balcony as she strained to catch their words.

The men spoke in hushed tones, barely audible over the gentle rustling of the palm trees swaying in the morning breeze. But Deanna immediately noticed that the soft melodic Portuguese she had been getting used to had been replaced by something harsher, more guttural. They held up their glasses in a toast, muttering something that sounded like *Blumen und Erde*.

Her mind scrambled for recognition – German? *Blumen und Erde* meant 'flowers and earth'. Perhaps it was a gardening club, but the intensity of their voices made her chest tighten. And why speak in German, here in Brazil?

Deanna's palms grew clammy as she eavesdropped, her secondary-school German coming back in disjointed flashes. She picked out a few words – Paris, music, *Kind* – child. The word was clear, but the rest was lost to her, except for one she couldn't quite place – *Verräter*. Anxiety bubbled up inside her. What could they possibly be discussing? And in German? It felt like a shadow had suddenly fallen over the sunny Brazilian morning.

The elderly man's voice carried a mix of anger and regret that sent a jolt of unease through Deanna. She leaned in closer, desperate to catch more of the conversation. Then, just as she thought she was piecing together their cryptic exchange, a sudden knock at her bedroom door snapped her away from her eavesdropping.

Her heart leapt into her throat as she spun around, nearly stumbling in her haste to retreat from the balcony. She forced herself to breathe, to calm the torrent of thoughts swirling in her mind, before opening the door to find Maria standing there with a bright, welcoming smile.

'Good morning, Deanna! I hope you slept well,' Maria said, her voice warm and filled with genuine kindness.

Dressed in a stunning blue batiste dress that flowed gracefully around her figure, with large gold hoop earrings peeking out from under her dark hair and colourful bangles jangling softly on her wrist, Maria glowed. But Deanna's thoughts were still trapped in that unsettling moment on the balcony.

Deanna forced a smile in return as Maria continued.

'I wanted to let you know that Carlos isn't working today and has organised a trip to the local market for us this morning. It should be a wonderful experience for you to immerse yourself in our vibrant culture.'

Deanna nodded, grateful for the distraction. 'That sounds lovely. I will be ready in a little while.'

When she returned to the balcony, she noticed that the men had moved away to a distant spot in the garden, their voices no longer audible.

Trying to push down her concerns, Deanna dressed in a light, breezy red cheesecloth sundress – perfect for the warm Brazilian weather. As she made her way downstairs to join Maria and Carlos for breakfast, the aroma of freshly brewed coffee and tropical fruits greeted her, momentarily lifting her spirits.

The dining room was bathed in sunlight, casting a golden glow over the table set with an array of local delicacies. Felicity was already there, teasing Carlos about his antique collection.

'Carlos, you can't *seriously* believe these will appreciate in value,' Felicity said with a sceptical chuckle, swirling her coffee. 'It's all about modern pieces now.'

Carlos grinned. 'You'd be surprised, Felicity. These old artefacts have more stories in them than anything you'll find in a gallery today.'

Deanna took her seat opposite them, pouring herself a cup of fragrant Brazilian coffee. She tried to focus on their conversation, nodding absently as Felicity laughed, but her mind kept drifting back to the mysterious exchange she had overheard.

Carlos greeted her with a warm smile that sent a flutter through her chest, his blue eyes catching the morning light. 'Morning, Deanna. Did you sleep well?' he asked, his voice smooth and inviting.

'Yes, wonderfully,' Deanna replied, her smile faltering slightly as she met his gaze, which lingered just a heartbeat too long. She felt her cheeks flush as she added quickly, 'And you?'

'Well,' he said, gesturing to the feast before them. 'When my sister makes a breakfast this good, it's hard to wake up in a bad mood.'

The spread before them was irresistible: *pão de queijo*, still warm and oozing with melted butter, decadent slices of cheese and ham, and a rainbow of tropical fruits – bright yellow pineapples, succulent mangoes and papayas.

Deanna cut herself a slice of pineapple, the sweet scent filling her nostrils and making her taste buds tingle with anticipation.

'I thought I caught sight of your father this morning outside,' Deanna started tentatively, trying to sound nonchalant, masking the curiosity that gnawed at her insides.

'Yes,' responded Maria. 'Once a month, he has a get-together with a number of his old friends.'

Deanna nodded, taking another sip of her coffee as she listened intently. Although Maria's explanation seemed plausible, a nagging sense of unease clung to her, refusing to be dismissed. She leaned forward, deciding to press further. 'It sounded as if he was speaking in... German.'

Maria paused for a moment, her dark eyes meeting Deanna's with a hint of hesitation before replying, 'Yes, he had to learn it for his Resistance work. He used to chauffeur the Nazis around, so he could eavesdrop on their conversations.'

Deanna's brow furrowed slightly as she listened, unsure

whether to feel relieved or more suspicious. 'So he kept up the language afterward?'

Maria nodded, a smile slowly spreading across her face as she explained further. 'Yes, it's funny, isn't it? After the war, he liked to keep up his German. He even joined a small club of German speakers – other immigrants who had lived through the war – just to practise. Apparently, he says it's good for his ageing brain.'

Deanna understood but something still didn't sit right. That look in Giovanni's eyes when she had asked about the violin, the strange intensity she had sensed in his demeanour below her when she had been out on the balcony – it all still felt off. She couldn't shake the feeling that there was more to the story, more to him, than Maria was letting on.

Felicity must have picked up on her concern, because she asked, 'Do you have pictures of your father when he was young? Maybe with the violin, so we can start a chain of verification?'

Maria's smile faltered slightly at the question, a flicker of uncertainty passing through her eyes before she recovered and said, 'I'm afraid I don't have any photos from his youth. He tells me there was a fire when he was young... and a lot was lost.'

A silence fell over the dining room, broken only by the squawking of birds outside and the distant sound of waves crashing against the shore.

As they finished their breakfast, Carlos stood up and announced that it was time to head to the local market. Deanna welcomed the distraction, eager to immerse herself in the vibrant culture of Brazil and put her nagging suspicions to rest, at least for a little while.

The bustling market was exploding with a vibrant array of colours and sounds, as vendors energetically called out to potential customers under their boldly patterned umbrellas. The air was saturated with an intoxicating mix of exotic spices, crisp produce, and sizzling meats on open grills. Deep red hues of the spices danced with the golden tones of freshly picked fruits and vegetables, creating a feast for all the senses.

As Maria began to try on hats and Carlos went off to buy some local artwork, Felicity pulled Deanna aside.

'What was all that about with Maria, about her father?' Felicity asked, her voice low. Deanna hesitated for a moment, trying to decide how to explain the unease that had been festering inside. She started by confiding in Felicity about what she had overheard on the balcony that morning.

Felicity listened intently, her brow furrowed in concern as Deanna recounted the snippets of conversation she had caught. 'It was these old men, all speaking in *German*,' Deanna began, her voice tight as the memory surfaced. 'And Giovanni... he spoke with such intensity. It felt wrong, and even Maria's explanation makes me feel they're not telling us everything. And then there were the words I caught – *Kind*... I know that means "child". But there was another word, something I didn't recognise – *Verräter*.'

Felicity's face went pale, her expression darkening as the word registered. She leaned in closer, her voice barely above a whisper. '*Verräter* means "traitor",' she said in a hushed voice, her eyes darting around to make sure no one else was listening.

Deanna felt a cold weight settle within her. 'Are you sure? That's what he said?' Felicity asked, her voice almost desperate.

'It was definitely *Verräter*... and the word *Kind*,' Deanna confirmed.

Felicity nodded slowly, the burden of the realisation settling in. 'If you heard correctly, he was saying "the traitor's child".'

Both of them widened their eyes as they processed Deanna's words. 'Do you think there's more to Giovanni than he lets on?' Felicity whispered, glancing over at Maria, who was trying on a colourful head wrap at one of the stalls.

Deanna nodded slowly, her mind racing with possibilities and suspicions. 'I don't know for sure, but there's definitely something off about the whole situation. Do you think it's possible he's not who he says he is?'

'I don't know,' Felicity responded carefully, 'but you should not hand over that violin until we've triple-checked his identity.'

Maria approached with a broad smile, a new head wrap in hand. Felicity and Deanna exchanged a quick glance, their unspoken understanding hanging heavy in the air.

After picking up all they needed from the market, they travelled back to the villa, the tropical heat clinging to their skin as they made their way through the lush gardens. Maria chattered excitedly about the new purchases she had made, but Deanna's mind was elsewhere.

They were taking some tea on the verandah when Maria floated into the room after checking on her father. 'I have good news: my father thought he would be out this evening but will be able to join us for dinner after all.'

'Good,' responded Felicity, 'we really need to start putting all these pieces together.'

The rest of the day, Deanna and Felicity basked in the sunshine, their books offering a quiet escape. But as the sun dipped below the horizon, casting a golden glow over the villa, a disquiet began to creep in once again. With dinner with Maria's father drawing closer, a sense of foreboding settled over Deanna, impossible to shake.

18

AUGUST 1941

Antoinette

The next day, after dropping Benjamin at school, Antoinette made her way to Emile's home, knocked out the code, and waited nervously.

Inside, Jacques was huddled with two other female agents, their voices hushed. The ramshackle kitchen was dense with the smell of black-market coffee and stale cigarettes and upon her entrance, the conversation halted, and Jacques nodded in her direction as he introduced her to the others.

'Melodie, I believe you've already met Florence and Alex.' She recalled them well from her training – two skilled agents she had encountered briefly. They offered her a guarded acknowledgment, their eyes briefly meeting hers before looking away. Antoinette nodded back, taking note of Alex's sharp-eyed, no-nonsense manner and Florence's striking auburn curls tucked under a black beret.

Serge gestured for Antoinette to sit. 'How did it go last night?' Serge enquired, pulling out a cigarette and lighting it up.

Antoinette recounted her tense interaction with Falkenberg, concluding with his unsettling invitation for her to become the permanent first-choice violinist at their events. The room fell into a thoughtful silence and Serge sat back, processing every detail with meticulous care.

'This could be very helpful to us,' Serge began, his voice low and deliberate. 'Falkenberg's reputation precedes him, and we may be able to use this to our advantage. But you need to be careful; he is known to be ruthless.'

Antoinette took a deep breath, considering the risks and potential rewards of getting closer to Falkenberg. The opportunity to gather intel from within his organisation was a rare chance that could significantly aid their cause, but still...

'Use any advantage with him wisely, but with caution,' Serge continued, maintaining eye contact. 'Your objective remains unchanged: obtain the documents revealing the whereabouts of our captured agents. But if you can gain Falkenberg's trust, who knows what else you might uncover.'

Antoinette's voice trembled as she spoke, her fear evident. 'I think Falkenberg wants more than just a *friendship* with me.'

Everyone in the room tensed up, and the two female agents exchanged a glance filled with silent empathy, fully understanding the grim sacrifices Antoinette might have to make.

'How far do you think I'll need to go?' Antoinette asked, desperation and fear lacing her tone as she sought reassurance.

Alex's expression hardened. 'I would do whatever it takes,' she declared firmly. 'Whatever is necessary to find our husbands and comrades. No one will judge you here.'

The thought of Falkenberg's advances made Antoinette's skin crawl, and she struggled to suppress the nauseating images of his touch. Her mind, unbidden, drifted to René – the warmth of his embrace, the gentle way he would tuck a strand of hair behind her ear, before he brushed her neck with a kiss, the love that had anchored her through this endless nightmare of this war. The idea of betraying that intimacy, even for survival, filled her with a deep, twisting guilt.

But then came the sharper, colder truth: if enduring Falkenberg's advances meant a chance of finding René alive, could she afford the luxury of hesitation? Could she face herself knowing she had failed to do all she could to bring him home?

Serge broke the heavy silence, his voice quiet yet firm. 'We all make sacrifices for the cause, but our ultimate goal is to bring down the enemy and save our comrades. Do only what you're comfortable with. We cannot lose ourselves in this fight for freedom.' His words were filled with compassion and understanding.

As she left the meeting, Antoinette's heart was torn between duty and personal values. She had never been intimate with anyone other than René, and the mere thought of such a betrayal sent a cold wave of dread through her.

Yet, she knew the crucial information she might gather was vital for saving René and many others.

The following month she was called again to play, and with mixed emotions she was glad to see that Falkenberg had been called away from Paris. She wouldn't see him again until the October concert.

Picking up Benjamin from school that afternoon, his cheerful chatter about his day contrasted sharply with the darkness clouding her thoughts. At her parents' house, her sister Charlotte eagerly took Benjamin for the evening, giving Antoinette the freedom to attend the reception.

'You're playing tonight?' her mother asked innocently. 'Is it for the Conservatoire?'

Antoinette forced a smile, guilt twisting inside her. 'Yes,

Maman,' she replied vaguely, avoiding her mother's penetrating gaze.

'Well, I'm glad you're playing, Antoinette. It's such a gift you have; don't let it go to waste,' her mother said, pride shining in her eyes. In that moment, Antoinette loathed her gift, the war, and the heavy burden it had placed upon her shoulders.

Later, as she prepared for the evening, Antoinette's heart raced. She fumbled with her delicate, shimmering light blue gown, feeling as if she were donning armour for battle. Sadness engulfed her as she remembered René giving her the dress for their first formal event together. His now distant smile and admiring gaze as he helped her fasten it felt like a painful reminder of what she was fighting for. She pinned her blonde hair into an elegant chignon, trying to focus on the task ahead despite the chaos in her mind.

As she reached for the crumpled Nazi armband, a surge of dread and guilt coursed through her. But this was necessary – it was her only way to infiltrate Falkenberg's inner circle and gather crucial information for the Resistance. As she fastened the swastika to her arm, conflicting emotions overwhelmed her. It felt like a shackle, a symbol of her deceit, yet also her ticket to victory against the enemy.

Pulling on a wrap to cover the hateful armband, she took a deep breath, steeling herself for the mission ahead. As Antoinette stepped out into the hall, her mother gave her a heartfelt hug.

'René would be so proud of you,' she whispered into her daughter's ear. Her mother's words felt like a slap, reminding her of the compromises and betrayals she was contemplating. How could René be proud of what she might need to do tonight? With each step towards the venue, the burden of her double life pressed down on her, a silent scream in the quiet evening.

Upon arriving at the hotel, instead of being directed to the main ballroom, she was met by another Nazi. He instructed Antoinette to follow him to the private rooms on the second floor. Clutching her violin case tightly, she ascended the ornate staircase, her nerves taut. The muted conversation and clinking glasses from the Nazis' private rooms drifted down the hallway as she approached the door.

Pushing back her personal fears, she slipped into her Resistance training mode. She meticulously noted the number and positions of the guards, the layout of the rooms, and the potential exits. Adjusting her wrap to ensure the armband was visible, she approached the door, where muted laughter spilled out. A guard noticed her violin case and motioned for her to enter.

The suite was lavish, filled with opulent furnishings and decadent decorations – a stark contrast to the horrors perpetrated by those within these walls.

With shock, she noticed Falkenberg was back at the Majestic. He stood across the room, his piercing gaze locking onto Antoinette the moment she entered. His smile was warm, but with the usual calculating glint in his eyes. With a graceful bow, he approached her, extending his hand in greeting.

'Ah, Melodie, I'm so glad to see you again. Your beautiful playing will surely enchant my guests tonight. As you can see, this is a much more *intimate* affair than the last time I saw you.'

He emphasised the word 'intimate' in a way that made Antoinette swallow hard. She fought to maintain a composed façade, her grip on the violin case tightening involuntarily.

Nodding respectfully, she replied with a forced smile, 'Thank you for having me, Commander von Falkenberg. I am honoured to perform for you again.' Her voice remained steady, belying the turmoil within her.

As Falkenberg led her further into the room, Antoinette's eyes darted around discreetly, taking in every detail. A side door opened and closed, revealing a desk cluttered with papers and two officers in conversation. She made a mental note to return later and investigate. The guests mingled, their laughter and chatter creating a veneer of normality that only heightened Antoinette's apprehension.

He removed her wrap without asking, and she shuddered as her bare shoulders were exposed to the cool air, feeling vulnerable under Falkenberg's lingering gaze. His fingers trailed along her arm, and she swallowed back her revulsion.

'Would you like a drink?'

'Yes, thank you,' Antoinette replied, her voice steady despite the unease tightening within her. As Falkenberg signalled for a servant, she subtly glanced around the room, searching for potential contacts to obtain information.

Accepting the glass of wine he offered her with a polite smile, she raised it to her lips, taking a small sip to calm her nerves. The liquid burned her throat, its taste bitter on her tongue. Falkenberg watched her intently, his eyes never leaving her face, studying every reaction, every flicker of emotion. He leaned in close, his breath hot on her skin.

'You look lovely this evening,' he murmured.

'Thank you,' she replied, feeling a surge of revulsion at his proximity, the cloying scent of his cologne suffocating her senses.

'I should probably set up to play for the guests,' Antoinette suggested, eager to create some distance between herself and the Nazi. With a nod, Falkenberg gestured towards a small area set up in one corner of the room. As she moved, Antoinette could feel his eyes boring into her back.

In the corner, a sallow-faced man was tuning a cello, and a balding pianist sat at a grand piano, rifling through music sheets.

She removed her violin from its case and began to tune it. The familiar notes brought a sense of comfort and strength to her, amid the chaos of the situation.

As she played the first hauntingly beautiful notes, the room fell silent, all eyes on her as the music filled the space.

Closing her eyes, Antoinette let herself be carried away by the melody, pouring all her conflicting emotions into each stroke of the bow. Beneath the surface of projected calm, her mind raced with thoughts of how to gain access to the room with the desk, how to discreetly gather information without raising suspicion. As she played, she opened her eyes and subtly scanned the room, taking in all the guests, and between sets, her ears strained to catch whispered secrets that might be useful to the Resistance.

During her break, she decided to make her move. With Falkenberg nowhere to be seen, she inched her way to the office door, her plan forming. Pushing open the door, she found a Nazi officer seated at the desk, who looked up in surprise as she entered. A mix of confusion and suspicion flashed across his features. She maintained her composure, offering a polite smile as she approached him, her heart pounding in her chest.

'Excuse me, I was looking for the toilet and must have taken a wrong turn,' she improvised quickly, her eyes darting around the room to note the documents scattered on the desk. A map of Paris on the wall, a filing cabinet marked 'Transit' in German, and a stack of papers bearing the insignia of the Third Reich.

The officer regarded her with a hint of scepticism but gestured towards a door at the far end of the room. 'It's down the hall, third door to your left,' he said curtly. Antoinette nodded her thanks, trying to appear nonchalant as she made her way in the indicated direction.

Once out of sight, she quickened her pace, her mind racing to remember all she had seen. She found herself in a narrow hallway lined with several doors. Opening what she thought was the third door, she was startled to find herself in someone's private room. But she wasn't alone. Standing by a window, smoking with his jacket off, was Falkenberg.

He turned to face her, mild surprise crossing his features as he took in Antoinette standing in the doorway. Before she could exit, he reached her and closed the door behind her.

'Commander von Falkenberg, I apologise for this intrusion,' she began, her voice steady but laced with tension. 'I must have taken a wrong turn. I was looking for the toilet—'

He interrupted her. 'Don't go. The view from here is quite spectacular, isn't it?' he said, his tone silky smooth as he stepped closer to her. She could smell the alcohol on his breath, mingled with a faint hint of tobacco.

His hand tightened around her arm, his grip firm and possessive as he guided her toward the window. The city of Paris stretched out before them, the twinkling lights casting a soft glow over the darkened streets below. Her breath caught – not from fear, but from the wave of memories that the view stirred. She thought of the evenings spent playing her violin in their small apartment, with her husband accompanying her on his piano. She remembered the sound of her son's laughter echoing in the park as they chased the last rays of sunlight, time laughing with her sisters. Those moments, fragile yet vibrant, reminded her of why she was fighting – why she had to keep fighting. Paris wasn't just a city. It was her home, her family, her love, and she would do anything to protect it.

As Falkenberg's proximity pressed against her, she felt a sense of danger pulsing in the air. His touch sent a wave of revulsion through her, and she subtly tensed her muscles, preparing for any sudden movements.

Keeping her voice steady, she spoke. 'Yes, it is quite a sight, Commander. Paris is truly a remarkable city. But I really should...'

Continuing to grip her arm, he turned her to face him. 'You are truly enchanting,' Falkenberg murmured, his voice low and intimate as he gazed into her eyes. His eyes drifted to her lips, and a sense of dread washed over her.

'I don't think you were *really* looking for the toilet, were you?'

Before she could answer, he pulled her close. Antoinette's heart raced with panic as Falkenberg's lips crushed hers, forceful and demanding. She tried to pull away, but his grip tightened further still, his other hand bruisingly cupping her face. The taste of alcohol and smoke assaulted her senses. She screwed her eyes shut and thought of René. She couldn't afford to offend this Nazi now. She reminded herself that there was so much to be gained from what she was doing. This was a small price to pay for the information she needed.

When he finally pulled away, he was smiling. 'I knew you felt the same way.'

She didn't trust herself to answer without showing her disgust, so she forced a smile, her body stiffened with suppressed rage and fear. As he released her, she backed away quickly. 'I really must return to the guests now. They will be expecting more music.'

He chuckled softly, a dark gleam in his eyes as he watched her retreat from the room.

In the bathroom, she closed the door behind her and leaned against it, her knees shaking beneath her dress. She felt a surge of anger and violation at Falkenberg's actions but pushed it down, focusing on the task at hand. She needed to find out whatever she could, and that forced kiss only strengthened her resolve. Scooping water into her mouth to wash away the taste of his kiss, Antoinette mentally replayed the details she had observed in his private office. The map of Paris hinted at strategic points of interest for the Third Reich, and the papers on the desk seemed to contain files that could be crucial for the Resistance. She was angry at herself for not taking in more in Falkenberg's bedroom, but there was no time to dwell on her frustration.

Determination burned in her eyes as she straightened her

posture, catching sight of herself in the mirror. She looked exhausted. Antoinette quickly composed herself and returned to the main room, where the guests were still mingling.

As she resumed playing her violin, her mind worked furiously to figure out how to walk this treacherous path without losing herself in the process. A picture of René and Benjamin floated into her thoughts, but she pushed it back.

She refused to feel guilt for doing what was necessary to keep both of them alive.

19

BRAZIL, 2012

Deanna

As they gathered around the table that evening for dinner and waited for Giovanni, the warm air carried the scent of tropical blooms drifting in through the open windows. The soft hum of crickets mixed with Felicity's bubbly laughter as she recounted a memory. 'You should have seen Deanna the last time we were on holiday,' Felicity giggled, eyes twinkling with mischief. 'She was determined to out-paddle a local in a kayak race down the river. Absolute madness!'

Deanna smiled. 'And we only lost because you *dived* into the water for that hat like it was a lost treasure.'

Felicity mock-glared. 'That hat was a limited edition, Deanna. Once it's gone, it's gone!'

'I understand the need!' confirmed Maria, who had a great love for fashion.

As laughter filled the room, the door creaked open, and Giovanni strode in, his presence commanding. 'Ah, my favourite people! I hope you haven't started the party without me!' His smooth, melodic Italian replaced the sharp German accent from earlier, his charm effortless.

Deanna tensed slightly, masking her discomfort with a smile. Why did he make her uneasy? He was a charming, harmless Italian man, she reminded herself.

Giovanni made his way round the table, greeting each of them and kissing Felicity on both cheeks. 'Felicity, *bella*! You're looking as red as a tomato. The Brazilian sun is not so forgiving, eh?'

Felicity giggled. 'Oh, Giovanni, my poor British skin can't handle this intense heat.'

He chuckled, then turned to Deanna, his eyes locking onto hers with unsettling intensity. 'And you,' he said, lowering his voice, 'you seem to be glowing tonight. Brazil must agree with you.'

Deanna's pulse quickened, but she forced a smile. His gaze lingered too long, the atmosphere around him suddenly too close. 'It's a beautiful country,' she replied lightly, hoping to shift the focus.

Giovanni poured her a glass of wine, his hand brushing against her arm with deliberate intimacy. 'Soon, you'll never want to leave,' he murmured.

The others laughed, but Deanna felt the seriousness of his words. Was he just talking about Brazil, or something else?

The conversation resumed, but Deanna's thoughts lingered on the odd tension from that morning. Perhaps she was overreacting, as Maria had suggested. Maybe it was nothing more than a language group meeting, nothing sinister at all.

Eventually, Carlos turned the conversation back to the real reason they were there. As he spoke, Deanna found herself studying his face – the way his jaw tightened slightly when he focused, the faint crease of concern that formed between his brows, and the way his piercing blue eyes caught the light, their intensity making it almost impossible to look away.

'Father, I know you love entertaining, but Deanna and Felicity have come a long way to verify that you're the rightful owner of the violin,' he said, his deep voice drawing her back into the moment.

'That's what I like to hear,' encouraged Felicity as she raised her glass, 'a man who gets *straight* down to business.'

Deanna immediately focused her attention on the older man, watching Giovanni closely.

He kept his easy smile, but Deanna noticed the slight stiffening of his posture. 'Ah, yes, information about the violin. I had almost forgotten with all this good company and wine!' He laughed, but there was a tension in his voice that hadn't been there before.

Carlos leaned back, his tone casual but firm. 'Yes, Father. I'm sure Deanna and Felicity would appreciate seeing the paperwork you mentioned – the documents proving your ownership.'

A moment of silence settled over the table.

Giovanni's smile remained, but it seemed forced now. 'Ah, yes... the paperwork.' His eyes flicked between Carlos and Deanna. 'I'm sure it's somewhere around here, though I haven't thought about it in a while. After all, the war was a long time ago.'

Deanna's suspicion deepened as her eyes met Felicity's briefly. She knew they were wondering the same thing. Why was he stalling?

Giovanni waved a hand, as if brushing off the seriousness. 'But of course, I'll look for it tomorrow. But for now...' He raised his glass. 'Let's enjoy tonight. There's plenty of time for old paperwork.'

He fixed his eyes on Deanna, and though his tone was light, the intensity of his gaze unnerved her once again.

The conversation shifted back to lighter topics, and more wine flowed, but Deanna couldn't shake her growing unease.

Deciding to probe further, she smiled and asked, 'Giovanni, have you ever been to the Infiorata festival in Spello? It's such a beautiful event. I was lucky enough to attend a few years ago.'

Giovanni's eyes lit up with enthusiasm. 'Ah, the Infiorata! Of course. It's one of those traditions that makes Italy so special.'

Encouraged, Deanna continued, 'I remember the vibrant carpets of petals lining the streets. And Todi, your hometown – it's not too far from Spello, right?'

For a brief moment, Giovanni's smile faltered. 'Ah, yes... Todi...' His tone shifted, slower now. 'A charming place. But, you know, it's been so long... the details are fuzzy.'

There was the crack she'd been waiting for.

'Well, I remember Todi vividly,' she pressed, her smile unwavering. 'The views from the hilltop were breathtaking. And the little café in the square with the griffin sculpture at the entrance... Do you remember it?'

Giovanni froze, just for a second. Then his smile returned, forced and strained. 'Ah, the café... Yes, though the name escapes me. Too many cafés, too many places.'

Deanna knew better. That café was famous, talked about by every local. Giovanni sounded as if he had never been there. He must be lying.

Later that night, after the others had retired, Deanna lay in bed, her thoughts racing. She replayed the conversation in her head – every hesitation, every forced smile. Giovanni was hiding something. She was certain of it. But as she stared at the shadowed ceiling, another thought crept into her mind, unbidden and unnerving: why had she really been brought here? Was it truly about the violin, or was there something deeper – something she couldn't yet see? The weight of the unanswered question settled heavily in her chest, keeping sleep far out of reach.

Just as she finally began to drift off, a sound broke the silence – a creak from the floorboards above.

She held her breath, listening.

Another creak.

Then footsteps, slow and deliberate, pacing back and forth. It was obvious that Giovanni couldn't sleep either.

The shuffling continued, steady and methodical. Deanna's pulse quickened, dread settling in her chest.

The footsteps paused. The villa was still, heavy with silence.

Then the pacing resumed, each step stirring her unease even further. Something was going on here – something far more than an old man looking for a family heirloom.

And the thought of what that could be filled her with foreboding.

20

FEBRUARY 1942

Antoinette

It wasn't until the February concert that Antoinette saw Falkenberg again. She arrived at the hotel to find a solitary red rose placed across her music stand. A wave of nausea washed over her. She knew exactly who it was from. Opening the attached note, her dread tightened like a vice as she read his words: *Meet me in my suite after your performance tonight.*

Jacques's warning echoed in her mind: *'Only do what you are comfortable with.'* Despite the disgust churning inside her, Antoinette understood the importance of this meeting for the Resistance. Falkenberg held crucial information, and she needed access to it. It had been challenging to get what she needed other ways.

As she played that night, her mind was a swirl of conflicting thoughts. Her fingers moved mechanically over the strings, the music flowing, but she was detached; every note seemed distant, drowned by her anxiety over the impending meeting. When the final note faded, she glanced up and saw Falkenberg watching from the back of the room, his lips curling into a knowing smile. It sent an icy shiver through her.

After her performance, she made her way up the gilded staircase toward Falkenberg's suite, dread clawing at her insides. She knocked on the door and when it opened, she was surprised to see not Falkenberg, but another officer – a man whose sharp gaze immediately made her uneasy.

'I'm here to see Commander von Falkenberg,' she said, her voice steady despite the growing sense of dread. 'He asked for me.'

The man looked her over with a hint of surprise but masked it quickly. 'I am Captain Vogelmann, his aide,' he replied. 'I wasn't informed of any plans,' he added, his tone edged with mild suspicion.

Antoinette held out the note Falkenberg had left her. 'I have a note from the commander himself,' she explained, as she passed it to Vogelmann.

As Vogelmann took the note, his fingers brushed against hers briefly, in what seemed like an intentional way. She withdrew her hand quickly.

His eyes flitted over the paper, and for a split second, a flicker of intrigue crossed his face, his guarded expression betraying a subtle recognition, or perhaps curiosity.

'You play in the orchestra?' he asked, his tone softening ever so slightly as his eyes settled on her, lingering.

'Yes, I am a violinist,' she responded, careful to keep her demeanour neutral.

For a moment, his expression softened, and the strict professionalism slipped as he seemed to study her more personally. 'I used to attend concerts in Germany before the war,' he said, wistfully. 'Classical music, of course. It felt like stepping into another world back then.' His eyes briefly clouded as if recalling a time when life was simpler – perhaps even beautiful.

'Come on in,' he said, stepping aside. 'You may wait here until he arrives.'

Antoinette hesitated just for a moment; this man didn't seem as controlling as Falkenberg but still she felt distrustful of him. She glanced around the opulent room, her eyes catching on the adjoining door that led to Falkenberg's private office. It was the room she needed to get into. For now, she had to play the part of an obedient guest.

'Would you like something to drink?' he offered, his words holding a warmth that felt slightly out of place in this formal setting. His gaze was attentive, as though he was waiting for her response with interest.

'A glass of wine, perhaps?' she replied with a polite smile, though internally, she fought the anxiety growing inside her.

Vogelmann turned to pour the drink, his posture relaxed yet precise. But as he handed her the glass, the phone rang sharply from an adjoining room. He hesitated, a reluctant look passing over his face before he offered her a quick, courteous nod. 'Excuse me for a moment,' he said, retreating to answer the call.

Placing down her glass after he left, Antoinette moved towards the door, listened carefully, the distant hum of his voice filtering through the thin walls. She couldn't make out the words at first, but then she realised he was speaking in Italian.

She strained to hear, hoping for something in French she might understand as she picked out snippets of the conversation: '*Si, tutto bene... No, nessun problema...*' The words flowed easily, as though it were his native tongue.

The conversation continued for another minute before it abruptly ended. Antoinette quickly moved back to the sofa, pretending to be engrossed in her glass of wine just as Vogelmann returned.

When he re-entered the room, she looked up, catching his gaze just as he seemed to pause in the doorway, studying her.

His eyes softened, and for a brief moment, he almost smiled – a gesture so fleeting it could have been imagined.

'I know you,' he said suddenly, his voice low. 'I saw you once before, at the Conservatoire.'

Antoinette's blood ran cold. She had a carefully constructed backstory given to her by the Resistance, and it didn't include being at the Conservatoire. This was in order to distance herself from René for his protection; she had to think quickly. She masked her shock, meeting his gaze with a steady calm. She was aware that one mistake in this moment could ruin all of her efforts.

With a mental prayer for composure, she replied, 'Ah, yes, I do occasionally attend performances at the Conservatoire to appreciate the talents of fellow musicians. It's always inspiring to witness such artistry.' Her voice remained steady, her eyes never leaving his face as she wove her impromptu tale.

'Yes, I remember now. You were there the night we rounded up the Jewish musicians,' he said with a chilling certainty.

Antoinette's heart pounded. Memories flooded back to her, the horrors of that night threatening to overwhelm her as she fought to keep her mask in place. But then another thought hit her like a punch to the gut – had he seen her with René and their son? Panic rose within her, but she knew that showing any sign of fear or guilt would only seal her fate. She forced herself to stay rooted where she was as every fibre of her being wanted to escape.

She was just about to answer when a rattle at the door diverted their attention. Her body tensed with the sudden interruption.

She never thought she would ever be glad to see Falkenberg, but in that moment, she felt a surge of relief as he entered the room, his imposing figure casting a shadow over the tense atmosphere. His eyes flickered between Antoinette and Vogelmann, immediately sensing the underlying tension.

'Forgive me for being late,' he said smoothly, his gaze lingering on Antoinette. 'I was tied up with urgent matters. Captain Vogelmann, arrange dinner for my guest and me, and then you are dismissed.'

Vogelmann gave a slight nod, his eyes lingering on her as he exited. Antoinette was left alone with Falkenberg and she steeled herself, ready to play whatever role necessary to extract information that could turn the tide in their favour.

Falkenberg approached her, his gaze intense as he studied her face. 'You played with such passion this evening,' he remarked, gesturing towards her violin that lay on a nearby table. 'I have missed seeing you play; my guests were very impressed.'

'Thank you, Commander,' Antoinette replied, her voice steady despite the turmoil inside her. She watched Falkenberg closely, trying to gauge his intentions. His eyes held a glint as he offered her a chair.

As they settled at the elegant dining table, the fine crystal glasses catching the soft glow of candlelight, Antoinette's mind continued to race after her revealing conversation with Vogelmann.

Over the course of the meal, braised veal and roasted vegetables were served. Falkenberg steered the conversation with practised ease, discussing music, art, and politics in a way that seemed almost too casual for the setting. Antoinette played her part flawlessly, echoing his sentiments and feigning interest where necessary. She drew on all the information she had learned in her Resistance training and found herself carefully steering the conversation towards the topic of the war, stroking his ego with compliments to gain any advantage.

Just before dessert, there was a knock at the door. Falkenberg raised an eyebrow in irritation at the interruption. It was Vogelmann, holding a telegram in his hand.

Falkenberg's expression shifted as he read the message, his

features darkening with each passing second. His jaw tightened, and his brows furrowed, creating deep lines on his forehead.

He asked something sharply in German. Vogelmann looked pale as he answered back also in rapid German, his eyes darting nervously between Falkenberg and Antoinette. The tension in the room was palpable, like a coiled spring ready to snap.

Falkenberg sighed heavily, and thrusting his serviette down onto the table, turned to Antoinette.

'Please forgive me for a moment, Mademoiselle Buchet, I must attend to urgent matters. I will be back in a moment.'

With a nod, Antoinette watched Falkenberg leave the room, Vogelmann following quickly behind him. Now alone, Antoinette moved swiftly to the door to listen and heard the two men in a heated conversation as their voices echoed down the hallway.

Assured they had gone to a different office, she moved swiftly to the room she knew was his office, anticipation coiling within her. Maybe this was it; she could get the information that was needed and never have to see this despicable man ever again. But as she attempted to open the door, it was locked. Antoinette cursed under her breath as she tried to force it, to no avail. Hurriedly, she began to search the room for a key. She had just finished searching a drawer when she heard the clipped steps of Falkenberg returning.

She didn't have time to get back to the table with ease, so she raced down the hall to the bathroom. She shut the door, quickly catching her breath, in a bid to appear nonchalant as Falkenberg re-entered the dining room.

She could hear his footsteps drawing nearer, the sound echoing in the silence of the hallway. She pretended to look startled as she opened the door to see him standing there, his eyes narrowing as they met hers. Antoinette quickly composed herself, as she stepped out of the bathroom.

'Ah, Commander von Falkenberg, you startled me,' she said

with a nervous chuckle. 'I was just freshening up. Is everything all right?' she asked, her voice steady, despite the nerves that threatened to unravel her carefully constructed charade.

'I'm afraid not. I am going to have to cut short our dinner,' Falkenberg replied with a tight-lipped expression. 'Urgent matters require my immediate attention.'

Antoinette feigned disappointment as she nodded understandingly, doing her best to hide her relief at the turn of events. 'Of course, Commander,' she replied smoothly. 'I appreciate your hospitality, and understand the demands of your position.'

Falkenberg's eyes searched hers for a lingering moment in a way that made her truly uncomfortable. 'It is most unfortunate; I was hoping for much more time with you this evening. I will have Captain Vogelmann arrange a driver to escort you back to your residence.'

He pressed his hand forcefully into her back, guided her towards the door of the suite, before grabbing her shoulders and kissing her roughly and without warning. Her body froze in place as he dominated her with cold, demanding lips. She fought back a wave of revulsion, trying to remain still as his hands roamed down her back. She held her breath, desperate to avoid showing any sign of disgust.

She finally managed to pull away as she mustered up the courage to speak. 'Please, don't let me keep you from your important work,' she muttered through gritted teeth.

'You are too irresistible,' he leered, gripping her head so tightly that he covered her ears with his hands so she could barely hear him. Antoinette could feel her skin crawling with repulsion as she forced herself to plaster on a smile, masking her true feelings.

Just then, a door closed down the hall and footsteps approached, saving her from any further unwanted advances.

Falkenberg appeared to swear in German before he bade her goodnight, moving away towards his office. She lingered in the doorway, pretending to fix her hair in a mirror as she watched him reach into his pocket and pull out the key to his office door. Now she knew where he kept it, but stealing it would be no easy feat.

Her mind shuddered at one possible solution, but she hoped more than anything that it would never come to that.

21

BRAZIL, 2012

Deanna

The next morning, the intense Brazilian heat was subdued, and the sun struggled to pierce through the heavy clouds hanging low over the estate. Deanna woke feeling unrested, the remnants of the previous night clinging to her thoughts like an unfinished puzzle. She needed answers and hoped she would get them today. Before heading downstairs, she knocked gently on Felicity's door.

'Fee, you awake?' From behind the door came a muffled groan.

'Barely... What time is it?' Her friend's voice was scratchy with sleep.

'Early, but I need to talk to you about something that happened last night.'

A few moments later, Felicity emerged in the doorway, hair tousled and squinting against the light.

Deanna stepped inside, feeling a sense of urgency. 'I heard footsteps pacing overhead for hours last night. It didn't feel... *right*.'

Felicity's tired expression mirrored the concern in Deanna's eyes. 'That's creepy,' Felicity said with a shudder. 'Are you sure it wasn't this old house creaking or maybe Carlos doing some sort of "midnight brooding bachelor" thing? He's always so secretive about his private life, have you noticed?'

Deanna crossed her arms, her tone becoming more serious. 'I don't think it was Carlos. But there is something about this family – especially the father – that feels off. He watched me at dinner last night, and not in a "wow, interesting guest" kind of way. More like he knows something I don't.'

Felicity's brow furrowed in worry. 'You mean more than just about your grandmother's violin?'

'*Exactly*,' Deanna replied. 'There's something deeper here. And I can't shake the feeling that it's connected to her in a way I haven't uncovered yet.'

Felicity shook her head in frustration. 'It's maddening how they keep stalling about showing you evidence that the violin was in their family.'

'I know, but honestly, Felicity, if for some reason they can't prove ownership, we lose nothing and just go home. But there's more here that I feel I need to uncover.' Deanna continued. 'Beside the fact I don't think the man has ever been to Italy, never mind being born there. He knew very little about his home town. I think he is hiding something about my grandmother; that's why he stares at me like that. Because I think I remind him of her. And if I don't figure this out, it's going to haunt me forever. I can't leave until we get to the bottom of it,' Deanna said firmly.

'Let's push for more answers today,' Felicity asserted. 'We need to break out of living in this carefree Brazilian vacation mindset; it's time to take control and be proactive.'

Over breakfast, after Maria asked her about her night, Deanna decided to approach the situation carefully. She glanced at Felicity, who raised her eyebrows as if to say, *Here goes nothing*.

'I had a bit of a restless night. I thought I heard someone moving around upstairs – was one of you up late?'

Maria's smile faltered ever so slightly, her eyes flicking toward Carlos. 'That must have been our father. He often paces at night when he can't sleep. Nothing to worry about.'

Deanna kept her tone light, though her curiosity sharpened. 'Is everything all right with him? He seemed a bit... preoccupied at dinner last night.'

Felicity chimed in, her tone casual but probing, 'And he seems reluctant to share any more information about his ownership of the violin.'

Maria's smile thinned as she glanced at Carlos, who had been silently listening. His expression tightened, his jaw setting with a hint of defensiveness.

'My father sometimes gets off-topic and can be easily distracted. He loves entertaining and having guests, and he gets caught up in all of that. I'm sure he will find the paperwork today.'

Deanna seized the moment. 'It's a lovely estate and we have enjoyed the hospitality, but I'm eager to sort everything out.'

Carlos glanced at the clock. 'He usually sleeps late, but I'll check on him soon. I'm sure he'll be ready to talk with you.'

'In the meantime, why don't we enjoy breakfast and take a walk around the gardens? They're beautiful this time of year,' Maria suggested.

Deanna nodded, though her thoughts were elsewhere, spinning with unanswered questions.

As they strolled through the estate's manicured gardens, the crisp air cleared Deanna's mind. Vibrant blooms framed the paths, and the distant hum of insects filled the silence. While Felicity, who shared a passion for gardening with Maria, strode off to admire a striking bush, Deanna wandered off down a pathway, drawn to a secluded corner. She found an old stone bench, surrounded by vines and blooming flowers, and sat down, hoping to find some peace. But her mind wouldn't settle.

Why hadn't her grandmother spoken of her work in the Resistance? Why had she never played the violin again after the war? What was Giovanni's connection to her grandmother, and why did he act so strangely?

She was so deep in thought she barely noticed the soft footsteps approaching.

Carlos sat down beside her, his presence magnetic in the dappled light. The open collar of his linen shirt revealed a hint of tanned skin, and his sleeves were rolled up casually, adding a relaxed charm to his usual polished manner.

'You seem... distant, Deanna. Is everything all right?'

His gaze, thoughtful and steady, made her stomach clench slightly with the intimacy of their surroundings, and she swallowed down her attraction, determined to speak with him seriously.

'Carlos, there's something I've been meaning to ask you.' Her voice was calm, but her eyes were searching. 'You once mentioned reconnecting with your father after years apart. Why did your mother keep you from him?'

Carlos's expression darkened. 'My mother... was a complicated woman. After the divorce, she took us away and never explained why she cut off contact. It wasn't until after her death that Maria and I sought him out.'

Deanna could feel the depth of sadness in his words. 'That must have been hard for you and Maria. So many unanswered questions for you both.'

Carlos nodded, his eyes drifting over the estate. 'It was. When we finally reconnected, our father was... different. Generous, but haunted. There's a darkness to him, something from the past he hasn't let go of.'

Deanna's pulse quickened. 'Do you think that has something to do with the war or the violin? I am really interested in its history.'

Carlos's gaze sharpened. 'It might... When I told him you found it, he became almost... obsessed. Like it was the key to unlocking something important.'

'*Obsessed?*' Deanna repeated, the word sending a chill through her. It was exactly how she'd describe the way Giovanni had watched her during dinner.

Deanna felt a surge of unease, her mind connecting the dots between Giovanni's intensity and Carlos's mention of their father's obsession with the violin. She turned to Carlos, her eyes wide with realisation. 'Do you think there's more to this violin than we considered? Something that ties all these mysteries together?'

Carlos furrowed his brow, deep in thought. 'It's possible...'

They both sat in silence, the weight of unanswered questions hanging heavy in the air.

'Do you think your father is awake yet?' Deanna asked, her curiosity pushing her forward. 'There are so many questions I'd like to ask him.'

Carlos glanced at his watch, then offered a thoughtful smile. 'He should be. Let's head back and find out.'

They met up with Felicity and Maria, and they made their way back to the villa, Maria excusing herself to attend to some household matters, while Carlos went to check on his father. He reappeared at the top of the stairs to announce, 'My father will be down shortly. He said he can meet you in the library, Deanna – there's something he wants to show you.'

The library was a warm and inviting space, with dark wooden shelves filled with leather-bound books and cultural artefacts. Soft light streamed through the tall French doors, casting golden patterns across the terracotta floors. Deanna felt an odd mixture of comfort and anticipation as she stepped inside.

Felicity disappeared, needing to grab something from her bedroom, and Carlos went to find Maria. Drawn by the view outside, Deanna wandered onto the stone terrace that overlooked the estate. The peaceful scene provided a brief moment of calm, but her mind continued to swirl with unanswered questions.

'Beautiful, isn't it?' A voice spoke softly behind her, pulling her back to the present.

She hadn't heard anyone enter. Startled, Deanna turned to see Giovanni standing a little too close, his gaze calm but intent.

'Indeed, it's stunning,' Deanna replied, feeling a slight flutter of concern.

He pierced her with his gaze. 'You look lovely today,' he said, his voice low and meaningful. The words, though harmless in themselves, held an undercurrent of energy that reminded her of the previous night. She shifted uncomfortably, silently grateful when the others came to join them behind him.

Felicity and Carlos entered chatting, and Maria brought refreshments. Giovanni moved away from Deanna's side and resumed his carefree Italian persona.

'Carlos mentioned you're interested in the violin's history.'

'Yes,' Deanna said. 'But I'm particularly interested in how it came to be in my grandmother's possession.'

Giovanni sniffed lightly, a subtle gesture of disapproval, as he motioned for Deanna to take a seat on the sofa.

The older man settled into his own chair, the leather creaking as he leaned back. 'This violin,' he began, his voice carrying the weight of time, 'is no ordinary instrument. Crafted by the Stradivari family in the late seventeenth century, it has passed through the hands of many people, each adding to its legendary story.'

Deanna tightened her grip on the side of her chair, listening intently.

'My grandmother Eleonora was a celebrated violinist.

During a tour in Venice, she met a relative of Stradivari, and they fell in love. And he gifted her this violin. But their love was doomed. He was killed in an accident the night they planned to flee together. Eleonora returned home to Todi, the violin her only reminder of their love.'

Giovanni's voice grew tight with emotion. 'When she died, the violin went to my father. He had trouble finding work and eventually moved to Paris for a job offered by an old friend. The violin came with us. Then the Nazis came. Von Falkenberg, obsessed with collecting valuable artefacts, found out about the violin and demanded to have it. We couldn't refuse.'

His fists clenched as he continued. 'I was livid and vowed to get it back for my family. I heard von Falkenberg had a suite at the Majestic, so I joined the Resistance in order to attempt to steal it back. But just when that was in my sight, one night, a woman stole it, leaving no trace of her whereabouts behind.'

'My *grandmother*?' Deanna whispered, a pang of undeserved guilt growing within her.

The old man's expression became tense. 'I believe so. Do you have a photograph of her?'

Deanna pulled out the photograph of her grandmother, taken at the party with the Nazi officer. She handed it to the older man, watching closely for his reaction.

He stared at the image for a long moment, a knowing smile curling his lips. 'This is her with von Falkenberg. But she went by Melodie when I knew her.'

'Yes,' Deanna confirmed, her pulse racing.

His eyes clouded with memory. 'I remember her well. She visited von Falkenberg's suite many times at the Majestic.'

Deanna felt a shockwave of realisation. She had suspected a connection, but hearing it confirmed was something else entirely.

'Do you know the nature of their relationship?' she asked, her voice barely above a whisper.

A slow smile spread across Giovanni's face. 'She was his lover.'

Deanna's chest tightened, a mix of horror and disbelief flooding her senses. Silence stretched between them, heavy and suffocating, as the weight of his words sank in.

'Are you sure?' she finally managed, her voice trembling as her thoughts raced to untangle the implications of what she had just heard.

'I am certain. Their relationship was passionate, but doomed of course.'

Felicity and Deanna exchanged a nervous glance.

'What do you mean, *doomed*?' Deanna pressed.

The old man leaned back, almost relishing her confusion. 'One night in a fit of jealous rage, Antoinette stabbed him to death.'

Deanna's mind reeled.

The idea that her grandmother had been involved in such a tragic affair with a Nazi officer was nearly incomprehensible. Shock, horror, and confusion swirled within her, leaving her grasping for understanding.

Felicity turned to Deanna, her eyes wide with disbelief, trying to process the bombshell that had just been dropped.

The old man leaned back, satisfaction evident in his posture. 'I think you'll find your grandmother is not the woman you thought she was. And her involvement with Falkenberg... well that was just the tip of the iceberg.'

22

APRIL 1942

Antoinette

The next time Antoinette saw Falkenberg was during the April concert.

Over the past few months, she had been able to gather and pass on valuable information to the Resistance, including details about attendees at the monthly concerts and conversations she overheard. However, she had not yet been able to access the floor of suites again where critical information awaited. Now, as Commander von Falkenberg approached her casually, she felt a mixture of emotions.

'Good evening, Mademoiselle Buchet. It is good to see you again.' His voice carried an unsettling ease.

Antoinette drew back slightly, looking up from the sheet music she was arranging. Forcing herself to meet his gaze, she replied evenly, 'Yes, thank you, Commander.' Despite her calm tone, her fingers trembled as they sorted through the pages.

'Good,' he said with a smirk. He began to move away, then paused, as if recalling something.

'I had an interesting conversation with my aide while we

were away,' Falkenberg continued, his voice casual, but with an underlying sharpness. 'He mentioned seeing *you* at the Conservatoire some time ago.'

Antoinette stiffened, unease coiling tightly within her as she braced herself for what was coming next. Where was this leading?

'He told me about your... enjoyment of the performances there.'

Her pulse quickened, but she kept her expression neutral. 'Yes, I do visit the Conservatoire when time allows,' she replied cautiously, uncertain of his intentions.

The commander's gaze lingered on her, his smile widening just enough to make her uneasy. 'Your passion for music is quite admirable. It's rare to find someone so deeply dedicated to their craft.' His words, though seemingly complimentary, chilled her. There was an edge to his tone that made her feel like prey being toyed with.

'Thank you, Commander,' she said softly, trying to steer the conversation away. 'Music has always been a source of solace for me.'

But Falkenberg wasn't ready to let go. 'I imagine you have many friends at the Conservatoire. Musicians are a close-knit group after all, aren't they?'

Antoinette opened her mouth to respond, but before she could, Falkenberg gave her a knowing look and strode off without waiting for an answer.

Her knees felt weak. *Does he know who I really am?*

Just then, the conductor tapped his baton on the music stand, bringing the orchestra to order. Antoinette swallowed hard, trying to focus on the notes swimming in front of her, but the mention of the Conservatoire continued to echo in her mind, chilling her to the bone.

As she raised her violin, preparing to play, another soldier approached the conductor, whispering in rapid German.

Antoinette waited, her violin poised, nerves fraying with each passing second. After a brief exchange, the soldier stepped toward a side door, which creaked open ominously.

Antoinette froze, her breath catching in her throat as a gaunt, pale man was escorted into the room. His ill-fitting suit hung loosely on his emaciated frame, but something in the way he moved – the slight stoop of his shoulders, the familiar angle of his jaw – was unmistakable. Her heart pounded against her ribs as she gasped softly, her blood running cold.

René.

A year. A full year since she had last seen him. She had feared he was gone, swallowed by the abyss of war. Yet here he was, her beloved husband, *alive.* Antoinette's heart surged with shock, disbelief, and a flicker of desperate hope.

Thank God... thank God he's alive.

Every fibre of her being screamed to run to him, to fall into his arms, to sob out his name. But her training slammed into place like an iron gate. She couldn't blow her cover – not now, not with the stakes so high.

Their gazes locked in a moment of intense connection, and she saw the raw and powerful emotions reflected in his eyes – an overwhelming love and relief that left her breathless. It was as if they were the only two people in the world, lost in a realm of their own making. Time stood still as they were stricken by the depth of their bond.

But then his eyes fell to the swastika on her arm, stark against the fabric of her dress.

And everything changed.

Horror. Betrayal. Fear. The emotions rippled across his face in waves of confusion and disbelief. His entire body stiffened as if he had been struck, and his hands gripped the piano for support.

Antoinette's heart shattered into a thousand pieces. She wanted to scream, to explain, to tell him this was a lie – a mask she wore to save him. But the room around her pressed in, its oppressive silence broken only by the murmurs of their enemies. She stood rooted to the spot, locked in silent agony as her world unravelled before her.

Everything else faded into a haze. The Nazis' voices blurred into background noise. The elegant chandelier above seemed distant and unreal. There was only René – his desperate expression, his trembling form – and the unspoken question searing through her mind like a brand:

Why was he here?

This wasn't coincidence. This wasn't mercy.

Had he been brought as a weapon? A test? A cruel game?

A chilling certainty settled over Antoinette, her chest tightening with the realisation that nothing about this moment was innocent. René wasn't just alive – he was a pawn, and she had no idea how to save him without damning them both.

Her breathing faltered as the room around her seemed to close in, the weight of this truth pressing in from all sides.

Tears threatened to spill from her eyes, but Antoinette forced herself to remain still, her nails digging into her palms. Whatever this was – whatever they wanted – she had to be ready. Because René's life, and now her own, hung in the balance.

She turned to see Commander von Falkenberg as he watched the scene unfold with keen interest, a slow, cruel smile tugging at his lips. He appeared to relish every second of her torment.

Summoning her last reserves of strength, Antoinette lifted her violin. She bit back the tears that threatened to fall, determined not to give Falkenberg the satisfaction of seeing her weakness.

In the moments before the concert began, she stole quick glances at René. The toll of incarceration was stark – his once-bright eyes now shadowed and hollow, his body marked with bruises, thinner and frailer than before. Yet a flicker of defiance lingered, a spark that gave her hope. René wouldn't break easily. But whenever his gaze drifted to the swastika band on her arm, Antoinette saw anguish and confusion wrestle in his expression, the love in his eyes dulled by what he perceived as her betrayal.

She longed to reach out, to reassure him, to explain. But any sign of affection would only feed Falkenberg's cruel game. Anger and fear surged through her at the thought of the man orchestrating this nightmare.

The orchestra leader raised his baton. Her hand trembled slightly as she brought the violin to her chin. Normally, the instrument was her solace, but tonight, it felt foreign and heavy. As she drew the bow, a single tear slipped down her cheek at the sound of René's playing – its beauty, a bittersweet ache.

Scanning the crowd, she found Falkenberg. His eyes were locked on her, glinting with malevolent satisfaction, as if daring her to defy him. The satisfaction of a man who believed he had her completely under his control. Her fingers tightened on the bow as she began Vivaldi's *Winter*, pouring every emotion into the music, letting it shield her from the darkness threatening to overtake her. Each note carried defiance, her gaze sharp and unwavering as she met his, silently declaring that his hold on her was far from complete.

Her fingers flew across the strings, the music swelling with intensity. Thoughts raced through her mind – had he uncovered her true identity? If so, why delay her arrest? He was toying with her, like a cat with a mouse, savouring every moment of control he held over her. But she would not be a passive victim. She would find a way to fight back, come up with a plan of her own.

The piece climbed to its crescendo, and her eyes briefly met René's, his pride and pain reflected in his gaze. No matter what, she would protect him – and their son.

As *Winter* came to its dramatic conclusion, the audience

erupted into enthusiastic applause. Her whole body ached to rush to René, to hold him and never let go. But she never had the chance because, before she could move, a chilling voice cut through the applause.

'Bravo, bravo! What a performance!' Falkenberg's voice boomed through the room, sending a wave of loathing rolling through her body as he strode toward the stage. Before she could react, he gripped her arm tightly, his touch cold and unyielding, like ice against her skin.

'I have some friends here I want you to meet.' Falkenberg's voice was smooth, but Antoinette could feel his desire to control her bearing down on her, suffocating her spirit. She didn't even bother to force a smile as she was introduced to the group of men Falkenberg had brought with him. They were all dressed in immaculate uniforms, their eyes cold and calculating as they scanned her up and down. These were high-ranking Nazi officials, and Falkenberg was parading her in front of them like a prized possession. She forced herself to maintain a façade of composure, even as her eyes desperately searched the crowd for René.

But her husband was nowhere to be seen, swallowed up in the sea of unfamiliar faces that surrounded her.

And her heart broke.

23

BRAZIL, 2012

Deanna

Deanna's mind reeled, trying to absorb the shocking revelation about her grandmother's past. The image of the fiery, independent woman she had known clashed violently with the dark affair the old man hinted at. It was almost too much to believe – her grandmother had stabbed her Nazi lover?

'What do you mean, "the tip of the iceberg"?' Deanna stammered, her heart racing. 'What else do you know?'

Giovanni's eyes glinted, his tone cryptic. 'Undercover at that hotel, I saw many things. Heard many rumours,' he murmured, his voice dropping to a whisper. But before Deanna could press for more, Maria interrupted with news of a phone call for him. The old man sighed. 'This business will take a while. We'll continue another time, and I'll keep looking for the paperwork you need.'

With that, he was gone, leaving Deanna frustrated and desperate for answers. Her heart ached for the safety and familiarity of home in England, but the whirlwind of questions kept spinning in her mind.

Felicity, sitting nearby, raised an eyebrow and sighed dramatically. 'We could be here *forever!*' She rolled her eyes as she sank back on the couch.

Deanna couldn't help but smile, despite everything. 'I can't believe it... my grandmother, involved in something so dark... it just doesn't seem... real.'

Felicity leaned over, nudging her gently. 'Hey, don't jump to conclusions just yet. She could've been tangled up in something she didn't want to be in.'

Deanna nodded, her head starting to throb. 'I just need to know the truth. But what if...' She hesitated. 'What if she was capable of... something terrible?'

Felicity's face softened, but she didn't drop her teasing tone. 'Deanna, your gran probably wasn't running around with a dagger and a trench coat. You need more facts before you start picturing her in some black-and-white murder mystery.'

Deanna sighed, her emotions churning inside her. 'You're right. I need to know more.'

'Exactly,' Felicity said, her voice calm and reassuring.

Just then, Deanna's headache worsened. The room seemed to spin, and she pressed her fingers to her temples.

Felicity's eyes narrowed. 'I know that look. Okay, migraine girl, let's get you to bed before you pass out on me. No arguing.'

'Wasn't planning on it,' Deanna muttered, already feeling the nausea creeping in.

Felicity helped her to the bedroom and returned moments later with a cold washcloth, some water, and Deanna's medication. She handed them over like a well-practised nurse.

'Thanks,' Deanna mumbled, grateful for the relief. She lay back, letting out a slow breath as the cool cloth soothed her forehead.

'Nurse Fee is on call,' Felicity teased.

Deanna managed a small smile. 'You can go now, Nurse. I'll just rest for a bit.'

Felicity chuckled, squeezing her hand. 'Okay, but don't even think about getting into more trouble without me.' She shot her a mischievous grin before slipping out the door, leaving Deanna in the quiet.

Once alone, Deanna's thoughts rushed back. The old man's cryptic words, her grandmother's secret – it all swirled in her mind. As the medication kicked in, Deanna slipped into a fitful sleep, her mind still wrestling with everything she had learned.

A while later, Deanna jolted awake, disoriented by a persistent buzzing. The migraine had subsided to a dull ache, but her mind was still foggy. She blinked against the dim light, realising the sound was her phone vibrating on the side table. Her heart sank as she saw her father's name flash on the screen.

'Hi, Dad,' she answered, trying to steady her voice.

'Deanna! I've been worried. Are you okay?' His concern was palpable, and Deanna felt a pang of guilt: she had meant to call him before now, but had been waiting to figure it all out herself first.

'I'm fine, Dad. Just dealing with a migraine and some... research. I've been a little out of it.'

'A migraine? Are you resting now?'

'Yes, I've got everything I need,' Deanna replied, keeping her voice light. 'Just taking it easy.'

'That's good to hear,' her father said, his voice softening. Then he asked, 'Any news about your grandmother's violin?'

Deanna's heart skipped a beat. 'I'm still looking into it. There's more to it than we thought,' she said quickly, then changed the subject. 'How's the new place?'

'Oh, fine, fine,' he said, launching into a detailed account of his day in the new warden-controlled flat – his neighbours, the garden, and the latest drama in the complex.

Deanna listened, but her mind wandered back to the secrets

she was uncovering. Finally, she interrupted. 'Dad, I need to go, but I'll call you soon, okay?'

'Of course, sweetheart. Take care of yourself.'

'I will. Love you.'

'Love you too,' he replied, and the call ended.

Deanna dropped the phone back on the nightstand, her chest tight with homesickness. But she didn't have time to dwell on it – she needed answers. Determined, she swung her legs over the side of the bed and got up. She had to find Felicity and figure out what to do next.

But as she walked through the villa, neither Felicity nor Maria was around. Stepping out onto the patio, she saw Carlos walking towards her, his head down, deep in thought. His dark hair was ruffled by the breeze, and his jaw was set. For a brief moment, Deanna felt a flicker of something – attraction, fascination– but she pushed it aside.

'Carlos?' she called out.

He looked up, and when their eyes met, his expression shifted, something unreadable in his gaze.

'Are you feeling better?' His voice was gentle, filled with concern.

'Mostly,' she replied, though the remnants of her headache lingered.

Carlos hesitated. 'There's something important we need to talk about. But not here. Let's go to my office.'

Curiosity stirred in Deanna's chest. 'Okay,' she agreed.

He led her through the town to an old building with wrought-iron balconies and colourful murals. Inside, the cool air was a welcome relief.

'Please, sit,' Carlos said, gesturing to a plush chair. He moved behind his desk, the seriousness in his eyes making Deanna's heart race.

Carlos paused before speaking, his voice hesitant. 'There's

something I've been wrestling with for a while now. And it's something difficult to confess.'

A wave of tension rippled through Deanna as she leaned forward, her eyes fixed on his, urging him to continue.

'My father always claimed he fought for the Resistance,' Carlos began, his voice heavy. 'But recently, I uncovered something... darker.'

Deanna's breath caught. 'What do you mean?'

Carlos clenched his jaw. 'Since reconnecting with him, I've noticed things in his stories that don't add up. At first, I ignored them. I didn't want to believe he wasn't the hero he claimed to be. But the more I listened, the more cracks appeared – especially when he talked about your grandmother.'

Deanna's breath hitched. 'Cracks?'

Carlos nodded. 'I've started to wonder if he wasn't just a Resistance fighter. What if he collaborated with the Nazis to get what he wanted? Including that violin.'

The room seemed to close in around her, the air thick and suffocating. Deanna blinked, her mind spinning as the implications crashed over her. Her chest tightened painfully; the thought of her grandmother – her fierce, courageous grandmother – being tied to a man who might have betrayed the very people she fought for was almost unbearable.

'So, it wasn't about the Resistance?' she asked, her voice trembling, laced with disbelief. Her fingers gripped the edge of the table, anchoring her against the tidal wave of doubt and fear threatening to pull her under.

Carlos exhaled, regret in his voice. 'I'm not sure any more. The violin became an obsession for him. To get it back for his family. I think he would've made deals with anyone, even the Nazis, to get it back. That's why he's so fixated on your grandmother; he knew she was the last one to have it.'

A chill ran through Deanna. 'But how can you be sure?'

Carlos slid a file toward her. 'I've found documents,

records... and *this*.' He hesitated. 'I didn't want to say anything before. Maria doesn't know, and I thought it didn't matter since it has nothing to do with the violin itself. But with all he is sharing, I thought you should know.'

Deanna cautiously opened the file, her pulse quickening as she stared at an old photograph. It had badly aged, but she could just make out two men – one a high-ranking Nazi officer in the foreground and the other a civilian looking away from the camera, with a build similar to Giovanni's – smiling, arms around each other. On the back, Carlos translated the words written in German: *With my good friend Otto von Falkenberg.*

A chill swept over her. 'What does this mean?' she whispered.

Carlos leaned back, his face troubled. 'Your grandmother could have been part of the Resistance, but I'm not sure about him. My father wouldn't admit that – not if it meant tarnishing his story. There's a reason for the secrecy, Deanna – something about that violin goes deeper than we realise.'

Deanna felt her need to understand clarifying. 'I have to know the full truth. Whatever your father is hiding, I need to uncover it before I can tell my dad.'

Carlos reached for her hand, his touch sending a shock through her. 'I will do all I can to help.'

The moment hung between them, their hands lingering for just a beat too long before Deanna pulled away, heat rising to her cheeks.

'We should get back before anyone starts to worry,' Carlos said, his voice tight.

Deanna nodded, still shaken. But as they made their way back, a deeper question burned within her: how far was she willing to go to uncover the truth? Was she ready to face the looming shadows that had haunted her grandmother and were now closing in on her?

24

APRIL 1942

Antoinette

As Antoinette continued to search the room for her husband, Falkenberg slipped his arm around her waist and pulled her close, a sickeningly sweet smile plastered on his face.

'What do you think of our first violinist?' he asked with false pride as he introduced her to another group.

One of the officials, a tall man with a scar running down his cheek, stepped forward and appraised Antoinette with a cold, lingering gaze. 'Her playing is quite lovely,' he said in a thick German accent. 'Wherever did you find her in France?'

The commander chuckled, his eyes never leaving hers. 'She fell into my *lap* unexpectedly, fortunately for us.' His words dripped with insinuation, and as he finished, he reached out to straighten her Nazi armband, his fingers lingering possessively on her arm. A triumphant glint shone in his eye, silently declaring, *You're mine.*

Antoinette's blood boiled with fury. She had complied with Falkenberg's demands for the sake of her mission with the Resistance, but now, with him parading her in front of these

Nazi officials and bringing René to the performance, it was all too much to bear. The fire of defiance burned bright within her as she met Falkenberg's gaze. She wouldn't let him play with her any longer, even if it meant risking arrest. Setting her chin, she spoke through gritted teeth.

'Let's hope I never give you a reason to be disappointed. That could end very badly, I fear.' She met his piercing gaze, her eyes locked on his. His eyes darkened for a fleeting moment, her unmistakable threat simmering just beneath the surface.

But before Falkenberg could respond, he was called away by an assistant. He excused himself to the group with a dismissive, 'Excuse me, I'm afraid duty calls,' before disappearing into the crowd.

Antoinette seized the brief moment to excuse herself. She frantically scanned the room, needing to find René, to explain why she was here, why she was wearing this despicable armband of the enemy. Through the sea of faces, she caught a glimpse of him being led from the stage by a guard toward a corridor on the other side of the room. A surge of determination coursed through her – she had to reach him before it was too late.

She swiftly made her way towards the corridor where René had disappeared, the sound of her heels clicking against the marble floor echoing through the grand hall, the urgency of the moment driving her forward.

As she turned the corner into the dimly lit corridor, she heard muffled voices and quickened her pace, her breath coming in short, sharp gasps. Peering around the corner, she saw René standing outside by the road, guarded by a stern-looking soldier who seemed to be waiting for a truck to arrive. The sight of René, so close yet still so far from her, filled her with both hope and dread. She knew she had to act quickly, or this might be the last time she ever saw him.

'*Monsieur!*' Antoinette called out in a frantic tone. Relief washed over her as René's head snapped up at the sound of her voice. His eyes widened in disbelief as she approached.

The guard turned, his hand instinctively reaching for his weapon. Antoinette slowed her pace, maintaining a safe distance.

'I just wanted to say how much I enjoyed your performance,' Antoinette continued smoothly, stepping closer to René, her heart pounding like a drum in her chest. The guard eyed her suspiciously, but she held René's gaze with unwavering confidence.

'You play with such passion and skill; it was truly captivating. I believe we once played together. I have missed... your music,' she said, her voice carrying a fragile tenderness. Then, after a beat, she added quietly, her tone bittersweet, 'Sometimes, we must play where we are asked to, no matter the stage.'

Her words were layered with hidden meaning, a desperate attempt to convey her love and reassurance while acknowledging the unbearable weight of their shared predicament. She prayed he would understand the message beneath her carefully chosen words, hoping to dispel any doubt or fear in René's mind.

René cleared his throat, and though it was heavy with emotion, he responded, 'Yes, we do. And I remember you too. I also miss your music.'

She nodded subtly, her eyes full of understanding. Just then, the truck arrived, and the guards pushed René towards it. Antoinette watched helplessly, her heart breaking with every step he took.

As René was led away, he craned his neck to shout back at her, 'Your son, Madame, is he...?'

Antoinette's heart clenched at the mention of Benjamin. She shouted back, her voice strained with emotion, 'He is doing well, though I know he misses your music, too.'

René's eyes softened briefly, but before he could respond, he was shoved into the truck, disappearing from view.

The pain of seeing René taken away for a second time cut deep within Antoinette's heart, but she knew she couldn't give in to despair. As she watched the truck drive away, carrying her beloved René with it, she realised with chilling certainty that her cover may well be blown. There would be no coming back here again. She might even need to go into hiding.

Panic clawed at her chest as she darted back into the ballroom, desperate to retrieve her violin and flee before Falkenberg could catch her. Every nerve in her body prickled with fear, knowing he must have discovered her connection with René. She moved swiftly through the dark, eerie streets, heart racing with thoughts of protecting her family from Falkenberg's wrath.

Taking every precaution, she navigated through back alleys and side streets, avoiding any contact with anyone. But just when she thought she had escaped his reach, her breath caught in her throat as she approached the road where he had dropped her off before. And there, leaning against his sleek black car, was Falkenberg.

The pungent stench of burning tobacco filled the air as he took a long, slow drag from his cigarette, his cold, calculating gaze fixed on her. His voice cut through the tense silence like a razor blade.

'You disappeared so quickly,' he said with a sinister smile. 'I wanted to know what you thought of our new pianist.' The ice in his tone was obvious, and she knew she was no match for this ruthless man. All she had were her wits and the knowledge that he desired her, even if it was just as a pawn in his dangerous game.

But if he was here to arrest her, he could have done it already. Instead, he was choosing to toy with her. Panic surged through Antoinette as she frantically looked around for an escape, just in case, relying on her training.

Falkenberg's eyes gleamed with cold amusement as he spoke again, his voice cutting through the night air like shards of glass.

'After my aide informed me that you have a fondness for musicians from the Conservatoire, I thought seeing him would bring you joy,' he drawled, his words dripping with malice. 'It is a shame he will be departing for a camp soon, far away from here,' he added casually, fully aware of the fear and dread creeping into Antoinette's heart.

Antoinette's body stiffened, her heart racing so hard she could feel it in her throat. A sense of dread washed over her as she stared at Falkenberg with his twisted smile.

A car slowly passed by, casting an eerie light on their faces. Antoinette cautiously inched closer, clutching her violin case like a shield.

'What do you mean?' she asked, her voice barely audible. She locked eyes with Falkenberg, searching for any hint of his intentions, but his inscrutable expression only added to the suffocating tension between them.

Falkenberg stepped toward her, his hand moving to cup her chin as he studied her face. The sharp scent of alcohol on his breath made her skin crawl as he leaned in, whispering in her ear. 'But maybe instead of sending him away, we could make use of him. Wouldn't it be thrilling,' he said, emphasising his words with a sickening sweetness, 'to see you play with the pianist, again?' His words sent a wave of terror through Antoinette, trapping her in her worst nightmare.

She swallowed hard, not trusting herself to answer for fear of giving herself away.

'I am hosting another dinner party in August, and I believe both your musical talents would be a *wonderful* addition,' Falkenberg stated, his words dripping with insinuation.

Antoinette felt a wave of nausea at the implication. She knew that if she dared to refuse him, René would be immediately shipped off to a concentration camp without a second thought. With a tight knot of dread forming in her gut, she knew she had no choice but to accept his demands. If it meant buying a few more months of René being close to her in Paris, she would pay the price.

Suppressing the bile rising in her throat, she forced herself to respond with a cool and steady voice. 'It appears you have already arranged everything,' she stated calmly, her words carefully measured.

'Nevertheless, I think we should meet for dinner when I am back so we can discuss it further,' he said, Falkenberg's smile stretching into a sinister grin at her compliance, making her feel like she might vomit. He slowly crushed his cigarette against the ground before slipping into his car. 'See you then, Mademoiselle Buchet – or should I say Madame *Kaplan?*' he purred smoothly, his departing words echoing through the stillness of the night informing her that her cover was indeed blown.

Alone on the deserted street, Antoinette felt the weight of the world bearing down on her shoulders. The stakes were higher now than ever before, and she knew that every move she made from this point on could mean life or death for her family.

Every action had to be calculated and precise – there was no margin for error in this dangerous game of survival.

25

BRAZIL, 2012

Deanna

As Deanna and Carlos walked back to the villa, the evening sky deepened into a twilight haze, casting the surroundings in a soft, ethereal glow. Her mind whirled, grappling with the shocking revelation about Giovanni Rossi that had shaken her to her core.

Could he have been a double agent for the Nazis? Could she trust anything he had said? Had Giovanni been Falkenberg's contact during the war? Was that his true motivation?

She stole glances at Carlos as they moved through the fading light, his profile sharp against the dusk. His silence carried an intensity that both drew her in and kept her on edge, a balance of allure and unease that made her question what his story was.

As Deanna stepped into the villa, the comforting aroma of sautéed onions mixed with the earthy scent of cumin filled the air, pulling her out of the heavy thoughts that had been swirling in her mind. The familiar sound of Maria and Felicity's laughter drifted from the kitchen, mingled with the sizzling from the pan on the stove. Deanna took a deep breath, savouring the warmth of the spices, feeling them ground her, even if only for a moment.

'Oh, look who *finally* decided to grace us with her presence!' Felicity teased, glancing up from the chopping board where she was dicing bright red bell peppers, their juicy sweetness adding to the rich scents of the kitchen. 'I went up to your room with a cup of tea, creeping in so as not to disturb you. Only to find your bed empty,' she added, a smirk tugging at her lips.

Deanna, caught off guard by Felicity's accusatory tone, blurted out, 'I was with Carlos,' before realising how it sounded.

Both women's eyebrows shot up in unison, but it was Felicity who spoke first, her voice dripping with mischief. 'Oh? And?'

Deanna, still reeling from her earlier conversation with Carlos, felt her cheeks flush as she fumbled for an answer that wouldn't betray his trust. 'We just... talked,' she said vaguely, praying Felicity wouldn't press her further.

Felicity narrowed her eyes, her grin widening as she pushed the diced peppers into a bowl. 'Uh-huh. Talked about what, exactly?'

Deanna waved it off, forcing a weak smile as she tried to steer the conversation away. 'Just family stuff, nothing important.' The truth was, she didn't want Maria to overhear. She wasn't sure if Carlos had told his sister everything yet, and the last thing she wanted was to risk saying too much. For now, she needed to tread carefully and keep the conversation light.

Felicity tilted her head, clearly unconvinced as she whispered out of Maria's earshot, who was leaning over the sizzling pan. 'You're hiding something. I can tell,' she teased.

Deanna managed a weak laugh, grateful for the humour but knowing she had to be cautious. 'Honestly, nothing exciting. Just boring family history.'

Felicity's eyes gleamed with mock suspicion as she leaned in. 'Sure!'

When dinner was served, Giovanni entered the room. Deanna's eyes were drawn to him immediately. She couldn't reconcile the man before her, so warm and genial, with the disturbing truth Carlos had revealed. If this man wasn't who he claimed to be, then what could she trust? His smile seemed genuine, his eyes twinkled with charm, but none of it could dispel the shadow of doubt that now coloured her every thought.

As they ate, the atmosphere around the table was light and filled with laughter. Even Giovanni seemed relaxed, occasionally nodding and laughing along with the others. Though she still caught Giovanni's gaze lingering on her longer than seemed comfortable.

As dessert was served, Felicity was mid-sentence, adding a final punchline to her latest tale, when Giovanni suddenly leaned forward, his tone cutting through the jovial chatter like a knife.

'Deanna,' he said, his voice smooth but commanding, 'I have something I want to show you. I found it earlier, although I thought I had thrown it out.'

The table fell silent, all eyes turning to Giovanni. Deanna felt the easy laughter drain from the room as her pulse quickened. She exchanged a brief, uneasy glance with Carlos, but even his reassuring smile did little to calm anxiety twisting in her gut.

With a sense of dread, Deanna watched as the older man left the room, went to his office, and returned carrying a small, timeworn box. He placed it on the table before her, saying, 'Open it.' The room seemed to fall into a hushed silence. The rhythmic crash of the waves in the distance was the only sound that broke through. She could feel the pressure of every gaze on her, expectant, as she slowly reached out and lifted the lid of the box, her breath catching in her throat.

Inside, the contents were a testament to time – old, yellowed documents with frayed edges, delicate as if they might crumble at the slightest touch. Among them lay faded photographs, and one in particular made her heart skip. It was a picture of her grandmother – eyes filled with a fierce determination that both mesmerised and unsettled her. Deanna's pulse quickened as she took in the setting – a lavish suite, her grandmother poised elegantly with a violin, surrounded by women in glamourous evening gowns and men in Nazi uniforms, including the now familiar sight of Falkenberg. The image was haunting.

Giovanni leaned in too, his voice a low whisper. 'Look carefully at the violin in this photo,' he urged. Deanna's gaze narrowed on the instrument, her eyes widening as she recognised its intricate carvings and distinctive markings. It was the very same violin she had discovered in the attic – a link that tied her grandmother directly to Falkenberg and the violin.

Carlos leaned in slightly, his voice soft but curious. 'That's... the same violin, isn't it?'

Deanna nodded, her throat tight. 'Yes, it is.'

'This is the night your grandmother played my violin for the Nazi officers. A night that would alter the course of her life forever. Because this was also the night I told you about, the night she killed Commander Falkenberg... in a fit of jealous rage.'

The room fell into an eerie stillness as the gravity of his words sank in, emotions flooding Deanna. She could feel Felicity shift beside her, her face tight with discomfort, and Carlos straightened in his chair, his brows furrowed.

Felicity's voice cut through, gentle but firm. 'This doesn't prove Antoinette was jealous of Falkenberg. She could have been helping the Allies.'

Giovanni's eyes flashed with anger, his voice biting. 'Then why didn't she return the violin to me if her motives were so noble? Why did she disappear with it without a trace?'

Deanna grasped at straws. 'Maybe you didn't know the full story. She might have been frightened, thinking the violin could be her only bargaining chip for safety.'

Giovanni's gaze hardened, his expression unyielding as he scoffed. 'Antoinette, afraid? You forget, my dear – I knew her better than anyone back then. We were together in the Resistance. She was brave, a master of deception, capable of anything. Ferociously protective. That's what made her so attractive.'

Deanna's voice was steady and sure. 'You're right. My grandmother was that way, and while I may never fully understand her choices, I know in my heart of hearts she wasn't a traitor. She loved my grandfather with a devotion that was unshakeable, and whatever she did, it wasn't out of malice or self-interest.' The room fell silent, the weight of Deanna's words hanging in the air, challenging everything that had been said.

Giovanni peered at her with a snide smile. 'You may be her granddaughter, but you can't possibly comprehend the darkness that lurked within a person during such a dark time – the secrets she harboured, the lies she spun.' His words cut through the air like a knife, each syllable laced with venom.

Carlos placed a hand on Deanna's shoulder, his voice calm but firm. 'Papa, enough. This is too much. Let's not forget we're talking about her family here.'

The old man shrugged as he reached into the box and pulled out a letter. The paper was brittle with age, the ink faded to a ghostly script. He handed it to Deanna, his expression unreadable. 'Perhaps this will convince you. I found this with her violin the night Falkenberg died.'

Deanna's hands shook as she unfolded the letter, a rush of emotions threatening to overwhelm her. The handwriting was unmistakable, a flowing script she had known since childhood. Her grandmother's.

It read in French:

My darling, I want you to know how much I truly love you and not being able to have you has consumed me. I fear that it may drive me to madness. I will do whatever it takes to ensure that we can be together, even if it means crossing lines I never thought myself capable of doing.

—*A*

Deanna read and re-read the words, each sentence a dagger twisting in her heart. Then, she handed it to the others, still reeling. The woman who had nurtured her with love and wisdom now seemed a stranger, her actions shadowed by desperation and regret.

It was like playing a game of chess. Just when she thought she knew what was going on, Giovanni pulled another rabbit out of the hat that seemed to prove what he was saying. And why did she feel he was toying with her, giving her this information like breadcrumbs?

Deanna's face reddened as she folded the letter with shaky hands. The tension in the room thickened as everyone absorbed the gravity of what had just been revealed.

For the first time since she had set out to clear her grandmother's name, Deanna felt a deep sense of uncertainty creeping in – a gnawing doubt that perhaps the truth was far more complex and painful than she could ever have imagined.

26

APRIL 1942

Antoinette

The events of the previous night weighed heavily on Antoinette's mind as she navigated the bustling morning streets, her thoughts consumed by the dangerous game she was now playing. Every glance from a passerby felt suspicious, every sound too sharp.

Why hadn't Falkenberg had her arrested? He knew her real name, her connection to René, and even hinted at Benjamin. What was he waiting for?

The question gnawed at her. She knew it wasn't mercy – Falkenberg didn't strike her as a man who dealt in mercy. If anything, the absence of immediate action was more unsettling. She couldn't shake the feeling that this delay was deliberate, a cruel game meant to unnerve her or test her limits. Was he savouring his control over her, using her as a pawn in a larger scheme she couldn't yet see?

When she arrived at Emile's house, she found Serge preparing for a mission. She pulled him aside and shared the tense conversation she'd had with Falkenberg the night before.

Serge listened intently, his brow furrowed with concern as he processed the seriousness of the situation.

'Do you think he knows about your involvement with the Resistance?' he asked.

Antoinette shook her head, taking a deep breath to steady herself. 'No, I don't think so. If he did, he would have had me arrested by now. He only seems to know about me through René. I think he sees a way to manipulate me, that's all.'

Serge let out a deep sigh of relief, though his expression remained troubled. 'At least we can be glad of that. Obviously, having you in there is a great asset, but we can get you away to the coast, keep you safe. But I have a feeling that's not what you want, is it?'

She shook her head firmly. 'No, my family is here and I want to try to save René. And the key to that lies in helping his escape. And in the meantime, I think there may be a way to use this to our advantage while the Nazi is consumed by his own desires,' she said, her voice laced with disgust.

Serge's jaw tightened. 'Be careful,' he cautioned. 'If he's as fixated on you as you suspect, what Falkenberg wants may be something you're not willing to give. And when you no longer serve his needs, he will think nothing of getting rid of you.'

Antoinette was fully aware of the risks, but she also knew she had to stay one step ahead of Falkenberg. 'I can take care of myself, and if I can continue to get access to his private rooms, I'm sure I will eventually be able to go through his files and get the vital information we need.'

Serge's eyes met hers, reflecting a mix of concern and admiration for her courage. 'I trust your instincts. I'm working on getting another agent in there to help you.'

Antoinette was grateful for the gesture, but she understood that this was a battle she would have to fight on her own, at least for the time being. Antoinette thanked Serge for his unwavering support, and as she made her way back to her apartment, her mind swirled with thoughts of Falkenberg that loomed before her.

The stakes were high, and with Falkenberg watching her every move, one wrong step could jeopardise not only her own life but also her family's. But this was her fight, and she would not back down.

In August, as they had arranged, she prepared again to go into the lion's den. The red dress she chose was bold, meant to exude confidence, but beneath it, her heart raced with the relentless rhythm of fear.

At eight, Antoinette arrived at Falkenberg's suite, her breath hitching with nerves as he greeted her with a charming smile that didn't reach his eyes. His gaze as always lingered on her body in a way that made her repulsed, his presence oppressive even before he spoke. He had shed his uniform jacket, holding a glass of whisky in one hand as he gestured for her to enter.

'Antoinette,' he drawled, his eyes roaming over her with predatory approval. 'Please, come in. I hope you have been well since I have been gone?'

She shuddered as he now used her real name. It made her feel exposed, vulnerable. He knew so much about her – too much – and yet, she wasn't in a cell. That truth gnawed at her. If her cover was blown, why was she still here?

The answer had come to her late at night in the dark silence of her apartment: Falkenberg *wanted* her. He wasn't keeping her around because of the Resistance or René. No, his reasons were far more insidious. She wasn't a prisoner in the traditional sense, but she was ensnared nonetheless – trapped in a game of power and control where he held all the cards.

Stepping inside, the scent of cigars and alcohol lingered in the air, creating an uncomfortable atmosphere. Antoinette forced herself to maintain her composure, masking her anger behind a façade of polite indifference. With a strained smile, she followed him into the lavish dining room, where a gramophone was playing, and a table was set for two. The intimacy of the setting only heightened her unease.

'Isn't this better?' Falkenberg's voice was smooth, almost coaxing, as he poured them each a glass of wine. 'Meeting earlier before the concert allows us to really get to know each other in a more... *private* way.'

Antoinette's hand tightened around her glass, her mind racing as she calculated her next move. She needed to gain his trust, to find a way into his confidences, all while suppressing the bile rising in her throat at the thought.

They began their meal with polite small talk, discussing music and art, but Antoinette's true focus was elsewhere. She subtly steered the conversation towards Falkenberg's work, probing for any information she could gather; his arrogance was his weakness and she searched for cracks in his armour, any vulnerability she could exploit.

Falkenberg's lips curled into a predatory smile, his eyes blazing with dark, possessive determination as he sliced into his chicken. 'You may be here tonight, Antoinette, but I can feel your resistance. Make no mistake.' He leaned in slightly, his voice a low, dangerous murmur. 'But I always get what I want. And I will make you *beg* for it.'

Antoinette's blood boiled at the sheer arrogance lacing his words, but she refused to flinch, meeting his intense gaze with her own unwavering defiance.

'Beg?' she responded, her voice icy, her tone dripping with contempt. 'Let's not waste time with fantasies, Commander. We both know why I'm here.' She set her glass down with calculated grace, her sharp words slicing through the thick tension between them. 'No more games.'

For a brief moment, Falkenberg's smile faltered, a flicker of surprise crossing his features before he composed himself. 'I assure you, Antoinette, this is no game,' he said, his voice laced with dangerous sincerity. 'I am very serious about this endeavour. I would hope you are too, for the sake of your... family.'

The mention of her family made her heart clench – he knew. She now knew for sure that he was aware of René being her husband, and by saying 'family', he implied he knew about Benjamin as well.

A tightness formed in her throat, but she forced herself to speak evenly, her voice barely above a whisper. 'How did you find out about me?' she demanded, though the answer terrified her.

Falkenberg's smile twisted into a cruel smirk, his eyes gleaming with malicious satisfaction. 'My aide remembered you from a concert at the Conservatoire; I spoke to the director there – a very accommodating man – who told me all about a young couple. A brilliant blonde violinist and a Jewish pianist who married against all the odds and had a child. Though your name was different I recognised you straight away. So, here's a question in return: why are *you* here at the Majestic and under a different name? Are you keeping secrets from us?'

Antoinette's thoughts raced as she came up with a plausible excuse; she managed to keep her voice steady as she answered.

'I needed the money, and I wasn't sure if you knew the truth that I would get a job,' she replied, her voice barely audible, 'because of my circumstances. I had no choice but to take work wherever I could find it to support my son.'

Falkenberg leaned back in his chair, his eyes narrowing. 'It doesn't have to be that way,' he said, his voice smooth, but the threat was unmistakable. 'I can offer you so much more than a broken-down Jewish piano player. Power, protection, and a life of luxury.'

Antoinette felt a fresh surge of revulsion, but she held his gaze steadily, her jaw set in defiance. 'I don't want any of that,' she responded, her tone unable to hide her disgust. 'I value something far more important – my integrity.'

Falkenberg's laughter filled the room, a chilling sound that sent a wave of fear through her body. 'You are feisty,' he remarked, swirling the blood-red wine in his glass. 'Bold words, but everyone can be bought, even *you*.' His voice dripped with a sinister intensity, wrapping around her like a vice.

He leaned in closer, his face mere inches from hers, his breath hot against her skin, the sickly-sweet scent of alcohol enveloping her. 'I feel a raw, deep connection between us, Antoinette. Something I've never felt with another woman. You must sense it too, and it could be mutually beneficial if you let it.' His eyes pierced hers, the implication unmistakable. 'All I ask is that you open yourself up to the possibility. Who knows, you might even grow to adore me. Tell me your desires, and I will fulfil them,' he slurred, his voice low and full of persuasion, pressing closer until she could feel the heat of his body against hers.

Antoinette refused to succumb to his manipulative tactics, her mind racing to find a way out of this nightmare. Her voice was cold as steel as she replied, 'My only desire is the safety of my family.'

Falkenberg leaned back in his seat, studying her with a calculating gaze. 'Is that so? If I were to honour such a request, I would need something in return.'

'What do you want from me?' she asked quietly, trying to maintain a façade of strength even as fear clawed at her insides.

Leaning in closer, Falkenberg whispered his terms like a sinister promise. 'I will ensure the Jew and his son's safety,' he murmured, his voice oozing with malice, 'but only if you agree to be my mistress, when I'm here in Paris.'

Antoinette snapped her head away, the gravity of his proposition sinking in. To betray her husband, to tether herself to this man who represented everything she despised – it was a fate she could hardly bear to contemplate.

She forced herself to meet his gaze, her mind a whirlwind of fear, anger, and desperation. Falkenberg's eyes gleamed with sinister satisfaction as he watched her struggle. He knew he had cornered her, trapped her in his web.

Antoinette's voice trembled as she spoke, her words heavy with the burden of what he was asking. 'And if I agree, you swear they will be safe? That you will never harm them?'

Falkenberg's smile widened, a predator sensing his prey's surrender. 'You have my word, Antoinette. As long as you fulfil your role.'

The room seemed to close in around her, the air thick with tension. Antoinette felt as if she were standing on the edge of a precipice, about to plunge into an abyss from which there would be no return. She clenched her fists, nails digging into her palms as she summoned the strength to do what he asked.

Her voice quivered as she tried to find the right words. 'I'll need some time to consider it,' she finally said.

Falkenberg took a sip of his wine, his next words a growl. 'Just don't take too long. I am not a patient man, and those trains leave daily for the camps to Germany.'

Their eyes hardened in a silent battle of wills when a knock at the door interrupted them. Falkenberg's expression showed frustration at the disturbance as he called out for the person to enter.

'Apologies for the interruption, Commander von Falkenberg,' Vogelmann began, his gaze flickering briefly to Antoinette before focusing back on his superior. 'We've received word about the Resistance cell you were interested in.'

Antoinette's heart slammed against her ribcage as she fought to keep her expression neutral, forcing her hands to remain still on her lap despite the instinct to clench them into fists. The mention of the Resistance sent a cold ripple of fear through her body, and she had to stop herself from darting a glance at Falkenberg for any hint of what he knew.

Falkenberg nodded before turning his gaze back to Antoinette. 'Our discussion will have to be put on hold until I am back here from my next assignment,' he stated firmly, as he bade her goodnight.

Later, as the car raced through the streets of Paris, the city lights a blur, Antoinette sat in silence, her mind reeling from the evening's events. A cold dread seeped into her core as she considered the sacrifices that might be demanded to protect her family. She felt trapped, with no choice but to comply. The weight on her chest grew heavier with each passing moment, suffocating her with fear and uncertainty.

Her thoughts churned relentlessly. What leverage did the commander truly have? What secrets about the Resistance had he uncovered? The possibility that Falkenberg held knowledge of who she was put everyone in danger. Every word he had spoken seemed laced with hidden meanings, calculated to unsettle her.

Antoinette clenched her hands in her lap, her nails biting into her palms as a chilling thought took hold. Was she already compromised, or was Falkenberg testing her loyalty? The idea that she could unwittingly betray the people she cared about most gnawed at her insides.

She stared out of the window, the glimmering lights shimmering on the Seine distorted through unshed tears. Her thoughts turned to René and Benjamin, her family's faces anchoring her resolve. No matter how deep the commander's knowledge ran, she would protect them – at any cost.

And as the car turned down the quiet, dimly lit street where she would be dropped off, a flicker of purpose sparked within her. She couldn't allow herself to be consumed by fear or guilt. Falkenberg had made his move, but this game was far from over.

She would bide her time, gather her strength, and when the moment was right, she would strike.

27

BRAZIL, 2012

Deanna

Deanna tried to sleep that night, but the Brazilian heat was oppressive, the stifling warmth before a storm.

She lay on her bed, tossing and turning, the thin sheet clinging to her skin as the ceiling fan lazily churned the heavy air. She glanced at the clock; it was 3 a.m. Her mind kept returning to the violin, to Giovanni, and to the puzzle pieces that just didn't seem to fit.

Frustrated, she slipped out of bed and tiptoed across the cool tile floor to the chair where she had thrown her dressing gown. She slipped out the door and down the stairs. Maybe she could find something out on her own? The villa was silent, the only sounds the distant hum of the sea rolling over the sand and the occasional croak of a frog.

The hallway outside was dimly lit, the ornate sconces casting long shadows on the walls. She hesitated for a moment at the top of the stairs, wondering if it was foolish to snoop around Giovanni's office in the middle of the night. But before she handed over a priceless violin, she needed answers. Answers he seemed reluctant to share...

The grand staircase creaked as she descended, but no one stirred. The villa's spacious living areas were bathed in the soft glow of moonlight filtering through the large windows. Deanna tiptoed to the office on the ground floor – the official office Giovanni used for receiving guests and handling family business. It was stately, with bookshelves that lined the walls and a heavy, dark wood desk in the centre of the room.

She pushed the door open, the old hinges protesting softly, and slipped inside. The room smelled faintly of leather and old paper, the kind of scent that felt like history was embedded in the very walls. Deanna stood for a moment, letting her eyes adjust to the low light before moving towards the desk.

A quick glance revealed little – just the usual papers and books stacked neatly on top. She rifled through the drawers, finding nothing of note: ledgers, family documents, mundane letters. But then, tucked between two books at the back of the drawer, her fingers brushed against a piece of paper. At first, it seemed unimportant – a crumpled newspaper cutting, old and well thumbed. She paused, hesitating before pulling it out.

As she unfolded the fragile paper, the headline caught her eye. It was an English newspaper: *Hunt for Nazis in South America Continues: Another War Criminal Captured.* Her breath caught in her throat as she scanned the article. It was dated from the late 1990s and detailed the capture of a notorious Nazi officer who had been hiding in Brazil for decades.

Deanna's eyes darted over the text, her mind racing. Could Giovanni have known this man from the war? Or worse still, was this something to do with the secret he was hiding? She skimmed the paragraphs quickly, looking for any familiar names or details that might connect to the violin, or to Giovanni himself.

The article described how the man had received plastic

surgery, lived under a false identity, his past hidden even from those closest to him. The authorities had been tipped off by a relative, and the discovery had shocked the local community.

As she read, Deanna noticed something odd – the article was torn. The bottom third of the page had been ripped away, as if someone had purposefully removed a section.

She turned the page over, hoping for more information, but there was nothing else. Just a jagged edge where part of the story had been lost.

Deanna's breath caught as she stared at the missing piece. Why would someone rip this out? What had been so important that it needed to be removed? The sensation of something being hidden crept over her again, stronger now.

Her fingers hovered over the torn edge. The ripped article had a title and she could just make out several Nazis by name at the top. One stood out to her – Johann Vogelmann.

Vogelmann? Where had she heard that name before? Then it came back to her: he had been the officer who was searching for the violin after Falkenberg's death. The one who had mentioned her grandmother in the letter Felicity had shown her in London. She could almost feel the pieces coming together, but there was no conclusion. The torn section was crucial.

Without hesitation, Deanna pulled out her phone, tension mounting as she typed 'Vogelmann Nazi South America' into the search bar. The results appeared almost instantly, and a wave of dread mingled with anticipation coursed through her as she scanned the screen.

Her eyes scanned the first few links, then stopped cold when she read *Johann Vogelmann, Missing Nazi Official Believed to Be Hiding in South America.*

Deanna's heart thudded in her chest as she clicked on the link and began reading. Vogelmann had been a high-ranking Nazi officer, serving directly under von Falkenberg. He had disappeared at the end of the war, like many others, and rumours had placed him in various countries in South America over the decades. But no one had ever definitively found him.

Until now, she thought grimly. *Could Giovanni be Vogelmann?*

Her mind raced. The implications were staggering. She had come here believing Giovanni to be an ally, a freedom fighter whose family had been victimised by the Nazis. But now, with the torn newspaper and his vague recollections of Italy, it seemed there was more to his story.

The final piece was missing. The ripped section of the article had most likely revealed that Vogelmann was still at large – still alive.

Deanna stared at her phone screen in horror, her breath shallow.

Suddenly, a creak echoed on the stairs. She quickly folded the newspaper clipping and slipped it back between the books.

She moved towards the door, careful to tread lightly as she glanced back at the desk one last time. Her suspicions had grown stronger now, but she needed more proof.

And one thing was certain – more and more she believed that Giovanni wasn't the man he claimed to be.

Just as Deanna turned to leave, the floorboards creaked again, louder this time. Her heart jumped into her throat. She held her breath, frozen for a moment, her mind racing with possible explanations. Was it Giovanni? Had he heard her snooping around?

The door creaked open just a crack, and then a familiar voice hissed in the darkness.

'Deanna, is that you?'

Deanna's heart sank with both relief and frustration. She knew that voice too well.

'Felicity!' Deanna whispered back, incredulous. 'What are you doing in here?'

Felicity pushed the door open a little more and slipped

inside, her eyes wide. 'I could ask *you* the same question! I thought I was the only one sneaky enough to come snooping around in the middle of the night.'

Deanna blinked at her, unable to stop the small laugh that bubbled up. 'Of course you'd be here too. I should have known.'

Felicity grinned, though there was a flicker of concern behind her eyes. 'What did you find?'

Deanna shook her head, the gravity of what she'd uncovered pulling her back into focus. She gestured toward the desk, lowering her voice. 'Felicity, I think Giovanni's hiding something... something *huge*.'

Felicity's playful expression shifted instantly to one of seriousness. 'What?'

Deanna reached into the drawer and pulled out the crumpled newspaper clipping again, showing it to Felicity. 'I found this. And it also mentioned a Nazi war criminal named Johann Vogelmann, who's been hiding in South America. And I think... I think Giovanni might be Vogelmann. It would certainly explain how he knew so much about my grandmother and Falkenberg.'

Felicity's eyes widened, as she grabbed the paper from Deanna's hands, scanning it quickly. 'Vogelmann? As in... the Nazi officer mentioned in that letter I showed you in London? The one connected to your grandmother?'

Deanna nodded, her pulse quickening. 'Exactly. It's all starting to make sense, but the article's torn. Whoever tore it out didn't want anyone to see something important.'

Felicity shook her head in disbelief, her brow furrowing. 'So, you think Giovanni – who's been playing the charming host this whole time – is actually this Nazi war criminal who's been on the run for decades?'

Deanna sighed, her voice tense. 'I don't know for sure, but it's starting to add up. And if it's true, then everything he's told us, everything about his past, could be a lie. He could have been after the violin all along – just like Falkenberg. Remember how concerned he was in the letter?'

Felicity stared at the torn newspaper, then back at Deanna, her voice low and sharp. 'We need to find out what was in that missing section. It could be the key to figuring out who Giovanni really is.'

Deanna nodded, a sense of urgency settling over her. 'But how? I've already searched online, but I couldn't find anything definitive. And if Giovanni is who I think he is... we can't exactly *ask* him.'

Felicity bit her lip, pacing the small office. 'Maybe we can find a copy of the full article somewhere – archives, old newspapers. I'm sure there's a way. But we can't let him know we're onto him.'

Deanna's mind raced. 'You're right. But we have to be careful. If he finds out we're suspicious, who knows what he'll do.'

Felicity nodded, her playful demeanour completely gone. 'Okay. I have contacts. Tomorrow, I'll look into it – discreetly. We can't make any moves until we're sure.'

Deanna took a deep breath, feeling a small sense of relief that Felicity was in this with her. 'Thank you, Felicity. I don't know what I'd do without you.'

Felicity smiled, the teasing glint returning to her eyes for just a moment. 'Well, for starters, you'd be snooping around in the middle of the night all by yourself. And let's be honest, you need me to make this whole espionage thing a little more fun.'

Deanna chuckled, despite the tension. 'I guess I do.'

They shared a brief, understanding look before Felicity gestured toward the door. 'Come on, let's get out of here before someone else decides to join us. And Deanna... don't worry. We'll figure this out.'

But as they crept back upstairs, once again she questioned

why she had really been brought here. Two thoughts echoed in her mind: did Carlos and Maria know? And how far deep did all these family secrets run?

28

AUGUST 1942

Antoinette

It was the summer when Falkenberg returned again. Antoinette arrived at the Majestic, as had been arranged, to play at his dinner party.

Entering his suite, Falkenberg stood at the far end, surrounded by a throng. A wave of tension rippled through her, but she refused to let his gaze unnerve her.

Hurrying to the spot where she had performed before, she stopped short and had to catch her breath; instead of the regular Majestic piano player, René was there once again.

Antoinette could barely breathe.

His once-vibrant appearance was gone – he was gaunt and pale in an ill-fitting suit and Antoinette's heart ached at the sight of him.

But as their gazes met, his face lit up, and all thoughts fell away, and time seemed to stand still for a moment. Despite the circumstances, the love between them shone through with an intensity that left Antoinette breathless. In that moment, they were no longer caught in the midst of a cold and cruel war – she was back on the rooftop of their apartment under a sky full of stars. Antoinette could almost feel the coolness of the rooftop under her bare feet, the warmth of his hand in hers. She could feel the familiar sensation of their bodies entwined, the heat of his lips pressing against hers.

She pulled her gaze away and quickly looked towards Falkenberg. His eyes were fixed on her with a palpable undercurrent of manipulation. She knew this reunion was orchestrated by him, using her own emotions as a tool to tighten his grasp on her.

With trembling hands, she quickly set up her music stand, her fingers betraying the conflicting emotions coursing through her body. As they began to play, it was a bittersweet experience that almost pained her with its exquisite beauty. The harmonies blended perfectly, creating an intoxicating melody that seemed to fill every corner of the room, revealing that this was a couple who had often made music together. Each note was played with such precision and emotion, it was as if the instruments themselves were alive and speaking directly to her heart. As hard as her life was now, this was a moment she would never forget, grooved into her memory with every stroke of the strings and sensitive movement of his hands on the piano.

In a breathtaking and unexpected moment, his fingers delicately danced over the keys in an impromptu performance of the enchanting melody of *Liebestraum No. 3* – a piece that held a special place in Antoinette's heart. It was the same song he had played on the day he proposed, which filled her soul with bittersweet memories. He was sending her a message of love. As she matched his impassioned performance, tears welled up in her throat.

And when she looked at him, she saw a single tear trailing down his cheek, mirroring the emotions that poured out through each note. As the last notes faded into the air, a heavy silence enveloped the room. The people in the room politely clapped, unaware of the depth of emotion that had just coursed through the music. Antoinette and René exchanged a wordless glance, a silent conversation passing between them, one that only they could understand. The weight of their shared history, the love and loss they had endured, was evident in their eyes.

But before they could say anything to each other, Falkenberg approached with a sinister smile playing on his lips. 'A mesmerising performance, my dear,' he remarked, his voice dripping with false charm, ignoring René completely.

'You must meet my new acquaintance,' Falkenberg exclaimed, his tone bordering on manic. He forcefully grabbed her by the elbow, hardly giving her time to place down her violin, pulling her away from René and causing her to stumble. With a look of disdain, Falkenberg turned to René and scanned him up and down, as if judging his worth. 'My cook has some scraps in the kitchen for you; I'm sure you would be most grateful,' he continued with a devious grin. 'We can't have you collapsing in front of our guests now, can we?'

Antoinette's heart tightened with a mixture of anger and fear, the sense of helplessness washing over her once again. She wanted to lash out, to defend René from Falkenberg's cruelty, but she knew that it would only make things worse for both of them.

As Falkenberg led her away, his grip tight on her elbow, she shot one last look over her shoulder at René, silently conveying her love and apology. The pain in his eyes mirrored her own, a silent connection passing between them.

Once they were out of earshot, Falkenberg turned to Antoinette with a smug smile. 'You see, my dear, I can be quite *generous* when it suits me,' he said as he guided her towards a group of his associates. 'Now I have something exciting for you; I have secured an invitation for you to perform at a gala next month. It will be a grand affair, and your presence will surely elevate the event to new heights of sophistication. The woman who is organising it wants to meet you.'

Falkenberg's words barely registered over the thundering of her pulse in her ears. The sight of René, so frail and diminished, still haunted her.

As they approached the group of Falkenberg's friends, Antoinette took a deep breath, forcing herself to regain her composure. With a practised smile, she greeted the men and women gathered there, her voice steady despite the turmoil within. But beneath her calm exterior, Antoinette's mind was racing. Why was René really here? Falkenberg was up to something – he always was; she had to be ready for whatever game he was playing, now.

'Thank you for the invitation,' she replied, her tone polite but distant, after the woman had given her all the details, 'I'm honoured to be considered for such an event.'

Falkenberg's smile widened at her words, clearly pleased by her apparent compliance. 'Excellent. I knew you would see the value in this opportunity.'

Antoinette swallowed her revulsion, nodding slightly in acknowledgment. 'Of course,' she said, keeping her tone light. Inside, however, she was seething. She knew she was walking a fine line, but she also knew she had no other choice. She needed to play along, if only to find a way out of this nightmare for her and René.

Falkenberg eventually turned to engage with another guest, and Antoinette saw her chance. 'Excuse me,' she murmured, her voice filled with feigned modesty. 'I need a moment.'

Falkenberg waved her off with a dismissive gesture, clearly confident in his control over her.

Antoinette rushed quickly down the hall and into the kitchen, desperate to speak to René.

But the room was empty. She moved with panic through the hallway, hissing his name.

All at once a door opened and a familiar arm pulled her inside.

It was René, his eyes wild with urgency as he closed the door behind them, cutting off any prying eyes or ears that might be nearby. Antoinette's heart leapt at the sight of him, relief flooding through her. Without a word, he pulled her into his arms, his lips meeting hers.

She melted into him, the fear and tension of the evening washing away in the heat of their embrace. René's kiss was desperate, filled with longing and unspoken words that hung heavy in the air between them. Antoinette clung to him, trying to anchor herself to this moment of stolen solace.

Antoinette could hardly believe she was in her husband's arms again. She felt such a sense of relief as she gazed into his eyes, seeing the love that had been absent for so long. 'Oh my darling,' he whispered, his voice thick with emotion. 'I can't believe you're really here. Why are you here? Did the director of the Conservatoire force you?'

Tears stung Antoinette's eyes as she struggled to find the right words. How could she explain everything that had happened without breaking her husband's heart? She took a deep breath and forced out a half-truth. 'No, nothing like that, I am here with the Resistance, trying to free you from this madness.'

René's expression shifted from surprise to concern in an instant. 'No, Antoinette,' he protested, his dark eyes filled with concern. 'I cannot let you risk your life for me.'

But Antoinette wouldn't let him continue. Placing a gentle finger on René's lips, she silenced his protests. 'We don't have much time,' she urgently whispered. 'Please, let's not argue. You know I was never going to lose you without a fight.'

With determination in her eyes, Antoinette hugged her husband tightly and felt him wince beneath her arms.

'What is it?' she demanded. 'Are you hurt?'

'It's nothing,' he grunted. 'I was just punished for something I did wrong. It is much better now.'

Antoinette's heart ached with his words. And all at once, the reality of his life under Nazi control crushed her. She felt a surge of anger toward these despicable people who had dared to lay a hand on her husband and a renewed determination to free him from this tyranny.

With a loud creak, the door swung open, light from the hall flooded in and a looming shadow filled the doorway. Antoinette and René immediately sprang apart, as Falkenberg flicked on a blinding light. He sneered at them with contempt, his gaze filled with malice.

'As much as I hate to interrupt what is most certainly a *heartfelt* family reunion,' he growled, 'my guests are getting impatient for more entertainment.'

Antoinette and René exchanged a quick glance, their expressions mirroring their defiance as they began to make their way towards the door.

'Interesting that you should choose my bedroom to bring your Jew to, Antoinette, especially when it has such special memories for *us*.'

Antoinette's blood boiled at his words, and she felt an overwhelming surge of anger and disgust towards the man standing before them. She glanced around, not realising where she had been in her desperation to find René. She remembered Falkenberg's forced kiss and shuddered, a cold fury rising within her.

She caught sight of René, and he looked crushed as he tried to make sense of what the Nazi was saying. Antoinette could see the turmoil churning within him and desperately wanted to explain herself. But she knew that this was what Falkenberg wanted – to see her husband's pain and her need to justify herself. Instead, she fixed Falkenberg with a hard-edged stare. 'You are mistaken, Commander von Falkenberg; this room has no special significance to me.'

She breezed past the commander into the corridor, as he chuckled in a low rumble.

They continued their performance, her heart heavy with the weight of their situation, and she could feel her husband's heart breaking as he played.

His fingers moved mechanically over the keys of the grand piano, producing a melody that should have been beautiful but instead sounded hollow and empty. Antoinette stood by his side, her eyes fixed on Falkenberg, her mind racing with plans to outmanoeuvre him.

As the final note of their music faded into silence, the people at the party erupted into thunderous applause. In that moment, she turned to her husband with a sense of urgency and whispered, 'Don't believe it, don't believe any of it.' Her words were muffled by the sound of the cheering crowd, but he appeared to feel the weight of their meaning. But she also saw his doubt, not in her love for him, but in her assurance. René knew her like nobody else, knew she would stop at nothing to get what she wanted, and his eyes showed the fear of where that might lead.

Before she had time to talk to him again, two guards at Falkenberg's request approached René and escorted him away. She watched him being taken from her again, her heart breaking once more.

On the way home in the car, she let the tears flow freely. Most days, it all made sense – what she was doing and why – but today it felt as if everything was falling apart. The burden of her decisions bore down on her, suffocating her with guilt and fear. Antoinette wiped at her damp cheeks and noticed the driver watching her in the mirror. He was new; she had not met him before and she attempted to hide her pain.

He spoke. 'Melodie?'

She looked up and nodded at him through tear-stained eyes.

He gave her his codename, saying, 'Serge sent me to help you.'

Antoinette stared at the man driving Falkenberg's car in the rearview mirror, her body still a tightly coiled spring, as the car sped through the city. She was so distracted by her thoughts it took her a moment to comprehend what he was saying.

'So, you are an *agent*?' Antoinette finally managed to stammer out, remembering Serge's promise of someone to help her, though it felt like a lifetime ago.

The man nodded, confirming her suspicions. He was in his late twenties, with a lean frame and sharp, angular features. His fair hair was neatly combed back, but a faint shadow of stubble softened his otherwise stern appearance. Though he spoke fluent French, his accent hinted at Italian origins. There was an alertness in his piercing brown eyes that revealed a man who had seen too much yet remained fiercely determined.

'I've taken a job working for Falkenberg. I'll mainly be his chauffeur, but I'm hoping to get more work inside the Majestic as well.'

Antoinette released a breath she hadn't realised she had been holding, studying the man in the mirror. Despite his intensity, there was a sense of friendliness about him.

'My family owned a valuable violin that I believe from my sources is earmarked for Falkenberg's possession,' he continued. 'I want to find it and steal it back.'

Antoinette was confused; as far as she knew Falkenberg had no interest in playing the violin. But then an unsettling thought dawned on her – had he procured it for her to play?

The memory of Falkenberg's presence consumed her – his piercing gaze, the sinister undertone of every word he spoke, and the lingering touch that made her skin crawl with disgust tormented her.

From the driver's seat, the agent's blue eyes flicked up to the rearview mirror again, concern furrowing his brow. 'Serge has come up with a plan,' he said, handing her a microfilm camera, his voice steady but laced with an urgency that belied his calm demeanour.

'A plan?' she repeated absently looking at the camera, remembering learning about using them during her training.

The agent gave a terse nod, his eyes locking onto hers in the mirror, dark and unyielding. 'Yes. He thinks we can use Falkenberg's... *interest* in you to our advantage.'

Antoinette felt her stomach cramp as the stranger's knowing gaze settled on her, leaving her feeling exposed and soiled somehow. She also felt disappointment; for a fleeting moment, she had dared to hope that the 'plan' would be an escape from the unbearable sacrifice she had to make month after month.

'But first, we'll need a copy of Falkenberg's office key, so we can get back in safely once you have left,' he continued.

Antoinette gasped. 'How will I get that? He keeps it in his trouser pocket,' she choked out, already knowing the answer deep down. The agent's gaze flickered away for a brief moment before locking onto hers again. His expression held an emotion that looked disturbingly like guilt.

'Serge said you'll have to get close to him,' he finally answered softly. 'Close enough to take the key from him.' Antoinette felt a wave of revulsion wash over her as the full implications of their plan sank in.

The words hung in the air between them, chilling her to the core. Falkenberg's leering face flashed in her mind, his hands on her body, the way his eyes lingered on her as if she were already his.

'You want me to...' She couldn't finish the sentence, the words too revolting to form, and her voice trailed off.

His face was pale, and his jaw clenched as he continued. 'Serge told me to tell you, it is your choice; he wouldn't ask you if there were another way. But this key... it could turn the tide if we had a copy. It could save countless lives.'

Antoinette's chest tightened, the moral lines blurring before her eyes. The war. The lives at stake. *René*. And her, caught in the middle of it all. The enormity of duty pressed down on her, but so did the revulsion. She pushed away the picture of her husband that hovered in her mind, his smile, the warmth of his touch, his words of love whispered in the darkness of Falkenberg's suite.

'I'm sorry,' the agent added, his voice barely audible as though he knew the toll his words were taking.

But apologies didn't make this situation any less difficult. They didn't change what she would have to do next.

'And once I have the key, how will I slip away without him waking?' Antoinette asked him, her voice barely more than a breath.

'We have something potent – it will dissolve easily in his wine. Once he falls asleep, he should remain unconscious until the morning. I'll be waiting outside in the alley behind the Majestic.'

Stepping out of the car, she hesitated, casting one last glance back. The agent's expression was unreadable, but she could see the tension in his clenched jaw.

'He is gone now for a few months and then he wants to see me again,' she informed him.

'I will be ready,' he said.

The door clicked shut behind her, and for a moment, the world seemed unnervingly still, as if everything held its breath. She stood frozen, staring into the darkness ahead, her mind spinning as the car drove away. What was being asked of her loomed like a storm gathering on the horizon – dark and inescapable.

Antoinette squared her shoulders, forcing her trembling hands into fists. The only way out was through this. That evening she wrote a note to René, which she tucked inside her violin case, hinting at what she was doing, in case she had the chance to see him again and if she got caught, at least she would know that he understood why she was doing it.

My darling, I want you to know how much I truly love you and not being able to have you has consumed me. I fear that it may drive me to madness. I will do whatever it takes to ensure that we can be together, even if it means crossing lines I never thought myself capable of doing.

—A

She reread it a couple of times, hoping her words would reassure him.

Then she prepared herself for the line she was about to cross.

29

BRAZIL, 2012

Deanna

The next day, as they sailed through the crystal-clear waters off the coast of Ponta do Arpoador, Deanna couldn't shake off her sense of unease. The ocean stretched out in a breathtaking display of vibrant blues and shimmering sunlight, but instead of feeling soothed by the beauty around her, her mind churned with half-truths and secrets she was struggling to unravel.

This trip to Ponta do Arpoador had been planned as a respite for the four of them – a chance to escape the oppressive atmosphere of the villa and the rising tension. But then Giovanni had insisted on joining them.

The night before, Deanna had overheard Carlos trying to convince his father to stay behind, to rest. But Giovanni had been unrelenting, determined to come with them.

And so, here they were, sailing toward Ponta do Arpoador with Giovanni at the helm, his sharp eyes fixed on the horizon.

The boat slid into a small, secluded cove, its motor humming softly as Giovanni guided it towards the dock. He leapt out to help them off, his movements deliberate, his frame still imposing despite his age. Even though he was in his eighties, the man was uncommonly strong, as though years of hardship had not worn him down but instead hardened him like stone.

Deanna followed the others along a winding path through thick greenery. The distant roar of the ocean was muffled by the dense foliage that surrounded them. Giovanni moved with purpose, and as they reached a wide terrace overlooking the sea, Maria made small talk with Felicity while Carlos kept a wary eye on his father.

They settled on a blanket Maria had laid out, surrounded by an array of Brazilian delicacies – *pão de queijo*, fresh fruit, and empadinhas. But as Deanna picked at the food, her appetite was nowhere to be found. The scent of salt and earth filled the air, mixing with the sound of the ocean crashing against the cliffs below.

'This is one of the most beautiful places in Brazil,' Giovanni remarked, breaking the heavy silence. 'Ponta do Arpoador,' he continued, his gaze never leaving the horizon, 'is a place where the past meets the present. A place where nothing can be hidden.'

His eyes found Deanna's, locking onto hers with an intensity that made her shift uncomfortably.

Deanna took a deep breath and decided to confront him with something that had been bothering her.

'Giovanni, there's something I've been struggling to understand,' she began carefully, meeting his gaze. 'You've told me a lot about my grandmother's time with Falkenberg, but there's one thing that still doesn't make sense. *Why* did she stab him? Why kill him at all?'

Giovanni's gaze darkened, his lips evened out into a thin line. He didn't answer for a long moment, and the weight of his silence only deepened the tension. Finally, he spoke, his voice low and gravelly.

'She had no choice,' he said, his eyes hard. 'Falkenberg lied to her, and when she found out... when she realised what he'd been doing behind her back, she snapped.'

Deanna frowned, trying to process his words. 'But... what *had* he done? What was so terrible that it drove her to murder?'

Giovanni's gaze turned icy, his voice cutting through the air like a blade. 'She was obsessed with him, and didn't want anyone else to have him.'

Deanna's breath caught at the harshness of his tone. But something in his sharp delivery made her doubt his words.

'So... she killed him out of *jealousy*?' Deanna pressed, her voice trembling slightly, unsure whether she was searching for confirmation or challenging his narrative.

'Jealousy, rage – call it what you want,' Giovanni said, his voice hardening. 'She took matters into her own hands. She stabbed him and fled, taking the violin as a twisted trophy of their love. She was drawn to power, to the promises Falkenberg had made her.'

Deanna shook her head, refusing to believe it. 'But she was part of the Resistance. Why would she care?' she whispered, her voice trembling.

Giovanni's gaze grew colder. 'She played both sides. Falkenberg offered her a way out – luxury, protection, influence. She took it, blinded by her desire for safety, for love. She betrayed the Resistance, betrayed her comrades – all for him.'

The words felt like a punch to the gut. Could it really be true? Had her grandmother been driven to murder, not out of necessity, but out of a desperate, personal rage? The more Giovanni spoke, the more her image of her grandmother seemed to crumble. She thought again of the letter he had shown her.

Almost as if sensing the shift in the conversation, the sky darkened, the sun slipping behind the clouds, casting the cliffs in shadow. Deanna stared out at the endless sea, her mind spinning, her heart breaking. Was this the truth – or lies? And what could Giovanni possibly gain from deceiving her?

As the moment stretched into a tense silence, Giovanni's voice grew softer, almost tender. 'Ask yourself, Deanna, why do you think your grandmother never shared this part of her history with you or your father? People don't hide things they're proud of. They hide their shame, and their mistakes.'

The question lingered in the air. She had never questioned why Antoinette had kept so much of her past shrouded in silence. But now, Giovanni's words unsettled her. Could Antoinette's silence have been born from guilt, not trauma? What had she truly been hiding?

Giovanni's gaze didn't waver, and his words struck her with the force of a hammer. 'She never shared this part of her life because she couldn't. She couldn't bear for you to see her for what she truly was.'

'I don't know what to believe any more,' Deanna whispered.

Giovanni's expression was grim as he replied, 'Believe the facts that can't be disputed. A man is dead, and a priceless violin was stolen. If she had been still working for the Resistance, why would she betray them like this?'

Felicity, who had been sitting quietly beside her, shifted. She glanced down at her phone, her eyes widening. As Giovanni turned to speak with Maria, Felicity tugged at Deanna's arm. 'Deanna,' she whispered urgently. 'We need to talk. Now.'

Startled, Deanna nodded, and together they excused themselves from the group, pretending to want to look at the view farther down the rocks.

They moved across the terrace, out of Giovanni's earshot, the wind whipping at their hair. 'What?' Deanna asked, confusion lacing her voice.

Felicity handed her the phone, her expression grim. 'After we found that article, I had a friend back in London dig deeper into the war archives. Information that isn't easily accessible online. He just sent me something.'

Deanna quickly scanned the message. It was a link to an old article, dated shortly after the war. Her heart sank as she read the first few lines.

Vogelmann, notorious for his role as a Nazi interrogator who tortured members of the Resistance, disappeared without a trace. It is believed that he fled to South America after the war.

Felicity leaned in closer, her voice urgent but hushed. 'It says Vogelmann was known for using personal details from his victims' lives to manipulate them. He knew their stories, their weaknesses. That's how he got people to break.'

Deanna's mind raced. 'So is this man Vogelmann? Is that how he knows so much about Giovanni's story?' she whispered. 'If he interrogated Resistance fighters during the war, he could've learned everything about Giovanni and Antoinette.'

Deanna swiped to an image from the article. The photograph was grainy, but it showed a group of Nazi officers. Behind them, hanging ominously, was a large banner.

A chill ran through Deanna as her eyes landed on the words printed on the banner: *Blut und Ehre.*

'What do those words mean, Felicity?'

Felicity translated softly. 'Blood and Honour. It was a Nazi slogan.'

Deanna's heart skipped a beat. '*Blut und Ehre...*' she whispered, the phrase triggering a memory.

'What?' Felicity asked, her eyes narrowing in confusion.

'I overheard Giovanni and his German friends. I thought they said "*Blumen und Erde*" – blooms and earth,' Deanna whispered. 'I thought they were talking about gardening. But they weren't. I think they were saying "*Blut und Ehre*"... Blood and Honour.'

Felicity's eyes widened in realisation. 'Oh my God...'

Before either of them could say another word, footsteps sounded behind them, making them freeze.

Giovanni appeared, his face calm but his eyes dark. His voice cut through the tension like a knife. 'Ladies,' he said smoothly, 'Maria wanted me to remind you that she brought dessert.'

Deanna forced a tight smile as Felicity slipped her phone into her pocket. 'We'll be right there,' Deanna said, her voice shaky.

Giovanni turned and strode back toward the blanket, his steps deliberate, each one echoing like a countdown in her mind.

'I'm sure he heard us,' Felicity whispered urgently, her voice trembling as she gripped Deanna's arm.

Deanna nodded slowly, her pulse pounding in her ears. The weight of everything – the lies, the fragmented truths, the shadowy past – pressed heavily on her chest. The lush beauty of the cove, once so picturesque, now felt like a trap, its isolation suffocating.

She glanced back at Giovanni, who had rejoined Maria and Carlos, his expression calm but unreadable. Why hadn't he confronted them directly? Why hadn't he acted on what he might have overheard? The question lingered, gnawing at her as she realised the answer might be even more chilling: because he didn't need to. He already had them exactly where he wanted them.

Deanna turned her gaze toward the sea, its vastness now a cruel reminder of how far they were from safety. Her voice was barely above a whisper as she said to Felicity, 'Whatever we do next, we can't let him know how much we've figured out.'

Felicity nodded, her lips pressed into a thin line. 'Agreed. But, Deanna...' She hesitated, lowering her voice even further.

'What if this isn't just about your grandmother or the violin? What if it's about something much bigger?'

Deanna didn't respond, but the cold realisation snaked through her, chilling her to the bone. She couldn't shake the feeling that they were walking deeper into a web they didn't fully understand – and Giovanni was the spider waiting in the centre.

The wind picked up, carrying the sharp tang of salt and something else – something metallic, faint but undeniable. She shivered as the sky darkened further, casting shadows that stretched like grasping fingers over the cliffs.

As she and Felicity began walking back toward the group, every step felt heavier, every sound amplified in the silence. And in the back of her mind, one relentless thought echoed, louder than the crash of the waves below.

How much longer could they play this game before someone got hurt?

30

JANUARY 1943

Antoinette

A few months later, Antoinette stood outside Falkenberg's suite, her nerves taut with anticipation. Dressed meticulously in a gown designed to allure, she felt it cling like armour rather than silk. She knocked, the sound tolling ominously down the hallway.

The door swung open to reveal Falkenberg, his presence as oppressive as his gaze, which roved over her with satisfaction.

'Antoinette,' he purred, his voice laced with sinister charm. 'You look exquisite tonight.' His words slithered over her, and her skin crawled. Despite the revulsion, she managed a brittle smile.

'Thank you, Commander,' she said, her tone steady despite the turmoil raging within.

He gestured for her to enter, and as she crossed the threshold, the scent of cigars and alcohol overwhelmed her. The room, thick with tension, felt like a cage, and with every step, the walls seemed to close in.

The evening unfolded in a haze of forced smiles and false

laughter, each moment stretching out like an eternity. Falkenberg was relentless, his advances growing bolder with each glass of wine.

At one moment he raised his glass. 'I have some good news for you; after this next assignment, my superiors have decided I will be assigned to Paris indefinitely. So we will be able to be together every day!'

Antoinette managed to hold back a gasp. His revelation made her feel sick. She pulled her focus back to the job at hand. The sooner she was away from this despicable man the better.

While he was distracted by a phone call at one point, Antoinette played her part, slipping the draught Serge had given her into his drink, and leaning in just enough to keep him interested, her mind always on the key in his pocket, the prize she had to secure.

As the evening continued, Falkenberg's movements grew sluggish, his words slurred as the drug took hold. Antoinette noticed it was already after eleven and the other agent would be waiting. When Falkenberg started to kiss her and suggested they move to the bedroom, she didn't fight him.

Falkenberg was elated. 'I take it you have made up your mind. I knew you would agree to our arrangement and wouldn't be able to keep your hands off me once you gave in to your true desires,' he slurred.

They stumbled into the room, Falkenberg's hands wandering over her body in a way that made her skin crawl. She guided him to the bed, her breath catching as she saw him begin to lose coherence, his eyes drooping as he struggled to stay awake.

He collapsed onto the pillows, reaching for her with a drunken grin. Antoinette steeled herself, playing along just long enough to keep him placated.

He pulled her down and began to kiss her greedily, but before he could proceed further he passed out on top of her.

She breathed a sigh of relief. Her virtue was at least intact for one more night. She carefully manoeuvred him off her. What she wanted was in his pocket – she reached inside, the cool metal of the key brushing against her fingers.

Just as Antoinette began to pull the key free, a sharp knock at the suite door shattered the silence, sending a shockwave of panic through her. Her heart lurched violently, and her fingers dropped the key. In a frantic motion, she threw the blanket over his unconscious form, her hands trembling as she pulled her clothes on and hurried to the door, every step feeling like a race against disaster. Her pulse hammered in her ears, drowning out all reason.

Vogelmann stood in the doorway, his presence charged with an unsettling intensity. His expression was polite, but his gaze held something darker, lingering on her dishevelled clothing with a mix of disgust and barely concealed jealousy. Beneath his formality, there was a glint of disappointment – a suggestion of thwarted desire that made the hair on the back of her neck stand on end. For a fleeting moment, she knew without a shadow of a doubt, he was disappointed because he'd wanted her himself, and the realisation sent a chill through her.

'Madame,' he greeted her, his voice smooth as he tried to control his emotions. 'I've come to discuss some final matters with the commander.'

Antoinette's blood ran cold; she forced a serene smile, masking the turmoil roiling inside her. 'He's already asleep,' she replied calmly, praying her voice didn't betray her racing heart-beat. 'Perhaps you can discuss it with him in the morning?'

His gaze shifted briefly to the bedroom door, hesitation flickering in his expression. She held her breath, silently pleading that Falkenberg remained concealed beneath the blanket, unaware of Vogelmann's presence. The seconds stretched painfully, and for a moment, she feared he would press further.

But then Vogelmann nodded, though his eyes lingered on her form a heartbeat too long, thoughtful and appraising.

'Very well,' he said finally, his tone clipped, a hint of resentment lacing his words. 'Inform him when he wakes.'

He gave her one last unsettling glance, a look thick with envy and unspoken frustration, before stepping back, leaving her alone with the thundering silence of the suite.

As the door clicked shut, Antoinette released a shaky breath. She leaned against the door for a moment, trying to steady herself, but the danger hadn't passed.

She had to finish the job.

A sense of dread filled her every fibre as she neared Falkenberg again, his unmoving form a stark contrast to the weight of his laboured breathing. Her trembling fingers reached for the key once more, with a primal fear unlike any she had felt before. But as her hand wrapped around the icy metal, Falkenberg's arm flung out, seizing her wrist in a crushing grip that sent a jolt of searing pain through her entire body.

A strangled cry escaped her lips as her body tensed with sheer terror. His iron-like grip crushed her delicate skin, leaving angry red marks in its wake. His fingers were like claws, piercing through her flesh with a possessiveness that struck fear deep into her core.

Her breath hitched. He wasn't fully awake – or was he?

Antoinette's heart continued to slam against her ribs as he pulled her to him, his hands roaming over her body, his touch possessive and heavy. He mumbled incoherently, clearly unaware of what he was doing, but the sensation of his hands on her made her want to scream. She clenched her fist around the key, forcing herself to endure his touch, knowing that if she gave in to the revulsion and panic now, everything would be lost.

At long last, Falkenberg's grip loosened as he fell back into unconsciousness, his breathing evening out.

Antoinette extricated herself carefully, her body moving

with agonising slowness, every breath held as she slipped out of the bed. One wrong move, one sudden sound, and everything they had planned would be for nothing.

She straightened her clothes quickly, her hands still shaking as she fumbled with the fabric. With the key clutched tightly in her palm, she slipped out of the suite and into the hallway, her breath uneven and her chest tightening with unease.

She glanced around, looking for the guards. The usual one was there, leaning out of a window, his cigarette glowing in the darkness. Antoinette held her breath and crept past him, her footsteps silent as death. She descended the back stairs and slipped through the rear door into the night, the cold air hitting her like an icy wall.

But when she reached the meeting place, the agent was nowhere to be seen. Panic seized her, her breath coming in short, shallow gasps. Each passing second felt like an eternity, her mind racing through a flood of worst-case scenarios. What if he'd been caught? What if this was a trap?

She paced the alley; it was freezing and she had not thought to grab her coat. As she walked in circles, her pulse racing, her grip tightened around the key so hard it hurt. The shadows seemed to close in around her, and her throat felt tight, her panic threatening to consume her.

Finally, after what felt like hours, but was probably no more than thirty minutes, the agent appeared out of the darkness, his face flushed with apology. 'I'm sorry I'm late,' he panted, his voice low and urgent. 'I was stopped and questioned.'

Relief washed over her, but the tension didn't fade. He took the key from her with a quick, reassuring squeeze of her hand. 'I'll be quick,' he promised, disappearing into the night before she could respond.

Antoinette nodded, though her heart was still pounding like thunder. She stood freezing in the alley, every sound of the night amplified, her nerves on high alert. She checked the time repeatedly, knowing that every moment of delay put her and her family's life at risk.

When the agent finally returned, the copied key in hand, Antoinette barely had time to whisper her thanks before sprinting back to the suite, her breath ragged and uneven, her legs feeling weak beneath her.

She slipped back inside as quietly as possible, her heart nearly stopping as she crept past the guard towards the suite. He was sitting back in his chair now, his eyes closed and head nodding. Inside, the bedroom was dim, Falkenberg still sprawled across the bed, snoring softly.

The door to Falkenberg's office loomed before her, the dark wood gleaming ominously in the dim light. She pulled out the camera hidden beneath her violin. Antoinette's hands trembled as she unlocked it, slipping into the darkened room with a sense of dread that gnawed at her insides.

The office was a stark contrast to the opulence of the suite, the walls lined with shelves of books and files, the desk cluttered with documents and papers. The air was thick with the scent of tobacco and leather, a combination that sent a wave of nausea rolling through her.

She knew she had limited time, so she quickly began searching through the papers on the desk, her heart racing with the fear of being discovered. Each document she picked up felt like a potential lifeline for the Resistance, a thread that could unravel the secrets of the Nazi regime. She came across a list of Resistance members, detailing their locations, and she hurriedly photographed each page with the tiny camera Serge had given her. She moved to the next stack, but her breath hitched when her eyes fell upon a single, unmistakable letter.

As she read the words on the official Nazi letterhead, her heart stopped. The letter was addressed to Falkenberg from a high-ranking officer, its contents chillingly clear:

As you requested, the transport of René Kaplan to Germany has been completed. His arrival was confirmed yesterday, and he is now in processing. Further instructions awaited.

The page slipped from her trembling fingers as the full weight of its meaning crashed over her. Despite every assurance Falkenberg had given, René had been sent to a German concentration camp. The realisation struck like a knife to the heart, cold and merciless. She had been clinging to the faintest hope, trusting the enemy promises in her desperation – and now that trust had been betrayed with terrifying finality.

A wave of nausea surged as she tried to comprehend the horror René was now enduring. Her mind filled with images of him, weakened and broken, facing the unfathomable cruelty that awaited him. Her knees nearly buckled, the betrayal stealing her strength, her spirit nearly shattered.

But then – *a sound.* A low murmur from the bedroom. Her head snapped up, blood turning to ice as she heard Falkenberg's voice, thick and drowsy with sleep, calling out for her. Panic surged like wildfire, igniting every nerve. She'd been gone too long. If he discovered her here, amongst his papers, the consequences would be unthinkable.

Swallowing her terror, she grabbed the letter, shoving it back where she'd found it, forcing herself to control her breath as her heart hammered painfully against her ribs. She turned towards the door, steeling herself, every step a desperate attempt to regain her composure before facing the man who had shattered her last hope.

Placing the camera back in her violin case and with one last glance around the office, she locked it and hurried back to the bedroom, her mind racing with a mix of dread and determination.

As she entered the dimly lit room, Falkenberg stirred on the bed, blinking blearily at her. 'Antoinette? Where were you?' he mumbled, his words barely coherent.

'Just in the bathroom,' she lied as she climbed back into bed, the sheer anger bubbling inside her.

She couldn't believe it: her husband was gone. In that moment, she made up her mind exactly what she was going to do. As soon as she could make arrangements to get Benjamin safely out of the city, she was going to kill Falkenberg.

31

BRAZIL, 2012

Deanna

The following day, as the morning sun warmed the patio, Deanna and Felicity sat in silence, sipping their coffee. The vibrant Brazilian morning felt at odds with the turmoil swirling in Deanna's mind.

Felicity's eyes narrowed as she broke the silence, her tone laced with suspicion. 'You know what I think? I don't believe Giovanni has any real evidence of owning that violin. He's just stalling and avoiding the issue.'

Deanna nodded, staring into her cup. 'You may be right. I came here to learn more about my grandmother's story, but now that I've found out Giovanni may have been a Nazi, I'm not sure I can trust anything he says.' Her gaze shifted toward the villa, and a heavy sense of unease settled over their otherwise peaceful morning.

Felicity reached out, giving Deanna's hand a reassuring squeeze. 'We'll figure this out.'

Their conversation was interrupted by Carlos, who stepped

onto the patio with a package in hand. 'This just arrived for me,' he said, handing it to Deanna. 'It's from Italy.'

Deanna noticed the official seal: *Archivio di Stato di Firenze*. She exchanged a glance with Felicity, who raised a curious brow.

'What is it?' Deanna asked softly. The stamp and return address were unmistakably Italian.

Felicity frowned as she answered her. 'It's from the official State Archives of Florence.'

Carlos opened the envelope and pulled out a collection of meticulously preserved documents, the kind that looked like they belonged in a museum. 'It's all in Italian...' he admitted, a sheepish smile crossing his face. 'Unfortunately, I can't read Italian.'

'I can!' Felicity chimed in, taking the documents from Carlos. She cleared her throat and began to read aloud:

To whom it may concern,

Thank you for your letter requesting documentation. After a recent reorganisation of our archives, we have unearthed several historical documents related to the ownership of your Stradivarius violin. These include personal letters, legal records, and certificates linking the instrument to Caterina Santos, an accomplished Italian violinist of the early twentieth century who had connections to the Stradivari family. Also enclosed is a copy of her will, deeding that same violin to her grandson, Giovanni Rossi.

We are providing these materials to assist in confirming the rightful ownership of the violin currently in your possession. We trust this will aid in your ongoing efforts.

Yours faithfully,

Paolo Esposito, Archivista Genealogico

Archivio di Stato di Firenze

Felicity paused, letting the weight of the words sink in. Deanna stared at the letter, her mind spinning. Beneath it were birth certificates, old letters, and official property records – all forming a chain of information, appearing to confirm Giovanni's family once owned the violin.

'This... this is pretty convincing,' Deanna said quietly, the realisation settling in.

Felicity leaned forward, her brow furrowed. 'Too convincing, if you ask me. How does all this surface now, just as we're trying to figure out the violin's history?'

Carlos glanced at the papers, his expression thoughtful. 'But if the Archivio di Stato di Firenze is legitimate, I don't think they would've sent this if they weren't certain.'

Felicity wasn't easily swayed. She tapped her fingers against the table, her scepticism deepening. 'But the timing is off.'

Before Deanna could say more, Giovanni stepped onto the patio, his presence commanding attention. He glanced at the package and smiled knowingly. 'Ah, good. It arrived.'

Deanna blinked, confused. 'You knew about this?'

Giovanni chuckled softly, his tone as smooth as ever. 'Of course. When we first started searching for the violin, I contacted them. I had heard nothing for months, so when I knew Deanna would be bringing my violin here, I called again. I even paid someone to dig deeper. I wasn't going to expect her to believe me without proof, now was I?'

Carlos nodded in understanding. 'But why didn't you mention it earlier?'

Giovanni shrugged, his expression casual. 'I wasn't sure it would get here in time, and frankly, I didn't expect them to find anything so quickly.'

Felicity shot him a wary glance. 'So, the timing really is just... *luck?*'

'Not luck, my dear – persistence,' Giovanni replied smoothly. 'When something as important as this is on the line, you push until you get answers.'

Felicity crossed her arms, eyes narrowed. 'Even if these documents are legitimate, it's still suspicious. We need time to verify this.'

Deanna pulled her friend aside, her voice low and tinged with exhaustion. 'Felicity, I can't drag this out any longer. If I take this violin to auction, my grandmother's past will be ripped apart. People will dig into her life, her secrets – and my father... he doesn't deserve that. He's already been through so much.'

Felicity leaned closer, her tone urgent and unyielding. 'But Deanna, this isn't just some keepsake. This is a priceless Stradivarius. Think about what that could mean – your money worries gone, your future secure. And what about our suspicions? What if he isn't Giovanni Rossi at all? What if he's the Nazi we think he might be?'

Deanna met Felicity's gaze, her own softening as sadness and determination mingled in her expression.

'I've thought about it – believe me, I have. But I can't keep money from selling something that doesn't feel like it's truly mine. I can't bear the thought of profiting from something that means so much to him, even if we have doubts. Carlos has offered some money for its return and I think I should just take that. And we have no proof, Felicity – no *definitive* evidence that he's anyone other than who he says he is. Those documents he provided are solid. Even Carlos's suspicions are just that – suspicions. Maybe he was a collaborator, but that doesn't make him the monster we're imagining.'

Her voice trembled, but she pushed on, her conviction unwavering. 'Do you remember how he looked that first night we arrived? It wasn't just relief – it was like he'd found a part of

himself he thought was gone forever. That kind of emotion...
you can't fake that, Felicity. Whatever the truth is, I can't let this
violin become a symbol of greed or vengeance. If it belongs to
him, it belongs to him. Holding on to it because of our wild
theories doesn't feel right.'

Felicity hesitated, the conflict clear on her face. But Deanna
pressed gently, her voice quieter now. 'I need to do what feels
right. For my grandmother, for my father, and for myself. I don't
want to carry this weight any longer. It's time to let it go.'

'But, Deanna!' Felicity sighed, frustration mixing with her
protectiveness. 'Once you hand it over, there's no going back.'
Deanna lifted a hand to stop her friend before she continued.

'Do you trust this Archivio di Stato di Firenze in Italy?'

Felicity exhaled heavily, her gaze shifting from Giovanni to
the documents she still held in her hand. She began sorting
through the papers, her brow furrowed in concentration. After a
moment of silence, she finally spoke in a measured tone. 'These
documents seem thorough and detailed. If they are indeed
authentic, then it appears Giovanni's claim is valid. But you
have some rights too, as you now have possession.'

'Then maybe all we were thinking was wrong. These look
pretty convincing to me. And it isn't mine to keep; it never was.
And it wasn't my grandmother's either. I don't know why she
never gave it back to him during the war. Maybe they were
separated, or maybe she was ashamed of what she had done and
didn't want to face him. I don't know, there could be so many
reasons.' Deanna's voice dropped to a near whisper. 'Even if
Giovanni was a double agent, it's not my job to judge him, is it?
Especially after all I've heard about my grandmother. I just
want to put this whole sordid episode behind me. We came to
authenticate that this violin belonged to his family, and to get
more information about my own. We've done both. All I want
to do now is go home.'

Felicity bit her lip, eyes flicking between Deanna and the

documents in her hand. After a long pause, she relented. 'If this truly is what you want.'

Deanna gave her a grateful smile, feeling the support of her friend despite their disagreement. 'Thank you. I just want this over.'

Giovanni, sensing the decision had been made, stepped forward. 'You've made the right choice, Deanna. This violin has always belonged to my family. And now, finally, it can return to where it belongs.'

Deanna made her way through the villa until she reached her room. She unlocked her suitcase and opened the lid of the violin case one last time and gently ran her fingers over the strings. She couldn't help but think that her grandmother might have been the last person to touch this instrument before her. A lump formed in her throat as she tried to push down her emotions. 'I love you, Grandma Netty, and I'm not sure why you kept this, but it is time for this violin to go back to its rightful owner,' she whispered before closing the lid once more.

As she presented the violin to Giovanni, his eyes lit up with satisfaction, and he extended his hand toward Deanna. A sense of relief washed over her as she handed him the precious instrument. 'Thank you,' he said, his voice filled with gratitude. 'You don't know what this means to me.'

Deanna hesitated for a moment before taking Giovanni's hand. She could feel the impact of her decision settling heavily on her shoulders as he held on to the violin with a firm grip. A slow smile spread across his face, and Deanna couldn't help but feel a sense of joy for returning something so important to its rightful owner.

However, even though she knew it was the right thing to do, an uneasy feeling remained within her. Conflicting emotions stirred inside her.

But looking at the letters now spread out on the table, and her need to put this all behind her, what else could she do?

32

JANUARY 1943

Antoinette

The morning light filtered through the curtains of Falkenberg's suite as Antoinette stood before the mirror, her fingers trembling as she fastened each button with deliberate care. Behind her, Falkenberg's presence was a shadow, his gaze like a burning brand searing into her back as he watched her dress.

The thought of René's fate smouldered within her, a wildfire of anger she struggled to keep from consuming her entirely. But she couldn't let it show – not yet. She had to play this deadly game a little longer, bide her time until she could destroy the man who had stolen so much from her. For now, she had to wear the mask of a woman seduced by power, all for the sake of her husband and son.

Falkenberg's breath was hot against her neck as he moved closer, his lips brushing her skin in a grotesque mimicry of affection. 'Last night was unfortunate, my dear Antoinette,' he murmured, his voice smooth, veiled with a threatening edge. 'Tonight, I'll be more restrained with my wine.'

Disgust coiled within her, but Antoinette maintained a

placid smile. 'Of course, Commander,' she responded, her voice steady. His smile broadened unnervingly as his hands slid down her arms possessively. 'Tonight will be memorable for both of us. As will every night from now on.'

Once Falkenberg left the room, Antoinette exhaled sharply, her fists clenched. She needed to protect the hidden camera in her violin case before he discovered it. As she moved to leave the suite, his voice froze her. 'Leave the violin.'

'But, Commander' – she feigned confusion – 'I need to practise.'

He snatched the violin, discarding it onto the sofa. 'You won't need it tonight. I have something special planned.'

Antoinette nodded, concealing her panic.

Did he suspect she was part of the Resistance, as well as married to a Jewish man?

Later, as the agent drove her home, his concern was evident in every glance he cast her way. Antoinette relayed the events of the morning, her voice barely above a whisper as she recounted Falkenberg's strange behaviour.

'How did everything go after I left; did you get into the room and photograph the documents?' the agent asked.

Antoinette shook her head. 'I have to go back again tonight. He made me leave my violin; the camera is hidden inside the case.'

'Do you think he's playing you?' The agent's tone was low, filled with unease.

Antoinette shrugged, uncertainty gnawing at her. 'I don't know, but I wouldn't put it past him. He loves the feeling of control.'

Once she got home, Antoinette's anger boiled over as she paced her apartment. Her mind raced with thoughts of René, Benjamin, and the treacherous world she was now entangled in.

She had risked everything for the Resistance, obtained the vital documents they needed, only to lose her beloved René. Tears burned down her cheeks as she recalled the last time they had been together and her heart ached with grief and sorrow.

But with her beloved husband gone, there was nothing left for her in that wretched place. Falkenberg's words echoed in her mind, a cruel reminder of what was in store for her: '*I will be assigned to Paris indefinitely. So we will be able to be together every day!*' She gritted her teeth, knowing that Falkenberg would never let her go. She was trapped in his clutches forever, a prisoner of his sick obsession.

Running was futile – he would hunt her down mercilessly and force her into submission once again. The thought made her blood run cold and fuelled her rage even further. There was only one way out of this that she could see. In her bedroom, she pulled up the floorboard and retrieved the knife given to her by Serge.

Her wedding ring glinted there, a mocking reminder of all that she had lost at the hands of Falkenberg's cruelty.

When Antoinette arrived at Falkenberg's suite that evening, she was met with a small gathering of guests. The room buzzed with conversation. Falkenberg's gaze found her instantly, a gleam in his eyes as he approached her.

'Ladies and gentlemen, I have a rare treat for you this evening,' Falkenberg announced, his voice a slick veneer of charm. Antoinette's chest tightened as every eye in the room turned towards her, the strain of their scrutiny almost unbearable.

Her mind raced, the knife in her handbag a constant reminder of what she had planned. She forced a smile, greeting each guest with practised ease, all the while keeping her guard up. But as Falkenberg left the room and returned with a violin case, her heart plummeted. *He knew.* He was going to reveal her secret, maybe have her arrested right here, right now.

But when Falkenberg thrust the case into her hands, she looked down and realised with a rush of relief that it wasn't her violin case. As she opened it, the sight of the rare, beautiful instrument inside took her breath away. The guests murmured in admiration, oblivious to the turmoil roiling within her.

It was a Stradivarius, unmistakable in its craftsmanship. The polished golden-brown wood shimmered under the chandelier light, every curve and contour exuding elegance and precision. The faint tiger-striped pattern of the maple back seemed to glow, as if it held its own light. The fingerboard, smooth and pristine, led to intricately carved scrollwork at the neck, where the pegs sat like sentinels, perfectly symmetrical. The varnish was flawless, giving the instrument a luminous, almost otherworldly sheen, as though it had been untouched by time.

'Tonight, my dear Antoinette,' Falkenberg purred, 'you shall grace us with a performance unlike any other. Play for us, and let this exquisite instrument's melody fill the room.'

A member of the party took a photograph of Antoinette with the incredible instrument as she brushed the strings, the beauty of the Stradivarius almost lost on her as she fought to maintain her composure. 'I will need my music,' she whispered, her voice barely audible.

'Yes, yes.' Falkenberg waved her away dismissively. 'It's in the corner.'

Antoinette moved quickly, retrieving her music from beneath her own violin that had been placed on the floor. She felt the pressure lift slightly as she saw that the case appeared unopened. Carefully, she opened the lid and saw the camera was still in its hiding place. She breathed a sigh of relief before closing the case, her heart racing.

Summoning every ounce of composure she could muster,

she delicately placed her fingers on the strings and began to play. Though her heart was racing with fear and anxiety, the moment she struck the first note on the Stradivarius, a wave of intense emotion overtook her. The rich, resonant tones filled the room, enveloping her in their beauty and power.

Despite the anguish of her life choices that constantly threatened to overwhelm her, this moment was pure and perfect. The exquisite balancing act between her life of horror and the transcendent sound of the violin was both excruciating and liberating. It was a reminder that amid all the darkness, there was still beauty to be found. In her defiance she played her and René's song, a lasting tribute to their love; tears streamed down her cheeks as she poured her soul into the music, every note a testament to the strength and resilience she harboured within. The guests were captivated, their hushed whispers falling silent as they listened, enraptured by the haunting melody that seemed to echo the turmoil hidden beneath Antoinette's elegant façade.

As the final notes faded into the air, there was a moment of stunned silence before the room erupted into thunderous applause. Antoinette lowered the bow, her hands trembling with a mixture of relief and adrenaline. Falkenberg's expression was a mask of inscrutable calm.

'Magnificent, my dear,' he drawled, his tone sending a chill through her veins. 'A performance to remember indeed.'

As the guests continued to lavish her with praise and adulation, Antoinette felt Falkenberg's eyes bore into her. She knew that despite the success of her performance, something had shifted between them. Falkenberg's demeanour was too controlled, too calculated to allow her any of her own freedom even in her music. He wanted to possess all of her and she sensed his desire to dominate her growing stronger with every passing moment. But instead of being intimidated she felt a sense of roaring defiance building within her as she remembered the dagger in her bag, and what she intended to do with it.

After the guests left, he immediately shed his jacket. He swaggered over to the bar and poured himself a generous glass of whisky, downing it in one swift gulp. He disappeared into the bedroom and emerged with a box, tossing it carelessly onto the sofa next to her.

'Put this on,' he commanded with a predatory glint in his eye. Antoinette's heart dropped as she opened the box, revealing a nightdress that was delicate and exquisite, made of the finest silk and lace. The implications were clear – he expected her to wear it for him. The revulsion she felt at the thought consumed her, but she had no choice but to comply.

He pulled her close and kissed her roughly, his unshaven face scraping against her cheek.

A wave of disgust rippled through Antoinette.

As Falkenberg's hands roamed over her, his touch leaving a trail of ice in its wake, she forced herself to endure it and maintain the mask of compliance she had crafted so carefully. Deep down, a fire burned within her, a fire fuelled by anger and defiance, her mind centred on the fact she was going to kill him, tonight. Now, she had no need of him. And would put her plan in place. In between his urgent kisses, she gently pushed him away and whispered, 'I need to put on your gift.'

He leered at her. 'That's right, my darling. Let me see you in it.' She made her way to the bedroom, her body tense with fear and anger. As she undressed, she pulled the knife from her handbag and placed it under the pillow.

When she emerged in the exquisite nightdress, Falkenberg's eyes widened with appreciation.

But Antoinette didn't care; she was too focused on the weapon hidden in his bedroom.

He arrived in the bedroom carrying the violin, and told her, 'I want to see you playing for me alone.'

With a forced smile, she raised the violin to her chin and began to play. The notes that filled the room were haunting, echoing with a sense of sorrow yet tenacity. As she played, her fingers moved deftly over the strings, each note a testament to the strength and resilience that burned within her. The melody swirled around the room, wrapping her in a shield of music that offered both solace and determination.

As the final notes of the melody faded away, Antoinette slowly lowered the violin, her gaze steady as she met Falkenberg's eyes.

He approached her and, pulling her onto the bed, pressed his lips to hers, his hands roaming over her body again. Antoinette's skin crawled at his touch, but she remained still, her mind racing with plans of escape. She knew she had to bide her time, to wait for the perfect moment to strike. And after he lay exhausted upon her and she could feel the heat of his breath on her neck, she reached beneath the pillow and with a steady hand, she gripped the handle of the knife. Her heart pounded in her ears as she slid it from beneath her.

She closed her eyes, envisioning René's kind eyes and gentle smile, only for the image to be shattered by the thought of him suffering in a camp because of this despicable person. She wasn't just fighting for herself but for him – for the love they had shared, the faint hope of a future together, and the desperate need to break free from this living nightmare.

And spurred by that thought and with a sudden surge of courage, she plunged the blade into his body.

Falkenberg's eyes bulged with shock and agony as the sharp steel pierced through his flesh, a guttural cry escaping his lips. As their eyes met, Antoinette leaned in close and spat out two words: 'For René.'

Her hands shook with the force of the blow, as adrenaline pumped through her veins. The Nazi gasped for air as blood gushed from his back, staining the sheets around him. His face contorted in disbelief and searing pain, a fitting end for a monster who had caused so much suffering.

As she launched herself from the bed, her hands wet with fresh blood and her heart racing, she desperately tried to drown out the sound of his choked gasps. The metallic taste of fear coating her tongue as she stumbled towards the door.

She had done the unspeakable, but there was no looking back now. Tears blurred her vision, the guilt and horror of what she had done weighing heavily on her. But she didn't care. She didn't wait to watch him die; she didn't want to spend one more minute in his presence.

Gathering her clothes quickly, she dressed, her movements driven by her urgency. As she fastened the last button, her eyes fell on the Stradivarius resting in its case – a symbol of everything Falkenberg and the Nazis had stolen, not just from her, but from countless others.

In that moment, her love for music surged through her like a lifeline. The violin, with its delicate craftsmanship and haunting beauty, deserved better than to be a pawn in the hands of those who twisted art for their vile purposes. It had played melodies that could stir souls, and she knew in her heart that it was her duty to save it from being silenced forever by the darkness of this regime. She would feel a great sense of pride as she handed it back to its rightful owner.

But there was something more. A spark of revenge ignited within her – a deep, burning desire to take something precious from Falkenberg, just as he had taken so much from her. It was a small victory, perhaps, but one that gave her a fleeting sense of control in a world where power had so often been stripped from her grasp. This was her chance to reclaim something, to assert her will against the man who thought he had broken her.

In one final act of defiance, she lifted the priceless violin and, removing her own, placed it in her own violin case, ensuring the hidden camera was still safely tucked inside. As she closed the case, she felt a wave of grim satisfaction wash over her. She had taken something of great value, not just an object, but a piece of the artistry and humanity that the Nazis sought to destroy.

It was a small, quiet act of rebellion. But it was hers.

33

BRAZIL, 2012

Deanna

That night, a storm outside the villa roared like a living creature, wild and untamed, lashing the walls with sheets of rain.

Inside, Deanna lay tangled in the damp warmth of her sheets, her mind spinning with fragments of memory, doubts, and unanswered questions: the violin, Giovanni, her grandmother's stories. Each time she closed her eyes, the questions tightened their grip, refusing her the sanctuary of sleep.

Finally, exhaustion overwhelmed her, but what followed in her dreams was far from peaceful.

She was in Paris – though not the Paris of café terraces and flower-lined boulevards. No, this Paris was broken. Bombed-out buildings sagged under the weight of war, their skeletons jutting out like broken ribs.

The air was thick with the smell of fire and fear. Deanna's pulse raced as she sprinted through the crumbling streets. But it wasn't the city's destruction that terrified her. No – it was a low, guttural growl behind her.

She stole a glance over her shoulder, dread gripping her. A

wolf, its eyes glowing like molten gold, prowled behind her, its powerful body moving with a predator's grace. Its presence was terrifying, with a silent promise that no matter how fast she ran, it would catch her. Panic surged through her body, but her legs felt like lead, weighed down by fear and the heavy smoke that hung in the air.

As the wolf closed in, Deanna heard a voice – a familiar voice – cutting through the chaos. *'He saved me, Deanna. The wolf saved me.'*

It was her grandmother's voice, soft but clear, a haunting whisper carried on the wind. Deanna stumbled, her legs giving out beneath her just as the wolf lunged, its jaws wide, teeth gleaming in the dim light of the shattered city. She screamed, but her voice was swallowed by the darkness.

Deanna awoke with a start, her body jerking upright as if she had truly been running for her life. Her breath came in short, sharp bursts, her heart hammering in her chest. The storm outside rattled the windows; its relentless howls had enhanced her nightmare. She assured herself she was no longer in the dream. Yet the images clung to her – Paris in ruins, the wolf's eyes, her grandmother's voice. It felt so real, like an echo from her own past.

She pressed her hands to her temples, trying to piece together the fragments of the dream. *'He saved me, Deanna. The wolf saved me.'* But what did it mean?

The question gnawed at her, relentless, the feeling that her grandmother had been trying to tell her something, something important that was hidden within those words. But the more she tried to grasp at the meaning, the more it seemed to slip through her fingers, like sand caught in the wind.

Deanna tossed the covers aside, her bare feet hitting the cold floor as she reached for her laptop. She wasn't going to find any peace tonight, not with these questions clawing at her mind. She opened it and typed in 'wolf symbolism in dreams'.

Her eyes scanned the results, but nothing seemed to resonate. Strength, loyalty, protection – none of it matched the primal fear that had gripped her in the dream. She scrolled further, frustration building, when a distant memory floated to the surface of her mind.

She remembered her father's voice, casual over breakfast one morning. 'Your grandmother once told me something strange. She said a wolf saved her during the war.'

At the time, Deanna had brushed it off as a one of her father's fantastical stories, a half-forgotten tale from another lifetime. But now, in the wake of the dream, the memory gnawed at her with a newfound intensity.

Could it have been more than a metaphor?

Deanna made her way to the kitchen, her footsteps silent against the tiled floor. The villa was eerily quiet, the air heavy with the storm's presence. She flicked on the light, its soft glow illuminating the polished counters and casting long shadows across the room. As she filled the kettle with water and set it on to boil, her mind whirred, piecing together fragments of conversations and stories. The weather outside seemed to howl in agreement with her swirling thoughts.

She dialled her father's number. It was early morning in the UK but not so early that she would wake him. The phone rang twice before he picked up.

'Deanna? Is everything all right?' His voice was warm, but tinged with concern.

'I'm fine, Dad. I just... I need to ask you something,' she said, tentatively. 'Do you remember when you told me that story about Grandma? The one where she said a wolf saved her during the war?'

Her father chuckled softly, the sound crackling through the phone like a memory brought to life. 'Yes, I remember. Always thought she was being dramatic, talking about someone who was strong, maybe cunning, like a wolf.'

'What if she wasn't?' Deanna pressed, the words rushing out before she could second-guess herself. 'What if it was a *person*? What if it was... a codename?'

There was a long pause on the other end of the line, the kind of silence that spoke of gears turning slowly, processing the implications of the question. When her father finally spoke, his voice was quieter, more thoughtful.

'I suppose that's possible. She did mention something about using codenames once.'

Deanna's pulse quickened, her mind racing with possibilities. 'Do you remember anything else? Anything specific?'

'I'm not sure. Just that she said, when her life was in the greatest danger, the wolf saved her.'

The words made her gasp. The *greatest danger*. That had to be the time when her grandmother had escaped from the Nazis – when she had killed Falkenberg. Did she mean Giovanni? He worked with her. Had he been The Wolf? But why had Giovanni never spoken about this codename while she had been here? Why had he never mentioned it if he was the one who saved her?

Deanna ended the call with a quiet goodbye, her thoughts buzzing with the implications. She felt sure now, the wolf wasn't a metaphor – it was real. A person. Maybe a Resistance fighter who had helped her grandmother escape.

Determined to find the answers, Deanna returned to her bedroom and pulled out her laptop, the storm's fury still raging outside. She opened it and typed 'The Wolf – Resistance fighter' into the search bar. Her fingers hovered over the keys as she scrolled through the results. Nothing. No one by that codename. Frustration prickled at the back of her neck. She had been so sure.

And then it hit her – she had been searching in the wrong language. If The Wolf was a French Resistance fighter, wouldn't the records be in French?

Deanna looked up the translation. The results filled the screen almost instantly: *Le Loup.* She stared at the name, her heart thudding in her chest. It was familiar – too familiar.

Where had she seen it before?

A sudden realisation hit her like a lightning bolt. The copy of the journal. The one Florence's daughter had given her in Paris. She had skimmed through it at the time, only focusing on the parts about her grandmother's affair. But now, as the torrential rain lashed the windows, she pieces began to fall into place.

Deanna raced to her suitcase, throwing clothes aside until she found the copies of the worn journal pages. She flipped through the papers, searching for the passage that had eluded her.

And there it was, a passage about The Wolf. Her breath caught in her throat as she painstakingly translated the message word by word online.

March 1943: Le Loup has been instrumental in our efforts. Without him, 'M' would never have escaped the hotel. We heard last night he was tortured and killed by the Gestapo.

The words blurred as tears filled Deanna's eyes. *Le Loup* – The Wolf, that had been the agent at the Majestic, it had been his codename and he had saved her grandmother and had been killed during the war.

Never escaped the hotel? Hadn't Giovanni told her he had worked with her at the hotel? Her world tilted, the weight of the truth crashing down on her like a wave. The real Giovanni wasn't alive. He hadn't been for decades.

So, if that was true, who was the man claiming to be him now? The newspaper clipping and the words Felicity had told her came back to her again. Vogelmann had been an interrogator.

As she absorbed this thought, her head started to pound,

and the familiar sense of nausea and light-headedness informed her she had a migraine coming on.

She understood his need to go to such lengths to escape detection. But something else gnawed at the back of her mind. And she couldn't help feeling it was something to do with her.

A second realisation hit Deanna like a punch in the gut. A gut she should have listened to in the first place. Felicity had been right to try and dissuade her from handing over the violin. Carlos's father had to be a Nazi imposter, capable of taking innocent lives without a second thought.

Fear and anger rose within her, knowing that she had put her trust in this man. But now she saw him for what he truly was – a dangerous enemy who would stop at nothing to achieve his twisted goals.

And with that realisation came the terrifying thought – if he had already taken one life, what was stopping him from taking another?

34

JANUARY 1943

Antoinette

Antoinette's entire body shook with the shock as she rushed through Falkenberg's suite.

The image of his eyes widening in shock and pain as the blade pierced his flesh kept flashing through her mind over and over in a loop. She could still feel how her hand shook from the force of her strike, the hot rush of shock coursing through her body as she had leapt off the bed, wiping the streaks of his blood from her skin.

Hurrying out of the door, she sprinted through the corridor and in her haste to get away forgot about the guard at the end who leapt to his feet as she approached. Her whole body tensed as she locked eyes with him, seeing suspicion flicker across his face.

'Why are you running?' he demanded, his hand hovering over his sidearm.

Antoinette's mind raced, desperate for an excuse as she slowed her pace, feeling exposed and vulnerable, all her Resistance training forgotten in the moment. Instead, she felt raw and unsteady as she struggled to keep control of her emotions.

'I need to get home,' she finally spluttered out, but she could tell he wasn't buying it. She had to come up with something better, fast.

'Commander von Falkenberg normally informs me when he needs a car for you. This is highly irregular. Come with me while I talk to him.' Before she could protest, he grabbed her by the arm and propelled her back towards the suite.

'But he's asleep!' she insisted, struggling against his grip. The guard only tightened his hold on her, his face hardening with suspicion as he marched her down the corridor.

'Commander von Falkenberg told me of this arrangement,' boomed a voice from behind them. The guard whirled around, and Antoinette felt a wave of relief wash over her as she saw the other agent standing at the end of the corridor. His eyes were impassive as he approached, commanding respect. 'I was told to report here now as his guest would need to leave in the early hours while he was sleeping.'

As the guard reluctantly released her arm, he noticed something. 'What is that on your arm?' he asked suspiciously.

With horror, she saw a smear of Falkenberg's blood she had missed. 'I had an accident earlier,' she managed to sputter out, but she knew now that her lies were unravelling.

'Wait here!' the guard snapped as he marched towards the suite.

But as soon as his back was turned, the agent hissed to Antoinette, 'Let's go!'

They raced towards the back stairs, taking them two at a time in their rush to escape.

'How did you know?' she asked between ragged breaths.

'I just had a feeling. I've been here waiting out of sight, listening all evening.'

'With that kind of cunning you suit your codename of The

Wolf,' Antoinette replied as they rounded the last flight of stairs. Suddenly, shouts erupted from the corridor behind the stairwell doors, followed by the sound of soldiers' boots rushing up the main stairs.

As they stood panting by the door, she turned to him and said, 'I have your violin.'

He answered her with a grateful smile. 'Thank you, unfortunately, the car is parked at the front of the hotel. Our only way out is through the main entrance.' Antoinette nodded in understanding, her lungs burning with the strain. They pushed open the door and started to walk as nonchalantly as they could towards the main entrance. Abruptly, a soldier in the foyer called out to them.

'No one is supposed to leave at this time!'

'*Run!*' the agent shouted at her, and they broke into a sprint towards the main entrance.

The soldier yelled for them to stop, but they paid no heed as they raced through the grand foyer of the hotel, pushing open the heavy wooden doors and bursting out into the cool night air. Their breath misted in front of them as they ran down the steps to where a sleek black car waited at the kerb. Without missing a beat, he yanked open the door and motioned for Antoinette to get in.

A deafening shot ripped through the air, and Antoinette's body froze in terror. Her eyes widened, darting around frantically as she searched for the source of the sound. Before her, the other agent crumpled to the ground, a dark pool of blood seeping from a wound on his leg as he howled in agony.

Soldiers materialised out of thin air, shouting orders and pointing guns at them. 'Go!' The Wolf screamed, his face twisted in anguish.

'I won't leave you!' Antoinette screamed back, trying desperately to lift him up. But the soldiers were closing in fast.

'Get my violin and yourself to safety,' he pleaded through gritted teeth. 'Keep it hidden, somewhere no one can find it.'

'No!' Antoinette protested. 'I won't abandon you!'

With a flick of his wrist, he tossed the car keys at her, his eyes pleading with her to save herself. She knew there was no time to waste trying to haul him into the car. With a heavy heart, she released him and sprinted towards the driver's seat, slamming the door shut behind her just as the soldier reached them. As she turned the key in the ignition, the engine roared to life, and she tore away from the chaos behind her. Tears streamed down her cheeks as she drove, fuelled by both fear and heartache over not being able to help the other agent.

As she glanced in the mirror, she saw the tiny specks of blood that peppered her cheeks. It was then that what she had done fully started to sink in. Antoinette stared at her reflection, her eyes wide with disbelief. She had killed a man. And it wasn't just any man; it was a Nazi – a monster who had hurt so many, stolen so much, and caused unimaginable pain. But he was still a human being.

She ditched the car a mile from her home. Arriving back at her apartment, she scrubbed her hands again and again until they were raw. She closed her eyes, trying to forget the feel of the knife in her hand, the cold breath of von Falkenberg, and the sound of his dying gasps.

She sank onto the bed, the events of the night replaying in her mind like a haunting melody, and as the horror of it hit her, she began to sob silently – not just from the terrible experience but also with relief that she had finally taken back some control from the monster that had taken everything from her.

Getting off the bed, she fumbled in the dark at the floorboards and pulled out her wedding ring. The small, gold band glinted in her hand – her one connection to her past, to her husband, to the life she had lost. She closed her hand around it tightly, trying to absorb the love and security it represented. She hadn't worn it for years, not since she had started playing at the hotel. Slipping it onto her finger, she felt a small, comforting warmth. It was a reminder that, despite everything, she still had a reason to keep fighting.

She was glad Benjamin was staying with the neighbours' child that night, and tomorrow he would leave on a train to safety with Charlotte. Then she must go into hiding, leave Paris forever.

She spent the rest of the night packing her things. She would never come back to this home – the home she had shared with her beloved husband and son.

In the morning, after Benjamin left she would head to the safe house to start her new life.

A few hours later, Antoinette shivered on the empty train platform, her body tense and aching, each breath a reminder of the nightmare her life had become. The acrid scent of his after-shave still clung to her neck, a suffocating reminder of what had transpired mere hours ago. She had meant to wash it away, but the need to get Benjamin to safety had been too urgent.

Beneath her coat, her blouse she had wore now felt like a straitjacket, constricting her with memories she wished she could erase. She could still feel the ghost of his hands on her skin, the unwanted touch repulsing her. Just then, a small hand squeezed hers, pulling her back to the present, reminding her why she had to flee.

'Maman, how much longer until the train arrives?' Benjamin's blue eyes, filled with innocent curiosity, looked up at her.

His black felt cap and coat, bought just last year, were already snug on his growing frame. A pang of worry struck her – he would need a new coat soon. How much would he change in the next year? Who would care for him if she couldn't be there?

She forced herself to push these thoughts aside. Her son was going away from Paris, away from danger.

'It won't be much longer,' she said, her voice steadier than she felt. The taste of last night's alcohol lingered on her breath, her throat raw from too many cigarettes. She reached out, brushing a stray hair from his cheek, clinging to the hope that better days were coming.

She would find her husband just as she had promised him – she had to believe that. She held on to that hope with every ounce of strength she had left.

Suddenly, the sound of footsteps echoed through the thick mist that blanketed the platform, the dense fog turning the world into a shadowy, eerie void. Antoinette strained her ears, trying to distinguish the muted sounds. A knot of nervous anxiety tightened in her chest.

She searched the hazy figures moving through the fog, her breath catching as she spotted her sister Isabelle leading one of her Jewish co-workers and a little girl down the platform. Relief washed over her, but it was tinged with deep sorrow. So many children, so many families torn apart on this long, uncertain journey. Brigitte's daughter, head bowed, hair adorned with shiny plaits and vibrant red ribbons, moved toward them with a sadness that weighed heavily on Antoinette's heart. As Isabelle approached, Antoinette saw the unspoken question in her eyes. She quickly wiped at her cheeks, hoping to conceal any trace of tears or smudged mascara from her emotional trip to the station.

Isabelle Valette reached out hesitantly, her arms hovering before enveloping her sister Antoinette in a warm embrace. 'Are you all right?' she asked with concern as she took in Antoinette's dishevelled appearance.

'We're fine.' Antoinette forced a smile, straightening her posture in a futile attempt to conceal the pain raging inside her. She knew she must look a mess after the night she had endured, but it wasn't just her appearance that troubled her – it was the searing disgust and self-loathing that gnawed at her insides. She continued to check her hands for blood as she longed to escape from her own skin, to be free of the choices that had led her here, but there was no escape. She was trapped in her own body, tormented by the decisions she had made.

But then she thought of Benjamin, her son, and her husband – the reasons she had made those choices. She swallowed her anguish, forcing a mask of normality onto her face as she focused on them. Isabelle spoke again, but Antoinette barely registered the words, her mind struggling to keep up the façade of composure. She glanced at Isabelle, her expression puzzled, trying to piece together what had just been said. 'I hope they are not late.'

Just then another sister appeared through the fog with two twin girls. Her sister Giselle moved gracefully down the platform, her impeccable attire and air of quiet confidence making her seem like a swan gliding across still waters.

Gigi's long, slender arms wrapped around Antoinette's shoulders in a tight embrace. 'You look chilled, Antoinette,' she said, her piercing blue eyes filled with concern. 'Did you forget to bring a warmer coat?'

The touch on her arm sent an icy shiver through Antoinette. The memories crashed over her – the rough grip of a Nazi soldier forcing her down onto a bed. She fought to keep her composure, nodding in response, desperately trying to push the haunting thoughts of the previous night out of her mind.

Antoinette felt a surge of relief as the rest of her sisters arrived, Madeline with her stepson, Kurt, and finally Charlotte, who would be accompanying all the Jewish children to safety at their aunt's house in the South of France. As her sisters gathered around her and Benjamin, forming a protective circle, Antoinette drew strength from their presence. In this moment of unity, she was reminded that she was not alone in this harrowing journey. Amid the hurried greetings and introductions, the sound of the approaching train grew louder, cutting through the mist like a beacon of hope.

The train's whistle pierced the air, signalling its imminent arrival, and the platform buzzed with activity.

Antoinette took a deep breath, steeling herself for what lay ahead. She glanced down at Benjamin, who looked up at her, bewildered by the chaos around them. She crouched to his eye level, mustering a reassuring smile that belied the nervousness in her voice.

'Are you ready, my darling?' she asked her son, her tone gentle.

Benjamin nodded, his young face brave but burdened. Antoinette's heart ached at the sight – her son, so innocent, yet already carrying the weight of a world in turmoil.

She handed him the violin. 'Take this with you, my love. One day you may need it, and I need you to really take care of it for me.'

As Benjamin grasped the violin in his small hands, a swell of pride and fear surged within Antoinette. The violin would be safe out of the city; no one was going to suspect a young boy of having such a valuable instrument. She prayed one day she would be able to hand it back to The Wolf, the agent who had saved her.

The train screeched to a halt in front of them, and a wave of frenzied energy swept through the crowd. Families clung to one another, desperate to hold on for just a few moments longer. Antoinette gripped Benjamin's hand with a force that turned her knuckles white, her body rigid with her pain.

'Remember, my love,' she whispered, her voice tight with emotion, 'no matter what happens, stay strong and know that I love you.'

She hugged him tightly, then with a final, lingering look, Antoinette gently nudged Benjamin towards the waiting train. She forced a smile as she waved to him, masking the pain and fear gnawing at her insides as she watched him step onto the carriage.

He disappeared into the crowd, swallowed by the throng of children with Charlotte, all seeking refuge from the nightmare that had become their reality.

A sob rose in Antoinette's throat as she stood on the platform, paralysed by her anguish. She had made this choice for Benjamin's safety, but the cost was almost more than she could bear. Would she ever see her son again?

Her sisters gathered around her, arms around each other, offering silent support as they watched the train pull away, carrying their loved ones to an uncertain fate. As the train vanished into the distance, Antoinette felt a numbness settle over her, a hollow ache where her heart once beat with purpose.

But now, with Benjamin safely away, the final piece of her plan could be put in place.

35

BRAZIL, 2012

Deanna

A soft knock on her bedroom door startled Deanna awake. She glanced at the clock – 4 a.m. Too early for anyone to be up. Her head was still pounding, the remnants of the migraine she'd been fighting off since the night before.

'Deanna?' came a faint voice from the other side. She immediately recognised it as Felicity's.

'Felicity?' Deanna called as she hurried to the door, her movements sluggish from the migraine's grip. She swung it open to find Felicity pale and swaying, her hand clutching the door-frame for support.

'I don't feel right...' Felicity whispered, her words trailing off as she stumbled forward, collapsing into Deanna's arms.

'Carlos! Maria!' Deanna shouted, her voice hoarse with panic. She struggled to guide Felicity back to the bed, as her friend slumped against her, barely conscious.

Within seconds, Carlos and Maria burst into the room. Carlos rushed to Felicity's side, his face tight with concern.

'What happened?' he asked, his eyes scanning Felicity's pale face.

'She just fainted,' Deanna replied breathlessly.

Maria, already thinking practically, spoke up. 'There's a hospital in town. We should take her now.'

'I'll drive,' Carlos said, his tone sharp with urgency.

'I'll come with you—' Deanna started, but as soon as she stood up, a sharp, stabbing pain coursed through her skull, forcing her to grab the edge of the nightstand for balance. The migraine surged back with a vengeance, making her vision blur momentarily.

Carlos saw her wince and shook his head gently. 'No, Deanna. You're in no condition to go out; stay here. Rest. We'll take care of her. We won't be long.'

Maria stepped forward, her eyes full of understanding. 'We'll call you the minute we know something. You need to stay behind and take care of yourself. The storm is starting up again, and travelling in your state could make you feel worse.'

Deanna hesitated, the urge to be there for Felicity tugging at her heart. But the pounding in her skull reminded her that she wasn't in any shape to go. She had to trust Carlos and Maria.

'Okay,' Deanna relented, helping them lift Felicity and guiding her as far as the stairs. She watched, her heart heavy, as they carefully helped her friend into the car, Felicity's form barely visible through the driving rain that had begun to intensify.

As soon as the car pulled away, the house felt unbearably silent. The wind outside lashed the palm trees, and the sound of rain pelting the villa echoed through the walls. Deanna sat on the edge of her bed, rubbing her temples, willing the pain to ease.

She should lie down. Just for a little while.

Easing herself onto the pillows, she closed her eyes, but

sleep didn't come. Her body ached with exhaustion, yet her mind wouldn't settle. The sound of the thunder crashed overhead – wind battering against the villa, branches scraping the walls, the distant rumble of thunder.

Her thoughts drifted to Felicity. What if it was serious? What if the weather stopped them from getting there? What if—

No. She forced herself to breathe, to slow the spiral of anxious thoughts. Carlos and Maria would call. There was nothing she could do but wait.

Somewhere in the background, the rain's rhythm became a lull, and she drifted in and out of restless sleep. Each time she surfaced, her head still pounded, and her stomach twisted with unease.

About an hour passed.

When she woke fully again, the thunder and lightening had intensified, rattling the windowpanes. The house was too quiet. She reached for her phone, but the screen remained dark. Dead.

Just as she plugged it in, a sharp, sudden sound shattered the silence – the sound of glass breaking above her. Deanna's heart leapt, and despite the pain coursing through her head, she stumbled to her feet and staggered to the window.

She threw open the balcony doors and stepped into the storm, the rain drenching her instantly. The wind whipped her hair across her face, but through the dark, she could see a large tree branch had crashed through a window on the upper floor – into Giovanni's room.

Her pulse quickened. She thought she heard someone cry out in pain, muffled by the wind's ferocity.

Ignoring the throbbing in her head, Deanna grabbed her robe and slippers, making her way up the stairs. Each step sent a dull ache through her skull, the pounding matching the rhythm of the rain outside. She clutched the banister for support, moving cautiously toward Giovanni's bedroom.

As she reached the top of the stairs, the wind howled through the broken window, rattling the villa. The darkness in the hallway made it feel like the house itself was breathing, alive with the weather's fury.

Deanna hesitated at Giovanni's door, her hand hovering over the knob. Her head throbbed so violently she could barely focus; she felt afraid, then reminded herself, *This isn't a horror movie; he could be hurt.* She knocked gently. 'Giovanni, are you all right?'

No response.

Her fingers trembled as she pushed the door open. The room was dark except for the occasional flash of lightning that illuminated the shattered glass on the floor. The bed was empty, the wind rushing through the broken window, making the room feel cold and eerie.

Deanna's breath came in ragged gasps as she stepped further inside, her head pounding with each step. As lightning flashed again, something caught her eye – a door, slightly ajar, concealed at the far end of the room.

A chill ran down her spine. 'Giovanni?' she called out again, her voice barely a whisper above the thunder.

No answer.

Her chest tightened with unease as she approached the door, the throbbing pain in her head intensifying and a wave of nausea threatening to overwhelm her.

She pushed it open, revealing a large, shadowy room behind it. The air was thick with the scent of dust, but as the next flash of lightning lit the room, what she saw made her blood run cold.

Fumbling for a light switch, she turned it on and gasped. Nazi memorabilia covered the walls. Swastika flags draped from the ceiling. Medals, armbands, and propaganda posters littered every surface. It was like stepping into a grotesque shrine, hidden within the house's walls.

Deanna stumbled backwards, her hand flying to her mouth.

Her mind reeled, trying to comprehend what she was seeing. *How could this be here?* She fought the urge to scream, her head spinning from the migraine and the shock.

Then she noticed something else. There were letters – dozens of love letters – all written to Antoinette. She looked at the end of one of them:

One day I know we will be together again. You're mine – Otto.

Her eyes fell on a photograph hanging on the wall, illuminated in the next burst of lightning. Her grandmother Antoinette, standing beside a man in a Nazi uniform – Falkenberg.

Otto von Falkenberg.

Her legs nearly gave out. The horrifying truth slammed into her. Carlos's father wasn't just someone who worked with Falkenberg.

He was Falkenberg.

Her head pounded harder as she tried to make sense of it. *He's alive. He's been here this whole time, pretending to be someone else. How could this be possible?*

Before she could gather her thoughts, she heard footsteps crunching on the broken glass behind her. Deanna whirled around, her heart in her throat.

Standing in the doorway, silhouetted by the storm, was Giovanni – or rather, *Falkenberg*. His cold, predatory eyes gleamed in the darkness as he stepped forward, his voice low and menacing.

'Antoinette,' he whispered softly, his voice dripping with venomous nostalgia. 'I always knew you'd come back to me.'

36

JANUARY 1943

Antoinette

As dawn broke at the safe house, Antoinette lingered in front of the mirror, the deep shadows under her eyes a constant reminder of the hardships she had faced. Whispering a vow to herself and to the one she longed for and the child she missed with her whole heart – 'I have not forgotten my promise to you. I will find you, Benjamin and René, but first I need to fight' – her voice was filled with conviction and a fierce steadfastness.

As she dressed in the clothes Serge had given her, she was reminded of how much she owed him. Serge had been more than just an ally; he had been a friend, a beacon of hope in her darkest hour.

Her new plan was as perilous as it was necessary. She would vanish into the countryside to live with a band of fighters who would sharpen her resolve into a weapon. This was no ordinary group – they were the spearhead of a major operation that could tip the balance of power. Antoinette knew the knowledge she had gathered was key to their success, but it also made her a target. There was no turning back now.

With a creaking echo, Antoinette descended the wooden stairs and was met by Serge, who handed her a steaming cup of dark coffee. For a moment, she allowed herself to savour the warmth, knowing that soon enough, she would need to draw on every ounce of her strength.

'We'll get you new documents soon, and remember, you are not alone. The information you got for us could change the course of this war. Your work now will be just as valuable.'

She pulled him into an embrace, the fear of finality gnawing at her insides. As the war was progressing, it was becoming increasingly dangerous for the members of the Resistance in Paris. She knew all too well this might be the last time she would feel the warmth of his friendship.

She whispered into his ear, 'I won't let you down.' The promise hung between them, fragile but unbreakable.

Before she left, she scribbled a note to her mother explaining she was going away for a short time and asked if they could close up things in her apartment, and collect the boxes she had left packed. She then slipped in the key, leaving it for Serge to post.

Serge's truck rattled through the early morning light; the villages with their red-tiled roofs and winding cobblestone streets seemed to merge together, a blur of familiarity and distance. She couldn't help but reminisce about her old life – the one where she was a devoted wife and mother, playing her violin at the prestigious Conservatoire. A wave of longing washed over her as she gazed out at the rolling hills and quaint farms, knowing that was all behind her now.

Now she was a murderer and a fugitive, her hands stained with blood she could never wash away. But for René and Benjamin, she would endure it all. She rolled her wedding ring around her finger, the only memento she had left of her husband, and drew strength from its presence. She pushed away thoughts of René waking up today in some terrible camp, or worse.

Orgeval was a place that time had forgotten, and the farmhouse stood at the edge of the village, a fortress for the Resistance fighters who called it home. Antoinette's heart warmed when she spotted Florence, her comrade from Paris, waiting in the doorway. Here, in this hidden corner of the world, they would work together, bound by the shared fire of rebellion.

They hugged one another and, arm in arm, they entered the farmhouse. Florence greeted her with familiar warmth. 'My God, Antoinette, you look *exhausted*!'

Antoinette managed a weary smile, responding, 'Tired is the least of my worries.'

Inside, the air was thick with the smell of gun oil and the lingering scent of cigarette smoke. The floorboards were scuffed and worn from the boots of many who had come and gone. Makeshift beds lined the walls, where some weary fighters lay in restless sleep, their faces shadowed by the flickering light of a single lantern. Weapons and radio equipment were scattered across a table, evidence of the constant preparations for battle. A large map of Paris, marked with pins and lines of attack, dominated one wall – an ominous reminder of the war that loomed just beyond the farmhouse's walls.

The two young women retreated to the kitchen, where the quiet allowed them to share the burdens of their journeys. The room was stark, lit by a single bulb that cast long shadows on the walls. The table they sat at showed remnants of the dinner from the night before.

'The Majestic,' Florence began, 'the last time I saw you, you were undercover, right in the lion's den.' She paused, lighting a cigarette, the smoke curling around her words like a veil.

As she took the offered cigarette, Antoinette began to recount the story, her voice low and controlled. Florence listened intently, her solemn nods and intense green eyes

reflecting the bond they shared – two women shaped by the fires of resistance, unyielding in the face of impossible odds.

When she finished her story, Florence reached out and grasped Antoinette's hand, her touch a reassurance that transcended words. 'My God, Antoinette. You have paid such a high price for this information. But it may save countless lives, including my own husband's.'

'I hope so,' Antoinette choked out, the words catching in her throat like a noose around her neck. 'Even if it is too late for mine. I saw a letter that said René was transferred to a camp in Germany.'

The gravity of those words hung heavily between them, both fully aware of the terrible fate that could await René in that distant place.

'You were brave. I still can't believe you managed to get close enough to *kill* one of them,' Florence said, her voice laced with a mix of admiration and disbelief.

Antoinette shrugged, trying to mask the guilt that gnawed at her. 'I had no choice. But it's still hard to kill a man, even when it's necessary.'

'You did what you had to do,' Florence replied, echoing Serge's earlier sentiment, though her tone carried a hardened edge. 'You may have saved countless lives, and you've taken back something for those who have lost everything. Besides, you'll get used to it.' Her voice turned cynical, a bitter smile tugging at her lips.

Antoinette took a long drag of the cigarette her friend had offered, the bitter taste a strange comfort as the smoke made her head spin. The room felt heavier, the air thick with their intense conversation.

'What about you, Florence? What have you been doing?'

Florence's voice was low and steady, almost conspiratorial. 'Since I last saw you, I've been working with this cell.'

'So, what will I be doing here?'

'Starting tomorrow, you'll begin your intensive combat and sabotage training,' Florence replied, stubbing out her cigarette with finality. 'Every member of our group has to be skilled in both physical combat and covert operations. You already have basic training from before; now it's time to hone those skills. We have little time, and even less room for error.'

Her words lingered like a warning as Antoinette exhaled, the smoke curling up to the ceiling, where shadows danced in the dim light. Tomorrow, everything would change again.

'The leader here is Louis,' Florence said, her tone carrying both respect and caution. 'He's a tough, no-nonsense man who has been fighting the Nazis since the very beginning. He's seen too much, lost too much, but he refuses to give up. He's a survivor, and he expects nothing less from those under his command. You'll be helping the cell with everything from blowing up bridges to disrupting Nazi supply lines, and rescuing downed Allied pilots.'

Antoinette's mind whirled with the implications of what her new life would entail. Images of her husband and son flashed through her thoughts, their faces blurring with the smoke and rubble of war. The cosy life they once had felt like a distant memory, almost a dream.

'I can do that,' Antoinette said, her voice steady, though her heart raced. The words felt like a promise to herself, one she was determined to keep, no matter the cost.

Florence gave her a small, reassuring smile, slipping her arm around Antoinette's shoulder. 'You'll do great, Antoinette. You've already shown more courage than most. Now, let's get something to eat. The rest of us are out tonight on a mission, but you'll start your training tomorrow.'

As they ate, the two women talked about their lives, their struggles, and their hopes for the future. Florence spoke of the dangers they had faced, the close calls, and the lives lost.

Antoinette spoke about the Majestic. But the mood was buoyant as they also joked with one another and connected like a family. Antoinette couldn't help but feel a mix of emotions as she looked around the room. She was both overwhelmed and excited by this new life she was stepping into.

She had left her old life behind, but in doing so, she had also left behind everything good about her past.

Later that night in the dim light of the kitchen, the other fighters gathered around the table for a quick meal before their mission. As they arrived and connected, Florence introduced Antoinette, and then as they ate, they told her their stories. There was Louis, the leader, a broad-shouldered man with a weathered face that spoke of years of hardship. His greying hair and deep-set eyes gave him an air of authority, and though his demeanour was stern, all of the cell knew his heart was as strong as his dedication, as Florence had explained.

Next to him sat Franck, a tall, lanky figure with a shock of dark hair that fell into his eyes. He had the quick hands of a pickpocket and the easy smile of a charmer, but his playful nature belied a deep-seated anger. Franck had lost his younger brother to a Nazi firing squad, and though he often masked his pain with humour, there was a hardness in his gaze that hinted at the grief he carried.

Across the table, Paul was sharpening a knife, his strong, calloused hands moving with practised precision. A former boxer, Paul's muscular frame and chiselled jaw made him an intimidating presence. His nose had been broken more than once, giving him a rugged look, but it was his quiet intensity that set him apart. Paul rarely spoke of his past, Florence informed her in a hushed tone, but everyone knew he had been a family man before the war took everything from him.

At the end of the table was Marc, a wiry man with sharp features and piercing blue eyes that seemed to see everything. He was the group's explosives expert, his nimble fingers always busy crafting bombs from whatever materials he could find. Marc had been an engineer before the war, and his meticulous nature made him invaluable to the Resistance. Yet beneath his calm exterior lay a simmering rage, fuelled by the loss of his fiancée.

As they shared their meal, the mood in the room was light, almost playful. Jokes were exchanged, and laughter echoed through the farmhouse, a brief reprieve from the darkness of their reality. Franck teased Marc about his latest explosive creation, while Louis, up till then so serious, cracked a rare smile as he recounted a humorous moment from a past mission.

Despite the camaraderie, there was an unspoken understanding, a bond forged through shared pain and sacrifice. It was obvious that each man had lost something to this war, but they had found a new family in each other. And though their lives were filled with danger, they faced it together, united by their cause and their unyielding determination to see it through to the end.

It was only as all the fighters left to complete their night mission and she headed for her bunk that the emotion of all Antoinette had been through hit her. In the quiet of the deserted farmhouse, she began to sob uncontrollably, the weight of her actions and the uncertainty of her future crashing down on her like a tidal wave. The tears came with fierce, silent sobs that wracked her entire body, releasing the pent-up tension and fear she had been carrying since the stabbing.

In the darkness of the room, Antoinette felt utterly alone, the sounds of her grief echoing off the walls of the farmhouse. She missed René desperately, his warm embrace and reassuring smile a distant memory in the face of the harsh reality of her war. Would she ever see him again? Would he understand why she had to do what she did? And would her precious son ever find out what his mother had become?

She wasn't sure, but what she did know was that she had made a choice and, right or wrong, she would have to live with the consequences.

37

BRAZIL, 2012

Deanna

Deanna's body was frozen in terror, her heart beating so loudly it drowned out all other sounds.

She tried to speak, but her voice was barely a whisper, her throat constricted. 'You're confused,' Deanna finally managed. 'I'm not Antoinette. My name is Deanna – Antoinette was my *grandmother*.'

A sinister smile crept across his face as he took a step closer, his voice lowering to a dangerous growl. 'You may have changed your name again, but I know that face. Even if you don't know mine. The plastic surgery has given me the freedom for a new life. Do you like it?' He sounded fully German now; the Italian accent was gone, as was the happy-go-lucky demeanour. His eyes gleamed with a dark and twisted madness, sending chills through Deanna's body.

Her mind frantically searched for a way out of this tense and terrifying situation. The storm outside raged on, the windows rattling with the force of the wind – a mirror of the turmoil brewing inside her. With only one door in the hidden room and Falkenberg blocking her path, and in her weakened state, she felt trapped and helpless.

Falkenberg's presence filled the entire room, suffocating and overwhelming. As he moved toward her, he slowly unbuttoned his shirt.

'Did you see all the pictures of us here on the walls? Such fond memories we shared, don't you agree?' He pulled down his shirt, revealing a jagged scar that ran across his back, as his voice took on a sinister edge. 'Do you remember this, Antoinette? The night you stabbed me in the back because of that pathetic Jew. You nearly killed me too. It took *months* for me to recover. And then when news of the war's end hit, it was easy to slip away, disappear, and become someone else. I knew Giovanni was dead – my forces took care of him after we tortured out all the information I needed to find you. Imagine my surprise when I found out who he really was – the only living relative connected to that violin. I knew that would help me find you again. I just had to wait. I kept myself fit. I look good for a man of my age, don't I?'

His eyes blazed with fury as he spoke, years of obsession and resentment bubbling to the surface.

Deanna's breath caught in her throat as she realised the depth of this man's delusion. He wasn't just a ghost from her grandmother's past – he was Deanna's living nightmare too.

'I've waited *decades* for this moment,' Falkenberg growled, his hand reaching out towards her.

Deanna's survival instincts kicked into overdrive as she ducked beneath Falkenberg's outstretched arm, sprinting towards the door with primal desperation. But her hopes of escape were quickly crushed as his iron grip closed around her arm, yanking her back with a force that shocked her to her core. Agonising pain shot through her shoulder as she stumbled and crashed to the ground.

'You think you can get away from me? You are mine! You always were.'

Falkenberg's voice was low, controlled, but laced with menace. His grip tightened, his fingers pressing bruises into her skin as he pulled her closer. The polished façade of Giovanni had crumbled completely, leaving behind something colder, something ruthless. The room felt smaller, the air thick with something more oppressive than the storm raging outside. Her pounding head and his unwavering determination held her in place – there was nowhere to run.

His breath was slow, deliberate, as if savouring the moment. 'Just like before... always causing trouble, Antoinette. Always fighting me.'

Deanna fought with every ounce of strength she had, fuelled by fear and desperation. The rain pounded against the windows, a symphony of chaos that mirrored the storm inside. She struggled against Falkenberg's grip, her eyes wild with terror. Heat radiated from his body, and the scent of sweat clung to the air, thick and suffocating. Panic surged through her. She screamed, but her voice was swallowed by the howling wind and relentless rain.

'I knew the violin would bring you back to me,' he rasped between bared teeth, revealing his true intentions. Deanna felt anger boiling inside her as the truth became undeniable. This man had not been her grandmother's lover, but her grandmother's tormentor. He was nothing but a monster in human form.

Suddenly, she felt an anger she had never known, not just for herself but for her own grandmother, who had suffered unimaginable horrors at this man's hands. This wasn't just about her survival now, but about avenging the past and bringing an end to this monster's reign. Deanna mustered every ounce of strength left in her and bit down viciously on Falkenberg's hand.

The shock on his face was fleeting, but it gave Deanna just

enough time to push him off her with all her might. Falkenberg rolled onto his side, momentarily off-balance. Deanna wasted no time, getting up and darting toward the door, her body shaking with anger and fear.

'You never had my grandmother, and you will never have me!' she spat back at him. 'I may not be Antoinette, but I certainly share her spirit.'

Just then, the distant crunch of tyres on gravel cut through the storm. Hope flickered in her chest.

She flung open the door and sprinted towards the window, her voice straining as she screamed. She prayed that her cries would be heard through the shattered glass.

Footsteps echoed through the house as Falkenberg lunged at her again. Carlos burst into the room. His eyes widened in horror as he took in the scene – Deanna struggling beneath his father's iron grip, Falkenberg's face twisted with mania.

Without hesitation, Carlos reached his father, wrenching Deanna free. Falkenberg staggered back, his hold on her finally broken as Carlos shielded her, his protective stance firm.

'What the hell are you doing?' Carlos shouted, his voice shaking with emotion, as he pushed his father down onto the bed.

Falkenberg's eyes darted between Carlos and Deanna, his obsession still burning in his gaze. 'She *belongs* to me, Carlos. She always has,' he spat out, his words venomous.

Carlos turned on the lights, and the room flooded with an eerie glow. Seeing the open hidden door, Carlos looked inside, shocked at the now fully illuminated shrine – a grotesque homage to the past. A chilling tableau, a dark tribute to a man obsessed with power and hate.

Carlos swore under his breath, stepping back in disgust. 'What the hell is all this, Papà?'

Falkenberg's eyes gleamed, the madness fully unleashed. 'This is my legacy, Carlos. This is what should have been mine

– ours. The world should have remembered Hitler not as a villain, but as a hero, a beacon of greatness!'

A voice called from the hallway. 'Carlos. What's going on?'

Carlos clenched his fists, rage and shame flickering across his face. 'It's okay, Maria. Stay there. I'll be right out.' He turned back to his father, eyes dark with fury. 'You don't ever bring her in here. You hear me?' His voice cracked, and Deanna could see the internal struggle – the pain of discovering his father's twisted reality and his desire to protect Maria.

Deanna, her body aching, looked at Carlos. Their eyes met, and in that moment, a silent understanding passed between them. Not to share this with his sister, at least not yet.

Sliding the hidden door shut, Carlos locked away the horrors within.

In the hallway, Maria hovered, her expression a mix of concern and confusion. 'I put Felicity to bed with the medication the doctor gave her. Is Papà okay? What happened?'

Carlos placed a hand on her shoulder. 'It's nothing, Maria. The storm shattered the window, that's all. I will clear it up and deal with my father. Why don't you go downstairs and get Deanna some tea?'

Maria and Deanna moved down to the kitchen, but the tension remained thick in the air. Deanna sat, trying to recover from what had just happened.

As the kettle whistled, Maria noticed the red marks on Deanna's arm. 'Deanna, what happened to you?'

Deanna winced but forced a smile. 'It's nothing. I just knocked into some furniture in the dark.'

Maria didn't seem convinced, but she didn't push further. They sipped their tea in silence, but Deanna's mind was still trapped in that dark room, haunted by the grotesque collection of memories and madness Falkenberg had displayed. Along with the feeling that this was far from over.

Later, when Maria went to check on her father, Carlos

came down and lingered. Once they were alone, he turned to Deanna. 'What happened up there?'

Taking a deep breath, Deanna recounted the terrifying encounter. With each word, Carlos's expression darkened.

'I'm so sorry, Deanna,' he whispered, his voice thick with guilt. 'I had no idea he was truly Falkenberg; how is that even possible?'

'You can't hold the truth back from Maria; she needs to know. He is a Nazi, Carlos. Your father is a Nazi. No wonder your mother left him and you were estranged for so many years. She must have found out somehow and wanted to protect you.'

Carlos nodded, his face a mix of sadness and anger. 'I'll tell her. I also feel an obligation to turn him in. He may still be wanted for his war crimes.'

Deanna placed a comforting hand on his arm, understanding in her gaze. 'I'm sorry this happened.'

Carlos sighed deeply and leaned back in his chair. 'No, I'm sorry you came all this way only to be assaulted by him. Looking back now, I should have seen the signs, but I didn't. I wanted to have a relationship with my father, even if it was late in his life. I just wanted... to believe in him.'

She reached out and took his hand, holding it for a moment longer than necessary, the warmth of his grip seeping into her skin.

'I should be comforting you, after what you've been through.' He sighed.

She smiled wistfully. 'As horrible as that just was, I know the truth now – that my grandmother was exactly what I always thought, a strong, resilient woman who would never back down from injustice or tyranny. I feel closer to her than ever. We both have that spirit, that fire, burning inside of us.'

Carlos drew closer, and Deanna's breath hitched slightly, the air between them suddenly thick with something unspoken. She looked into his eyes – saw the vulnerability there, the gratitude, but also something more. The intensity of the moment sent a pulse of awareness through her, a realisation that maybe, just maybe, there was something more between them than she had been willing to admit.

She pulled her hand back, the loss of his touch immediate and unsettling. 'I'm just glad you heard me. I'm not sure what would've happened if you hadn't...'

Carlos stood, and for a moment, the space between them felt electric. He hesitated, his eyes lingering on her, his expression conflicted. 'Deanna... I know this isn't the right time, but... after everything we've been through today, I need you to know – you've become more important to me than just as a friend to my family.'

Deanna's heart thudded in her chest, his words hanging in the air, heavy with meaning. She opened her mouth to respond, but the words wouldn't come.

Carlos's gaze locked on hers. For a moment, Deanna was lost in the depth of his eyes, the connection between them palpable, undeniable. She nodded, unsure of what to say but certain that something between them had shifted.

As Carlos turned to leave, a new question bubbled to the surface: What exactly was growing between them? And where would it lead?

38

JANUARY 1943

Antoinette

The dawn light barely penetrated the thick forest canopy as Antoinette stood at the edge of a small clearing, her breath forming misty clouds in the cool morning air. Her bed in the farmhouse was a distant memory, replaced by the stark reality of the rough training ground laid out before her.

Louis, ever the stoic leader, was already waiting, his broad shoulders and greying hair making him an imposing figure against the backdrop of dense trees. He was flanked by Franck, Paul, and Marc, their expressions a blend of curiosity and scepticism as they watched Antoinette take her first steps into the crucible that would forge her into a fighter.

'Today, we start with the basics,' Louis announced, his voice carrying the authority of a man who had seen too much, lost too much. 'Combat, sabotage, survival – these are the tools of our trade. You'll learn to use them, and you'll learn fast. There's no room for error in our line of work.'

Antoinette nodded, her throat dry as she struggled to mask her anxiety. This was not the life she had envisioned for herself

– a life of music, love, and family. But that life had been torn away, and now she had to adapt, to survive.

Louis led her to a patch of bare earth where a series of crude dummies had been set up, each marked with vital points. 'We start with hand-to-hand combat,' he said, demonstrating a series of strikes, blocks, and counters with the precision of a seasoned warrior. 'You need to be quick, decisive. Hesitation will get you killed.'

Franck stepped forward, his lanky frame deceptively agile as he began to spar with Louis. Antoinette watched, absorbing every movement, every tactic. Franck moved with the fluidity of a dancer, his dark hair falling into his eyes as he ducked and weaved. But there was an edge to his movements, a barely contained fury that hinted at the pain he carried inside.

'Your turn,' Louis said, stepping back to give Antoinette space.

She swallowed hard and faced Franck. He offered her a small, almost teasing smile, but his eyes held no humour. This was a test, and she knew he wouldn't go easy on her.

The first blow came fast, a jab aimed at her midsection. Antoinette barely blocked it, the force of the impact sending a shockwave through her arms. Franck followed with a swift kick, and she stumbled, barely maintaining her footing.

'*Focus!*' Louis barked. 'Don't think – just react.'

Gritting her teeth, Antoinette steadied herself, her mind racing to keep up with Franck's relentless assault. She managed to deflect another punch, then ducked under a swing aimed at her head. Franck's movements were almost too fast to follow, but she began to see patterns, openings in his attacks.

She struck back, a quick jab to his ribs. It connected, and Franck grunted, but he didn't stop. He pressed harder, forcing her to adapt, to fight back with every ounce of strength she had.

By the time Louis called for a break, Antoinette was drenched in sweat, her muscles aching. But she had held her own, and that small victory filled her with a fierce sense of pride.

'Not bad,' Franck said, wiping sweat from his own brow. His voice was light, almost playful, but there was respect in his eyes. 'You've got potential.'

Before she could respond, Marc appeared by her side, handing her a canteen of water. His fingers brushed hers briefly as she accepted it.

'You did well,' Marc said, his voice low and encouraging. 'Franck likes to show off, but you held your ground.'

Antoinette managed a small smile, grateful for his kindness. 'Thank you. I think I'm going to need all the encouragement I can get.'

'You'll get there,' Marc assured her, his tone carrying a personal warmth that set him apart from the other men. 'If you need help with anything, let me know.'

The morning passed in a blur of drills and exercises. Louis pushed her to her limits, showing no mercy as he drilled her in close combat, knife fighting, and basic sabotage techniques. Paul, with his quiet intensity, taught her how to handle a knife – how to throw it, how to use it to kill. His hands, rough and calloused, guided hers with surprising gentleness, and she found herself learning faster than she had expected.

'Don't think about the target as a person,' Paul advised, his voice low and steady. 'Just focus on the task. It's about survival, nothing more.'

But Antoinette found it impossible to disconnect the two. Every time she aimed the knife, every time she imagined plunging it into flesh, she saw the face of the man she had killed – the Nazi officer whose life she had ended in a moment of desperation. The memory gnawed at her, a constant reminder of the darkness she had stepped into.

Louis seemed to sense her struggle. During a brief break, he pulled her aside, his gruff exterior softening slightly. 'I know what happened in Paris. You did what you had to do,' he said, echoing the words Florence had spoken to her. 'We've all done things we never thought possible since the war. But you can't let that thought consume you. You have to find a way to live with it, or it will destroy you.'

Antoinette nodded, though she wasn't sure she believed him. The guilt was a heavy weight on her soul, and she didn't know if she could ever shed it.

As the week wore on, the training intensified. Louis introduced her to the art of sabotage – how to rig explosives, how to disable vehicles, how to bring down bridges. Marc took the lead here, his sharp features softening slightly as he patiently walked her through the process.

'This is where precision matters,' Marc said, his voice calm and methodical as he demonstrated how to set a charge. 'A single mistake can cost lives – yours and others.'

Antoinette watched closely as Marc's nimble fingers worked with the explosives, turning them into deadly tools of resistance. There was a cold efficiency to his movements, a reflection of the detachment that simmered beneath his calm exterior. She wondered what had happened to him before the war, what had turned him into the man he was now.

'You try,' Marc said, handing her the components of a small explosive device.

Her hands shook slightly as she took the pieces, but Marc's steady gaze gave her the confidence to continue. She followed his instructions carefully, focusing on each step, each connection. When she was done, Marc inspected her work with a critical eye, then gave a small nod of approval.

'Good,' he said. 'You're learning.'

Antoinette exhaled, relief flooding through her. It was a small victory, but in this world, every victory counted.

· · ·

At the end of the week, the fighters gathered around a small campfire they had built near the edge of the clearing. The day's training had pushed them to their limits, their bodies aching from relentless drills, but exhaustion gave way to a quiet solidarity.

Antoinette sat between Florence and Franck, the warmth of the fire a welcome comfort against the cool evening air. The group spoke in low tones, their laughter occasionally breaking the stillness as they recounted stories of past missions.

'You did well this week,' Florence said, her voice soft as she nudged Antoinette with her elbow. 'I think you even surprised Louis.'

Antoinette smiled faintly, the lingering doubts still occupying her thoughts. 'I'm not sure I'm really cut out for this,' she admitted. 'I am a musician after all, not a soldier.'

Florence's eyes softened with understanding. 'None of us were born for this, Antoinette. But this war didn't give us a choice. We all had to become something we never imagined. The important thing is that you're here, and you're fighting.'

Antoinette nodded, as she glanced around at the others – at Louis, who stared into the fire with a faraway look in his eyes; at Paul, his hands always busy to keep away his fears; at Marc, who sat quietly, his thoughts unreadable. They had all been ordinary people once, before the war had twisted their lives into something unrecognisable.

As the night deepened, the conversation turned more serious. Louis leaned forward, his expression hardening as he spoke. 'We've received word that a supply convoy will be passing through a nearby village tomorrow, and we need to intercept it.'

Antoinette's heart skipped a beat at the gravity of his words. This was it – her first real mission.

'We'll be splitting into two teams,' Louis continued. 'Marc and I will handle the explosives. Franck, Paul, and Florence will take out the guards and secure the area. Antoinette, you'll be with me and Marc. Your job is to cover us while we set the charges.'

The weight of the assignment settled on her, but she nodded, determined not to let her fear show. 'I understand,' she said, her voice steady.

Louis met her gaze, his eyes searching hers for any sign of hesitation. 'Good. We move at dawn. Now, get some rest.'

The group dispersed, each fighter retreating into their own thoughts as they prepared for the mission ahead. Antoinette lingered by the fire, her mind racing with a thousand what-ifs. What if she failed? What if she made a mistake that cost lives? What if she couldn't go through with it?

Florence found her, sensing her turmoil. 'It's natural to be scared,' she said gently. 'But you're not alone. We're in this together.'

Antoinette looked at her, grateful for the reassurance, but the fear gnawed at her. She had never been more terrified in her life.

The night was restless. Antoinette tossed and turned on her makeshift bed, her mind refusing to quiet. Memories of René and Benjamin haunted her – images of their faces, their smiles, the life they had shared. She rubbed her wedding ring, drawing strength from the memory of her husband's love.

But the guilt was always there, lurking in the shadows of her mind. The image of how Falkenberg's life had drained away beneath her hands. It had been necessary, she knew that, but it didn't make it any easier to bear.

Finally, unable to sleep, Antoinette rose and slipped outside, seeking solace in the cool night air. The forest was quiet, the only sound the rustle of leaves in the gentle breeze.

She walked to the edge of the clearing, her heart heavy with what lay ahead.

As she stood there, lost in thought, a rustle of leaves announced company. Turning, she saw Marc approaching, his wiry frame cutting a lean silhouette in the muted moonlight. His sharp features were accentuated by the soft glow, and his piercing blue eyes, which always seemed to see everything, locked onto hers with quiet intensity.

'Couldn't sleep?' His voice was low, threading through the quiet night.

Antoinette shook her head. 'Too much on my mind.'

Marc nodded, stepping closer, his presence both commanding and comforting. 'You're worried about tomorrow.'

'Aren't you?' she replied, her voice barely above a whisper.

He gave a small, knowing chuckle, his smile tinged with melancholy. 'Fear has been a constant companion on too many nights to count. But I've learned it's not the presence of fear that defines us; it's how we wield it.' His gaze was steady, piercing through the darkness. 'Fear sharpens us, Antoinette. It hones our instincts. If we let it, it can guide us to do things we never imagined possible.'

Antoinette looked up, looking for the sorrow she had seen before in his eyes, but finding instead a purpose that mirrored her own burgeoning determination.

'I'm scared of who I will become after today, of who I have become already,' she admitted, her voice quivering with uncertainty.

Marc reached out, his hand resting reassuringly on her shoulder. 'Every one of us has faced that moment, standing on the precipice, unsure if we could step off.'

His eyes softened, the moonlight illuminating the profound sorrow returning. 'I lost someone once,' Marc whispered, his words carrying the gravity of his untold story. 'She was everything to me. Her loss... it didn't just bring me here; it ignited a fire within me that burns relentlessly. This fight, it's more than just survival or vengeance. It's about shielding others from the agony of such a loss.' He paused, his voice firm yet thick with emotion. 'I'll do whatever it takes to end this war. If that means killing the enemy, so be it. My hands carry the stains, but if it means saving the innocent, preserving even a fragment of what we once called normal, then I'm willing to bear that burden.'

Antoinette felt a resonance deep within her soul, a shared ache with Marc's revelation, reflecting her own harrowing losses. His dedication fortified her own, binding her to this cause not just through shared duty but through a profound understanding of what was truly at stake.

He gave her a small, reassuring smile. 'Rest now. We need you sharp tomorrow.'

As Marc walked away, a quiet strength settled in Antoinette's bones. The night remained dark, the path uncertain, but a resilient flame had been kindled within her. She wasn't just fighting for survival now; she was fighting for a cause, for all their loved ones, for every moment René and Benjamin deserved.

She returned to her bunk, her steps lighter than before. Tomorrow would indeed be a long day, and as sleep finally claimed her, she clung to the image of René's face.

His love would be the armour she'd wear into battle.

39

BRAZIL, 2012

Deanna

The next morning, Deanna sat at the breakfast table, her body still tense from the events of the night before. Every movement felt mechanical, as if her mind had yet to process the terror she had just survived. Felicity sat beside her, pale, her eyes speaking volumes – they needed to leave, and quickly.

Felicity reached out and squeezed Deanna's hand briefly, offering silent support. 'Are you okay?' she asked in a low voice, her gaze sharp with concern. Deanna had already filled her friend in on what had happened.

Deanna nodded, though the tightness in her chest made it hard to breathe. She glanced at Carlos across the table, where he sat with his head down, fingers tracing the rim of his coffee cup. Maria moved around the kitchen, setting out plates of fruit and bread. Her usual cheer was dimmed, her eyes red from crying. Carlos had obviously told her who her father really was.

Deanna exchanged a glance with Felicity, who gave her a small, encouraging nod. Taking a deep breath, Deanna spoke up. 'Carlos, Maria, we need to talk.'

Carlos's head lifted slowly, his eyes meeting hers with a grim understanding. Maria, on the other hand, turned from the counter, concern already clouding her features. 'What is it?' she asked, her gaze moving between them.

Deanna hesitated. She glanced at Carlos, but his expression remained unreadable.

'We've decided to leave the villa. It's time.'

The room fell silent, the only sound the gentle clatter of plates as Maria placed them on the table. Her eyes widened in surprise. 'Leave? But why?' she asked, her voice wavering. 'Is it because of Papà?'

Carlos tensed, his grip tightening on his cup. Felicity shifted uncomfortably beside Deanna, her eyes narrowing as the tension in the room built.

Maria's legs gave out, and she collapsed onto the nearest chair, her face pale and stricken. 'How could he do this? How could he lie to us like this?' Her voice broke as the tears began to fall, her sobs filling the quiet kitchen.

Felicity was at her side in an instant, placing a comforting arm around her shoulders.

Deanna's heart ached for Maria. She had only known this family for a short time, but already felt so close to them; the pain of betrayal was written so clearly on Maria's face. Deanna had witnessed the truth unfold last night, but it was Maria who would have to live with it now, and forever.

Carlos moved to his sister's side, kneeling beside her as she sobbed into her hands. 'I'm so sorry, Maria. I didn't want to believe it either. But we can't hide from the truth any more. I need to call the police.'

Maria shook her head, her sobs growing louder. 'I don't understand... how could he have done this? How could I have not known? So many years we never had a relationship with him, and then when we found him he lied... I love him, Carlos.'

Carlos placed his hand over hers, his voice gentle but firm.

'He's still our father, but he's also someone else – a man with a terrible past. We can't ignore what he did. He may still be wanted for his crimes.'

The room fell into a heavy silence, broken only by the sound of Maria's quiet sobs. Deanna sat frozen in her seat, watching the siblings struggle to come to terms with the truth. Felicity remained close to Maria, offering what comfort she could, though it was clear that no words could truly heal this.

Later, when the police arrived, the procedure was swift but harrowing. Falkenberg was questioned and escorted away, but he showed no remorse. His eyes gleamed with the same twisted obsession as before, and as they led him out of the villa, he shot one last venomous glance at Deanna.

'This isn't over, Antoinette; it never will be over,' he hissed, his voice filled with delusional certainty.

Deanna shivered at his words as Felicity put her arm around her. But as the police car disappeared from sight, she knew it was a lie. She had confronted the ghost of her grandmother's past and survived.

Carlos placed his arm around his sister. Maria had been through a storm of emotions, but there was a strength in her now, a determination. She looked at Carlos and Deanna, her eyes red-rimmed. 'We'll get through this,' she said, her voice strong.

Carlos gave her a small, sad smile. 'Yes, we will.'

That evening was calm, a stark contrast to the chaos that had engulfed the villa earlier. The police had kept Falkenberg overnight. The storm of the night before had passed, leaving behind a gentle breeze that rustled through the trees and carried the faint scent of saltwater from the nearby coast. The air was crisp, refreshing, and full of the kind of peace that Deanna hadn't felt in what seemed like days.

Inside the villa, Felicity was bustling about in her bedroom, packing the last of her things for the next day's departure. Maria had gone to bed early, worn out from the emotional toll of the day.

Needing a glass of water, Deanna went down to the kitchen. Seeing the balcony door open, she was drawn to the cool embrace of the night. The stars were scattered like diamonds across the velvet darkness, and the cool air beckoned her outside. Without a second thought, she stepped out onto the balcony, drawn to the serenity of the moment.

The stone beneath her bare feet felt cool, grounding her as she breathed in the night air. The soft sounds of the ocean in the distance, the rustling of leaves, the occasional croak of a distant frog – it all combined to create a stillness she desperately needed. Even with all the turmoil, she realised she was going to miss Brazil. Her mind still swirled with all that had happened, but out here, she felt a momentary release, like she could finally exhale.

As she walked out to the balcony, she noticed she wasn't alone. Carlos was standing near the edge, his silhouette illuminated by the moonlight. His hands rested on the railing, his gaze fixed on the horizon, lost in thought.

Deanna hesitated for a moment, unsure if she should intrude on his solitude. But before she could retreat, Carlos turned, sensing her presence. His expression softened when he saw her, a faint smile crossing his face.

'It's beautiful, isn't it?' he said, his voice low and gentle.

Deanna nodded, walking slowly to stand beside him. 'It's hard to believe so much beauty can exist after a day of so much turmoil,' she admitted, leaning her arms on the railing next to him.

Carlos nodded, his gaze returning to the distant sea. 'Yeah, I know what you mean.'

For a moment, they stood in companionable silence, both of

them taking in the beauty of the night. The breeze played with Deanna's hair, and she pulled her sweater tighter around her, feeling a strange mixture of calm and restlessness.

After a while, Carlos spoke again, his voice softer this time, as if he were revealing something he hadn't shared with many. 'You know, I haven't told you much about my past... but there's something I want you to know.'

Deanna turned to him, sensing the weight behind his words.

His voice was suddenly tinged with sadness. He took a deep breath, his eyes still focused on the dark horizon. 'I was married once,' he began, his voice steady but laced with emotion. 'Her name was Camila. She was everything to me. We met when we were young, grew up together really, and fell in love over time. She had this way of making the world feel brighter, like no matter how bad things got, there was always hope. We were very happy.'

Deanna listened quietly, her heart aching at the pain she could hear in his voice.

'But five years ago,' Carlos continued, his voice faltering slightly, 'there was a car accident. She was driving home from work, and it was raining. Another car lost control and hit her. She didn't... make it.'

Deanna felt a lump rise in her throat. She reached out and placed her hand on his arm, offering silent support. 'I'm so sorry, Carlos,' she whispered.

He nodded, his eyes glistening in the moonlight. 'After that, I shut down. I didn't want to feel anything. I couldn't. I lost myself in work, in distractions... anything to avoid facing the fact that she was gone. And when my mother passed not long after, I felt like I had lost my anchor. That's when I started looking for my father. I thought... maybe if I found him, I could feel like I belonged somewhere again. Like I could rebuild my life.'

Deanna squeezed his arm gently, her heart aching for him. 'It must have been so hard,' she said softly.

Carlos turned to look at her then, his dark-eyed gaze intense and searching. 'It was. And when I found him, I thought Maria and I would finally get that chance to have a family again, to have someone in our lives. But then everything I've learned about him... it's shattered that hope. It's like losing Camila all over again.'

Deanna knew that pain – losing something you thought you had, the dream of what could have been. 'You're not alone, Carlos,' she said quietly. 'You have Maria. And... you have me. I hope we can continue to be friends.'

Carlos's gaze lingered on hers, and for a moment, they were suspended in that quiet understanding. He reached out and took her hand, his touch warm and steady. 'I've been thinking a lot about that lately,' he said, his voice a little shaky. 'About how much you've come to mean to me. Even in the short time we've known each other.'

Deanna's breath caught in her throat. She hadn't expected such an honest response and as she looked into his eyes, she saw the vulnerability there, the raw honesty he was offering her.

Carlos continued, his thumb brushing softly over the back of her hand. 'After losing Camila, I never thought I could let anyone in again. But you... you've changed that. Our growing friendship means a lot to me.'

Deanna's emotions swirled in her chest, her cheeks flushed as she swallowed down the lump in her throat. From time to time, she had seen something warm towards her in his eyes, but he had kept his emotions carefully guarded, his focus always on protecting and providing for Maria. She didn't know how to respond – this man, who had been through so much, was opening up to her in a way that felt real. And she couldn't deny the pull she felt towards him, the connection that had grown between them.

'To me too,' she finally stuttered out.

Carlos smiled, a soft, almost relieved smile, and for a moment, the weight of everything they had been through seemed to lift, leaving only the quiet promise of something new.

Something unspoken between them, but undeniably real.

40

JANUARY 1943

Antoinette

The predawn light was a dim, ghostly grey as Antoinette and the others silently prepared for their mission. The air was thick with tension, each fighter moving with a quiet efficiency, born of countless similar mornings. Antoinette felt the weight of her rifle in her hands, its cold metal a reminder of the grim reality she was stepping into. She had trained for this, had been pushed to her limits, but she knew nothing could fully prepare her for the real thing.

Louis stood at the centre of the small group, his presence commanding without a word spoken. His greying hair was slicked back, his eyes sharp and focused. He glanced at each of them in turn, a final, silent check to ensure they were ready.

'Remember the plan,' he said, his voice low but firm. 'Marc will handle the explosives. Antoinette, you're with us. Your job is to cover his back while he sets the charges. Franck, Paul, and Florence will take out the guards and secure the area. No unnecessary risks, no heroics. We get in, we do the job, and we get out. Understood?'

A chorus of nods followed. Antoinette felt a surge of fear tighten within her, but she forced herself to focus, to push the fear aside. She was no longer a musician, no longer a wife and mother – at least not in this life.

She was a Resistance fighter, and she had a job to do.

As they moved out in silence, Marc fell into step beside Antoinette, glancing her way for the briefest moment. 'You ready?' he murmured, his voice low enough that only she could hear.

She nodded, the tension in her chest making it hard to speak. Marc offered her a faint smile, a small gesture of reassurance that steadied her nerves more than she cared to admit.

The forest enveloped them in its dark embrace, the heavy canopy above muting what little light the early morning offered. Every snap of a twig, every rustle of leaves, set Antoinette's nerves on edge. The rifle in her hands felt alien, yet she gripped it tightly, determined to prove she could do this.

As they neared their destination, Louis signalled for them to stop. They crouched low behind a thicket, peering out at the small cluster of buildings that made up the sleepy village. The convoy hadn't arrived yet, but it wouldn't be long.

'Marc, you know where to place the charges,' Louis whispered. Marc nodded, his piercing blue eyes scanning the area with the precision of a hawk. 'Antoinette, you stay with him. Keep watch and be ready to move when I give the signal.'

Antoinette nodded, her throat too dry to speak. She could feel the sweat on her palms, the tension growing but she forced herself to remain steady. For a fleeting moment, she could hear Benjamin's squeals of laughter as René chased him through the park, their faces lit with pure joy. The innocence of that life felt painfully distant now, a cruel contrast to the dark reality she faced. The ache of what she had lost threatened to overwhelm her, but she pushed it down, and calmed herself ready for what she needed to do.

Louis gave the signal, and they moved out. The village was eerily quiet, the kind of quiet that preceded violence.

Antoinette followed Marc closely as they slipped through the shadows, moving from cover to cover with practised ease. The village was a stark contrast to the dense forest they had just left – its cobblestone streets and old stone buildings seemed almost dreamlike in the early morning light.

Marc led her to a narrow alley between two buildings, out of sight from the main road. He crouched low, unpacking the explosives from his bag with the precision of a craftsman. Antoinette kept watch, her eyes darting back and forth, her grip tight on the rifle.

'How long will it take?' she whispered, her voice barely audible.

'Not long,' Marc replied, his focus never wavering. Then, as if sensing her unease, he added, 'You're doing great.' His words, though simple, carried a warmth that momentarily eased the tension in her chest.

The moments stretched out, each second feeling like an eternity. She could hear the faint rustling of Marc's movements as he worked, the distant calls of birds, the soft rustle of the wind. But then, another sound – a low, rumbling noise that grew louder with each passing second.

The convoy was approaching.

Marc finished setting the last charge and stood up, giving her a quick nod. 'It's time. Stay close to me.'

As they moved back towards the main road, Marc placed a steadying hand on her arm for the briefest moment, guiding her to a better vantage point. The touch was fleeting, professional, but Antoinette couldn't help noticing how deliberate it felt – as though he was silently offering her something more than just strength.

The first truck came into view. Louis was already in position, hidden in the shadows of a building on the opposite side of the street. Franck, Paul, and Florence were further down, their silhouettes barely visible in the dim light.

The convoy rolled toward the village, the heavy rumble of the trucks reverberating off the stone walls. Antoinette counted three vehicles – two cargo trucks and a smaller car, likely carrying the officers. Her breath caught in her throat as the convoy slowed to navigate a tight corner right in front of them.

Louis raised his hand, the signal they had been waiting for. The next few moments would decide everything.

In a fluid motion, Marc stepped out of the alley, detonator in hand. He pressed the button.

The explosion was deafening, a burst of fire and smoke that tore through the first truck, flipping it onto its side. The blast wave knocked Antoinette back, but she scrambled to her feet, blood surging through her veins. The second truck skidded to a halt, its occupants disoriented by the sudden attack.

'Now!' Louis shouted, emerging from his hiding place, gun in hand.

Antoinette didn't think – she reacted. She took aim at one of the German soldiers who was stumbling out of the second truck and pulled the trigger. The recoil jolted her shoulder, but she barely felt it. The soldier crumpled to the ground, and she shifted her aim to the next target.

The firefight erupted in full force. Bullets flew through the air, pinging off the stone walls and kicking up dirt from the cobblestones. Franck and Paul were already in the thick of it, their movements swift and lethal. Franck, with his quick reflexes, took down two soldiers in rapid succession, his anger fuelling his every move. Paul was a force of nature, his knife flashing in the morning light as he took down a soldier who had got too close.

Florence, meanwhile, was working her way around the

convoy, her movements precise and calculated. Antoinette watched her taking out the driver of the third truck, a quick, efficient kill that prevented any chance of the convoy escaping.

But it wasn't over yet. The officers in the car had recovered from the shock and were returning fire. Antoinette saw Marc take cover behind a stone wall, exchanging shots with one of the officers. Louis raced toward the car, his expression grim as he fired with deadly accuracy.

Antoinette realised that one of the officers was aiming at Marc. Without thinking, she raised her rifle, her hands steady despite the chaos around her. She squeezed the trigger.

The officer's head snapped back, and he crumpled to the ground. Marc glanced at her, a flash of gratitude in his eyes before he turned his attention back to the fight.

The battle was brief but brutal. One by one, the German soldiers and officers fell, their resistance futile against the coordinated attack. The noise of gunfire gradually died down, replaced by the crackling of the burning truck and the moans of the wounded.

Antoinette stood frozen, her rifle still raised, her breath coming in ragged gasps. She had done it. She had killed again. The realisation hit her like a punch to the gut, but there was no time to dwell on it.

Louis moved swiftly, checking the bodies to ensure none were left alive. 'Marc, secure the explosives. Make sure there's nothing left behind that can be traced back to us.'

Marc nodded and set to work, his movements efficient and quick. Franck and Paul began searching the bodies, taking anything that might be of use – documents, weapons, ammunition. Florence joined them, her face expressionless as she rifled through the pockets of a fallen officer.

Antoinette's body shook as she lowered her weapon. The adrenaline was wearing off, leaving her shaky and nauseous.

She turned away from the carnage, trying to steady her breathing.

'Antoinette.' She looked up to see Louis standing beside her, his gaze steady and unreadable. 'You did well,' he said, his tone calm. 'But just know, I'm afraid it doesn't get easier.'

She nodded, unable to find her voice. Louis didn't press her further; he simply placed a hand on her shoulder, a gesture of quiet solidarity, before moving to help the others.

The mission had been a success, but the cost weighed heavily on Antoinette. She had survived her first real test, but at what price? The faces of the men she had killed would haunt her, just as the memory of the first man she had killed did. But this was the reality she had chosen – or rather, the reality that had been thrust upon her.

As they gathered their spoils and prepared to leave, Antoinette felt a cold steadfastness settle over her. She had stepped into the darkness, and there was no going back.

The journey back to the farmhouse was silent, the significance of their actions weighing down the whole group like a blanket. The adrenaline that had fuelled them during the mission had dissipated, leaving only exhaustion and a grim sense of duty.

When they finally arrived, Antoinette was too tired to do anything but collapse onto her makeshift bed. She lay there, staring up at the ceiling, her mind a jumble of conflicting emotions. The day's events played out in her mind on a loop – the explosion, the gunfire, the faces of the men she had killed.

Sleep didn't come easily that night. When it did, it was filled with nightmares – René's face pleading with her, Benjamin lost and alone, her family frantic with worry. She woke with a start, sweat drenching her, the taste of fear bitter in her mouth.

Antoinette sat up, rubbing her hands over her face. There was no time for self-pity, no time to dwell on what was lost. She had to be strong, for herself, for René, for Benjamin. She dressed quickly and left her room, the echoes of her nightmares following her like shadows. The farmhouse was quiet, the others still sleeping or lost in their own thoughts. Antoinette made her way to the kitchen, where she found Florence sitting alone, a cup of coffee in her hands.

Florence looked up as she entered, her expression softening when she saw the turmoil in Antoinette's eyes. 'Couldn't sleep?' she asked gently.

Antoinette shook her head, sinking into a chair across from her. 'Nightmares,' she admitted, her voice strained.

Florence nodded, her gaze understanding. 'They don't go away, but you will learn to live with them.'

'Will I?' Antoinette enquired, her hands betraying her fear as she wrapped them around the cup of coffee Florence offered her.

'You will,' Florence responded firmly. 'We all have them.'

Antoinette looked at her, seeing the truth in her words. She wasn't alone. She had found a new family in these fighters, in their shared struggle, their shared pain. She took a deep breath, finding strength in the simple act of breathing.

She would carry on. She would fight. And she would survive and then she would find René and Benjamin, as she had promised them. But she would never forget the cost.

41

BRAZIL, 2012

Deanna

The next day, as she hugged Carlos and said goodbye to Maria with tears in her eyes, it felt like a heavy burden had settled in her chest. The shocking revelations about her grandmother's past and Falkenberg's devastating confession still lingered, leaving them all feeling raw and exposed. Even after he was taken in for questioning, Deanna was still shaken by what had occurred.

Maria pulled her in for one last embrace, her voice barely above a whisper as she pleaded, 'Promise me you'll come back?' Deanna nodded, but her throat burned with the uncertainty of that possibility.

As the taxi pulled away, Deanna kept her gaze fixed on the villa until it blurred into the horizon. Carlos was still standing on the patio, his face as unreadable as ever, but his eyes... His eyes were etched with a sorrow that mirrored her own. The promise of something between them lingered in her mind.

Maria stood beside him, her hand on his arm in an attempt

to comfort him, but Deanna knew better. She hated leaving them to face the storm alone, but she had no choice. There were other ghosts waiting for her at home, and she dreaded telling her father all she had learned.

São Paulo's airport was a blur of movement, the cacophony of voices and footsteps a harsh contrast to the storm swirling inside Deanna. As Felicity navigated the crowd beside her, Deanna let the noise wash over her, almost grateful for the distraction. While she waited to check in, Deanna pulled out her phone and scrolled through photos – snapshots of a world that already felt too distant. Images of Carlos and Maria, the villa, the beach bathed in a golden sunset... a bittersweet ache rose in her chest.

How had everything unravelled the way it had?

Deanna's thumb hovered over the screen as she paused on a photo – the three of them standing by the shore, the sun casting a molten glow over the water. Carlos's arm was around her and Felicity's shoulders at Ponta do Arpoador, his eyes dark and intense in the fading light. Her chest tightened with the memory, but the sudden ping of her phone jolted her out of the past.

She glanced down at the message, her breath catching as the words blinked up at her:

I hope you have a safe journey back. Thank you for everything.
– Carlos.

Felicity leaned in closer, her eyes flicking between the phone and Deanna's face. 'It's been one hell of a week, hasn't it?' she said softly. 'Now that you know Carlos's father doesn't have a right to the violin, what are you going to do?'

Deanna let out a slow, shaky breath, her mind still reeling. 'I don't know yet. But I'm sure of one thing now – whatever my grandmother went through with that man, it was much darker than I can ever imagine.'

The boarding announcement echoed through the terminal, and as she handed over her boarding pass, a single thought anchored in her mind – there were still too many questions without answers, and she was determined to find them.

When they landed at Heathrow, the city was draped in grey, a familiar mist hanging over the skyline as they collected their luggage. Deanna hadn't realised how much she had missed England.

When she finally got home, the front door groaned as she pushed it open, the silence inside wrapping around her like a heavy blanket. She dropped her bags to the floor, her eyes sweeping over the room. Everything was as she had left it, yet nothing felt the same.

The solitude she once embraced now pressed against her chest like a vice. She had grown accustomed to being alone since separating from Glen, finding solace in her routine of caring for her father and tending to her garden. But now, the quiet was unbearable. She longed for the roar of the ocean, the salty breeze whipping against her face, the horizon stretching out endlessly before her. Brazil had left its mark on her, and no matter how hard she tried, she couldn't shake the feeling that she was trapped here, in this small, still world.

Making herself a hot drink, she took the letters that had gathered on her doormat outside to open, seeking refuge in her garden. The familiar blooms greeted her, their colours vivid against the backdrop of her sadness. Sipping her tea, she flicked through the stack of mail until an unfamiliar envelope caught her eye. Deanna's hands trembled as she tore it open, revealing an official-looking letter inside.

Her breath hitched as her eyes darted over the text. 'This can't be real...' she whispered aloud to herself. The shock was immediate, crashing over her in waves, and she shot to her feet, her hand colliding with the teacup, sending it tumbling to the ground. The hot liquid spilled across the grass, but Deanna barely noticed. All she could see were the words, as a new truth appeared before her eyes, tearing her world apart again.

Deanna reached for her phone, her fingers fumbling across the screen. She couldn't think straight, couldn't breathe. There was only one person who would understand. One person who could help her make sense of this madness. She barely managed to dial the number, her pulse quickening with each endless ring.

'Miss me already?' Felicity asked as she answered the phone, a smile in her voice, unaware of the storm brewing on Deanna's end.

Deanna swallowed hard, the words catching in her throat. 'Felicity... I – I need to come and see you tomorrow.'

There was a pause on the other end. Deanna continued, her voice shaky. 'I've got a letter. I – I don't even know how to explain this over the phone. I have to show you.'

Felicity's voice shifted instantly, her lightheartedness replaced with concern. 'Deanna... what is it? Is it bad?'

Deanna's breath came in shallow bursts. 'I wouldn't say it was bad, just shocking. It – it confirms something Giovanni – I mean *Falkenberg* – was saying.' The name felt heavy on her tongue, as if speaking it aloud gave him power over her even now.

Felicity was silent for a long moment. Then, her voice was gentle but urgent. 'Okay. Come tomorrow. I'll meet you off the train. And, Deanna, whatever it is, I'll help you get through it.'

Deanna nodded, even though Felicity couldn't see her. 'I'll be there by noon.'

They hung up, and Deanna let the phone slip from her hand, clattering softly onto the table. The letter lay open beside her, stark and glaring under the sunlight. She stared at it, her mind still struggling to comprehend everything it contained.

She couldn't stop reading the lines over and over again, her mind refusing to accept what they meant.

The next day, Deanna sat stiffly on the train, the soft hum of the engine beneath her clashing with the wild, erratic beating of her heart. The letter was tucked safely inside her bag, but it felt like it could burn through the fabric at any moment. She hadn't dared open it again. Not yet.

When she arrived, Felicity was waiting for her just outside the station, a coffee in hand. Her bright smile faltered when she saw Deanna's expression.

Felicity looped her arm through Deanna's as they made small talk on their way towards Sotheby's. The office was a world of its own, gleaming and polished as usual. It was strange, Deanna thought, to be here with something so personal, so raw, while the rest of the building buzzed with auctions and valuations. Deanna dropped into one of the plush chairs in her friend's office, her heart racing.

Felicity closed the door softly behind her. 'Okay, tell me. And take your time.'

Deanna let out a shaky breath, her fingers fumbling as she reached into her bag for the infamous envelope. She knew it was just in her imagination, but it felt heavier as she handed it to Felicity, the paper crinkling slightly under her grip. She couldn't bear to look at it again; she knew what it said. Every word had carved itself into her memory.

Felicity took the letter with a quiet nod, her fingers deftly opening the envelope. The seconds stretched into an eternity as she read, the only sound the soft rustling of paper.

Felicity's expression shifted slowly, her brows knitting together in confusion before her eyes widened in disbelief. 'Oh my God...' she whispered, shaking her head as if trying to make sense of it. Her voice tightened with shock as she looked up. 'Deanna, this – this can't be right. It just can't. It confirms...'

She paused, unable to finish her sentence, so Deanna finished it for her. 'Without a shadow of a doubt, it confirms everything I feared it would.'

42

MARCH 1943

Antoinette

As the days blurred into weeks, Antoinette transformed from a novice fighter to one of the group's most skilled and valuable members. Each mission sharpened her abilities and strengthened her commitment. The camaraderie she forged with her fellow fighters solidified into a tight-knit bond, forming a family united by a fierce drive to help win this war. For her it was a beacon of hope during the darkest of times.

Antoinette's reputation among the group soared. She was known as the member of the team able to move undetected among her enemies and deliver lethal attacks with precision. She frequently partnered with Marc, her agile hands – once adept at coaxing perfect notes from a violin – now just as skilled in delicate explosive work.

But even as she earned the respect and admiration of her comrades, there was a part of her that could never fully be released from the reality of what she had become.

It was during a particularly gruelling mission – a daring raid on a Nazi ammunition dump – that Antoinette first felt the cracks in her seemingly impenetrable armour. The night was thick with tension as they ran through the underbrush, fighting through obstacles in their path. And despite being weighed down by exhaustion, she continued to push forward.

She didn't realise she had blacked out until she awoke moments later, disoriented, her head spinning.

When her vision cleared, she found herself cradled in Marc's arms, his face laced with concern. 'Antoinette, are you all right?' His voice was steady, but his eyes betrayed his worry.

'I'm fine,' she murmured, attempting to shrug off the incident as she sipped the water Florence offered. But the tremor in her body told a different story.

Florence's brow furrowed as she shook her head, her tone firm. 'You've been pushing yourself too hard. You need to rest.'

Antoinette wanted to argue, to insist that she was strong enough, but she knew her friend was right.

The next morning, she barely made it to the toilet before a wave of nausea overtook her, leaving her retching and weak. As she knelt on the cold floor, her body shaking with each successive heave, Florence hurried to her side, her face a mask of concern.

'What's wrong?' Florence asked softly, helping her friend to steady herself.

Antoinette sipped water, trying to push away the growing sense of dread. Her voice filled with uncertainty as she attempted to force a smile. 'Probably Louis's cooking,' she said in an attempt to lighten the mood.

But Florence didn't smile. Instead, her expression softened with understanding. 'We have a doctor who helps the Resistance,' she said gently. 'I'll go and fetch him.'

The hours dragged on as Antoinette lay in bed, her mind racing. When the doctor finally arrived – a kind-faced man with gentle hands – he examined her with a thoroughness that only heightened her anxiety. Each question he asked seemed to pierce through the fog of her thoughts, bringing her closer to a truth she wasn't sure she was ready to face.

Finally, the doctor straightened as he turned to Florence and Antoinette. The room seemed to shrink, the air thick with anticipation. 'You're not sick,' he said quietly, his voice gentle but firm. 'You're pregnant. And too far along than is safe for me to do anything about it.'

The words hit her like a physical blow, knocking the breath from her lungs.

Pregnant.

The world seemed to tilt on its axis as she struggled to process what this meant – for her, for the group, for the fight they were in the middle of. Her mind raced, a storm of emotions battering her from every side – fear, confusion, guilt and finally disgust.

'That's impossible,' Antoinette whispered, her voice weak as she clutched the edges of the bunk, her knuckles white with the force of her grip. 'My husband... he was taken years ago...'

Her words faltered, fading into a hollow silence as an icy realization gripped her. The unthinkable took shape in her mind, a dark and terrible truth that tightened around her chest, sending a shiver of dread coursing through her.

Memories she had fought so hard to bury surged to the surface, crashing over her with the force of a tidal wave, threatening to drag her under. She could feel Falkenberg's cruel hands on her again, his presence suffocating as he forced himself upon her, leaving invisible scars that had never truly healed. She had pushed it all down, locked it away in the deepest corners of her mind, unwilling to revisit the horrors of that night. But now, the walls she had built to protect herself crumbled, leaving her defenceless against the onslaught of pain and fear.

Antoinette's breath hitched as the truth struck her with

merciless clarity: she was carrying the child of the man she had stabbed to death – the man who had shattered her life in more ways than one. The realisation was a knife to the heart, twisting cruelly as she struggled to comprehend the terrible turn of fate that had brought her to this moment.

Florence, who knew the whole story, reached for her hand, her touch warm and firm. 'Antoinette, don't be scared,' she said, her voice filled with quiet determination. 'You're not alone in this.'

But even as she nodded, Antoinette couldn't shake the cold, creeping fear that had taken hold of her heart. How could she continue to fight, to kill, with a new life growing inside her? What would this mean for her role in the Resistance, for the future she had fought so hard to reclaim? For René?

The days that followed were a blur of anguish and confusion. Antoinette wrestled with the shocking news, her emotions a tangled mess of anger, fear, and despair. The life growing inside her felt like a betrayal, a constant reminder of the worst night of her life. How could she give birth to the child of a man who had caused her so much suffering? The question gnawed at her constantly, leaving her sleepless and hollow.

Yet, amid the storm of her emotions, she found herself surrounded by the unwavering support of her fellow fighters. Florence, always perceptive, offered quiet reassurances and a steady presence that calmed Antoinette when she felt like she was spiralling. Marc, too, had shown a rare tenderness, his normally sharp eyes softened with concern. 'You're one of us, Antoinette,' he had said, his hand resting lightly on her shoulder. 'We'll support you. This child doesn't change who you are, or what you mean to us.'

Even Louis, who rarely displayed emotion, had spoken up, his gruff voice tinged with an unfamiliar warmth. 'You've proven your strength time and again,' he said, his gaze steady. 'Don't doubt yourself now.'

Antoinette found solace in their words, their solidarity giving her the strength to face the days ahead.

One evening, as the sun dipped below the horizon and the sky was painted in hues of pink and orange, the group were all resting, before a late-night mission. Antoinette slipped out of the farmhouse, seeking solace in the cool twilight air. She found herself at the edge of the clearing, tears she had been holding back all day finally spilling down her cheeks. The burden of her situation felt unbearable, crushing her beneath its relentless pressure.

She didn't hear Marc approach until he was right beside her, his presence both startling and comforting. 'Antoinette,' he said softly, his voice low and full of concern. She quickly wiped her tears, but it was too late – he had already seen her pain.

'I'm fine,' she lied, her voice shaky as she turned away from him, trying to hide her vulnerability.

'You don't have to pretend with me,' Marc said, stepping closer. He hesitated for a moment before gently placing a hand on her arm, his touch warm and steady. 'It's all right to not be all right. When I lost... Sarah, my fiancée, to these animals I thought I'd lost everything worth living for. But then I realised that it was just the beginning of a new fight. You're still you, Antoinette. This is just another battle you have to win.'

The gentleness in his voice broke through the walls she had tried so hard to keep up, and before she knew it, the tears were flowing freely again. Marc didn't say anything, just took her in his arms as she sobbed, offering silent support.

'I don't know what to do, Marc,' Antoinette whispered, her voice thick with emotion. 'How can I bring a child into this world? How can I raise a child whose father was...' Her voice trailed off, the words too painful to speak aloud.

Marc was silent for a moment, and when he spoke, his voice

was filled with a quiet persistence. 'You don't have to do it alone,' he said, his hand slipping from her shoulder to gently take her hand in his. 'I could help you, Antoinette. We could raise this child together, if you want.'

She looked up at him and noticed something in his eyes she had been avoiding. Love, and not just as a fellow fighter. The sincerity in his voice and this realisation took her by surprise, and for a moment, she allowed herself to imagine it – someone who knew the horror of all she had done, yet accepted her. The two of them out here in the countryside after the war, raising the child together, finding some semblance of peace and happiness after the chaos of war. It was a tender, fleeting fantasy, one that almost felt real in the quiet of the twilight.

But as Marc leaned in, his gaze softening as he looked at her, Antoinette's heart clenched. The warmth of his breath on her skin sent a shiver through her, and for a brief, heart-stopping moment, she thought he might kiss her. She found herself leaning in, drawn to the comfort and safety he offered.

But then, just as their lips were about to meet, Antoinette pulled away, a picture of René flashing before her, a sob catching in her throat.

'I can't,' she whispered, her voice trembling with guilt and longing. 'I still love my husband, Marc, and I have a son who depends on me. Even though I don't know if René is alive or dead... I can't betray him. Not again.'

Marc smiled, a mix of understanding and regret in his eyes. He didn't push her, didn't try to convince her otherwise. He simply nodded, his hand slipping from hers as he stepped back, giving her the space she needed. 'I'm sorry,' he said quietly. 'I didn't mean to make things even harder for you.'

Antoinette shook her head, wiping away the last of her tears with the heel of her hand. 'You didn't.' Her voice was barely audible. 'I just... I just know that this would be wrong.'

Marc nodded again, his gaze lingering on her for a moment

before he turned to leave. 'I'll be here, in any way you need me,' he said softly, his footsteps fading as he walked away, leaving Antoinette alone in the gathering darkness.

As she stood there, the twilight deepening into night, Antoinette felt the weight of her choices pressing down on her once more. But this time, there was a flicker of something else – determination.

She wouldn't allow herself to be broken, not now, not when her own personal fight was only just beginning. And now she wasn't just fighting for herself, but also for the innocent young life growing inside her.

43

OCTOBER 1943

Antoinette

Over the months that followed Antoinette struggled to come to terms with the shocking news of her pregnancy. The emotions that churned within her – anger, fear, confusion – all threatened to consume her, leaving her questioning everything she thought she knew about herself and her future.

Despite the turmoil, Antoinette found herself wrapped in the unyielding support of Florence and the other fighters. They rallied around her, their camaraderie offering a lifeline in her darkest moments. And though Antoinette often felt like she was teetering on the edge of despair, the unwavering presence of her friends gave her the strength to carry on. In their eyes, she saw not pity, but respect and understanding – a silent vow that they would stand by her side, no matter what.

As her pregnancy progressed, Antoinette threw herself into the Resistance work with a fervour that bordered on desperation. Each mission became an escape, a way to drown out the overwhelming emotions that threatened to engulf her. Each operation was a temporary reprieve from the reality she faced.

She moved with a newfound ferocity, striking with deadly precision, her body driven by a determination that verged on obsession. Even as the physical toll of her pregnancy grew more pronounced, Antoinette refused to slow down. The war was her battlefield, and each mission was a fight not just against the Nazis, but against the demons that haunted her nightmares.

But as her due date drew near, the reality of her situation became impossible to ignore. The other fighters, once merely concerned, now grew openly anxious about her well-being.

'You're risking too much,' Marc had said one night, his voice tinged with worry as he watched her from across the room. They all knew the dangers of bringing a child into a world consumed by war, but they also seemed to recognise the tenacity in Antoinette's eyes. She was a fighter, but even she couldn't deny the strain her body was under.

In the final months, when her growing belly made it impossible to continue on missions without endangering everyone, Antoinette remained at the farmhouse. The missions may have been out of reach, but she refused to be sidelined. She immersed herself in Resistance work – creating forged documents, intercepting enemy communications, and gathering intelligence for future operations.

Each task became a lifeline, a way to stay connected to the fight, even as her body demanded rest. The work gave her purpose, a distraction from the weight of her reality. Yet, with every passing day, a gnawing fear grew in her chest: would she have the strength to protect her child if the enemy finally came knocking?

One evening, the group returned from a mission with a wounded downed pilot in tow. The young man, barely conscious, was carried into the farmhouse, and Antoinette, despite her condition, rushed to assist.

As she knelt beside the doctor, her hands steady as she helped tend to his injuries, the British pilot's eyes fluttered open. He had a shock of curly brown hair and green eyes that met hers with a mix of pain and gratitude. 'Thank you,' he whispered, his voice hoarse but sincere.

The connection was brief, but in that moment, Antoinette felt a strange kinship with the young man. He was a reminder of the countless lives that hung in the balance, and of the fight that still lay ahead. She worked tirelessly alongside the doctor, her focus unwavering despite the fatigue that exhausted her.

As the night wore on and the pilot's condition stabilised, Antoinette finally allowed herself to step back, her hands aching from the exertion. Florence, who had been watching from the doorway, approached her with a look of concern. 'You need to rest, Antoinette,' she said softly, her voice firm but gentle. 'You've done enough for tonight.'

Over the weeks that followed, as Thomas recovered within the comforting walls of the farmhouse and his proficiency in French emerged, an unexpected bond began to form between him and Antoinette. Amid the chaos of war, they shared a friendship that, for Antoinette, wove a fragile tapestry of hope and understanding against the backdrop of despair.

One crisp morning, with the sun casting a golden hue over the dewy landscape – a brief respite from the encroaching winter chill – Thomas sat outside on the weathered stone wall of the farmhouse compound. A thin spiral of smoke rose from the cigarette between his fingers, his gaze distant, reflecting shadows of battles fought and losses endured.

Antoinette, emerging from the farmhouse, cradled two steaming mugs of rich, aromatic black market coffee. Her steps were measured, the weight of her growing belly making each movement deliberate. As she approached, Thomas's sombre expression softened into a genuine smile.

'Thought you could use something to warm you up,' Antoinette offered gently, extending a mug toward him.

'You're a lifesaver,' Thomas replied, as he took the mug. As she settled beside him on the wall, a sharp kick from the baby made her gasp, her hand instinctively moving to her abdomen. Noticing her flinch, Thomas's brow furrowed with concern.

'Are you all right?' he asked, his eyes searching hers with genuine worry.

'Just someone reminding me they're here,' Antoinette laughed softly, trying to mask the complex emotions swirling within her as she rubbed circles over her belly.

Thomas watched, curiosity and tenderness flickering across his face. 'May I?' he asked hesitantly, gesturing toward her stomach.

She hesitated, the unexpected gesture making her feel vulnerable. But there was a kindness in Thomas's eyes that eased her apprehension. Nodding slowly, she guided his hand to rest atop her belly.

They sat in silence, the world fading away as they focused on the subtle movements beneath their hands. When the baby kicked again, Thomas grinned, his voice filled with quiet admiration. 'Strong little fighter you have there.'

'Yes, quite the fighter,' Antoinette echoed softly, her smile waning as she gazed toward the horizon where dark clouds gathered ominously.

Sensing the shift in her mood, Thomas withdrew his hand with a smile. After a sip of coffee, he ventured cautiously, 'Do you have anyone waiting for you? Family?'

Taking a deep breath, Antoinette unlocked a floodgate of emotions. 'I have a husband, René, taken by the Gestapo early in the war, and my son is in the South of France with family. Since then, it's just been me and now the Resistance.'

Thomas's empathy was palpable. 'I'm sorry, Antoinette. War tears lives apart.'

She adjusted her grip on the mug as painful memories surged. 'As you have probably guessed, this baby... it's not René's,' she confessed in a whisper, the admission hanging heavy between them.

Thomas remained silent, allowing her to continue.

'I was part of an underground mission. The man responsible... a Nazi, took more from me than I thought possible,' she continued, her voice strained. 'So, this child is a constant reminder of that time in my life.'

A tense silence fell between them, the distant sounds of the countryside filling the quiet. Thomas's jaw tightened briefly, his eyes reflecting a mix of anger and deep compassion. 'You've endured more than anyone should,' he said softly, his voice firm yet gentle. 'But look at you, still standing, still fighting. That's truly a testament to your strength.'

Tears welled in Antoinette's eyes, his words unexpectedly comforting. 'Some days, I don't feel strong at all. I don't know if I can love this child, knowing its origins. And what if René returns? How can I explain... this?'

Thomas set his mug aside and took a deep breath, giving himself a moment before responding. 'War forces us into unimaginable situations, introduces us to horrors we never thought we'd face,' he began, his tone soft. 'It's stolen a lot from you, but it doesn't have to define your future.'

A single tear rolled down Antoinette's cheek, which she quickly wiped away, her breath shaky. 'I just don't know if I'm capable of the love this would require. And I'm terrified of what the future holds.'

Thomas nodded understandingly, then paused as if considering his next words carefully. He leaned back, taking another sip of his coffee. 'I don't know if I've ever mentioned this to you yet, but I was adopted,' he said quietly, almost contemplatively.

'The woman who gave birth to me was very young, far too young to take on such a responsibility. Though I've never met her, I often think of her decision as the greatest gift. She gave the gift of life not just to me, but to a family that desperately wanted a child. I grew up in a wonderful loving home, and whenever I think about her, I thank her for making such a self-less choice. Sometimes the greatest act of love is knowing when to let go. Even in this great darkness, you can have the power to light the way for this child's future.'

They sat together in shared silence, allowing the weight of his words to settle between them. For the first time in a long while, Antoinette felt a spark of clarity cutting through her confusion, comforted by what Thomas had said.

Two days later, the farmhouse buzzed as an extraction point was secured for Thomas's safe return to Allied territory. Preparations were swift, mixed with relief and melancholy ahead of his departure.

As the sun set the day he was leaving, casting long shadows across the courtyard, Antoinette was drawn to the garden behind the farmhouse, the sadness at losing her new friend over-whelming. She knelt among the plants, her hands methodically harvesting, finding solace in the simple, repetitive motions.

The crunch of gravel announced Thomas's approach. He stood there, a packed rucksack over his shoulder, a soft smile tinged with sadness. 'I figured I'd find you here,' he said warmly.

'Leaving our hotel so soon?' Antoinette tried to sound light, but her tone fell short.

Thomas nodded. 'The sooner I'm back, the sooner I can continue the fight.'

Pride flickered in Antoinette's smile. 'Always wanting to play the hero,' she teased.

He chuckled, then became serious. 'Just doing my part, like

everyone else.' A pause followed before he reached into his pocket, pulling out a polished compass that had nestled there. The metal gleamed softly in the fading light, its surface etched with intricate designs worn smooth by time.

'This belonged to my father,' Thomas explained, his voice thick with emotion. 'He carried it through his own battles and passed it down to me. It's guided me through some of my darkest moments, and now I want you to have it for your own.'

Antoinette's eyes widened, her gaze flickering from the compass to Thomas's earnest face. 'I can't accept this. It's too precious.'

'But so are you,' he replied softly, gently pressing the compass into her hand. 'Let it guide you when things seem impossible. Let it remind you that even in the darkest times, there's always a way to find your own true north.'

Tears blurred her vision as she closed her fingers around the compass, its weight anchoring her amid her emotional turmoil. Overwhelmed, she wrapped her arms around him in a heartfelt embrace.

'Thank you,' she whispered into his shoulder, 'for everything.'

He pulled back slightly, his hands lingering on her arms as he looked deeply into her eyes. 'Take care of yourself, Antoinette. And remember, no matter what happens, you have the strength to face it.' She nodded, unable to find words that could adequately convey the gratitude and affection she felt in that moment.

As Thomas turned to leave, he hesitated, casting one last glance over his shoulder. 'I hope our paths cross again, in a world at peace.'

'Me too,' Antoinette replied softly, watching as he walked away, until he disappeared from sight.

Left alone in the quiet garden, Antoinette gazed down at the compass cradled in her palm. Gently, she opened its lid, watching as the needle quivered before settling, pointing stead-fastly north. A sense of calm washed over her, mingled with a renewed commitment.

She looked up at the sky where the first stars were begin-ning to twinkle, their light piercing through the encroaching darkness.

In that moment, she made a silent vow – to not doubt her ability to do the right thing. With a deep, steadying breath, she turned back toward the farmhouse, ready to face whatever tomorrow would bring.

44

OCTOBER 1943

Antoinette

Two days later, as Antoinette stood in the farmhouse kitchen washing dishes, a sharp pain suddenly shot through her abdomen.

She froze, feeling the unmistakable gush as her waters broke. The dish she had been holding slipped from her hands, shattering on the floor, but she barely noticed. Gripping the edge of the sink, wave after wave of contractions wracked her body, each one more intense than the last. Panic surged within her: this was it – the baby was coming.

With body convulsing, she stumbled her way up to her room, each step a struggle against the relentless pain. This labour was nothing like the slow, agonising hours she had endured with Benjamin. This was already swift and brutal, catching her off guard just as the conception had.

She barely made it to her bed before another contraction hit, doubling her over in agony. A guttural scream tore from her throat, echoing through the empty farmhouse. Sweat dripped from her brow as she tried to recall the steps from her first labour, but fear and confusion clouded her thoughts. The room spun, her vision blurring as another wave of pain slammed into her.

Antoinette crawled into bed, clutching the pillow as the contractions intensified. She closed her eyes, focusing on her breathing, trying to push aside the terror that threatened to overwhelm her. Minutes felt like hours in the haze of labour, and she lost track of time entirely.

Finally, she heard the door to the farmhouse creak open and she heard Florence's voice calling out. Relief flooded through her as she summoned the strength to respond. 'I'm up here, in my room,' she managed between ragged breaths.

Florence's footsteps were quick and urgent on the stairs. She burst into the room, eyes wide with shock as she took in the scene. 'Oh my God, you're in labour!' she exclaimed, immediately moving to support her friend.

Without hesitation, Florence took charge, calling out to one of the other fighters to fetch the doctor. She stayed by Antoinette's side, offering steady words of encouragement as the contractions came faster and harder. The doctor arrived shortly after he was summoned, his face calm and composed, despite the urgency of the situation.

Antoinette clung to Florence's hand, her knuckles white as surges of pain washed over her. The doctor's voice was a lifeline, guiding her through each contraction.

'Your baby is ready to come, Antoinette. You're doing great. Just keep breathing.'

With Florence by her side, offering quiet reassurance, Antoinette drew in every ounce of strength she had left. She pushed, her body trembling with the effort, her screams filling the room as she fought to bring her child into the world.

Then, in a rush of overwhelming sensation, the room was filled with the piercing cry of a newborn. Antoinette collapsed back against the pillows, gasping for breath. The world around her seemed to blur, the pain of labour fading into the background as the doctor placed the tiny, wriggling form of her son into her arms.

For a moment, everything else ceased to exist. Antoinette's gaze locked onto the tiny bundle cradled against her chest. The baby was impossibly small, a perfect creation of new life, his skin soft and pink, with delicate fingers that curled instinctively around her thumb. His other tiny fist waved in the air, a cry escaping his rosebud lips – so fragile, so pure, so helpless.

A torrent of emotions crashed over her like a wave, pulling her into a maelstrom of love, fear, and anguish. This was her child, her flesh and blood, a life she had brought into the world. His little body was warm against hers, his heartbeat steady, a rhythm of life so starkly contrasted with the cold, dark memories that haunted her.

She studied his face again, every tiny feature etched with perfection – the soft curve of his cheeks, the flutter of his eyelids as they struggled to open, the small tuft of fair hair atop his head. Yet, as she traced the lines of his face, she saw the faintest shadow of someone else – someone who had left a scar so deeply on her soul that it might never fully heal.

Her thoughts whirled in a chaotic storm, torn between the joy of new life and the horror of its origin. She could see it already – the shape of his nose, the line of his jaw. Would he grow up to sound like his father? To look like him? To carry that same darkness? That same intense gaze that had once stolen her peace and shattered her world?

The thought froze her to the core, cold and unrelenting. How could she raise this child, knowing who his father was? Every time she looked at him, would she see Falkenberg's cruel eyes staring back at her? Would she relive the terror of those nights, over and over, with each cry, each smile, each innocent question about the man who had fathered him? Worse still, what if she couldn't love him in the way he deserved?

Her heart twisted painfully, the ache spreading through her chest as if it would crack her ribs and split her in two. She knew this child was a part of her – a part that was innocent, that had done nothing wrong. He was blameless, a perfect creation born out of the most horrific of circumstances. But how could she reconcile that innocence with the darkness that lurked in his blood?

Antoinette's tears fell silently, wetting the baby's head as she held him close, feeling the warmth of his tiny body against hers. Her mind screamed at the injustice of it all – how could something so pure, so perfect, be born of such violence? And how could she ever be the mother he deserved, when every glance at him would tear open the wounds she had fought so hard to close?

Yet, the thought of giving him up was just as unbearable. How could she hand him over to strangers, never knowing if he was loved, if he was cared for? He was her son, and to lose him would be to lose a piece of herself – a piece she wasn't sure she could live without.

But as she stared down at his innocent face, the choice became clearer, even as it shattered her heart into a million pieces. She had to protect him – from the world, from herself, from the shadow of the man who had fathered him. To raise him would be to condemn them both to a life of pain and reminders of what had been stolen from her. The scars on her soul would only deepen, and she feared they would consume her, leaving nothing left to give him.

Florence, sensing her turmoil, placed a gentle hand on her shoulder. 'Antoinette... what are you thinking?' she asked softly, her voice filled with concern.

Antoinette's voice was barely more than a whisper with the weight of her decision. 'I... I can't keep him, Florence. I can't do this. I... I just can't.'

Florence's eyes widened with shock, but she quickly hid it

behind a mask of understanding. 'Are you sure?' she asked gently, though the sorrow in her voice was unmistakable.

Antoinette nodded, tears streaming down her face, her heart breaking with every beat. 'Every time I look at him, I see... his father and what happened. I don't know if I can live with that. He didn't ask for this... he didn't ask to be born into this.'

The doctor, who had been quietly observing, stepped forward, his voice calm and compassionate. 'Antoinette, you've been through something no one should ever have to endure. It's not wrong to feel the way you do. If you truly believe you can't raise this child, there are families who would love and care for him. I can help find one, if you want.'

Antoinette nodded slowly, her decision made, though it felt like it was ripping her apart from the inside out. With trembling fingers, she reached up and untied the compass from around her neck, the one Thomas had given her, a symbol of hope and guidance. She tucked it into the blanket around the baby, her tears falling onto the soft fabric as she remembered Thomas's words: '*Sometimes the greatest act of love is knowing when to let go. Even in this great darkness, you have the power to light the way for this child's future.*'

She whispered into the neck of the baby, 'I promise you one day when all of this is over, I will find you. Please, please forgive me.'

As she handed the baby to the doctor, her hands shook, and she felt as if her very soul was being torn from her. This was the right decision – she knew that – but it didn't make it any less agonising. It felt as though she was giving away a piece of her heart, a piece that she would never get back.

Florence squeezed her shoulder gently, offering silent support, but Antoinette barely felt it. Her eyes were fixed on the tiny bundle in the doctor's arms, the last piece of her heart leaving the room with him.

As the door closed behind him, the silence in the room was

deafening, echoing the emptiness that now consumed her. She had made her choice – one born of pain and necessity – but the weight of it threatened to crush her. And as she lay back against the pillows, her stomach roiling with exhaustion and grief, she knew that this was a burden she would carry with her for the rest of her life.

45

BIRMINGHAM, 2012

Deanna

The next day, Deanna woke with a jolt, her mind already thick with dread. For a moment, she couldn't remember why. Then her eyes fell upon the neatly folded letter on her bedside table, and it all came back to her, reminding her it hadn't been a dream as she had hoped.

She hesitated, her fingers fumbling for it to read it one more time, and even though she knew it would shatter her father's world, she couldn't put it off any longer. She would have to tell him what she had learned.

On the way, the winding roads of Wales were lined with lush green fields and grazing sheep, a peaceful scene that usually brought her comfort. But today, her mind was consumed with one recurring thought as she drove to her father's new flat. Pulling up at his home, surrounded by beautiful gardens, she couldn't bring herself to get out of the car for a moment. She just sat there, watching the leaves rustle in the trees and the birds chirping, but no matter how long she sat, none of it seemed to calm her jangled nerves.

Taking a deep breath to steady herself, Deanna mustered the courage and made her way towards the entrance. Her father opened the door with a warm, unsuspecting smile that only deepened the ache in Deanna's heart.

'Deanna, what a lovely surprise!' he exclaimed, his eyes crinkling with joy.

He launched into his usual ramble, guiding her down the hallway. The scent of sandalwood and freshly brewed coffee hung in the air, the flat neat and welcoming. Family photos smiled down from the walls, and a deep ache settled in Deanna's chest as her gaze lingered on one of her father as a child, laughing with his mother in his grandmother's garden. The guilt gnawed at her, knowing she was about to rip the veil from his carefully constructed past, exposing something neither of them could have anticipated.

In the cosy living room, her father continued chatting, unaware of Deanna's internal struggle. As they settled down with cups of coffee, he pulled out a letter, his face lighting up with a surprising excitement. 'I almost forgot to tell you, Deanna. I got the most interesting letter a few days ago.'

Glad for a moment more before sharing what she found out, Deanna tilted her head. 'Who from?'

'A woman named Esther. Her mother, Sophie, was on the same train as me during the war. You remember, when Aunt Charlotte took me and the other children out of Paris? She wants to reunite us. Can you believe it? I haven't heard from any of them in so many years. Apparently, Esther's been organising it for a while now.'

Deanna's heart clenched at the innocence of his words, her mind racing ahead to the news she was about to deliver. She forced a smile, masking the turmoil churning inside her. 'That sounds incredible, Dad. You should go.'

He beamed at her, the excitement in his eyes shining brighter than she'd seen in a long time. 'I think I will. I've always wondered what happened to the others. Maybe it's time we reconnected after all these years.' His gaze grew distant as he reminisced about those difficult times, his tone filled with a quiet sense of sadness.

Deanna's chest constricted. How could she bring herself to shatter his fragile state? She placed her cup down, her hand shaky. She had to do it. There was no turning back now.

'Actually, Dad, there's something important about that time I need to talk to you about.' Her voice wavered, shaky, betraying her nerves. His smile faltered, concern knitting his brow. She took a deep breath, forcing the words out before she could second-guess herself.

'You know I've been looking into the history of the violin your mother gave you. Well, I have some results back from your DNA test.'

Her father blinked, confusion flickering in his eyes. 'A DNA test?' he repeated, setting his coffee cup down with a soft clink. The room seemed to grow smaller, the air thicker.

'We needed to see if we were related somehow to the last known person who owned it. But the test revealed something else, something unexpected.' She paused, watching his face for any sign of understanding, but only saw the growing shadow of confusion.

'And what did it reveal?' His voice was barely a whisper now, tension creeping into his every word.

Deanna's throat tightened as she forced the words out. 'The test... it showed a match. Not with the original owners of the violin, but with someone else – someone named Alex, whose mother was Antoinette and father was a man called Otto von Falkenberg.'

The room fell into a heavy silence. Her father's face drained of colour. 'What do you mean, a match?' His voice was hoarse, strangled by disbelief.

She took another breath. 'Dad... the test showed that your

mother and Otto von Falkenberg had a child together. A son. Born in 1943.'

His eyes widened, filled with shock and incomprehension. 'That's impossible,' he whispered, his voice cracking. 'There must be a mistake. Von Falkenberg? That sounds German.'

Deanna nodded, her heart aching for him. 'He was German, Dad. He was a high-ranking Nazi officer. I met him in Brazil.'

Her father stood abruptly, knocking his coffee cup, and Deanna reached to steady it as he turned away, pacing the small room. 'No,' he muttered, his voice shaking with desperation. 'That can't be right. My mother... she would never...' He trailed off, as though the words were too painful to say out loud.

'I'm so sorry,' Deanna whispered, tears stinging her eyes. 'I know this is hard to hear, but the DNA test doesn't lie.'

He stopped pacing, his back to her, shoulders hunched as if carrying the weight of the revelation. 'So, what are you saying?' he finally asked, his voice hollow. 'I have a half-brother? A brother who is the son of a Nazi?'

Deanna nodded, struggling with the pain in his voice. 'Yes, Dad. His name is Alexander.'

Her father turned to face her, his eyes brimming with unshed tears. 'How could she keep this from me? My whole life... everything I knew about my family... was a *lie*?' His voice broke, the heaviness of the truth pressing down on him.

Deanna wanted to reach out, to comfort him, but she knew there was no way to soften this blow. 'It's not Alexander's fault,' she said quietly. 'He didn't choose his father, just like you didn't choose this.'

A long silence stretched between them. Her father's face hardened, his grief turning into something colder. 'No,' he said sharply. 'I don't want to meet him. I can't.'

Deanna's breath caught in her throat. She had hoped he would be open to moving forward. 'Dad...'

'No!' His voice was firm, final. 'I don't want anything to do with him. I don't care who he is.'

She stared at him, heart aching, but nodded. She knew it was his way of keeping the memory of his mother alive, untainted by the sins of the past.

The rest of their visit passed in a heavy, suffocating silence. Deanna tried to engage her father in small talk, to lighten the atmosphere, but he remained distant and withdrawn. His pain was palpable.

When Deanna finally left, her father stood in the doorway, watching her go with a hollow expression. She drove home in a daze, her mind spinning with everything that had happened. But one thought stayed with her, clear and insistent: even if her father was resistant, she couldn't just let this go.

As soon as she arrived home, Deanna sat down at her desk, opened her laptop, and logged into the Ancestry website Felicity had told her about before she had left London. Her fingers hovered over the keyboard for a moment before she typed out a message to Alexander. She didn't know what she would say, didn't know if he would respond, but she had to try.

The truth, she had learned, couldn't stay buried forever.

46

BIRMINGHAM, 2012

Deanna

Deanna composed her message to Alexander, deciding to keep it brief and friendly. She mentioned that they might have ancestors in common and asked if they could speak over the phone. After hitting send, she waited anxiously for a response. Minutes ticked by, then hours, but there was no reply. Doubt crept in, and she questioned whether reaching out to him had been the right decision. Just as she began to give up hope, a new message notification popped up on her screen. Quickly, she clicked on it.

Alexander had replied with a short message and a phone number. Even though it was after nine – ten in Paris – she knew she wouldn't sleep if she didn't call, so she dialled immediately.

The line rang once, twice, each sound tightening the tension within her. Then, a voice answered, deep and unmistakably French. *"Allo?'* The accent was sharp yet smooth, carrying a hint of curiosity that sent a shiver through her. Deanna's breath hitched – this was real.

'Hello, is this Alexander Dural?' Deanna asked, her voice steadier than she felt. Her nerves fluttered in her stomach like trapped butterflies, but she forced herself to stay calm, to focus. Silence lingered on the other end, long enough to make her pulse race before the voice replied.

'*Oui*, this is Alexander.'

Deanna took a moment to gather her thoughts, knowing there was no easy way to say what needed to be said. 'I believe we may be... related.' The words felt fragile, too small for the weight they carried.

There was another pause, longer this time, followed by a sigh heavy with meaning. 'Are you related to Antoinette?' Alexander asked, his voice low, as though the name itself carried a reverence.

Deanna's breath hitched; hearing her grandmother's name caught her off guard. A chill swept through her, goosebumps rising.

'Yes,' Deanna managed, her voice cautious. 'Her son, Ben, is my father. Antoinette was my grandmother.'

A beat of silence, then Alexander spoke again, his tone softer now. 'Then I suppose that makes you Deanna.'

Her heart stuttered. He knew her name. The realisation hit her like a cold wave. 'Yes, that's right. I'm Deanna. Do you know about me?' she asked, barely able to form the words. She had expected Alexander to be in the dark, as she and her father had been, but his certainty unnerved her.

Alexander let out a long, slow breath, full of meaning she couldn't yet decipher. Then his tone shifted, sharpening, as if the burden of the past had settled even more heavily upon him. 'Is your father, Benjamin, still alive?'

Deanna swallowed, her pulse quickening. 'Yes, he is,' she replied, bracing herself for what was to come.

On the other end, there was a long silence, and Deanna could feel the impact of her words landing like a blow. When Alexander finally spoke, his voice was different – frayed, raw, as though he'd been holding back a flood of emotion. 'He's alive,' he repeated, the sound of his disbelief washing over her. 'Thank God, after all these years, I had hoped...' His breath hitched audibly, and Deanna imagined years of silence unravelling for him in that moment – the brother he had thought lost, suddenly within reach.

'If you knew about him, why didn't you ever reach out to us?'

Another long pause. Deanna could hear him struggling on the other end, could sense the decades of longing and confusion beginning to rise to the surface.

'My mother made me promise to wait for *him* to contact *me* first,' Alexander said, his next words thick with emotion. 'It has been a hard promise to keep all these years. If you're both willing to come to Paris, I have something important to tell you about her time during the war – something your grandmother made me swear never to tell her son, not until she was gone.'

Their conversation concluded with the agreement to call him again once she had made arrangements, but a larger concern loomed over the joy of reconnecting with her newly discovered uncle: whether to tell her father.

He had been so adamant about avoiding a meeting, and now the weight of that secret pressed down on her even more.

After a few days of inner turmoil, Deanna finally decided to tell her father about finding Alexander. Despite the conflict she felt between honouring his wishes and seeking the truth, she knew he deserved to know. Although it might be difficult for him to hear, her father was not one to hold grudges or let pride get in the way of doing the right thing.

Taking a deep breath, Deanna picked up her phone and dialled her father's number. The line rang for what felt like an eternity before his familiar voice finally answered, weary and guarded.

'Hello?'

'Dad, it's me,' she said softly. Steeling herself, Deanna plunged straight into the truth, her words spilling out in a rush of emotion as she explained everything she had learned.

The silence on the other end was deafening. Deanna could almost feel the enormity of her father's internal battle, emotions raging within him as he processed what she had just told him.

Finally, after what felt like a lifetime, he spoke, his voice strained. 'I see. So, what do you want to do?'

Deanna took a deep breath, her voice steady as she responded. 'I think we should go, Dad. If your mother met with him before she died, he knows things. He might have some of the answers we need, and I think it would be good for both of you.'

Her father's silence stretched on, and Deanna's heart ached as she waited for his reply. Then, at last, he spoke, his tone subdued. 'Can I take some time to think about it?'

'Of course, Dad,' Deanna said gently, though the emotions inside her threatened to burst. 'Take all the time you need.'

As she ended the call, Deanna sat in the quiet of her living room, tears welling up in her eyes. The end of this difficult journey was now within reach.

And yet, amid the sadness, there was a flicker of hope – a hope that by confronting the past, they could finally heal the present.

47

MAY 1945

Antoinette

Antoinette was in the farmhouse kitchen, peeling potatoes, her fingers stiff in the cold water, when Franck burst through the door, breathless and wild-eyed, clutching a newspaper.

'It's over! The war's over!' he exclaimed.

She froze, the words echoing in her mind like a distant hope. '*Over?*' she whispered, barely daring to believe it.

'Yes! It's happening. It's really happening!' Franck's eyes shone with a mixture of disbelief and joy.

Antoinette's gaze dropped to the paper in his hands, its headline bold and clear despite the tears that blurred her vision. *Could it be true?* The relentless march of time and terror was finally slowing.

'René,' she murmured, his name a fragile prayer on her lips.

She thought about the cost – the killing, the horror, the baby given up for adoption to protect him, and the nights spent clutching her empty arms, imagining his tiny form. There had been no other way. The doctor had assured her the family he had found would love him, care for him. It was the only way she could survive, to fight, to find René if he was still alive, to see Benjamin again, to be his mother, if fate allowed.

Hope surged through her, timid but undeniable. They had gained their freedom, and maybe now, she could too. The farmhouse erupted in celebration, wine poured with reckless abandon, victory toasts mingling with laughter that felt foreign after so much despair. Antoinette joined the others, her heart lightened for the first time in years, the heavy burden of the past momentarily lifting. Across the room, she caught sight of Marc, tears of relief glistening in his eyes. Their gaze locked, and in that shared glance, Antoinette felt an unspoken connection – a bond forged in the crucible of shared danger and suffering. She knew how he felt about her, but also that she could never consider returning those feelings if there was a chance her husband was still alive.

As the night wore on, filled with music and the promise of peace, Antoinette allowed herself to believe it was real – that she was finally free. But as dawn broke and the remnants of the night's revelry faded, reality crept back in.

Over breakfast, as Marc fried eggs with practised ease, the conversation turned to the future. 'What will you do now, Antoinette?' he asked.

She paused, letting the question settle in the air. Her gaze drifted to the window, the sunlight warming the room with a deceptive calm. 'As soon as the border is open, I'm leaving. I made a promise to my husband, and I'll start by finding René,' she replied, her voice steady, though her heart trembled with the weight of the decision.

Marc looked up from the stove, his eyes dark with concern. 'You're really going to search the camps?' His voice was soft, almost as if he didn't want to ask.

'Yes,' she said, her tone unwavering. 'I need to know what happened to him. I owe it to him, to myself... and to Benjamin.'

'How will you get there?' he pressed gently, his concern evident in the way his brow furrowed.

Antoinette met his gaze, feeling the quiet strength in his eyes. 'My father taught me to drive, and there are abandoned Nazi wagons everywhere. I'll find a way,' she asserted, her tone unshakeable. Facing the truth, whatever it may be, was no longer an option but a necessity.

Marc set down the frying pan and turned to face her fully, his expression softening. 'I could come with you, at least to the border. I've got family I want to see there.'

Her heart lightened at the offer. It was more than just concern; it was the unspoken care of a man who had stood by her side through the darkest of days. She nodded, a faint smile tugging at her lips. 'I'd like that, Marc. Truly.'

As they prepared to leave, Antoinette packed her few belongings with care, savouring the bittersweet memory of their time together. She hugged each of the Resistance cell deeply, feeling a deep gratitude for the bond they had formed. These people were more than comrades – they were her family.

'Thank you, all of you,' she said softly, emotion thick in her voice. Franck stepped forward, wrapping her in a tight embrace, his warmth a stark contrast to the cold reality outside.

'You better come see me in Paris when you return, okay?' Franck whispered, his voice rough but full of genuine concern.

'I will,' she promised. She and Florence wept and then laughed, wiping the tears from each other's eyes. With a final nod, Antoinette stepped into the morning light. Climbing into an abandoned Nazi wagon, its roof newly emblazoned with *Vive La France – Freedom Fighters*, she was ready.

Marc joined her in the passenger seat, his presence a silent reassurance as they drove through the shattered landscape. Antoinette's thoughts drifted to René. She couldn't allow herself to hope too much, yet hope was all she had left.

As they approached the border, Marc filled the wagon with

stolen petrol. 'To Germany,' she said when he asked where she was headed first. 'It's where my husband was sent.'

He nodded, a look of deep understanding passing between them. 'Take care of yourself, Antoinette. And if for some reason, you don't find what you are looking for, know I am always here for you.'

Her eyes met his, and for a moment, they stood there, two souls bound by the trials of war and the uncertain future ahead. 'Thank you, Marc. For everything,' she said, her voice tinged with the weight of all they had shared and all they had yet to face.

He held her in his arms one last time before reluctantly pulling away. 'Go find your answers, Antoinette,' he said, his voice filled with hope. 'I hope for your sake your husband is still alive, and he is a very fortunate man.'

She watched him retreat with a mixture of emotions swirling in her chest.

As Antoinette crossed the border, she was met with a land-scape scarred by war. The remnants of conflict were apparent in the shattered buildings and haunted faces of the people she passed.

The journey was gruelling, the roads treacherous, but Antoinette pressed on, her persistence unyielding. As she passed refugees, their hollow faces and ragged clothes mirrored the suffering etched into the land.

Each nod of solidarity she offered was a silent promise to herself and to them – she would find René.

Days turned into a blur of uncertainty and exhaustion. Sleeping rough, scavenging for food, she relied on the skills honed during her time in the Resistance. At a refugee camp, she met a woman who spoke French, who told her the German camps had been liberated. Antoinette's heart leapt, only to be crushed by the woman's grim tales of death and horror.

But she couldn't stop. She wouldn't.

Arriving at each displacement camp, the sight of survivors – mere shadows of their former selves – brought tears to her eyes. At one, she approached a tent marked with the Red Cross, her stomach clenching. 'I'm looking for a man named René Kaplan,' she said to a weary nurse.

The nurse's eyes were kind but burdened with the strain of bad news she often had to deliver. 'We'll check, but it may take time. And... I need to prepare you, I am afraid many didn't make it.'

Antoinette's breath caught in her throat. Minutes felt like hours until the nurse returned, her face solemn. 'I'm sorry, there's no record of your husband here.'

The words struck like a hammer, shattering the fragile hope she had clung to. Was this how it would end – never knowing, never finding him? As she turned to leave, the nurse called after her. 'Don't give up. Records are still incomplete, and some survivors may yet be found.'

Antoinette paused, a flicker of hope reigniting within her. 'I won't give up,' she whispered fiercely. 'I'll search every camp, contact every organisation. I have to believe he's alive, because I can't imagine my life without him.'

With renewed determination, Antoinette left the camp, setting out on a relentless quest. She would not rest until she found René, no matter how long it took, or how far she had to go.

48

PARIS, 2012

Deanna

A week later, Deanna sat on a plane to Paris with her father, the tension between them as heavy as the clouds outside the window. Paris – once a symbol of romance and beauty – now felt like a city haunted by family secrets waiting to be unearthed.

Her father was beside her, fingers drumming an anxious rhythm on the armrest, his eyes distant and hollow. Deanna had never seen him look so lost, and her heart ached for him. An only child all his life, he was about to meet a half-brother he'd never known – a man tied to a buried part of their history. She reached for his hand, offering silent reassurance. He turned to her with a small, tight smile, but the tension between them stayed, ready to snap.

'I still can't quite believe it,' he whispered, as if saying the words might make the truth disappear.

Deanna squeezed his hand.

The taxi ride from the airport to the café near Notre-Dame blurred by. Cobblestone streets and ornate buildings passed in a haze; while Paris bustled around them, vibrant and alive, Deanna felt disconnected, as though moving through a dream. Her father stared out of the window, silent, his mind clearly elsewhere. She could feel the full weight of his apprehension as they neared their destination.

When the taxi stopped outside the café, Deanna's stomach twisted into a knot. The charming bistro, adorned with flower boxes bursting with colour, was a stark contrast to the nervousness gnawing at her. She followed her father inside, the scent of coffee and pastries doing little to calm her nerves.

It didn't take long to spot Alexander.

At a corner table, a man sat with a newspaper folded in his lap. His silver hair mirrored her father's, but his face was more weathered, shaped by a life Deanna couldn't imagine. His pale blue eyes – so much like her father's – caught her off guard. Two halves of the same coin, yet so different.

Her father froze beside her, staring at Alexander with the intensity of someone confronting a long-lost reflection. Slowly, Alexander stood, and the three of them were locked in a tense silence, bound by invisible threads of shared blood and a history none of them had chosen.

'Thank you for coming,' Alexander said, his voice low and hesitant. 'I wish I could've come to England, but... my wife's sister lives with us, and she needs constant care.'

Small talk felt painfully inadequate for the magnitude of the moment. Deanna watched her father nod, his lips pressed into a thin line, his usual calm cracking at the edges. His hand twitched – a telltale sign he was holding back a flood of emotions.

They sat, and Deanna barely registered the clatter of cups or hum of conversation around them. The café faded as she watched the two men – brothers, yet strangers – navigate this fragile terrain.

Her father spoke first, his voice barely above a whisper. 'All my life, I thought... I thought I was alone.'

Alexander's expression softened. 'I always knew I was adopted, but I never knew the full story. Not until I found your mother... well, *our* mother.'

Deanna's father tensed, gripping his coffee cup so tightly she feared it might shatter. The betrayal was written all over his face. How could Antoinette have kept this from him?

Alexander continued, his tone measured but heavy with his own history. 'I found out through an article about the Resistance. There was a photo of her with a group of fighters. I knew she was part of a Resistance cell not far from my home. And there was something about the way she looked... I just knew. I tracked down the journalist, pieced the story together. That's how I found her.'

Her father's voice tightened. 'And she told you everything?'

Alexander nodded. 'She told me about my birth, about Otto von Falkenberg, and everything that happened.'

Deanna's heart clenched at the name. She saw the wave of emotion wash over her father's face, his knuckles white against the table as he absorbed the truth. 'So it's true, then,' he muttered, barely audible. 'She was with him.'

Alexander hesitated. 'Not by choice. She told me she was with my father to save yours.'

The words hit like a blow, and Deanna saw the air leave her father's lungs. His shoulders slumped under the burden of it, and for the first time, she saw him as fragile, more human than she'd ever allowed herself to see.

'She was brave,' Alexander said softly. 'She did what she had to do to survive.'

Her father's eyes flickered, as if some fragile thread of closure had appeared. 'But why didn't she tell me? Why didn't she tell me about *you*?'

Alexander sighed. 'She made me promise. She wanted to

protect you from the darkness of her past. She thought you deserved a life free from that.'

Silence stretched between them, thick with everything that had been uncovered. Deanna watched her father wrestle with his emotions, his eyes glistening with unshed tears.

Finally, Alexander spoke again, his voice raw but hopeful. 'We can't change the past, Ben. But we have a future now. We're family. No matter what, we have each other.'

Deanna saw the hope slowly replace the pain in her father's eyes. In that moment, she knew they would face whatever lay ahead together – as a family.

49

EUROPE, 1945

Antoinette

Antoinette pressed on from camp to camp, her heart bruised but her will unbroken. The endless parade of displaced faces both haunted and strengthened her, each person a reminder of her own missing René. She navigated through the ruins of Europe with one goal – to find him, no matter the cost. The devastation around her mirrored her inner turmoil, but Antoinette refused to let the war take what little hope remained.

In every camp, Red Cross workers looked at her with pity, but never with answers. Days blurred into weeks, her body aching from exhaustion, her eyes hollow from sleepless nights spent scanning lists of names. Yet her hope, though fragile, burned stubbornly. The weight of loss pressed on her shoulders, but it was hope, that thin sliver, that kept her feet moving forward.

On a bitter evening, the wind howling through the remains of a dilapidated hotel turned into a refugee camp, Antoinette entered with her heart as heavy as the rain soaking through her clothes. The building, once grand, was now a skeletal reminder of the past. She moved like a shadow through the wreckage, her footsteps echoing off the crumbling walls as she scanned the bulletin boards yet again. With every name not his, the walls seemed to close in; her throat constricted with despair she couldn't afford to feel.

The thought began to gnaw at her: *René could be gone.* Forever.

Her mind resisted, but her heart faltered, just for a moment. All at once something familiar reached her from the void – a sound, a familiar sound that calmed her. Music. Someone was playing music. It drifted through the air from somewhere deep within the hotel. It sounded odd in this place of such desolation and despair. The experience dragged her back to her life in the Conservatoire, stirring memories of another time, a life before guns and sorrow, when her violin had been her world. The melody – out of place, impossible – pulled her back, its notes like an outstretched hand offering comfort.

Antoinette followed, the sound drawing her deeper into the forgotten hallways. The notes seemed to wrap around her, urging her forward. She turned the final corner and there, half-hidden in shadow, was a door left ajar. Taking a deep breath, she pushed it open, the melody spilling out like a secret whispered just for her.

Inside, it looked as if the room had once been a ballroom, its grandeur now faded and tarnished by years of neglect. Dust motes floated in the air, illuminated by a soft, ethereal light filtering through the cracks in the walls. In the centre of the room, a small group of musicians had gathered, their music filling the space. Antoinette's eyes instinctively sought the piano, her heart clenching when she saw that the man playing wasn't René. The familiar shock of black hair she yearned for was missing; instead, an older man, his hair grey, sat at the keys.

With a heavy heart, Antoinette found a seat, the weight of

her unfulfilled hope bearing down on her. The music surrounded her, stirring memories and long-buried emotions. Though this man wasn't René, he was playing his song – the song René had played when he proposed to her. The irony was almost unbearable. Yet amid the pain, there was a flicker of hope, as if René himself were sending her a message, reminding her to keep going.

As the notes washed over her, Antoinette allowed the music to fill the emptiness inside her. It felt like an embrace, both comforting and bittersweet. Tears slid down her cheeks as she closed her eyes, letting the music carry her back to a time when the world was whole, when love wasn't shattered by war. In her mind, she was once again with René, laughing, dancing, and holding each other close. The haunting beauty of the melody made her long to pick up her violin and join them, to feel the strings under her fingers and let the music speak what words could not. For a brief moment, the room, the war, the pain – all of it faded away, leaving only the echoes of the life she once knew.

As the final notes lingered in the air, the group of refugees that were gathered in the ballroom broke into applause, their weary faces briefly lit with joy, a fleeting respite from their daily struggle. Antoinette's eyes fluttered open, still wet with tears, and she found herself facing the musicians. The pianist stepped forward, and her breath caught in her throat. Even in the dim, candlelit room, there was something about him – his walk, his demeanour – that mirrored René's. Not his face, but the way he carried himself. Antoinette's heart began to pound in her chest. Could it be? Was her mind playing tricks on her again? She had thought she'd seen him so many times before at every camp. But this time, despite her exhaustion, her feet carried her towards him. A few feet away, he finally saw her.

As the man turned to face her, Antoinette's heart stopped. The resemblance was so striking that she couldn't help but hope, her breath catching in her throat. His eyes widened, taking in her tear-streaked face and trembling hands. For a moment, the world around them seemed to fall away, leaving only the space between them charged with unspoken emotion.

'René?' Antoinette's voice was barely a whisper, as fragile as the hope burning inside her. She searched his eyes for a flicker of recognition, praying this time it wouldn't be another cruel mirage.

The man looked at her, his brow creasing in confusion. For a moment, her heart sank. And then, slowly, something shifted in his expression. His eyes softened, and a spark of realisation flickered.

'Antoinette?' His voice cracked, disbelief and raw emotion washing over his features.

She stumbled forward, her chest tight. 'Yes. Yes, it's me.' Her voice broke, as tears welled in her eyes. Before she could say another word, René crossed the distance between them and pulled her into his arms.

They clung to each other, both laughing and crying as they held on to each other. For a long time, neither of them spoke, too afraid that this moment would vanish if they let go. The warmth of his touch, the sound of his ragged breath – everything about this felt like a dream. But the solid weight of him in her arms grounded her, made her believe that this – after all the pain, all the years – was real.

When they finally pulled apart, Antoinette cupped his face in her hands, tracing the lines that the hardship had carved into his skin. His once-dark hair was now mostly grey, his face worn by the years and the horrors he had endured. But his eyes... those were still René's eyes.

'How is this possible?' René whispered, his voice heavy with disbelief. 'What are you doing here?'

Antoinette swallowed hard, fighting back the sob that threatened to rise. 'I promised you I would find you,' she said, her voice shaky but unyielding. 'And I *never* break a promise. I've been searching for you for a very long time.'

He stared at her, his own eyes brimming with tears. 'I should have known you would never give up.'

She nodded, a smile breaking through the tears. 'I have come to take you home, René.'

René took a deep breath, glancing at their surroundings – this dilapidated, war-torn world they had both survived. '*Home,*' he repeated, his voice soft. And in that word, Antoinette heard everything he hadn't said – the years of fear, the nights of hopelessness, the agony of believing they'd lost each other forever.

They stood for a moment longer, hand in hand, as the past slowly slipped away. And then, together, they stepped forward – towards a future that, for the first time in years, held the promise of hope.

50

PARIS, 2012

Deanna

The concert hall in Paris was breathtakingly grand, its crystal chandeliers casting a warm glow over the luxurious red velvet curtains and plush seating.

Deanna fidgeted on the edge of her chair, nervously tapping her fingers on the armrests. Beside her, Ben sat with his hands clasped tightly in his lap, his tension matching hers. On Deanna's other side sat her great-aunt Madeline, her weathered hands resting calmly in her lap, though her eyes held the weight of thoughtful reflection. Her presence tonight brought with it an air of quiet strength, a testament to the sacrifices of that era.

Across the row, Alexander and his wife sat quietly, their eyes scanning the double doors at the back of the hall, waiting for Carlos and Maria to arrive.

Finally, the doors swung open. Carlos entered first, towering over the room in a sharp suit, guiding Maria gently down the aisle toward their newly found family. Tears welled in Deanna's eyes as she watched them approach, unable to believe that this moment – this family reunion – was finally happening.

The siblings embraced, their laughter laced with the disbelief at the improbable circumstances that had brought them together mingling their newfound joy with the sorrow of lost years. In that moment, an overwhelming sense of peace washed over Deanna. All of the secrets and lies that had haunted her through this journey were finally out in the open, and it had all been worth it.

As everyone settled into their seats, the lights dimmed and the room fell into a hushed silence. An older man in a dark suit approached the podium, his presence commanding yet gentle.

'During the 1940s, this very hotel – then called the Majestic – was a stronghold for Nazi officers. The walls here still bear witness to the unimaginable horrors committed within them, forever stained with the shadows of those dark days. But tonight, we are not here to fear those shadows. We are here to remember and honour those who stood against tyranny, those who sacrificed so much for our freedom.'

A collective shiver seemed to ripple through the audience, and Deanna felt the enormity of the old man's words settle over her. She glanced at Carlos and Maria, and her heart ached at the sight of them. Maria's eyes were bright with unshed tears, her lips pressed together in an effort to keep her emotions in check, while Carlos's face was a mask of sadness. Deanna knew they were thinking about Otto – he was talking about their father, one of the men responsible for the very horrors being described.

The old man's voice grew more sombre, deepening the sense of gravity in the room. 'Among those who dared to resist was a woman named Antoinette Kaplan. She risked everything – her honour and her life – to aid the Resistance. In this very hotel, she stabbed a Nazi officer to provide the Resistance with a crucial advantage in their fight against oppression. But her bravery did not end there; she stole a priceless violin to return it to its rightful owner, another Resistance fighter. Unfortunately, that man was killed, and the rest of his family perished in a death camp.'

Deanna felt a powerful connection to her grandmother, whose courage now seemed more tangible than ever. She glanced at her great-aunt Madeline, watching her reaction. Madeline's eyes glistened, her expression a mixture of pride and grief. This wasn't just history – it was their family's legacy.

'The violin, lost for many years, was recently discovered by Antoinette's family, who have made the decision to sell it, with all proceeds going to the Jewish War Foundation in honour of the family that owned it and the millions who perished under that evil regime.

'Tonight, we are privileged not only to have Antoinette's descendants with us but also to hear the violin she once played – a melody that defied the silence of oppression.'

The audience clapped softly as the violinist took the stage. The room held its breath as the young woman lifted the bow and released the first haunting note. The music was a cry from the past, a lament for the lost, and a tribute to the brave. Each stroke of the bow seemed to transport the audience back in time, weaving a tapestry of pain, resistance, and hope.

Photographs from the era flickered onto a screen behind the violinist – images of the Resistance, showing those who had fought and suffered. When a picture of Antoinette and her sisters appeared, Deanna heard her great-aunt gasp softly, the sound barely audible over the music. Deanna turned to see tears slipping down Madeline's cheeks as she stared at the photograph of her and the other Valette sisters, standing side by side. Deanna reached for the older woman's hand, squeezing it tightly. In that moment, the past felt achingly real.

The mournful notes of the violin continued to fill the hall, and as the music swelled, Deanna closed her eyes, allowing herself to be transported back to that era – a time when every breath was a battle, and love and loss were intertwined. She brushed away her own tears, noticing her father's glistening eyes, as well.

As the final note faded into a poignant silence, Deanna felt a deep peace settle over her. The journey to uncover her family's past had led them here, to this moment of unity and remembrance. The shadows of the past had been confronted, honoured, and woven into their future.

Carlos reached for her arm, his grip warm and reassuring. 'Thank you for doing this,' he mouthed, his voice a soft breath against the lingering echoes of the music.

As the performance ended, the audience rose to their feet, the applause swelling through the hall, each person swept up in a collective wave of raw emotion.

When the applause subsided, Deanna was invited to take the stage to speak. Her whole body trembled, but she knew that if her grandmother could face a ferocious enemy with nothing but her courage, she could find the strength to speak her truth.

Clearing her throat, she unfolded the piece of paper that held the words she had carefully crafted. Her voice wavered at first, but with each word, it gained in strength and conviction.

'The grandmother I knew when I was young was creative, fiercely protective, and a force of nature who instilled in me a love for stories and a thirst for truth. But she never spoke of the war. I grew up knowing only that she and her sisters had been part of the Resistance, and little more. I had no idea, until recently, that Antoinette was a woman of remarkable courage and unwavering determination. As we uncovered her harrowing story, we learned of the risks she took, the lives she saved, and the price she paid.

'Tonight, as I stand in this place that holds both darkness and light, I am reminded of the power of confronting our past, of acknowledging the shadows that linger in the corners of our lives, and of what it took for a young woman barely in her twenties to stare hatred in the face and defy it. The lessons of history are not always easy to bear, but they are necessary if we are to forge a future rooted in compassion and understanding. My grandmother's silence over the years was not just a withholding of words – it was a shield against the horrors she had witnessed. And as I listen to the violin that she played, I feel her spirit all around me.'

Deanna paused, taking a deep breath as she gazed out at the audience. She caught sight of Carlos as he nodded silently, a look of unwavering support in his eyes.

'If you truly want to honour my grandmother and the brave souls who stood against tyranny, then let us carry their legacy forward by standing up against injustice wherever we find it, by speaking out against oppression, by choosing love over hate, compassion over cruelty. Let us be the torchbearers of a brighter future, guided by the unwavering courage of those who came before us.'

As Deanna finished her speech, a profound silence hung in the air, the weight of her words settling deeply in the hearts of those present. Then, the room erupted into applause, a thunderous wave of support that carried her back to her family.

Later, as people mingled and exchanged words of gratitude after the concert, Deanna found herself alone with Carlos. Without hesitation, he wrapped her in a warm, heartfelt hug. The embrace felt both grounding and electric, stirring emotions she hadn't felt for a long time.

'How are things with you and Maria?' she asked softly, pulling back just enough to meet his gaze.

'Things have been difficult, but Maria is strong,' Carlos

replied, his voice soft yet filled with quiet resolve. 'We're still trying to come to terms with everything we've learned about our father's past. With him arrested, it's... a lot to process.' His eyes darkened for a moment, reflecting the significance of recent events. 'But there's a silver lining in all of this. Meeting Alexander has been a gift – he's truly wonderful. And I have to admit,' Carlos added with a small smile, 'I'm grateful that even though we have a half-brother and uncle in common, you and I aren't *directly* related.'

Deanna shifted slightly, feeling a blush rise to her cheeks. 'Why is that?' she asked, her voice barely above a whisper.

Carlos hesitated, a glimmer of vulnerability in his eyes. 'Because... I'd love a chance to get to know you better, Deanna. To see where things could lead between us.'

Her heart skipped a beat, the sincerity in his words leaving her momentarily speechless. She took a deep breath, her gaze meeting his. 'I'd like that too, Carlos. But right now, I need to be there for my dad. And I've got to focus on finding work. But... who knows? In time... maybe a new life in Brazil could be on the cards for me. I really loved it there.'

Carlos's smile widened, a flicker of hope lighting up his eyes. 'In the meantime, I'm often in the UK for business. Maybe we could meet up – grab a drink or dinner sometime?'

Deanna felt a warmth spread through her, her heart fluttering with anticipation. 'I'd like that,' she said softly, her voice tinged with quiet excitement at the possibility of what the future might hold.

Their eyes lingered on each other, and for the first time in a long while, Deanna felt something hopeful bloom within her – a sense that, despite everything, the future might just hold something beautiful.

. . .

Later, as they stepped out into the cool night air, Deanna paused at the bottom of the steps. An elderly man approached her, his face lined with age but his eyes sharp. There was something in his gaze that drew her in.

'You remind me of her,' he said softly. 'My name is Marc and I fought alongside your grandmother in the Resistance. We lived together, side by side, through some of the darkest days of the war.'

Deanna was surprised to find another person still alive who had a connection to her grandmother.

Marc's voice shook slightly as he spoke, but there was a deep affection in his tone. 'I was in love with her, you know,' he admitted, his eyes glistening. 'I offered to marry her, to raise her son as my own. But Antoinette... she was fiercely loyal to your grandfather, René.'

Marc paused, the memories washing over him. 'When she gave up her son for adoption it was the hardest decision she ever made, and it cost her dearly. But she did it out of love.'

Deanna felt a lump form in her throat as she caught sight of Alexander, his eyes brimming with tears, and as Marc's words dissolved the last remnants of any lingering doubts about her grandmother's character during that time.

'She was a remarkable woman, your grandmother. Brave, selfless, and utterly devoted to those she loved. She fought not just for the Resistance, but for her family, for a future she believed in. Don't ever doubt that she was a hero.'

With that, Marc reached out, gently squeezing Deanna's hand, his eyes holding hers for a moment longer before he turned and walked away into the night, leaving Deanna standing there, tears streaming down her face, feeling closer to her grandmother than ever before.

She looked up at the stars, the night sky clear and endless above her. 'Thank you,' she whispered. 'For your strength, your sacrifice. I promise you, we won't forget you. We won't forget any of you.'

And with that, Deanna knew, without a shadow of a doubt, that she had finally come to understand the true depth of her grandmother's courage, and that the legacy of her grandmother would live on in her heart, guiding her as she stepped into her own future.

EPILOGUE

PARIS, 2001

Antoinette stood outside the Majestic Hotel – now called a different name– her whole body a tightly coiled spring as her feet shifted restlessly in the shadows of its arches. Time had softened the edges of the hotel; new coats of paint, polished windows, and subtle renovations hinted at an attempt to erase its darker history. Yet beneath the fresh façade, the bones of the building remained the same. Like her, it had been forced to wear the scars of those who had walked its halls with sinister intent.

She had come here today hoping to leave those shadows behind, to find the courage to reclaim something that had been stolen from her. She was no longer the young, naive woman who had once trembled in these very walls, yet standing here now, facing the building's imposing frame, she felt the same familiar chill. As if the hotel itself were holding its breath, waiting to see if she would be brave enough to step inside and confront the ghosts of their shared past.

In mere moments, she would see her son – the baby she'd given up during the war, under circumstances too painful to remember, yet impossible to forget. *Alexander.* Just his name felt heavy, echoing in her mind like a call she'd been waiting to answer for a lifetime. Her breath shuddered as memories surged up, unbidden, searing her with guilt and fear. Falkenberg with his leering grin and piercing gaze, and the shock on his face when she stabbed him. Antoinette clenched her fists, steeling herself against the onslaught of emotions threatening to overwhelm her. Today she refused to give his memory any power over her. Today was about reclaiming her own narrative, rewriting the ending that had haunted her for far too long.

As she scanned the crowd, a man emerged with a measured stride, his gaze fixed on the hotel's entrance, oblivious to her presence for now. She froze, her breath catching like shards of glass in her chest, where a thousand fears and hopes collided. Even from this distance, she recognised him – broad-shouldered, golden hair catching the afternoon light, his features carved in familiar, sharp lines. She swallowed, fighting the rising nausea, the sense of past and present blurring. He was every inch his father's son, and yet, as his gaze swept across the crowd, there was no icy glint, no cold calculation in his eyes. Instead, she saw a flicker of warmth, of something gentle and uncertain. *Valette eyes.* Relief surged through her in an overwhelming wave. Despite everything he was, he was also hers.

As Alexander drew closer, she forced herself to stand tall, though her knees felt weak. She closed her eyes for a moment, took a trembling breath, and whispered inwardly, *Let him be kind. Let him be nothing like his father.*

When she opened them again, Alexander was nearly in front of her, his steps slowing as he caught sight of her. In that instant, it felt as though the crowd around them dissolved, leaving only the two of them suspended in this fragile, trembling moment. Her heart thudded painfully, her lips parting as she struggled to find words, to find courage.

'Antoinette?'

Her son's voice trembled with a mixture of longing and disbelief.

Slowly, she nodded, and he extended his hand towards her – a simple, polite gesture, a tentative bridge across years of silence. But something broke loose within her. Instead of taking his hand, she reached out and pulled him into a tight embrace, fierce and desperate, as if holding him tightly enough could bridge the chasm of time that had kept them apart.

For a heartbeat, he stiffened, his body tense against hers. Then, she felt him exhale, his frame softening as he wrapped his arms around her, holding her with a quiet strength. A sob clawed its way up her throat, and she could feel his shoulders shaking slightly, the emotions cracking open, spilling out in gentle, soft sobs of his own.

'I'm so sorry, Alexander,' she whispered into his shoulder, her voice barely more than a breath. 'So, so sorry.' The apology was raw, too large to contain in words alone.

He responded with gentle firmness. 'There's nothing to be sorry for.'

Antoinette pulled back slightly, her hands on his arms as she searched his face for any sign of accusation, of blame. Instead, she found only compassion in his eyes, a reflection of her own pain and longing.

'Are you happy?' she blurted out.

'I am now,' he replied, his voice warm with hope.

'No, I mean, was life good to you?'

His voice was soft but steady, his gaze unwavering. 'I had a good life, with people who loved me, if that's what you mean.'

Tears stung her eyes again as relief flooded through Antoinette like a warm embrace. She realised in that moment that she had carried the weight of his potential unhappiness for so long, in that time she had forgotten to consider the possibility of him finding joy and it felt like a balm, soothing the pain that had been festering inside her for so many years.

'Shall we go inside?' he asked, his voice a gentle invitation as he offered her a tissue.

Nodding, she rolled back her shoulders, ready to face head-on the ghosts she'd tried so hard to leave behind.

The lobby of the hotel was breathtaking as always, an opulent blend of marble and gold, chandeliers hanging like constellations above. Antoinette's gaze drifted upwards, tracing the gleaming crystals as they caught the soft afternoon light. For a moment, she was back in the past – the scent of cigar smoke, the sharp click of heels on polished floors, the pungent tang of military leather, and the murmur of low voices echoing in German. Memories of uniforms and authority, of fear that had compressed the very air.

She blinked away her vision, inhaling the delicate aroma of lilies that were in abundance in the foyer, grounding her in the present. As her vision dispersed she noted the light was soft, inviting, the room no longer casting sinister shadows but offering a gentle illumination that beckoned her in.

As they settled at a table near the window in the restaurant, Antoinette's eyes wandered around the room, a sense of eerie familiarity creeping over her. The striped chairs and pristine white tablecloths were a stark contrast to the utilitarian furnishings she remembered from decades ago. Now, it was a sanctuary of luxury and tranquillity filled with the delicate aromas of fine cuisine – freshly baked bread, rich sauces, and the subtle hint of truffle.

But it was as though the shadows of the past were still lingering, just out of sight, reminding her of everything she had endured. But for the first time, she felt that she could face them, that she could reclaim this space as her own – a place of healing rather than fear.

'What are you thinking about?' Alexander asked after they ordered lunch, his voice pulling her from the reverie, his gaze gentle, his tone curious.

She hesitated, a lifetime of instinct pushing her to hide, to deflect. But today, she was done hiding. Her voice was strained as she began, 'There's a reason I asked you to meet me here.' She felt her pulse quicken, the weight of truth pressing on her chest. 'This... this is where I met your father. The place where you were conceived.'

She saw the words settle over him.

His expression shifted, his eyes widening as he absorbed the revelation. Yet his gaze didn't waver, and in the depths of his piercing blue eyes, she saw a quiet understanding, a patient acceptance that steadied her trembling nerves.

Reaching across the table, Alexander's hand found hers, his fingers warm and soft as they intertwined her own. The simple gesture was both comforting and encouraging, giving her the strength to continue.

'This place has changed, but it holds so much of who I was. And you deserve to know the truth.' She looked directly into his eyes, her voice steady now. 'All of it.'

And so, she began to speak, her words a delicate thread weaving through the years of silence. She told him about René, his life and his death just the year before. About Benjamin, about the Resistance, and the choices she'd made that had cost her everything. She did not hold back, telling of how he was conceived. At her confession, Alexander's breath hitched, his eyes widening as he absorbed the revelation. A flicker of pain crossed his face, his jaw tightening as he grappled with the truth of his origins. But even through the shock, he kept his gaze steady, a quiet strength in his expression that softened as he reached out to take her hand. Each word was a weight lifted from her heart, each memory a step towards healing. She could feel his gaze on her, unwavering, absorbing every detail, every painful nuance of the life she had lived and the sacrifices she had made.

As she spoke, the memories surged, relentless and vivid,

dragging her back to that time. She finally told him of how she had stabbed Falkenberg, and she saw Otto's face again, his eyes cold and possessive, his words a cruel reminder of his manipulation. The nausea crept up her throat, the room around her dimming as the shadows of the past tried to pull her under. But then she felt Alexander's hand squeeze hers, pulling her back into the present, into the warmth of his quiet understanding. In his gaze, she found an anchor, a tether that kept her steady amid the storm.

When she finally fell silent, her voice hoarse, she felt both hollow and whole. Across from her, Alexander's eyes shone with unshed tears.

'I always hoped that even though what I did to you was horrendous, somehow, some way you would know that I have always loved you with every fibre of my being,' she said.

He reached into his pocket, his movements slow and deliberate, as though handling something fragile. When he withdrew his hand, he held a small, worn compass, its metal scuffed and battered. Antoinette's breath caught as he placed it on the table between them.

'This compass...' Her fingers trembled as she picked it up, memories flooding her. 'I placed this in your blankets the day I...' Her voice cracked, but she forced herself to continue. 'The day I said goodbye.'

Alexander's hand closed around hers, his voice thick with emotion. 'I've carried it with me my whole life,' he whispered. 'I knew one day it would lead me back to you.'

In that moment, Antoinette realised that the compass was more than just a relic of the past. It was a symbol of the bond that had always existed between them, a bond that time and distance had never truly severed.

Tears spilled over, but they weren't just tears of sorrow. They were tears of hope, of a love that had survived against all odds. 'I've carried so much guilt,' she began, her voice soft. 'Not for what happened with your father – I've forgiven myself for that; it was war. But for how easily I gave you up. How could I let you go...? I was your mother, how could I...?' She looked down at the table, the weight of her shame pressing on her chest like a concrete weight.

Alexander rose from his chair and moved around the table, coming to kneel in front of her. He reached up, his fingers gentle as he stroked away the tears from her cheeks. '*Maman*,' he murmured, his voice like a warm embrace, 'you did what you had to do to protect me. You sacrificed everything to give me a chance at life, a chance to grow up safe, with people who could care for me when you couldn't. I always knew in the depth of my heart that you didn't let me go because you didn't love me. You let me go because you did.'

His words pierced through the armour of guilt she'd wrapped herself in for so many years, breaking it open with a compassion that left her raw, vulnerable, and strangely free. She looked into his eyes, searching for any trace of resentment, of blame, but found only love – pure, unwavering love that softened the pain she had carried.

His voice dropped to a whisper, thick with emotion. 'I can only imagine how hard that decision was for you, the strength it took to let me go. To know you'd never see me grow up, never hear my first words, never hold my hand when I was afraid.' His thumb brushed across her cheek, his eyes shining with tears of his own. 'But you did it so I could live, so I could have a future. And because of that, I am here now, with you. That sacrifice – it's the greatest gift a mother could ever give.

'Now, it's time for you to forgive yourself, Maman, please, let the past go,' he continued, his voice a gentle plea as he pulled her gently into his arms.

And as she felt the warmth of his love surrounding her, she realised the truth – Alexander had inherited none of his father's darkness. He was kind, loving, and compassionate, just as she had always hoped he would be.

As if sensing her very thoughts, he whispered into her hair, 'You're safe now, Maman. He can't hurt you any more.'

And with that realisation, she sobbed in his strong arms, releasing years of pent-up pain.

In his arms, the final chains of her pain and guilt fell away, and in their place, she felt a fragile but growing peace – a peace she had never believed she deserved. In his arms, she felt the shadows of the past finally recede, leaving space for something new – a love unburdened, a bond that, at last, felt whole.

As they finished their meal, she asked only one thing of him. 'Please don't seek out Benjamin. Let him find his own way to this truth. It would break his heart to know that I betrayed his father. Let's leave your meeting in God's hands. I believe, if you are meant to find each other, fate will find a way.'

And as they stepped out into the sunlight, her burden lightened as the modern world swirled around them, Antoinette felt a deep and abiding peace settle within her. She had fulfilled her responsibilities to both her family and her country, and the heavy weight of the secrets she had carried for so many years no longer held any power over her. Forgiveness, both given and received, had set her free. She had come here prepared to face her demons alone, but in her son, she had found an unexpected ally.

As they hugged goodbye and promised to keep in touch, Antoinette looked up at Alexander and she realised that nothing in her life would ever compare to the love and freedom she felt in this moment. The future, unknown and full of promise, stretched out before her, carrying with it the hope of things to come – hope that she had never dared to dream of until now.

A LETTER FROM SUZANNE

Dear Reader,

I sincerely hope you enjoyed reading *The Paris Promise*. If you did enjoy it and want to keep up to date with my latest releases, just sign up at the following link. Your email address will never be shared, and you can unsubscribe at any time.

www.bookouture.com/suzanne-kelman

As you close the final pages of Antionette's story, I want to take a moment to thank you for walking alongside me through her journey. Writing this book was deeply personal and, at times, emotionally challenging. Antoinette's path led me into moments I approached with great care and trepidation – moments that tested her spirit and resilience. Her story, as you know, took her to unimaginable places, including the bed of a Nazi. Writing those scenes felt like balancing on a tightrope. I wanted to honour her strength and ensure that, even as she faced the impossible, her unbreakable spirit shone through. I hope I've done justice to her courage.

In crafting this story, I was inspired by the remarkable bravery of real-life heroes like Simone Segouin, a teenage French Resistance fighter who refused to stand idly by. Simone's story stayed with me as I wrote, her determination a guiding light for Antoinette's journey. In August 1944, a journalist described her standing fearlessly with her FTPF armband

and revolver, fighting alongside Allied forces during the liberation of Chartres. It's this kind of bravery and resilience that I wanted to capture in Antoinette's character and share with you.

Another inspiration came from the real-life events at the Paris Conservatoire during the early years of the war. When Henri Rabaud, its director at the time, collaborated with the Nazis, identifying Jewish students and teachers to ensure the school's survival, it broke my heart to research. But in spring 1941, a glimmer of hope arrived for the members of the Conservatoire in the form of Claude Delvincourt, who fought tirelessly for the rest of the war to protect his students. Though, because of the timeline of my book, Antoinette's fictional story couldn't benefit from his heroism, his actions were a reminder of the courage it took to resist oppression in even the smallest of ways.

One of the key settings in the story, the Majestic Hotel, holds its own haunting history. During the Occupation, it became the headquarters of the German Abwehr, its luxurious halls transformed into places of espionage and interrogation. Today, the building is home to The Peninsula Paris, a luxury hotel that now stands in stark contrast to its wartime history. Writing scenes in this setting allowed me to explore the complexities of Antoinette's relationship with Otto von Falkenberg, a character who exists in the shadows of moral ambiguity. While Otto is fictional, his story parallels the very real truths of that era. Many high-ranking Nazis escaped to South America after the war, often living in anonymity. These dark echoes of history became the threads that tied Antoinette's to Deanna's contemporary story – a tale of secrets, redemption, and the search for truth.

Writing *The Paris Promise* was a journey of discovery, sorrow, and hope for me. My deepest wish is that Antoinette's story resonates with you, not just as a tale of war, but as a testament to the resilience of the human spirit. The people who lived through those harrowing years – ordinary individuals in extraordinary circumstances – found ways to resist, to love, and to endure. I hope Antoinette reminds you of their strength.

Thank you for spending time with these characters and for letting me share their world with you. Your support means everything. If Antoinette's story moved you, I encourage you to explore my other stories in this series, *The Last Day in Paris* and *The Bookseller of Paris*. There's so much to learn from the courage of those who came before us.

With gratitude and warmest wishes,

Suzanne

www.suzannekelmanauthor.com

facebook.com/suzkelman
x.com/suzkelman

ACKNOWLEDGMENTS

As I reflect on the journey of bringing *The Paris Promise* to life, I am filled with gratitude for the remarkable individuals who have supported me every step of the way.

To my phenomenal editor, Jess Whitlum-Cooper: your encouragement, sharp insights, and boundless enthusiasm have been transformative for my writing. Working with you has been an absolute privilege, and I feel truly fortunate to have you as part of this journey. Thank you for your unwavering dedication and for always inspiring me to reach new heights.

To my incredible publisher, Bookouture: your unwavering encouragement, expertise, and enthusiasm have been the foundation of my work. Every member of your team works tirelessly to bring these stories into the world, and I am endlessly grateful for your dedication.

A special thanks to the talented individuals who continue to make my dreams a reality: Jenny Geras, Peta Nightingale, Lizzie Brien, Mandy Kullar, Hannah Snetsinger, Occy Carr, Melanie Price, Alex Crow, Alba Proko, Ria Clare, Sally Partington, Richard King, Saidah Graham, Sinead O'Connor, Melissa Tran, Lauren Morrissette, Hannah Richmond, Imogen Allport,

Debbie Clement, Mark Alder, Mohamed Bussuri, Becca Allen, Ciara Rosney, Martyna Młynarska, Marina Valles, Stephanie Straub, Joe Morris, Nadia Michael and Jess Readett and everyone at Bookouture who has contributed to this book's journey. Your hard work and passion are deeply appreciated.

I owe a heartfelt acknowledgment to Kim Nash, Noelle Holten, and Sarah Hardy – your steadfast support and ability to connect readers with my stories is nothing short of extraordinary. Thank you for your belief in me and my work.

To my husband, Matthew Wilson: your steadfast support and patience remain my greatest blessings. Through every twist and turn, you've been my anchor, and I am forever grateful for you.

To my son, Christopher: watching you grow into the incredible person you are fills me with pride and joy. Your thoughtful feedback, encouragement, and belief in my work inspire me daily. Thank you for always being my sounding board and my greatest champion.

To my dear friends – Melinda Mack, Eric Mulholland, Shauna Buchet, and K.J. Waters – your friendship and unyielding support mean the world to me. Thank you for cheering me on every step of the way.

And finally, to you – my wonderful readers. Your loyalty, enthusiasm, and love for these stories are the heartbeat of my writing. Thank you for choosing to spend your time in the worlds I create. It's a privilege to share this journey with you, and I am forever grateful for your support.

Here's to more stories, more connections, and the continued joy of storytelling.

With love and gratitude,

Suzanne

PUBLISHING TEAM

Turning a manuscript into a book requires the efforts of many people. The publishing team at Bookouture would like to acknowledge everyone who contributed to this publication.

Audio
Alba Proko
Sinead O'Connor
Melissa Tran

Commercial
Lauren Morrissette
Hannah Richmond
Imogen Allport

Cover design
Debbie Clement

Data and analysis
Mark Alder
Mohamed Bussuri

Editorial
Jess Whitlum-Cooper
Imogen Allport

Copyeditor
Sally Partington

Proofreader
Becca Allen

Marketing
Alex Crow
Melanie Price
Occy Carr
Ciara Rosney
Martyna Młynarska

Operations and distribution
Marina Valles
Stephanie Straub
Joe Morris

Production
Hannah Snetsinger
Mandy Kullar
Ria Clare
Nadia Michael

Publicity
Kim Nash
Noelle Holten
Jess Readett
Sarah Hardy

Rights and contracts
Peta Nightingale
Richard King
Saidah Graham

Made in United States
Orlando, FL
26 May 2025

61596980R00218